Lake of Secrets

Shay Lee Giertz

LAKE OF SECRETS
BY SHAY LEE GIERTZ

Published by Late November Literary
Winston Salem, NC 27107

ISBN: 978-1-7352800-3-5
Copyright 2020 by SHAY LEE GIERTZ
Cover design by Sweet N' Spicy designs
Interior design by Late November Literary

Available in print or online. Visit latenovemberliterary.com

Library of Congress Cataloging-in-Publication Data:
Library of Congress Control Number: 2020944765
Giertz, Shay Lee.
Lake Of Secrets / Shay Lee Giertz 1st ed.

Printed in the United States of America

Dedicated to both my grandmothers—Shirley Giertz and Darlene Jones—who taught me and loved me unconditionally.

1

The last-minute of the last day of school defies the law of physics. I'm not a physics expert. But I do know enough to embrace the possibility that the last-minute lasts much longer than sixty seconds. And the longer I stare at the enormous clock over the doorway, the more I'm absolutely certain of it.

It doesn't help that my uniform sticks to me, and my legs stick to the wooden chair. Thanks, of course, to the wonderful St. Francis Catholic School where air conditioning is right there next to the antichrist.

When Sister Mary Lucia finally checks the time—and even that seems in slow motion—she clears her throat and says with a slight Irish accent, "All right, put down your pencils. The exam has come to a close."

Every student in the room had already put down their pencils. I go to stand up but hear Sister Mary Lucia cough again. "A final prayer to Saint Joseph for protection as you leave here for the summer months."

I groan.

One look from the nun and my head is bowed. She draws in a deep breath and begins.

My hand rests on my camera, as I sneak a peek at her. I'm tempted to pull out my Nikon and frame the shot. The lighting may be off, but it would make a great black-and-white. Better yet, I could pin it on my dartboard and use it for target practice.

Her chubby face snaps up, and her beady eyes glare at me like she knows what I'm thinking, and she disapproves. Her prayer continues, but the temptation is too much.

I slide the camera out and pull off the lens cap. I raise the camera and focus the shot. The nostrils on her pug nose slightly flare with each intake of breath, and I smirk. Perfect. I wait for it…

I take the picture, lower the camera, and bow my head.

She gives a slight pause, and I can feel her penetrating gaze scan over me and the rest of the class. She finishes reciting the prayer. Now all of us stare at her like we're ready to pop.

"Class Dismissed."

Amen.

I peel my sticky legs away from the chair and push out of class without bothering to tuck in my white shirt or to fix the length of my skirt. Normally, a few of the nuns walk around with a ruler for that very reason, but I'm on a mission. Once outside the door, I pull out the Nikon and study the picture. I can feel the slow smile spread across my face.

"You look quite sinister right now," Alisa says. I glance up quickly but look back down. She pushes herself against me and stares at the picture. "Oh, that is riotous."

"Isn't it?"

"What are you going to do with it?"

"There are endless possibilities." I put the camera away and grin at my best friend. Alisa and I found each other back in primary school when we were the last to be picked for a schoolyard game. I don't even remember what the game was, and neither does Alisa, which shows how unconcerned and inept the both of us are when it comes to team sports.

Now my red-headed friend and I hug and squeal simultaneously. "It's finally here! Our last day of this awful place. Well, at least for a few months," she says. "Maybe forever for you. Did you find out yet?"

"Not yet."

"Early acceptance into the university is huge. How can they keep you waiting?"

"They already told me everything will go through. It's just not official yet."

Alisa squeals again and nearly jumps on me.

Someone coughs behind us, and we immediately separate. Sister Mary Lucia lifts her eyes to mine. When standing, I'm a good couple inches taller than her, then again, so is everyone else. After a few awkward seconds, she hands me a manila envelope with the school's official seal. "I was supposed to give this to you, but you left my class before I could."

"Thank you, sister." I reach for the envelope.

She pulls it back and does that eyebrow thing. "Taking pictures is an enjoyable hobby, I'm sure, but it is terribly distracting. Especially during prayer."

I swallow and instinctively rest my hand on the school bag that holds my camera. I give a slight nod, which seems to satisfy her, and she extends the envelope again.

Once I have the envelope in my hand, I let out the breath I'd been holding.

"Happy summer, girls," she says with her slight Irish lilt before waddling away.

"That Irish Abbey she came from needs to take her back," Alisa says under her breath.

"I'm only glad she didn't ask for the picture." I glance at the envelope, then stuff it in my bag.

"What are you doing? Take that back out right now and

show this delinquent how smart girls finish first." When I don't move to show her, she sets her hands on her hips. "You show me that, and I'll show you this." she pulls out a piece of paper from her pocket.

My eyes widen and my palms start to sweat. "Is that—?"

"The list? But of course. You will be the envy of all of London."

I turn to see Alisa wave a sheet of paper in front of my face. I pause to scan it. "You invited everyone," I say. "There are at least a hundred people on this list."

"Yes, that is the point of a party, isn't it? And since I'm assuming that envelope in your bag contains the wondrous news of you never having to step foot in this place again, I say that a party is in order."

"I can't have that many people in our townhouse."

Alisa sighs. She takes being my best friend way too seriously. Almost like it is a burden she must bear. The martyr. "Ginnie, this is what you wanted, remember? *I want to have fun this summer*," she says, trying to mimic my voice. She's not very good at it. "*I want to have adventures. To show Leo that I'm more than a girl who attends Catholic school, takes pictures, collects bugs, and sometimes takes pictures of bugs!*"

"Shh!" I look around to make sure no one heard. "Lower your voice. And don't make me sound weird." Leo is my crush. My lovely, blonde hair, blue-eyed heartthrob. The boy who could be Justin Bieber's younger brother. But he's also the one who doesn't know I exist. Well, technically, he knows I exist. Mostly because during our first year at Saint Francis he paid me to complete his school work for the entire year. It was quite lucrative, but my father found out and ended that.

Alisa gives me an exasperated expression. "You *are* weird. Anyhow, this is the list. Your Dad will be out of town for three weeks. That means you have more than enough time to party, snog, and put the house back in tip-top order."

My face heats up at the idea of kissing Leo. "But a hundred people? I don't know half of them! And the half I know, I don't talk to!"

Kids walk by, and one says, "Thanks for the invite, Ginnie. It sounds posh. See you Saturday."

I wave and mumble something incoherent.

"See," Alisa says in excitement. "This is it. The start of our lives."

I have never understood Alisa's fascination with crowds of people. Alisa attends every party and tries to persuade me to join. Occasionally I will, but I would much rather stay home and document the new inventory Dad brings home from the lab. He is an entomologist, not that Alisa could even say the word. Part of documenting the bugs is taking pictures. I go a bit overboard and add some flair to it, but just because they're bugs doesn't mean they shouldn't have a decent picture taken of them, right? Just the same, I would have to lock our study. Other kids might not appreciate Dad's and my fascination with insects.

But I do want Leo to notice me. My geekdom has kept me dateless for far too many evenings.

"Come on," she says, "You know you're just as excited as I am. Three weeks without parental supervision."

Technically, Mum would be watching me, but that's *technically*. She's a model. Not one of those big-wig ones who are size negative two, but she likes to think she is. Her big contract is with *Sally's Apparel* catalogue. No one under fifty has ever heard of it. Their biggest sellers are girdles, minimizers, and muumuus. Still, she is so self-centered, she left me and Dad because we weighed her down. Dad and she have stayed friends, more for my benefit, but she definitely isn't going to be watching me too closely. Her idea of adult-supervision is to call me periodically to make sure I am alive.

"Okay, I'm a little excited." I glance at the list again and shrug. Might as well live a little. Leo may show up, and if Leo showed up… "Can I borrow one of your dresses?"

Alisa throws her arms around me and squeals. "Everyone will be drooling by the time I get done with you. You will look more gorgeous than Cinderella. Not that you look anything like her."

"I look nothing like her, and which Cinderella are you talking? There're hundreds of versions."

"Any of them. Your hair is dark, and your skin is olive, not to mention you're a bit curvier…"

"Hey! Curvy is another word for chubby!"

"No, it's not. Are any of the Kardashians chubby? I think not."

"I don't look like any of them either."

"Maybe like a distant cousin."

"You are horrible! Anyway, it doesn't matter what I look like because my Prince Charming is going to love me for me?" At least that's what I've told myself since I was five.

"My sentiments exactly. But who wants Prince Charming when there's Prince…*Leo*?"

We're giggling and acting completely childish when Leo— yes, that's the newly coined *Prince* Leo—stands in front of us.

"So, I hear you wenches are throwing a party."

Alisa and I act a bit shell-shocked, but eventually, Alisa recovers enough to nod.

"See you there," he says and gives me a lopsided grin. "Bye, Ginnie."

Alisa shoves her elbow into my ribs.

"Bye!" I shout.

Leo laughs and leaves. I, however, nearly die from the gorgeousness of him. And the pain in my ribs, of course.

"Thanks a lot, you loon. My ribs will be bruised."

"We have work to do," Alisa says and pulls me out into the hot afternoon sun.

"Ugh," I moan. "This heatwave is killing me." I

surreptitiously sniff at my armpits.

"Stop smelling your nasty pits."

"Shh!" I order her, embarrassed at her lack of tact. "I'm checking to see if they're fresh."

"You don't stink. Your hair, on the other hand, looks awful. Must you always wear it in a ponytail?"

"I like my hair." I spot the motorcycle and slow down.

"Why is your father at school?" Alisa's eyes widen. She grabs the list from my hands and shoves it in her front pocket. "He does realize that you're eighteen, practically in college, and no longer need an escort, right?"

He never picks me up at school. I normally take the London bus to the house or walk on the rare occasion I want the exercise.

Dad sees me and waves me over. He looks ridiculous. He still has on his white lab coat, and his one pant leg is partly tucked into his frayed sock. How he managed to score with my mother might be a mystery until you took off his helmet. With his strong chin and wavy black hair, he doesn't necessarily appear as nerdy as he is. But trust me when I say he's as nerdy as they come. He's tried to date a few women after Mum, but when they find out what he does for a living and just what a nerd he is, they don't stay for long. Dad says he's given up on women and is focusing on bugs. I told him to never tell anyone else he said that.

"Hi, Dad," I say, wondering if he's already found out what my plans are for the next three weeks.

"Hi, Mr. Paxton," Alisa smiles and waves. With her two red braids and wide grin, she appears as innocent as a little school girl. But she's the president of our thespian club, so she's quite good at acting. That party list is no doubt burning a hole in her pocket.

"Say good-bye to Alisa," Dad says and hands me my helmet. "We need to hurry."

I look from him to her. "I guess I'll see you later."

"I'll stop by."

"No can do," Dad says impatiently. "We need to leave

immediately."

Panic settles in, but I have no time to contemplate anything because Dad revs the engine and motions for me to hurry.

Alisa throws me a worried glance. "Call me!"

I nod and get on the motorcycle. Now all the students in the schoolyard are watching. I even see Leo out of the corner of my eye pausing to take a look. I turn away in complete humiliation. What a sight my Dad and I must make. Especially Dad. Couldn't he at least have taken off the horrendous white lab coat?

I make sure my bag is secure, then yell over the engine. "So, what's going on? Where are you taking me?"

"America," he yells back. "Your grandmother had a heart attack."

The words sink deep inside me. I wonder if it is possible for a person to feel total disappointment and complete horror at the same time.

One thing I know for sure. My plans for the most amazing summer have just been sucked down the loo.

2

Dad's back is to me as he packs his bag. "This is not up for discussion."

"But you said that you're hopeful Gran will make a full recovery."

"Yes. So?"

"Wouldn't it be less stressful if your whiny daughter wasn't there?" It is a selfish argument. What kind of person am I? My grandmother—the only one I have a real relationship with—just had a heart attack, and my thoughts keep traveling back to Leo and the thought of what it would be like to kiss him. Trust me, I am not proud of myself at the moment.

"The real question is why you're standing there arguing with me when you should be packing."

"Explain why I have to go? You were leaving for three weeks anyway." He's not listening to me, which annoys me even further. I am in full tantrum mode…and it isn't pretty. I resist the urge to stamp my foot.

"It's a little different when I'm only an hour's drive away. Not an entire continent apart!"

"We wouldn't be a continent apart. More like an ocean ride apart. And an ocean is nothing more than a really big lake filled with salt."

"The ocean is bigger than the continents! Now go pack your bags."

"What about Aunt Sue? She's right there in Michigan."

"She's already with her. Does that excuse us from our responsibility?"

"You could go. It's a great idea. Mum is watching me, so I have one parent here." This is a weak argument, and one look from Dad says it all.

"Virginia," he starts.

Let me just say that my father is the only person in the history of *ever* that I allow to call me by my birth name. A girl cannot live in London and be named after one of the first states on the continent of America. Dad thought he was paying homage to his birth country since he had to live over here to be with Mum, but I have never been appreciative. Mum doesn't even call me by my birth name. She says she was half-drugged when Dad asked her to name me that.

Dad walks over to me where I stand with my arms crossed and eyebrows furrowed in anger and rests his hand on my shoulder. "Virginia," he says again in a softer tone. "If your mother agreed to let you stay over with her, I would be tempted to let you stay. I've already tried to contact her. Three times."

That hits my heart like a flaming arrow.

Dad must sense that because he changes the subject. "Your Gran is very sick. Wouldn't you want to see her?"

Oh, lovely. *Guilt.*

"Of course I would," I say, truly meaning it. "I haven't seen her since Christmas holiday, but..."

"This isn't the whole summer. I'm going for a couple of weeks. Martin's taking the conference, so it works out perfectly. That means we'll be back in London before July."

I feel my resolve evaporating.

But the party…*Leo*…

Then Dad throws in the clincher. "I know that your relationship with your mother is…complicated. But Gran was a wonderful mother to me, and I need to be there for her. And I need you to be there for me."

What is a girl supposed to say to that? Ever since Gramps passed away two years ago, I've sensed Dad's restlessness here in England. He's never fit in with the English culture, not that we're terribly different, well, not me at any rate. He, on the other hand, has never even tried. He works in the lab and comes home to study more bugs with me, or to plop into his chair with a beer and the remote control. Gran talks with him all the time via phone or video chat, but I try to avoid much of the conversation because she will invariably ask me about the University of Michigan and when will I follow in my father's footsteps and carry the Paxton family maize-and-blue banner. My father, along with the rest of his family, seems to forget that I am perfectly content in *my* homeland. If I had my way I would apprentice under some high-end travel photographer and work my way up to my dreams. No college required. But Dad is the only family I've got. The only one who's ever been there for me.

I swallow back the disappointment and nod. "But it's just a couple weeks, right? I can come back here and hang with Alisa."

"Yes. Maybe even have that party you're keeping from me." Dad gives me a sly grin before going back to his packing.

I press my lips together because I have no idea how to refute that. Lying has never been one of my strengths. Keeping it from Dad was one thing; bold-face lying about it is completely different.

Dad takes a shirt from his bottom drawer and stops. With a sigh, he says, "Why the Debbie Downer expression? You enjoy going to America. Think of all the bugs you've never observed. You've never been to Michigan in the summer. You can take your camera, and you and I can go explore the Pigeon Forest."

His words garner the desired effect. My heart lifts. Of course I enjoy visiting family. Especially if my cousin, Cassie, would be there. And the bugs would be fascinating; all of the wildlife would be. He pulls me in and hugs me. "Thanks, sweetie."

Dad smells of his aftershave and the spearmint gum he always chews. I lean into him and rest my head on his shoulder.

"I have to run back to the office and go over a few things with Martin. I will be back in time to pick you up and get us to the airport for the Red Eye. Please be ready."

After he leaves, I head to my room, drag my suitcase out from underneath the bed, and toss it on the mattress. My letter of university invitation still rests open on the bed. Dad hadn't even noticed or asked. But that is okay. That letter weighs heavily on me, and with everything happening, talking with Dad would have to wait. I shove the letter back in the envelope and toss it in the bottom of the suitcase. A large part of me shudders at the thought of four to five years of additional schooling. Especially when photography doesn't require a degree.

That is definitely not a subject to broach with Dad. At least not yet.

I toss my clothes into a suitcase with no rhyme or reason. A couple of t-shirts and shorts. Some jeans. A summer dress I bought on clearance, just in case. My one-piece bathing suit Dad insists I wear, and the bikini I bought with Alisa that has stayed hidden in a drawer for almost a year. After I pack my panties and bras, I decide to throw in a few sweatshirts. Dad told me many times that Michigan weather is unpredictable.

When it's done, I stare at the suitcase and allow myself to wallow in disappointment for a few minutes. I feel bad that Alisa went to all that work, only for me to drop the plans. It would have been wonderful. She would have made sure of that. I think of Mum, and how she hadn't answered any of Dad's calls. The hurt shouldn't be there, but it is. I pick up my cell phone and call her. It goes straight to her sodding voicemail. "Mum, it's Ginnie."

Exasperation drips from my words. "I need you to call me back. Immediately. It's important."

The computerized voice cuts me off and tells me if I need more time to press "one." I close my cell phone and sit on my half-stuffed suitcase.

Someone pounds on the front door. I wonder if it's Earl, our neighbor, coming over to complain again. Dad says only three things ever come out of Earl's mouth: complaints about the weather, complaints about the government, or complaints about the stray dog who haunts our neighborhood and likes to scare Earl's cat. Either way, we avoid talking with him if at all possible. I think he's figured that out because he's become prone to coming over for his weekly venting sessions without an invitation.

I fling open the door, ready to tell him to hit the road and am surprised not to find his bald head and flappy jowls in front of me. Instead, it's Alisa.

"Tell me it's not true," she says and pushes past me and into our front hall. "Your father can't be so daft as to take you halfway across the world the last day of our classes!"

"It's true." I sigh and head into my bedroom. She follows me and mutters a string of curses when she spots the suitcase. "We're leaving when he gets back from his lab. I guess we're taking a Red-Eye flight."

"No, no, no, no!" Alisa grabs my shoulders and turns me to face her. "We've already planned out this next month. We have a party every weekend. A few parties, in fact. One just happens to be your party! Two nights from tonight! Or have you forgotten about that little tidbit of information?"

"And what am I supposed to do?" My heart beats faster in my frustration while at the same time feeling like a sumo wrestler just crushed it in his fat paws. The irritation had begun to lull until Alisa showed up. Now it rears its monstrous head. Again. I press my lips together and close my eyes. Alisa is my best friend, but I don't want her to see me have a complete meltdown. From Mum ignoring me to Gran having a heart attack, I'm not too sure I can take the disappointed look on my best friend's face.

She pinches her nose and scrunches up her eyes in apparent concentration. "What about your Mum?"

"Won't return any of my calls." I flop down on my bed defeated. "So much for hanging with Leo."

"Oh, you are going to hang with Leo by summer's end if I have anything to do with it." Alisa flops down beside me and crosses her legs Indian-style. "What would your Mum do if you showed up on her doorstep? 'Hello, Mummy dearest, you've been nonexistent in my life these eighteen years, and I'm here to call a favor.'"

I shrug my shoulders, not sure if I would want to do that. I take issue with feeling unwanted. I'm not about to throw myself at her if she doesn't want me. I've got my pride, after all.

"Then you will have to stay with me."

"No…bloody…way." Alisa shares a room with her annoying ten-year-old sister. Her mum and pop seem to have a hazy understanding of birth control or how to properly use it because they have six children. Alisa is the oldest, which means their small cottage with three smaller bedrooms is one big noise. It never shuts off. Someone is always shouting, crying, running, farting, or picking their nose. How Alisa has not gone completely insane is a mystery. One time was enough for me, thank you. Alisa has always crashed over here, and we've been perfectly fine with the arrangement.

"We don't have any other options."

"I could barely stand one night over there, let alone three weeks!"

"Artie and Angus are going to summer camp in a few days. Those boys are the worst of the bunch." She smiles in a way that even she doesn't believe her lie.

"Can't we just postpone the party?" I ask, not thrilled with the idea, but seeing it as a possibility. "Dad promises we are only there for three weeks. We can change the date to the end of June."

"We are solidly booked, Ginnie. As in there are loads of parties going on after this weekend. We won't have nearly the showing."

"So? A hundred kids is a lot to have in this place. Besides, if we're going to the parties, I'm bound to run into Leo."

"What are you saying? Give up the most amazing, delicious, sensational party we will have attended, only to satisfy ourselves with other poorer quality get-togethers?"

Now I'm the one smiling in a falsely reassuring way.

"So I get to go to all of these parties by myself? While you're having a dandy time in America?"

"Well, I've never been there during the summer months. Who knows what specimens…"

Alisa throws a pillow, smacking me in the head. "I cannot believe you're thinking about bugs at a time like this!"

"I'm not! Okay, I am, but only a little."

Alisa glares at me before rolling her eyes.

"So there are some interesting insects in Northern Michigan. At least that's what Dad tells me. But I would much rather stay here, and that's the truth of it."

My cell phone rings, and we both jump to grab it. Only it's not Mum. It's Cassie, my cousin. "Hello?"

"Is it true?" she yells into the phone. I hold the phone from my ear. "Are you coming to visit? Mom just told me, and I am seriously freaking out!"

Alisa stands with her arms crossed. I'm not sure how a person can intensify a glare, but Alisa has mastered the talent. Then again, I know she can hear Cassie. Shoot, my neighbor can probably hear her.

"Well, is it true?" Cassie's asking.

"Um, yeah, maybe. I don't know all the particulars yet." I try to turn from Alisa because her glare is making me uncomfortable, but she only maneuvers herself to be in front of me again.

"She's not going anywhere!" Alisa yells into the phone. I turn, but she's too quick. "We are planning the best three weeks of our lives, thank you very much!"

"Let me call you back." I flip the phone closed and toss it on the bed.

Alisa and I stand there as the weight of the inevitable settles between us. She blows out a breath. "Your cousin's annoying."

"She's not that bad."

"I don't trust blondes."

I glance over at the picture of me and Cassie at Christmas time. She *is* blonde and perky, and my only cousin on Dad's side, so I refrain from saying anything more.

After another moment or two of silence. Alisa throws her hands up in surrender. "I can't believe it. The best summer of our lives has sodding runoff and had an illicit affair with Major Inconvenience."

We look at each other, and I can't help it. I break into a grin. "Don't be so dramatic."

Now she's grinning. "They have an illegitimate love child. Do you know what they name it?"

"Inglorious Bastard?"

Alisa snorts out a laugh. "Oh, that's a good one. I was thinking Forest Dump."

I start giggling. "That doesn't make sense."

"I know." She pulls the list out of her pocket. "I made a list for you. I've got the original at home." She hands me the paper. "Look at it and think of me. Three weeks. We can handle that."

"Definitely. Maybe I'll gather enough courage to talk to a guy before college."

Alisa wraps her arms around me and gives me a bear hug. "I love you bunches, and I will miss you bunches. If you need anything, call me. I'll put my coins together and round up a plane ticket. But only if it's an emergency."

"That'd be fun. You'd like America."

We release each other, and I see Alisa wrinkles her nose. "American men look bizarre. I mean, their teeth are straight. I bet that means they're lousy kissers."

"Like we would know."

"Hey, by the end of this summer, we'll be experts, and that's a promise. And not by no straight-teeth-American-men. We have standards, after all."

We walk back to the front door. Alisa opens the door when we hear my cell phone going off again. "I'm going to leave without any more delay. It'll be easier." Alisa rolls her eyes, blows me a kiss, and shuts the door behind her.

I run to my room, annoyed that Cassie calls back so quickly. I pick up the phone and say, "I said I was going to call you back!"

"Don't come over here."

The voice is raspy and brittle. I check the phone and see it's a number I don't recognize.

"Who is this?"

"Listen to me. You need to stay put!"

"Gran?" She hardly sounds the same, but I do recognize the familiar ring of her voice. "We want to come for a visit. We miss you." I stop because I think I hear her laughing, but then I realize it is sobs. Now I feel like a selfish pig for even thinking of staying back. "Gran? What's wrong? Oh, please, stop crying. We're taking the Red Eye. We'll be there soon."

"N-o," she moans. "This isn't supposed to happen. Stay there. Promise me…"

The phone clicks, and the line is dead.

3

Dad is a whirlwind, moving at least 90 kilometers a minute. Maybe that's an exaggeration, but only a slight one. I've tried to bring up the phone call, but I can't get him to stand still for ten seconds. "Taxi's here," he says as he comes into my room. "Perfect timing if I say so myself. I've only been back for fifteen minutes. Just enough time to grab our stuff and get moving."

"Dad."

Dad grabs my suitcase. "What did you pack?" he asks in surprise. "It must weigh over fifty pounds!"

"Dad." I have to follow him out of the bedroom.

"Seriously, Virginia. What do you have in here?"

"I had to bring clothes for hot days, semi-hot days, normal days, cooler than normal days, plus it's got my camera equipment. But Dad, I've got to talk to you."

"Let's get going, then you can tell me in the cab. Oh, grab the laptop and its case. I'll need to work a bit while I'm there."

Once in the study and packing the laptop, I hear the cab's horn.

"Virginia, you ready?" Dad calls out from the front room.

I race out to the foyer where Dad had the door open waving at the cabbie.

"Come on, come on," he says and gently pushes me out the door. He sees our neighbor and tells me to get in the cab. "I've got to tell Earl to check our mail."

By the time, I'm situated in the cab, I'm a frazzled mess. I check to make sure I remembered my purse. I hear the truck slam shut, then Dad slides in beside me. "To the airport." He glances over and says, "You all right? You look kind of green."

"I've been trying to talk to you."

"Sorry, hon, traveling overseas is hectic. Did you grab the passports?"

"Yes. Dad!"

"What?"

"Gran called me."

"She did? Good. How is she doing?"

"No, not good. She acted scared and told me not to come."

Dad's facial expression changed to one of disbelief. "I can't believe you're still trying to get out of going."

Now my expression changes to disbelief. "Dad, I'm here, aren't I?"

"True. Well, maybe she didn't want you to go through all the trouble of coming just for her. You know how she is. Aunt Sue says she's trying to act like nothing happened."

"But she acted strangely. Like she was scared and was trying to protect me."

"She was a teen once, too. She probably doesn't want to bother you. It'll be okay. We'll get there and make sure she's all right. Don't worry."

I shrug and look out the window. Tears threaten but I hold them back. It must not have hit me that I would be flying to America so soon until I sat in the cab. Now I have Gran's warning echoing through my brain. Too much too fast.

"How was school?" Dad asks.

I know he's trying small talk, and I don't feel like a conversation. Still, I suck in a breath and say, "I think I pulled off a high mark in Literature class."

"So?" Dad says with a chuckle. "I wouldn't expect anything less."

"It was quite difficult to read Chaucer, you know."

"With your brains, you could have memorized Chaucer and wrote a doctoral dissertation on his use of language."

"What have you been snorting?" I chuckle and shake my head. Dad may be a genius, but I have always had to work hard to maintain high marks in school. "I may get some of my brains from you, but I got a few traits from Mum, as well. Procrastination and disorganization being two of them."

Dad shakes his head. "You're not that disorganized. You keep excellent records for your scrapbook."

"My scrapbook is one thing, but I can never find my homework."

"If you were truly that disorganized, I doubt you would have received that early admission letter."

I pause and glance over at him. "You saw it?"

"Of course. A lot's happened this afternoon, but something like that would not have escaped my notice."

I smile despite myself. "Thanks for noticing."

Dad put his arm around me and squeezed. "I think it's terrific. Gran will be thrilled."

I decide not to say anything about photography and the whole I'm-not-sure-I-want-to-go-to-college talk. Instead, I change the subject. "Gran's going to come through, right?"

"She's stable. Aunt Sue is the one who called me. She's Gran's emergency contact. The hospital called her and told her Gran had been rushed there. Sue jumped in her car and drove the two hours up to Pigeon Lake."

"Poor Gran."

"She's a tough nut, sweetie. She's not going to go down

without swinging a few punches."

I smile. Gran *is* tough, as feisty as they come. "That's not what I was referring to. I'm talking about Aunt Sue and Gran together alone. No wonder Aunt Sue wants you to come. For reinforcements!"

Aunt Sue and Gran always argue about something. Mostly it's good-spirited, but it can get carried away.

"Sue will behave," Dad says. "At least until I can get there and be the mediator."

The next several hours go by in a blur. We barely make it to the flight on time. Dad has to shove me through security and pull me toward the gate while I'm still trying to put back on my shoes. Once we're seated and in the air, I pass out. Dad wakes me for dinner. I start watching the in-flight movie with him, but I fall asleep again somewhere in the middle of it.

All in all, by the time we land in Detroit, I'm a disheveled wreck who hasn't had a shower in the past twenty-four hours and with a mouth that feels and probably smells like a nuclear bomb just exploded.

Dad hands me a coffee. It tastes weird. Everything about America is slightly weird. Not unpleasant weird. Just *off*…a little. But Dad, on the other hand, acts like he's in heaven. He inhales his coffee and sips it, a slight smile on his face.

"It's coffee, Dad," I snap. I don't know why I'm pissy, but I am. "It tastes the same in London."

"No," Dad shakes his head. "I can't put my finger on it. But this stuff, this stuff is good. It's *American*."

I roll my eyes. Any moment I expect him to go skipping down the corridor singing *Oh Beautiful for Spacious Skies*, or whatever other American patriotic song there is out there. I'm sure there's a few. "Can we get our bags and get out of here?"

We find the baggage area and wait around the turntables while everyone around me talks in an American accent. Funny, they sound a lot like Dad. He never really picked up the London accent. He would mimic me sometimes to be funny, but eighteen years later, he stands out like a sore American thumb. And I think he likes it.

Since Dad is in his element, I follow him around.

"Which car would you like, Virginia?" Dad asks at the rental car counter.

"One that drives us to Gran's really fast."

The guy behind the desk smiles at me. He's young—mid-twenties—and a little cute, but I probably resemble a hideous creature, so I turn away. They take off outside, and I hurry to catch up. The guy walks us right up to a red Mustang convertible.

"How's red?" he asks me as if impressed with himself.

Buggers, I am impressed.

"A convertible?" I glance at Dad.

"Sure, let's live it up a little. What do you say?"

He's grinning at me. The cute guy is grinning at me. And all I manage to come up with is, "How in the world do you people drive on the wrong side of the car?"

Dad laughs, signs the paperwork, and throws our luggage in the trunk. "You act like you've never been here."

"I'll never understand it, I guess. Just like you hate to drive a car in London even though you've been there for over eighteen years."

"Motorcycles are better. Get in," he says, already opening the—on the wrong side—driver's door. "We'll be at Gran's in less than four hours."

I get in the car and buckle up. Okay, the convertible is cool. Dad wiggles his eyebrows in my direction. I giggle and shake my head. "You act like such a child sometimes. And for a worried son, you are rather happy."

"Of course I'm concerned about my mother, but I'm *here*. Home. Can't I be a little excited?" Dad has to be tired, but he doesn't show it. He sings to the radio the entire trip up to Northern Michigan. He gets like this every time we come. It makes me feel a little bad every time we leave because I know he only goes back to London for me.

"Isn't it crazy," he's saying, "The United Kingdom is small enough that it can fit into the state of Michigan?"

"Yeah, it's crazy," I agree. America is big. That's all there is to it. There's so much *space*. In London, everything is crammed together. And the funny thing is all my "America" experience has been Michigan. I've heard other parts of this country are breathtaking, too. Not that London is all bad. I rather enjoy it.

We drive past rolling fields and an occasional farm, and jet lag sets in. With the sun over us and the warm June air blowing, I lean my seat back and fall asleep to Bon Jovi's, *Living on a Prayer*.

For some reason, I dream of Dad standing over me. "What's in the box?" he asks.

I'm sitting at Gran's table. A box rests on my lap. Is it a present for her?

When I glance back up, I see Gran in a hospital gown standing on the other side of the table. Her appearance startles me. She whispers, "I told you not to come."

The box lid flies off as thousands of beetles tip the box off my legs and onto the floor. I scream as Gran steps away from the table. The bugs head toward Dad.

"Dad!"

The beetles crawl up his legs, but it isn't until they are on his stomach and moving fast, that he realizes the swarm of insects. I'm finally free from the chair, and I race over to help. He tries brushing them off, but they completely cover him, and he falls to the floor. I wipe at the beetles furiously, but it's no longer Dad's face I'm looking at. It's my own. I watch as the beetles swarm my face. My eyes stare out at me, mirrors of the shock and fear I am feeling. I watch still frozen as the other me falls back until all I see are the beetles.

4

"Virginia? We're here."

I hear a car door open and close. My throat feels like I swallowed a bunch of bugs, so I cough and grab my water bottle to chug away the after-effects of the dream.

There's a shout and something drops, and then I hear Aunt Sue cry, "Brother!"

I drag myself out of the car, feeling groggy and irritable. Still, I inhale deeply. London is smoggy and stinks of exhaust and the vendors' stalls. Outside my Gran's house, it smells of forest and leaves and fresh dirt and flowers.

"Ginnie!" After she's done smothering Dad, Aunt Sue embraces me. "Look at you! You get more beautiful every time I see you."

I hug her in return as Dad goes into the house then goes back outside pushing Gran who sits in a wheelchair. The image of Gran from my dream resurfaces in my brain, but I mentally push it back down. She looks well as she smiles up at Dad. "Hi, Aunt Sue,"

I say as we walk over to the porch. "Have you been behaving yourself?"

"No," Gran interjects. "She refused to take me to mass this morning."

"The doctor said to keep you home until she gives you the okay. You're lucky they let you leave the hospital at all."

Gran rolls her eyes. "Pish-posh. I'm just fine. And you shouldn't neglect religion."

Aunt Sue starts to say something, but I quickly say, "Gran, you look fantastic." I walk up the steps to where she sits on the porch and hug her. Her dark hair mixed with gray is still thick and wavy, resting at her shoulders. The lines around her eyes seem a bit more pronounced, but her smile is wide and her cheeks have some color. She shows no sign of the agitated grandmother who had been on the phone not 24 hours earlier.

"Of course I look good. When have I ever not looked good?"

"But you were also just released from the hospital. I'm sure God understands that you need to stay home and rest." Aunt Sue turns to me. "Cassie wanted me to tell you that she'll be here in a few days. She has some graduation parties to attend. She said she tried to call you."

I force myself not to look at Dad. "That's great that she gets to go to some parties."

"Well, let me look at you," Gran says, holding my hand in her left and Dad's in her right. "I'm perfectly fine. It's good to see you both, but you should go back to London and enjoy your summer."

"We only just arrived," Dad says. "You're stuck with us for a little bit."

"How long are you here for?" Gran acted antsy.

"As long as I'm needed."

I glance at Dad but turn back to Gran and smile. *As long as I'm needed?* Dad and I would talk later.

"There's evening mass. Take me to mass." Gran lets go of my hand and pats Dad. "You're still Catholic, aren't you?"

"Of course I am, but we just got here. How about we make some lunch, then we'll see how everyone's feeling?"

Gran shrugs. "Fine, but don't talk to Sue. She'll talk you out of it."

Dad motions for me to push Gran back inside.

"Gran, do you have any of that mint sweet tea?"

"We'll have to make some more, but I'll show you where everything is."

I wheel Gran past the door and into the large hallway with the staircase right in the middle of the house. Gran has always called their home a cabin, but if it is a cabin, it's taking some major steroids. Her office sits on the left side of the stairs with double-glass doors; she writes a housekeeping and gardening column for newspapers in the northern state area. It has been Gramps' office, too. Before he passed away, he had been a real estate contractor and developer. Gran still kept his desk and all his mess in there.

Gran says he died in his sleep like an angel came down and took him without stirring him one bit. I think when I go, that's what I want too. Just take me before I know what hits me.

Then I think of my dream about being swallowed up by beetles, and I keep walking past the staircase into the kitchen.

To the right is the sitting room, complete with a fireplace that takes up half of the far wall and a piano that has been in the family for generations. With three bedrooms upstairs and a modernized basement—complete with a home theater and game room—I can see why Dad has a hard time leaving this for our two-bedroom townhouse in London.

"All right, stop this nonsense." Gran puts her feet on the floor to slow the wheelchair. I slow down, and she stands up. "Ah, this is better." She walks over to the cupboards and opens one up.

She has already pulled out a pitcher and has started to heat the water on the stove before I say, "Are you allowed to do this?"

Gran gives me a hard look and laughs. "I'm only sixty-five, Ginnie. I've still got another twenty to thirty years in these bones!"

"But the heart attack…"

"My chest felt tight, so I went to the hospital to be safe. I didn't know everyone was going to treat me like an invalid."

She looks fine to me. Her mop of curly dark hair is in clips and her jean overalls make her appear as I remember her: vibrant and full of life.

"But if my chest pain is what you brought you here, then I'm glad for it," Gran says and pats my cheek. "But you shouldn't be here."

Her severe tone surprises me. "We're here for you."

"You told me not too long ago that you had your entire summer planned."

We did have that conversation. I didn't divulge all of the information, but I had told her some of my plans. Now, I can only look away and busy myself by pouring tea.

"And wasn't there a boy?"

I swallow hard. "You matter more than any boy, Gran."

"Don't you worry." Gran kisses my cheek. "I'm going to talk to your father. In the meantime, I wouldn't go swimming if I were you. This lake is a fishing lake. It's full of seaweed and leeches."

I make a face. "Not a chance. But if Uncle Doug brings his boat, maybe I'll go for a ride."

Gran's features turn guarded. "I need to talk to your father. Now go and tell your Dad and Aunt Sue that the tea's ready. And, if anybody asks, you made it."

I go to get Dad, but before I do, I ask, "Do you remember calling me yesterday? You were frantic. At least that's how it seemed. You told me not to come."

"What?" Gran pauses for just a second before she continues spooning fruit salad into a bowl. "Did I? Oh, Ginnie, I have no recollection of that. It must have been the pain meds talking.

Although it might have been me trying to spare you from wasting your summer plans."

Of course, Gran would want me to enjoy my summer, and the thought makes me feel guiltier. "I'm glad to be here. We wanted to see you." I walk back to the front porch but stop before opening the screen door. Dad laughs with Aunt Sue. Neither of them acts too worried. Did he purposefully make Gran sound worse than she is? All of a sudden, just thinking about Leo and Alisa and my three weeks of freedom makes me homesick. It's not as if I don't want to be here, but couldn't we have visited after the three weeks of his conference? Gran's health seems fine. Even Cassie gets to have some time to go to parties.

Then I hear Dad and Aunt Sue talking in low voices. I walk closer to listen in.

"She won't talk about it at all," Aunt Sue is saying. "I even have a hard time getting her to take her pills. Not that I blame her. Some of the pills make her loopy. She was practically begging to talk to you at the hospital, but this morning when she woke up, she acted like she remembered none of it."

"You got to give in a little," Dad responds. "Some of those medications are worse than what they're trying to fix. Not to mention, she'll just push back, which might turn out worse."

Aunt Sue sighs. "That's why I'm glad you could come. She needs you. You're not nearly as stubborn or argumentative as she is or I am."

Aunt Sue hugs Dad, and I feel guilty again. I reassure myself that it's only because I'm over-tired and irritable that I would question Dad's honesty.

I open the screen door and step out. Dad smiles over at me. "There's my girl. How's Gran?"

"She wanted me to tell you tea is ready."

"She got up and made it, didn't she?" Aunt Sue asks.

Before I can respond, Dad says, "I'm thirsty. I'm going to grab our suitcases and meet you inside."

When I open the door I see Gran hurry to the wheelchair and sit down. Once we're in the kitchen, I notice Gran has set out a spread of lunch meats and slices of bread, along with the fruit salad.

"Didn't our girl do a great job?" Gran pats my hand from the wheelchair.

"She sure did," Aunt Sue says. She chuckles, but I can't bring myself to say anything.

What I want is a shower and a change of clothes, but I sit down at the table with the others.

Dad joins us and has his sandwich halfway to his mouth when Gran asks, "So, have you met a woman yet?"

Dad stops and says, "No, but if I ever do, you'll be the first to know."

"You're going to be forty years old in a week. You need to find a good woman."

"Thank you for pointing that out. I will get right on it."

"I only want you to be happy."

"I am happy."

"Happier."

"She wants more grandchildren," Aunt Sue interjects. "She's been nagging me these past two days to start popping out some more kids."

"Your clock is ticking," Gran shrugs. She looks at me and says, "Both of my children give me only one grandchild apiece. This does not make me happy, Ginnie."

"I'm ...sorry?"

"Think of how many Ginnies I could have as grandchildren? And Cassie, too, and when is she coming?"

"Soon. She'd have come with me, but she had already R.S.V.P.ed to a few parties. She got out of a few of the commitments, but she still had to stay back a few days."

"I can't wait." I take the last bite of my sandwich and ask to be excused.

I nearly barrel down the hall and up the stairs to the shower.

My manners could only last so long. Once in my room—the room I share with Cassie when she's here—I grab a change of clean clothes, then a towel from the linen closet, and head to the shower. Dad's room has an attached bathroom. So does Aunt Sue's and Uncle Doug's. But Cassie and I have to share the bathroom at the end of the hall. Not that I care because I'm the only one up here.

The shower is nice and hot when I step in. I wash off the travel grime and possible phantom residue that feels very real as I scrub with the washcloth. Everything has happened so fast that it weighs on me like a barrel of dead, stinking fish. I need to call Mum. After the dream, I need to make sure she's okay. Then there's Alisa. I had to drop her and our plans like a bad date. Her three weeks of wonderfulness have been ruined, too. She would now be stuck babysitting her younger and rather irritating younger siblings. I try not to think of Gran downstairs and how healthy she looks, or of the strange phone call she made to me yesterday. I try not to think of the betrayal that's lurking somewhere inside of me that Dad would make everything sound so urgent when it's not. More importantly, I try not to replay the horrible dream I had in the car. I try not to think about any of these things.

But I do. I think of every one of them.

5

Alisa or Mum?

I drop onto the bed and dial Mum's number. Her conversations never last more than five minutes. If she answers the phone.

"-Ullo?"

"Hey there, Mum. I've been trying to reach you."

"Ginnie? Dear, is that you?" Mum shouts into the phone. I can hear the voices in the background. "Hold up a sec." She asks someone to hold her ciggie, and then I hear her walking away from the noise. "Ginnie!" she is talking loudly. "What a horrid night. Me and Marty stop by the boozer for a few, and who do you think I happen upon?"

"I don't know, who?"

"Marty's wife! Can you believe it? He said it was over, but she mustn't have got the memo, let me tell ya'. She threw her drink on me! *Me*! The nerve! I'm a frightful mess, that's for sure."

"Maybe you shouldn't hang out with Marty anymore. Who is he anyway? Another model?"

"Oh God, no. I would never date any of them wankers. No,

this is the same Marty who works with Sam."

"You mean Martin? As in Dad's best friend?" Sometimes I could not believe my mother. "Isn't he supposed to be at a convention covering for Dad?"

"Easy does it, love. He leaves tomorrow. And we have all been the best of friends for the longest time. Having a drink isn't for derelicts. It's his wife who needs to mellow."

I rub my head. "I wanted to make sure you got the message that I'm with Dad in America."

"Of course," she says distractedly. "Where's my cig?" she asks someone. "Have a good time, love. Meet a boy. Have fun. You're only eighteen once."

"I want to fly home soon. That'll be okay, right? We can hang out until Dad gets back?"

Mum's laughing with others before saying, "What? Tell me later. Got to run. Kiss, kiss!"

She hangs up. I glance at the clock. Yep. Five minutes tops.

I rest my head on the pillow. It's only four o'clock in the afternoon in Northern Michigan, but I could sleep. Would Mum want me to hang out with her? Of course, I tell myself. But as I take a deep breath, I realize I don't feel like I fit anywhere. Not here in the boonies. Not with Mum and her crazy lifestyle. Covering my face, I tell myself it's the jet lag talking. I'll feel better in a day.

I call Alisa. She picks up on the first ring. "It's about time you call me! I have been waiting, you know!"

I grin and turn on my side, propping up my head with my hand. "Sorry, sorry, it has been nonstop since Dad picked me up from school."

"Everyone is royally peeved you ran out on us and the party. I explained it was an emergency, but no one's buying it."

"This is not happening." I groan in frustration.

"No worries. Leo saved the day. He's having the party at his house. And guess what? He called me and invited me personally."

I sit up. "He called you. Did he say anything about me?"

"Not really, but he probably called everyone," Alisa says, but I can tell she's hiding something.

"What are you not telling me?"

"I told you everything. What's the issue? You seem jumpy."

"Sorry. It's been a long twenty-four hours. I wish I was there."

Alisa chatters—she's good at that—about the party and how horribly boring it has been and how I need to call her every day. This horrid depressive blanket seems to fall on me, and I feel as if I might cry. Not to sound childish, but I wish Leo had called me. He has never talked to Alisa, yet he calls her? This bothers me, and I'm upset it bothers me, and I'm getting more upset because I'm upset.

Dad gently knocks on my open door and steps in, holding a small box.

"Alisa? I've got to go. Dad just walked in."

"Hugs and kisses," she says before hanging up.

Dad sits on the edge of my bed. "You're in your pajamas at four-thirty in the afternoon?"

"I'm tired."

"Want to talk about it?"

I shrug.

"Aunt Sue is leaving. She's got to head home, and it's a two-hour drive. Gran wants to go to evening mass. Would you like to go?"

"No." I refrain from adding that I had to go to mass every day for the entire school year, so I'm probably well caught up for the summer months.

But Dad laughs as if he understands.

"Did you know that the heart attack was only chest pains?" I blurt out. I want to make sense of why we had to hurry out of our life in London to come here.

"Gran doesn't want to admit what happened. Aunt Sue says

she's been having some irregular pains for a few months. Good thing it was a mild heart attack, and she could call 9-1-1."

"She looks fine."

"Yes, she does, but she can't be by herself. Doctor's orders. Aunt Sue can't be here every day. She has to work." Dad rubs his face. I can see now that he is tired.

I lean forward and hug him. "I think I'm cranky, that's all. I'll be right in the morning."

Dad's hugs are warm and strong, and tears threaten, but I refuse to make him feel any worse. Especially if the poor guy has to endure mass.

"Oh, I almost forgot. I brought you a present." Dad releases me and hands me the small box he's been holding.

I open the box, then quickly shut it and hand it back. It's the same beetle from my dream.

"What?" Dad laughs. "Isn't it fascinating? This little guy is rare. He has yet to be documented." He opens the box and studies the beetle.

"Why's that?" I ask, still creeped out in a really big way.

"I'm not sure," he says. "The carrion beetle feeds on the decaying carcasses of animals and such. This is similar to that, but yet it's different. I've found these before up in this area. Mostly when I was younger. This time around, I'm documenting it. I'm going to send Martin a picture and see if he can't figure it out either."

Dad glances up and must see my freaked out expression because he quickly puts the beetle back in the box. "Virginia, what's wrong? I thought you'd want to document it."

"Yes, I do." I press my fingers against my eyes, then run them through my still-damp hair. "Of course I do. Just not now."

Securing the box, Dad sets it down on the table by my bed. "Maybe later then. You sure I can't tempt you to go with us?" He grins and raises his eyebrows like he's trying to sell me a used car.

"I think I'm saved."

Dad laughs, and I smile.

"Well, sit back and relax. Or go for a walk around the lake. There's a trail that winds around the whole five miles of it."

"Miles?"

"Yes, *miles*. We're in America now. Remember?" He winks then stands up.

"You keep reminding me."

"Since you're here, try to have a good time."

I nod, and he leaves. I notice he's left the box on the bedside table.

Eventually, I hear Dad and Gran leaving. I fall back onto the bed and stare at the ceiling. "Great," I say to the ceiling. "I'm here in America with no one around and nothing to do."

Sleep doesn't come, so I decide to get out and roam around a bit. After I throw on shorts and a t-shirt, I put on socks and my tennis shoes. I know better than to walk in these woods with flip-flops. The last thing I want is for those God-awful ticks Dad tells me about to crawl up my legs. Investigating them in a scrapbook is one thing, having one suck my blood is another.

The minute I'm outside, I feel better. It's not terribly hot, and the breeze is perfect. I inhale deeply and set out toward the lake. I pass the fire pit and lounge chairs and take the small hill down to the dock. I stand there for a minute, taking in the scenery.

All right, fine, I admit it. It's beautiful. Dad and I normally come here for the holidays, so I can't remember the last time I was here during the summer months. There's not another house along the lake, at least from what I can observe. Just layers of thick trees and forestry. I take a deep breath and then another. "So much better than London's pollution," I say out loud. But thinking of London leads me to think of Alisa, and thinking of her makes me think of Leo, and thinking of him reminds me that he called her and not me. So, my volatile emotions rule out any appreciation of Pigeon Lake for its aesthetic qualities. Perfect.

The water ripples below. I look down and see nothing but

murky, dark water. Yuck. "Swimming is out of the picture."

The water ripples again. There's no wind and no boats. Even though I rationally know it's nothing more than fish, I still turn around and head back to shore, marching toward the trail.

After several minutes of marching and muttering under my breath, it dawns on me that I am in insect heaven, and I didn't think to bring Dad's book or my scrapbook or anything to capture one to bring back. At least I brought my camera. I bring it out of my bag and snap the lens cap off. Once it's ready, I study trunks of trees, leaf piles, and dead logs. I lose myself in nature and snap pictures to preserve what I see. I inspect a centipede resting on the limb of a thin birch. I hold the camera steady and decide for a close-up.

A cold wind blows from behind me sending shivers up my spine. I turn quickly, but all is still.

My shivers are still there; my senses on alert.

A part of me tells my brain to go back. I've seen one too many scary movies, and my imagination is revisiting every horrific detail from each of them. Maybe I've had enough of the forest. But I haven't. I want to observe more bugs, so I tell myself to stop being a sissy and get going.

A monarch butterfly flutters around me, and I stop to watch it, then frame it, then take the shot. It lands on my finger; its wings never quite still. Suddenly, it flies away as a cold wind comes up again, pushing me from behind. Its force catches me off guard, and I stumble forward, accidentally taking another picture.

Goosebumps burst onto my skin.

"Stop it!" I tell myself. "You are such a wimp. There are no such things as ghosts."

The nuns at Saint Francis whisper it in my ear. *The only spirit you need to concern yourself with is the Holy Spirit.*

But I'm not buying it at this moment. Something is with me. Maybe an animal? I hear scampering across some dried leaves. I focus my Nikon in that direction, and being ever the documenter, I snap another shot. But pretending not to be nervous isn't working.

My knees knock, and I swallow the lump in my throat.

That's when I hear some children playing. I hope there's not a bunch of children ghosts around here. They're the worst. I decide I'm no longer interested in bugs if they came with *whatever-this-is-that-I'm-experiencing*.

It is stubbornness that has me moving forward. It's like a game I'm playing with myself to make sure I'm not chicken. The cold wind has let up, which isn't entirely reassuring. "I'm going to be surrounded by a group of witches and a cauldron, and I'll be their lunch."

A scream rips through the trees, and I turn full-circle, completely panicking. The scream's close…

Another scream. Then high-pitched laughter.

I push through a dense clump of bushes and stumble upon a couple of erected tents. Children run around with squirt guns. I lean against my knees to catch a breath. And gather my wits, too. Some men stand over a small fire pit with beers in their hands. Some women chat beside them. All is well.

Looks like I'm the only nutcase.

I wave at one of the women standing there and keep moving, following the trail. I will not let my crazy imagination get the better of me. No, sir. These woods are not scary.

I have to remind myself of that sentiment as I continue to hike, but all in all, I'm proud of myself. I observe a range of insects that fascinate me, have documented them with dozens of pictures, but I need Dad's help to double-check the species on each. I'll develop the pictures and maybe he can hike with me later.

The trail winds for another half kilometer or so until I can barely make out the water. I leave the trail and notice the tree line falls into a steep hill down to the lake. I slip on the ledge and fall with a thud.

I get up and wipe the dirt off my shorts. Still curious, I hold a slim tree trunk, leaning over the steep hill down to get a good look at where Gran's house might be. The late afternoon sun hits the trees like a poet's words on paper. With one hand holding on to the limb, I bring up my camera. That's when something crawls across my hand.

I drop my camera back into the bag and release the tree at the same time. Not a good idea.

I start to plummet down, but my hand reaches out and catches the thin trunk. Now I'm hanging over this steep drop down with one hand—and not my strong one, mind you—barely hanging onto a tree.

"Breathe, Ginnie," I say. I also tell myself not to look down. With a somewhat normal heart rate, I throw my other hand around the thin trunk and pray it doesn't break from my weight. Glancing at the tree, I nearly let go again.

Beetles crawl around the trunk. The weird ones Dad said aren't documented yet.

This shouldn't bother me. It shouldn't. It doesn't. It's a beetle. Who cares?

I force myself to close my eyes as I pull myself up until I'm lying flat on the ground. My heart pounds so loudly, it rattles my brain. My eardrums even pulsate. Without losing my nerve, I take some pictures of the beetles around the trunk of the tree. But my hands are shaking, and I already know the pictures won't turn out.

It's at this moment that the longing for home hits me hard. I hug myself tightly and breathe in deep breaths. I want to be in my house, in my room, hanging out with Alisa. I want Leo to call *me*, for him to come to *my* party. What I don't want is to be in some creepy forest alone with some psycho beetles that seem to be everywhere I am.

It's then I realize I'm crying. I wipe my eyes annoyed with myself and with my Dad and with a lot of other people.

Cold wind or not, I'm turning around and going back to Grans. It may not be home, but it's as close as I can get right now.

6

A tree branch snaps. I whirl around. "Who's there?"

I hear leaves rustling as something moves closer to me. I find a stick on the ground and poise it for an attack. "I'm armed," I yell. "And I'm not afraid to fight."

"Don't shoot," a voice says.

I see a head poke out of the trees. It's a boy, probably a little younger than me. He steps out from behind a tree, holding his hands up. He has a goofy grin on his face, but he doesn't make eye contact. "I'm innocent, your honor."

I drop the stick. It's hard to put my finger on what's different about him. Nothing major. It may be the whole eye contact thing. He looks off to the side of me.

"My name's Ian," he says.

From his mannerisms, I can tell he's nervous or anxious. "Are you lost?" I ask him, concern winning out. "Can I help you find your way somewhere?"

"My brother told me not to go far, but I didn't listen. Hi, my name is Ian." He pauses, then adds, "When I say my name, you're supposed to say yours."

"Oh, I'm sorry." I wipe my hands on my shorts, and then extend one to him. "I'm Ginnie. It's nice to meet you, Ian."

Ian shakes my hand, still not making eye contact. "Where are you from? Your dialect is a mix of British and American."

"London. My Dad's from here, so I probably do have a mix of the two."

Ian glances up, meets my eyes, and then looks away. His eyes are green. "I'm from here. America. Home of the brave. Did you know we defeated England in 1776?"

"Yes, that's the rumor."

"It's not a rumor. It's historically factual. It is why our country is independent of yours."

"Right. Well, no worries though, we don't hold a grudge."

He doesn't seem to understand my humor. "Why would you hold a grudge? It was over two hundred years ago."

"You're correct." I watch him and try to recall what I know about different types of behavior. He takes things literally and doesn't quite understand tone of voice.

"I saw you looking at bugs," he says quickly. "You had a butterfly on your finger."

I breathe a sigh of relief. Okay, no ghosts in the forest. Only young teen boys. *Harmless* young teen boys. "Bugs are kind of cool."

"So are trees. That one you were holding on to is a white birch. They normally don't have thick trunks. I'm glad you didn't fall, but I would have got you help. I saw everything. What bug were you looking at?"

"Here." I lead him to the tree. I spot some beetles. "See these? They are gross, don't you think? And I like insects, too. Just not this one."

"There's a decomposing carcass just off the trail." Ian acts proud of himself for knowing this. "I bet these beetles are here because of that."

"Right," I say, feeling strangely reassured.

"Want to see?" he asks. "I think it's a dead deer."

I crinkle my nose. "No, thanks. Want to walk with me?" I don't want to admit how much I want the company.

Ian acts surprises and makes brief eye contact again before looking away. "You want me to go with you? On a walk?"

"Yes."

"Most girls don't talk to me."

"Why?"

"I'm too weird for them. I have Asperger's, but you'd think I was an alien." He grinned at his metaphor.

Asperger's. That's it! One of the boys in my younger years had similar mannerisms as Ian, which is what I must have been trying to remember. "Well, I don't think you're an alien. Come on, you can tell me more about trees."

And he does. As we continue down the trail's path, he quizzes me on coniferous and deciduous trees. "This is a black willow." He stops our hike and points out a tree. "The trunk is dark with black ridges. They like to be around lakes." Then he shows me the leaves, and I point out an Asian beetle that he thinks is a ladybug. I show him some of my pictures.

The cold wind moments have disappeared, and I have chalked it up to an overactive imagination when I hear a faint shout. "Did you hear that?"

Ian listens.

The shouting gets closer. Someone is calling for Ian.

"I'm here!" Ian shouts.

"Do you know what direction you came from?" I ask.

Ian turns in a full circle confused. The shouting doesn't help. "I'm here!" Ian yells.

"Whoever's calling you is back in the other direction. We'll meet up with them."

Ian and I walk back through the trail, as the voice gets closer to us.

"Isaac's going to be mad," Ian says. "I wasn't supposed to

go this far."

I am about to ask "Who's Isaac?" when the words suspend in my mouth. He's tall with broad shoulders and a lean frame, and he's jogging toward us, looking in every direction until he spots Ian waving at him.

"That's Isaac. He's my brother."

My eyes widen, and I try to push down my wavy, frizzy mess of hair. But I'm sweaty and dirty, and yeah, well, I definitely don't look as beautiful as this male approaching us. He has what might be sandy-colored hair, but it's cut close, with the same green eyes as Ian's.

"Ginnie?" Ian drags me back to reality.

I pull myself away from the fantasy. "Yes?"

"That's your name?" the tall guy asks. Boy, is his voice deep.

Stop it, Ginnie! Stop it!

"Yes, I'm Ginnie." I extend my hand, but it's dirty. I wipe it off nervously. "Sorry. We've been hiking the trail. Ian's been showing me trees."

"Ginnie's showing me bugs."

The guy raises his eyebrows.

I laugh and shrug and wish the ground would open up and swallow me whole.

"You weren't supposed to go far," Isaac says to Ian.

"I didn't go that far."

"At least a half-mile, Ian. Where were you headed?"

"Around the lake," I say, trying to get Ian out of trouble. "I asked him to come with me."

"Where are you from?"

"She's from London," Ian answers. "She has a mix of a dialect from both London and America. Her Dad's American. She's visiting."

"There you have it," I say. "Wow, Ian, you pay attention."

Ian grins. So does Isaac.

Oh, dear Lord.

"Well, let's get back. Mom and Dad are in a panic." Isaac turns and leaves with Ian following him.

I stand there. It's not like I'm going to follow them. That would appear stalker-ish. Maybe I should move in the other direction, but my feet stay put. Instead, I look at the pictures on my camera, acting preoccupied.

"Ginnie?" Ian stops talking to Isaac and looks in my direction. "You're coming with us, right?"

Isaac stops and glances over, too. He doesn't repeat the invitation.

"I'm going to finish the hike," I say, hoping I can tame my overactive imagination, especially now that I know there are no ghosts or weird supernatural specters.

"You sure?" Isaac asks. "I can walk you back to wherever you came from."

"You're going to walk her back to London?" Ian laughs.

"Ha, ha." Isaac pretends he's going to wrestle his brother, while Ian runs from his grasp. Isaac pauses long enough to say, "Come with us, you probably shouldn't be walking this trail alone. You're not from here and might get lost."

That's all the invitation I need. I jog over to them and pretend not to notice Isaac looking me over.

Oh please, Lord, don't let me look like a madwoman.

Isaac brings his hand up to my hair. My heart beats faster, but instead of pulling me toward him in a rapturous kiss, he pulls a long twig out of my hair.

Lovely.

7

The Fulton family doesn't live on the lake but on a dirt road beyond the forest. That meant leaving the trail to follow a "shortcut," which Isaac says he knows by heart.

In the middle of the wooded terrain, we come to a halt.

Isaac studies the scene. "I think we went too far east."

"This is right," Ian says. "This is the way."

"I'm thinking we went too far east."

"No, we didn't," Ian insists. "That is a Balsam Poplar tree and there is a Black Ash tree, which I thought was funny because they are both right next to each other in my tree book. Those are the same trees. I am right. Don't argue."

I laugh because Ian is adamant, and actually, his reasoning is sound. "There you have it. Trees that start with a B."

Isaac shrugs. "I'm not sold yet, but we'll see."

Ian keeps walking. Isaac falls behind with me. "He's probably right," Isaac whispers. "But I don't tell him because he'll get a big head."

"Good idea," I agree with mock seriousness. "And you didn't have a big head when you said that you knew this 'shortcut'

44

by heart."

"I do," he says in defense. "I've just been a little preoccupied."

He glances in my direction, and my insides are ablaze. Maybe this guy likes dirty girls with twigs in their hair.

"So London, huh?"

"Born and raised."

"You probably get told this a lot, but your accent is sweet. I've never met an actual English person before."

"I don't have an accent," I say in all seriousness. "You do. With your drawn-out words and nasal tones." I fake an American accent, repeating one of Dad's favorite lines when he's homesick. "Boy, what I wouldn't do for a chili dog and some cheesy nachos and a nice cold beer." I say the last word, "beeeeeeer," which has Ian snickering in front of us.

Isaac shakes his head but grins anyways. "Who would ever say that?"

"My Dad."

"Oh, come on. Can't he get some dogs and nachos and beer in London?"

"Yes, but he says it's not the same. He wants to take me to a Tigers game where I can try a 'real' hot dog."

"So, your Dad misses America but stays in London anyway? Why not just move back here?"

"Because of me. My Mum's over there, and I have friends, plus Dad's job is there, and it would be hard."

Isaac acts like he wants to say something more, but he seems to stop himself.

"It's not as if I don't like America. It's complicated."

"I understand. How long are you staying?"

"We're not sure. Gran had a heart attack, so we're taking it one day at a time." For some reason, I keep my mouth shut about the whole three-week thing.

We make it out of the trees and onto the dirt road. "See, told you," Ian says and crosses the road to a two-storied home surrounded by more trees. "Come on, Ginnie. I want you to meet my parents."

"All right," I agree. "I can't believe all the space that's around here. That's one thing about London that isn't my favorite thing, and that's everything is so crammed together."

"I'd hate that," Isaac says as we cross the road. "We live on two acres here, but we have another property in the U.P. which has twenty acres of land. That's where we do our hunting and fishing."

"Hunting and fishing? There's a lake right here? And there's deer and all sorts of animals."

"Yeah, but there's more space in the Upper Peninsula. Besides, most of the land around Pigeon Lake is protected by some Ancient Indian pact or something. The fines are huge if you get caught. Not to mention that weird stuff happens at the lake."

"What weird stuff?"

"I'm not going to freak you out just yet. I just met you. Maybe one day I'll tell you ghost stories."

"Ghosts?" I give a little laugh then steal a glance at the woods. My eyes stop scanning, and I freeze in place.

Something in the woods moves. Not something. Someone. Someone whose eyes are looking right at me.

"That's why Ian is not supposed to go into the woods by himself. You've got to be careful. The woods give some people the creeps." Isaac touches my arm. "Are you coming?"

I turn around and move past him to the house. I'm not about to admit being spooked.

"Don't go scaring her," a lady says from the porch.

Isaac laughs. "I didn't get to tell any of the ghost stories."

"My grandparents have lived here for almost forty years, and they've never said anything about ghosts." I still look over my shoulder one more time.

"Are you going to introduce us to your friend, or are you going to stare at her for the rest of the evening?"

"I told you," Ian says. "Her name is Ginnie, and she's from London. Her Dad is from America. And Isaac has been looking at her the entire way back."

Heat rushes to my cheeks, and I look away from Isaac embarrassed. "Hello," I say. A man and woman smile at me from the porch. He's got a close hair cut like Isaac's, but both boys resemble their mother in the face. Their height they get from their father. She is short and plump but pleasantly so. "It's nice to meet you."

Their mother gives me a greeting, only to turn and give Isaac a stern expression. "By the way, Isaac, go clean that mess you left before you headed out to find Ian. You know I don't like you fixing your cars on the driveway and not putting the stuff away."

I follow Isaac with my gaze and see what might have been a red, rusted-out Jeep now covered with mud.

"Please stay for dinner," their mother says. "It's not often we get guests that both our sons like. Do you need to call your parents?"

I press my lips together and weigh my options. These people are strangers, but they seem nice. On the other hand, I am filthy and want to develop my pictures. That's the best part of taking them. "Maybe another time. My Dad is probably back from taking my grandmother to mass."

"Rose? Is Rose Paxton your grandmother?"

I nod slowly, not sure whether he's happy excited or angry excited. "How'd you know that?"

"Everyone knows each other in the Pigeon Forest area, especially this side of the lake, and everyone from about a twenty-mile radius knows Rose," the lady says.

"Is Sam your Dad?" The man rubs his hands together like he already knows the answer.

I nod again.

"Call that rascal, and tell him to get over here. He owes me a rematch on the basketball court. Tell him the message is from Ted

Fulton."

Isaac stands next to me again. "I'm going to go clean up."

"Show Ginnie where the phone is."

I follow Isaac in, and Ian follows me. "It's in the kitchen," Ian says. "I'll show her, Isaac. You should shower. You smell like sweat and oil."

Isaac shoots his brother an annoyed look. "You don't have to say everything that comes to your mind, remember? We talked about this before."

"Yes, I remember. It was when you brought Bethany over, and your zipper was down, and I told you about it."

Isaac stops and shakes his head. "Whatever, Ian." Isaac takes the stairs two at a time.

"I am working very hard at the present moment not to say everything that is in my mind," Ian says and motions for me to follow him. "I think I've embarrassed him."

"He seems like a good brother. I'm sure he forgives you."

Ian hands me the phone but doesn't make eye contact. "So if I tell you that your face and hands are smudged with dirt, and your hair has leaves in it, will I need you to forgive me, too?"

I blink in surprise. "I should go home and shower."

"We have a shower here."

"I'm not comfortable taking a shower here." I dial Gran's number, resolved to go back to her house and scrub down. Dad answers on the first ring. "Virginia May Paxton, where in the world have you been?"

"Um, out," I say. "How'd you know it was me?"

"A father's intuition," he says gruffly. "I have been worried sick. No note. No nothing. And then you leave your cell phone!"

"Sorry. I went for a walk in the woods, that's all."

I could hear Dad breathe into the phone. "The woods are deep, and you've never walked them. Probably best not to do so alone."

"Gran says there's a trail around the lake. I followed the

trail. And I didn't get lost."

"The trail forks near the creek. It can get confusing."

"I didn't make it to the fork, and are you trying to freak me out?"

He exhaled slowly. "People have gotten lost in the woods. Please, at least remember your cell phone next time."

"Fine."

"Do you need me to pick you up? Where are you?"

"I met some guys in the woods, and I'm at their house."

"Are they potheads? You got to be careful because there're a bunch of potheads in this area."

"Dad, there are potheads everywhere. And no, I'm at the Fulton's house. Ted Fulton told me that you owe him a basketball game."

There is a pause before Dad laughs. "Ted Fulton! Tell him anytime, anyplace."

"He wants you to stop over for dinner. Gran, too. But can you come to pick me up first? I need a shower."

"Perfect," Dad says. "Aunt Sue called and said she couldn't come up until later this week, so we have the evening free."

"Okay, but I need to get clean."

"Do they not have a bathroom?"

"Yes, but that's beside the point. I would rather clean up at Gran's."

"I'll bring you a change of clothes. Tell him to get his basketball ready."

Dad hangs up before I can get another word in. No need to tell Mr. Fulton about basketball. I spot him from the window practicing lay-ups outside. Mrs. Fulton has entered the kitchen, so I resist the urge to find Isaac and instead ask if Mrs. Fulton needs any help.

"Thank you, but I'm all set. Could you ask Mr. Fulton to get the grill started? We're grilling homemade pizzas tonight. And Ginnie, I overheard you with your Dad. We have a second restroom if you'd like to freshen up."

I head back outside. Ian sits on the front porch reading a book so thick he needs both hands to hold it. I stop myself from saying anything; he seems completely drawn into the pages, and I don't want to interrupt. As I step off the porch, I glance across the road and into the trees. Nothing out of the ordinary.

"Mr. Fulton? Your wife asks that you start the grill."

"Okay," Mr. Fulton says. "I'm about as ready as I'm going to get."

A red Mustang drives into view and pulls up into the Fulton driveway.

That was rather quick. I hope he remembered my clothes.

"Sam Paxton!" Mr. Fulton calls.

Dad's out of the car, and the two men meet, shake hands, and embrace. Dad's laughing. "Ted Fulton! Long time, no see, my friend!"

I go over to Gran to see if she needs help. "Lord, child, what happened to your hair? And did you go roll in the mud or something?"

Isaac comes over next to me, all showered and clean, and completely mouth-watering, which only embarrasses me more. "I went hiking through Pigeon Forest."

"And what? The dirt was glad to see you, so it kissed you all over the face?"

Isaac laughs. All right, it *is* kind of funny. "Sure, Gran. That's exactly what happened."

"Hello, Isaac Fulton." Gran changes the subject. "I had to get a new young man to mow my lawn because you never seem to be around."

"Gran!"

"I apologize. I'm not hiding, I promise. I've been working at the golf resort. And since I start basic training in another two months, my parents seem to have a to-do list that's ten miles long."

Mr. Fulton calls over to us, "Isaac, bring Rose to the porch and get our visitors something to drink. Sam, you can come with me and help me grill up some pizzas."

Dad follows Mr. Fulton, and it's then I realize he hasn't said two words to me. "Glad you missed me!" I yell out.

He turns and waves. "Your clothes are in the back." Then keeps talking to Mr. Fulton.

"Where is the love?"

"What are you talking about? You've been out kissing the dirt all day. How much love does one girl need?" Gran chuckles and follows Isaac to the porch.

I lean into the back seat and grab the plastic bag Dad threw my stuff in. I say a silent prayer that he remembered to bring my antiperspirant.

Nope. He brought my dark green shorts and a hot pink hoodie. "It doesn't even match," I say through gritted teeth. It's no wonder I've never dated. My Dad's been sabotaging me for years. First bugs, now mismatched clothes.

Dinner is anything but ordinary. I was able to clean up and brush my hair. I had no choice but to wear the shorts and hoodie, my hiking outfit had been too dirty. No one said anything when I sat down, so hopefully, I'm the only one off-put by the color scheme.

Dad and Mr. Fulton talk most of the meal, telling their high school stories.

"You set off the fire alarm because you didn't want to take the English exam."

"Because you dared me!" Dad exclaims. "And I'm the one that gets busted."

"How do I not know about this?" Gran asks.

"I didn't tell you," Dad says. "There're a lot of things I didn't tell you."

Gran acts surprised.

"Don't worry," Mr. Fulton jokes. "Nothing too illegal."

The good thing about the adults carrying on most of the

conversation is that I get to sneak peeks at Isaac. Sometimes I feel him sneaking a look at me, but I pretend to be immensely fascinated by the conversation. Still, I'm glad to have found an opportunity to go to the loo before dinner for a chance to freshen up. At least there are no more twigs in my hair. My reverie ends when I hear the word "ghost."

"Oh, don't start this again," Mrs. Fulton says, pointing a finger at both my dad and Mr. Fulton. "You two and your ghost stories."

"I never heard about a ghost story." Gran is no longer smiling. "When did this happen? What happened? Has it been recently?"

"Mom, relax." Dad patted her arm. "It was after high school graduation."

"You were going to a friend's house."

"Yes, that friend was me. We decided to spend the night in the woods to see who could brave the night."

Dad and Mr. Fulton started laughing simultaneously. They started talking at the same time about dares and who ran the fastest. "I'm telling you, I saw something," Mr. Fulton says.

"You chickened out first. I won."

"This is upsetting," Gran says.

"It's fine. It was years ago. Besides, you always told me that all the ghost stories weren't true."

"You still should have told me." Gran still acted displeased.

"So, Ginnie," Mrs. Fulton says, "Have you graduated?"

It takes a second to realize she's talking to me. "I'm sorry. Can you repeat the question?"

"She's too busy looking at your boy," Gran says with a chuckle.

My face heats up. Now Isaac is watching me. So, is Ian.

"School? Are you done? Do you go off to college this fall?" Mrs. Fulton graciously ignores Gran.

"It looks like it."

"Virginia has been accepted early into college."

"Will you go to school in London?" Mrs. Fulton asks.

"I haven't really thought about it."

"University of Michigan." Gran keeps eating her pizza. "Any grandchild of mine goes to the only school whose degree means something."

"I haven't made any decisions."

"It's paid for," Gran tells the Fultons. She doesn't even look at me. "I will pay the whole way, but I will only write a check to the Maize and Blue."

"I don't think you can write a check out to the Maize and Blue," Ian corrects Gran. "You would need to write it to the University of Michigan."

I smile at Ian and bite my lip to keep from laughing.

"There are good schools everywhere," Mrs. Fulton says.

Gran snorts in derision. "There are only two types of schools. University of Michigan…and everybody else." She shakes her fork at everyone, especially shaking it at me.

Isaac looks over and makes a face that I read to mean glad-it's-you-and-not-me.

"Well, I guess it's settled," Dad says with a laugh. "Virginia, you're going to be a wolverine."

Can I crawl under the table? Or, better yet, can I throw my corn-on-the-cob at my father's head?

I don't know what humiliates me more, the fact that they have already decided my future, or the fact that he calls me Virginia in front of them.

"That's funny," Ian says. "Virginia lives in England." He starts laughing, and his laugh has this high-pitched squeaking sound, which makes Dad start laughing, then just like Dominoes, one-by-one everyone's laughing. Even Isaac thinks it's funny. I try hard to hide my grin because I'm rather annoyed, but Ian's laugh squeaks and pretty soon, I'm giggling with them. Only Gran sits there, eating her pizza, muttering about wolverines.

8

After dinner, Dad and Mr. Fulton head outside for their basketball one-on-one.

I help Isaac and Ian clear off the table.

Isaac sets the dishes down in the sink. "Want to go do something fun?"

My heart jumps into my throat. What kind of fun is he referring to? "Sure."

Ian walks into the kitchen and asks if I want to play *Spoons*.

I look from Isaac to Ian.

"Hey, Ian, I'm going to take her mudding first. Want to come along?"

"You both just cleaned up. That would not be logical to get dirty again."

"Nothing about mudding is logical. That's what makes it fun."

Ian sighs and shakes his head. "No, Ginnie and I should stay and play *Spoons*. She would like it, and she would stay clean."

I try to come up with a good excuse to go because I don't want to hurt Ian's feelings, but the thought of being alone with a boy—I mean, a man—is way too alluring to pass up. A guy like Isaac has never asked me to do something like this with him.

"How about I take her mudding, then we will come back and play *Spoons*."

"I think that's a great idea," Mrs. Fulton has entered the kitchen and has started running the water. "It's Ian's turn to help me load the dishwasher."

"Does that sound like a plan?" I ask, still not wanting to hurt the boy.

Ian's muttering under his breath while his mother is directing him with the dishes. Isaac gently pulls my sleeve, and we leave quietly. Once out of earshot, Isaac whispers, "He'll be fine. He mutters like that to work out the answer he wasn't expecting."

"He was expecting me to play with spoons?"

Isaac grins and shakes his head. "It's a game called *Spoons*, and yes, that's what he thought would happen. It will still happen, but I thought you might want to get out of everyone's scrutiny for a little while." He opens the passenger door for me. The outside of the Jeep seems to be layered with mud, but the inside looks spotless. "You may get mud on you," he says, watching me. "We don't have to go if you'd prefer."

"No!" I say a little too quickly. "I've never been…mudding, so I say let's give it a go." I slide in, and Isaac shuts the door. I have no clue what I just agreed to do. Would it be like a mud fight?

Isaac jumps in and revs the engine. Hard rock pumps through the speakers. He gives me a sly grin that melts my insides to liquid lava. He backs out and zips down the road. I glance back to see my Dad watching us. He seems perplexed. I laugh out loud.

"What?" He turns down the volume.

"My Dad doesn't quite know what to think."

"Yeah, he already talked with me."

My mouth drops open. "Please, tell me you're joking."

"No, I'm not joking. He told me while you were cleaning up that any son of Ted's is a friend of his, but that if I touch you, he will cut off the body part that was doing the touching."

"I'm going to strangle him."

"Don't worry about it. He's being a good Dad. If I ever have a daughter, especially one that looks like you, you better believe I will protect her."

I would be flattered by his words, but there's no time. He turns down a narrow path, smack in the middle of the woods. "Is this a road?"

"It's a two-track."

"So? Is it a road?"

Isaac laughs. "You're funny, you know that?"

I give a half-laugh but clutch the seat as the Jeep bobs through the very narrow trail. Tree branches are slapping the doors, and I find I'm holding my breath. A couple turns later, we are in the middle of thick woods, and I have lost all sense of direction.

"Are you ready?" he asks.

"Uh…"

He laughs again, then guns the engine. I shriek as he plows through a mud trench, and the mud splatters the windshield. He puts the wipers on, which do little more than smear it. "Don't worry, I can see where I'm going." The Jeep jumps from the bumps and slides through mud that looks like mini-lakes. Before I know what I'm doing, I'm holding on to his arm and shrieking through every bump and slide. At one point the Jeep is airborne, and we both yell like we're on a roller coaster. By the time, the Jeep slides to a stop, I am grinning and breathless.

"That was crazy."

"Crazy fun?"

"Yes!"

"Good. I didn't know if you'd want to come after I tried to spook you with ghost stories."

"Ha, ha, let's not bring that up now, shall we?" I take a glance at the forest around us.

"Yeah, let's keep moving before the tires get stuck."

"That doesn't sound too good. Have you been stuck before?"

"It comes with the territory. But I know exactly what to do if it happens."

"Seems like you go mudding quite a bit."

"Honestly, it gives me space to think and relax and not be, you know, 'on' all the time." Isaac shifts gears, and we slide out of the mud and onto another trail.

"Like with Ian?"

He nods. The sun is setting, but I can still see his features through the dusk.

"I think you're a good older brother. You have a lot of patience."

"Sometimes. And sometimes I have to come out here and release the tension." He grins in my direction. "So, why have I never met you?"

"I've only come to Michigan during Christmas holiday. Normally, Gran and Gramps would spend their summer holiday out in London. But then Gran had the heart attack, and well, here we are."

"What happened to her was awful. My Dad responded to her call, you know."

"Really? He's a doctor?"

"A police officer. Chief of Pigeon Forest. When the call came through, he knew it was Rose, so he went over there to assist EMS."

"Where did they find her?" I am intrigued at what happened, especially with her cryptic call still lingering in my mind, and her acting like it never took place.

"Outside. She was working on her garden or something, thought she heard something, went to stand up to check it out, and saw someone approaching her. She was so shocked, she stumbled back. Dad says they don't know if she had a heart attack first, or if seeing someone caused her to have a heart attack."

My gut feels queasy. "Who did she see?"

"We don't know. The police checked the perimeter several times. There was no evidence of anyone being there. No footprints. Nothing. Rose told us not to worry, that she probably didn't remember too clearly."

I open my mouth to tell him about her phone call to me, but I shut it before I say anything. It's better to think first and talk later. "I had no idea. Poor Gran."

"She'll recover. She's the toughest lady we know."

The engine sputters, then lurches forward. "Oh no," Isaac says and switches gears. "Come on, Daisy, don't do this to me now."

I remember the tools he had to put away when we came back from the hike. "Was it having problems before?"

"It's a fuel line issue." Isaac glances over at me apologetically. "I'm sorry. I thought I fixed it. Fixing cars is kind of my thing."

"Mudding, fixing cars, and didn't I overhear that you have a job?"

"Yep. Up at the golf course. I'm one of the mechanics. I make sure the golf carts are good, along with the company vehicles."

The engine keeps sputtering, but Isaac seems to know how to keep it moving. "So, what about you, Virginia from London. What's your thing?"

Having him say my full name seems very intimate, and I feel my cheeks redden, especially because I'm not sure I should tell him about my bug fascination. "I'm into photography. For Christmas, Dad bought me a Nikon D7000 and the set-up equipment."

"That's a nice camera?"

"The best. It's about a thousand euros."

"Wow. Sounds like an awesome present. You'll have to show me sometime."

"It's at your house. I took a bunch of shots today that I need to develop." I decide not to admit that I take it with me everywhere I go, and the only reason I didn't have it with me is that I was in la-la-land when Isaac asked me out.

This time the Jeep sputters to a halt. Isaac tries to start the engine, but it chokes and turns over.

The sun has all but disappeared over the horizon. It hits me that I am alone in the forest with a hot guy. I don't know whether to be terrified or exhilarated. At the moment, with the creepy trees and forest sounds, terrified wins out.

"Stay here," Isaac says, as he reaches behind us for a flashlight. He pops the hood and disappears into the darkness.

I keep my eyes focused on the hood in front. I hear snaps of branches, and sounds of things that I'm not sure what they are, and I refuse to find out tonight.

The door opens and I jump.

"Sorry," Isaac says. "Do you mind holding the flashlight? I have to pull out the fuel line and make sure it's not clogged."

"Sure," I say a little too brightly. I try to open my door, but it's too close to a tree.

"Here, climb over on this side. There's more room."

I push myself up and climb over the stick shift, allowing Isaac to hold my waist as he helps me out of the Jeep. For a second, we both stand there. His hands linger on my waist, and my hands linger on his chest. "Thanks," I say to break the silence.

He releases me but holds my hand to help me walk to the front of the automobile. "Just hold this right here, so that I can see to the side of the calibrator."

I have no idea what a calibrator is, but I hold the flashlight exactly where he showed me.

Some bird flies through the trees, and I jump again, moving the flashlight. "I'm sorry."

"You don't have to apologize. I'm the one with the crap car. You're stuck out here because of me, but don't worry. I've camped in these woods before. It's your basic forest life, that's all. Besides, we're only about a mile from my place. If we have to, we can walk back."

"We don't have Ian to help with directions."

"Ha, ha. Okay, the line looks good. There might just be an air pocket in the gas. I'll be right back."

"Where are you going?" I hold the flashlight on his face.

"I have a gas can in the back. Would you like to go with me?"

Yes, yes, I would, but I don't say that. I tell myself to be brave. "Don't be long."

"It'll take me about thirty seconds." He takes off down the side of the Jeep.

My official freaking out begins. The woods seem alive, and they're watching me. That may be my Londonite-self talking, but it's the truth. So when I feel the cold wind lick against my legs like it did earlier in the day, I start to tremble. I hear Isaac talking and then he's standing there again. I push down the terror and try to hold the flashlight steady, my hand can't hold it still.

"A few minutes more," Isaac says and holds his hand over mine. "I'm going to make this up to you, Ginnie, I promise."

I nod, still unsure of myself to speak.

Something moves out of the trees with a start. I grab Isaac and whip around with the flashlight. A deer stands directly behind us. He seems to take us in, then runs back into the woods.

Isaac starts to chuckle.

"Not funny," I say, but at least I'm able to breathe again.

"I think I've got it. Here, let's get back in the Jeep."

A part of me wonders if he's saying that because I'm acting like an imbecile, but I'm not about to argue. He leads me to his door, and I climb in and back over to my side. I cross myself without him noticing and pray that whatever he did works.

"Do you know how to start a car?" he asks.

"I think so, but normally it's on my side over here."

"You press down on the clutch and turn the key. Got it?"

No. No, I have limited knowledge of vehicles, but I nod because I want more than anything to be out of these dark woods. I climb back over to the driver's side. "Press on this? This is the clutch?"

"Yep. You've got it. Then turn the key when I tell you to."

I sit there while he goes back out.

"Try it now."

I do as he told, and the engine turns over.

"Stop," he says. "Count to ten, then try it again."

This time, the engine chugs to life. I sigh in relief and am smiling when Isaac drops the hood down. He grins at me and gives me a thumbs-up sign.

My smile fades and fear takes over. Directly behind him stands a girl. But she's not looking at him, she's only looking at me. Her hair is long and dark, and even though she's darker-skinned, her face is very pale. Isaac must see my frozen expression because he turns to see what I'm looking at. He turns back to me confused. "Are you all right?" He makes his way back to his door.

I shake my head, unsure of how to answer. Because whoever that was has disappeared.

9

I sit in the back of the red Mustang with Grandma in the front seat. Dad stands at his door still chatting with Mr. Fulton. If I had one of those long canes, I'd wrap it around his waist and yank him inside the car. I have one desire, and one desire only, and that is to go back to Gran's house where I can be alone.

There may be more desires on my list, such as locking myself in my room in London and never traveling here at all. Since I can't change the past, going to Gran's and locking myself in my room is what tops the cake. Just reliving the events of the evening brings me to tears and makes my throat all stuffy and choked up. After seeing the girl on the trail, my brain, my mouth, everything froze up. Isaac kept asking what was wrong, and all I could do was keep my eyes shut and shake my head in response. He eventually stopped asking. When we got back to his house, Gran was with Mrs. Fulton on the porch waiting for us. She took one look at me and told Dad we needed to leave. Isaac had been polite enough to say good-night, but then he holed himself up. Which is what I want to do. And yet, here we are. I'm freaked out and unsettled, and Dad won't shut his mouth.

"What the bloody hell, Dad," I say under my breath.

Gran turns around in the seat. "What happened? Tell me everything."

I should be polite, but every nerve ending seems to be on edge. "It's nothing. I'm only tired and jet-lagged."

Gran leans over the seat. "Samuel Paxton, get in the car now. I need to go home, and you have kept your daughter and me waiting long enough."

I hear Dad and Mr. Fulton say something and laugh, and I wonder if they are going to ignore Gran, but then Dad's sliding in the driver seat and starting the car.

As Dad reverses, he asks, "What's the problem, Virginia? It's not like you to be so rude."

"Leave her alone," Gran says. "She doesn't want to talk about it."

"There's no excuse not to speak. You didn't say one word to anyone when you got back with Isaac, you just climbed into the car. Isaac probably thinks you're some uppity London girl."

I can't stop them. The tears leak from my eyes. I know what Dad says is true. Isaac will probably never talk to me again. But they hadn't seen what I had. Nor do they understand that I need to hide, to pretend that what I saw is only a figment of my imagination, and that conversation is the last thing on my mind.

"Well?"

"She doesn't want to talk about it," Gran says with an edge to her voice. "Leave her be."

Thankfully, the ride back around the lake is not even five minutes. Since the top is down, I don't wait for either of them to get out. I jump out and run into the house.

"We're not done yet!" Dad says, but I'm already in the house and on my way up the stairs.

I peel off my clothes, throw on my pajama bottoms and a tank top, and fall onto the bed. I should be exhausted, but I'm too keyed up. I check my phone for messages. None. That upsets me more than anything. I toss my phone back on the bedside table and sulk. No friends to call me. Not even Alisa. When I finally meet some nice people, I have to act like an idiot. It's not my finest moment to be a sodding mess, but I hold the pillow and cry. How do I fix this?

Deciding that a list is in order, I sit up and rifle through my things for my notebook. I hear Gran's phone ring downstairs, but don't try to answer it. It's probably Aunt Sue. I'm partway through my list of how to fix things with Isaac when there's a knock on my bedroom door.

"Virginia, you have a phone call."

I set my notebook down and open the door. Dad's standing there with a wireless telephone in his hand. His eyebrows are doing this thing where he's trying to figure out what is going on. It's his scientist look, but I don't enlighten him. I grab the phone, mutter a "thanks," and shut the door.

"Hello?"

"Hey, Ginnie."

My heart seems to pound ten times faster.

"It's Isaac."

"I know." Stupid thing to say, but his voice is deep and smooth, and I haven't heard anything like it.

"You left your bag here."

My stomach flips. "My camera!" How could I have been that out of it that I ran to the car without my bag? "I can't believe I forgot it."

"Well, you seemed in a hurry, but anyway, I can drop it off tomorrow morning on my way to work. I won't wake you. I'll leave it on the porch."

"No," I say too fast. "I mean, it's really expensive. I can't be having someone snatch it."

"This is Northern Michigan. Stealing isn't too big of a thing here, but whatever you say. I have to be at work at eight in the morning, will you be up by then?"

I crinkle my nose. "No, probably not."

"If you'd like, I can drop it off right now."

"Yes," I say too fast again. "If it's okay with you, I'd appreciate it."

"Sure. I'll be there in a few." He hangs up without a good-bye, but I shouldn't be surprised. I treated him like one of the ten lepers. I vow to apologize when he stops over. Now that I have my wits about me, I can explain—or at least partly explain—my bizarre behavior.

I brush my hair and check my reflection. My eyes are a wee bit puffy from the tears, but it'll have to do. I hear the Jeep's engine before it pulls into Gran's driveway. Wanting privacy, I run down the stairs and am on the porch when he steps out of the Jeep.

Thinking about what happened makes me nervous, but I tell myself that he deserves an apology. It's not his fault, I'm seeing things.

"Hey," he says, stopping at the bottom of the steps. He holds out the bag.

I step toward him and take it. "Thanks."

He nods and turns to walk back to Jeep.

"Wait!" I step down, but it is dark, and I'm still not over what happened. I stay on the safety of the bottom step. Isaac stops but doesn't move toward me. "I w-w-ant to thank you for this evening. I know it doesn't seem like it, but I had a lovely time. Up until, well, that doesn't matter. I'm sorry if I acted weird. Dark forests aren't my thing."

"I'm the one who's embarrassed." He rubs his hand on his neck. "I thought the Jeep would be fine, but I should have run it through once to be on the safe side. Not exactly impressive, is it?"

"What are you talking about? You somehow managed to get that big lug down some very tiny trails, and you drove through mud better than anyone I know, and you single-handedly fixed your Jeep in the middle of the creepy, dark forest with a crazy English girl adding to your headache. If that's not impressive, I don't know what is."

Isaac steps closer to me and gives a slight smile. "When you put it that way…"

"Exactly."

He pauses before saying, "You sure you're okay? Don't take this wrong, but you acted freaked out. I felt so bad. I had to hear it from my mother, my father, and even Ian."

"Ian?"

"He said if you would have stayed and played *Spoons*, you would have enjoyed it more."

I cringe because I know I made a jerk of myself. I contemplate telling him. Instead, I say, "After I saw the deer, I kept thinking there were things out there, so I kept my eyes shut until we got back." Sighing, I'm resigned when I say, "Too many ghost stories, and I feel pretty dumb."

"You're a city girl out of your element. If you were to take me to a big city, I might act the same way."

I laugh at the visual.

"Well, I've got to go, so I'll see you around. Good night." He pauses before heading to the Jeep. I want there to be more, for us to make that contact like we did tonight when his arms were around my waist.

I may want to tell him that, but reservation stops me. He's seen too much of my crazy side tonight; I don't want to add hapless school girl crush to the list.

When he gets into the Jeep, the moment's passed, and I realize I'm outside in the dark. I race into the house and slam the door and lock it. I take a deep breath. I glance up the stairs, but I'm still wired. It's a good time to use Gran's computer and scanner and check out my pictures. That'll help me unwind.

First, I run up the stairs and press my ear to Dad's door. He's snoring. Of course. He's been going nonstop since he picked me up from Saint Francis. Once I get downstairs, I turn on one lamp in Gran's office and start-up the equipment.

As I'm scanning the digital pictures, I minimize the screen and start perusing the Internet. I can only stand to be on Instagram for a few minutes because it makes me miss home more. I click on the History icon out of habit with my own computer and feel as if I unearthed something secretive. Recent websites looked up are ones on tribal curses and Ancient Indian pacts. Now I'm perplexed. Gran writes a newspaper column about gardens and home projects, so I'm drawn to these sites that seem out of place with the other sites on the History list.

"Can't sleep?"

I whirl around in the chair to see Gran standing in the doorway.

"I can't either." She comes to sit down in a recliner next to her bookshelves.

The office is cozy, and eclectic, like Gran, with soft colors contrasting vibrant pictures on the walls. I notice one of mine hanging between bookcases. I took the picture at Christmas with the new camera. It had just snowed, and the sun had shown through the trees onto the iced-over lake. It had been the most serene scene, and I had captured it. "You hung up my picture."

"Yes, I went and got it enlarged and framed. It's a beautiful shot. There's a great photography program at the University of Michigan."

That is one subject I don't want to discuss. "I see here on your history list that you were looking up Ancient Indian pacts. Is this a new assignment at the paper?"

Gran furrows her brow, then shrugs. "Well, I guess you're old enough to know, but I haven't explained it all to your father yet, so you'll have to not say anything until I can have that conversation with him. Deal?"

"Deal."

"A little over forty years ago, Grandpa and I decided to raise our family here. Aunt Sue was on the way, and we were tired of living in a spare apartment in Bay City. So, Grandpa took the meager savings we had and drove us up to where he would spend his summers as a boy. At the time, all of the land around Pigeon Lake was protected under tribal laws. The U.S. government gave certain Chippewa tribes most of the land around the lake to settle some type of tribal disputes. Who knows? What I do know is that your Grandpa made a sound, valid business contract with two of the Indian leaders for three acres of land at the water's edge. Since then the tribes have been fighting us to get the land back."

"The contract's binding, right?"

"Yep. Your Grandpa knew what he was doing. We paid a fair price for the land, most of our savings, and slowly built the house. He took odds and ends jobs fixing things until people in the community were calling him directly to do the jobs. I started substitute teaching until the newspaper hired me, and we were able to take the money and voila. Here's the result." She holds out her hands.

"So why look up tribal curses?"

Gran releases a sigh and a little laugh. "Don't think your old grandmother as a superstitious fool, but the man who is wanting this land back said something about a curse on the land. I know it's probably scare tactics, but I wanted to find out if there might be any truth to it."

I think of the girl I saw in the forest, and a chill runs up my spine.

Gran seems to sense that. She watches me closely, "Are you superstitious?"

For some reason, I want to change the subject again. "No, not really. This land is too beautiful to have any curses on it, so that guy's feeding you a pile of bollocks." I see that my scanning has been complete for some time. "Want to see some of the pictures I've been taking?"

Her smile returns, and it's as gracious as always. "Of course." She leans forward and says, "Oh my."

I laugh. Sister Mary Lucia's photo turns out perfect. "I have to send this to Alisa."

"What is the nun doing?"

"She's praying."

"Well, I don't approve of you not praying, but my, look at those nostrils."

We laugh, and I click through more, mostly of the hike. The pictures aren't my best work, but I can't wait to show Dad.

"I will never understand yours and your father's fascination with insects."

"It's a whole other world. These ecosystems have survived and thrived for millions of years. Like this butterfly. She doesn't need us to exist. It's almost as if we're a part of her world not the other way around."

Gran stifles a yawn. "I'm sorry, but that's my cue. The meds are finally kicking in." She stands up and kisses my forehead. "'Night, Ginnie."

"Good night."

"Oh, and Ginnie?"

"Yes?" I glance up from a picture.

"Just…be careful, okay? Maybe not go out into the woods by yourself. That way you won't get so easily spooked."

"Got it." I resist saying that there was no way in Hades that I'd go back into the woods again. At least not without someone else and never in the dark.

She gives a slight wave before leaving the office.

When I turn back to the computer, I think about what Gran just said. *That way you won't get so easily spooked.* How does she know I got spooked?

But I can't dwell on the question for too long because I get distracted by the next picture. It's a blurry shot. It must have been when I fell. The edges seem defined, but not the center, which is a blob of white, like someone smudged it in the wrong place. That's when I remember accidentally snapping the shot when the cold wind hit me. Feeling my hair stand on end, I hurry and click to another shot. And I pretend that underneath the blur is not the outline of a person.

10

Today, there will be no hikes.

Today will be a lie-on-the-beach-and-work-on-my-tan kind of day.

I put on my bathing suit and throw on a pretty deep purple swimsuit cover my Mum gave me from the catalogue. I comb out my long hair until it shines, add some product to make it not frizz, then put on my sunglasses.

"You will do just fine," I say to my reflection in the mirror. If Isaac sees me today, there will be no twigs in my hair and no dirt on my face.

Grabbing my cell phone, my camera, a book, and a beach towel, I head toward the kitchen for a few snacks.

Gran's outside on the deck that faces the water. I say good morning.

"There she is," Gran says. "Will you be a dear and make me an English muffin with peanut butter? My energy hasn't recharged yet."

"Of course."

Deciding on one myself, I make two, slather on the peanut

butter, and then pour two cups of coffee. Gran likes her black, but I throw in several spoonfuls of sugar and creamer for mine.

Once outside, I notice she already has a coffee.

"That's okay," she says. "This one's all done."

I sit down next to her and think about last night, wondering if I could pry some more info out of her.

"Oh, I wanted to ask you. You flirting with that Isaac Fulton?"

I'm sipping my coffee at that moment, so of course, when she asks me, I gulp too much of it, coughing violently.

Gran throws her head back and laughs. "Oh, dear! Oh, dear! My sweet Ginnie has a crush."

I shake my head, but she just laughs and laughs. I cover and say, "There's a boy back home I like. His name is Leo." Interesting that it is the first time I've thought of him since meeting Isaac.

She pats my arm. "There's no reason you can't like two boys. Isaac's a good one. As good as they come. I didn't want to pry last night, but I can only hold out for so long. What happened that you were behaving so badly?"

Gran's word from last night replay in my head. I have a feeling she knows more than she's saying. "Did something happen in the woods?"

Gran stops smiling and furrows her eyebrows. "What?"

"Do you know anything about the woods? Isaac was joking around yesterday about them being haunted. Then Dad and Mr. Fulton tell some story about a ghost. What's it all about? You've lived here the longest, you should have the inside scoop."

"I thought you weren't superstitious?"

"I'm not. Not really. More curious."

"I've lived here for a long time, and I've hiked the trails, and there's nothing in the woods other than God's beautiful creation."

"So, no one might have died in there and is now looking for revenge?"

Gran blinks at me in surprise, then starts howling in laughter.

"What's so funny?" Dad steps outside.

Gran is still chuckling, so I answer, "I'm ever the jokester."

"Glad to see you're not as cranky as you were last night." He pulls up a foldable chair and sits down.

"I was overly tired, and Isaac's Jeep broke down in the middle of a dark forest. Forgive me that I can't be eternal sunshine when I'm fearing for my life."

Gran starts laughing all over again, as does Dad. "Oh no," he says. "Poor Isaac."

"Is that why you asked me about someone dying in the woods?" Gran wipes at her eyes.

"Forget I said anything. I'm going to sunbathe." I stand up to leave. "Oh Dad, I took some interesting photos yesterday from my hike."

His eyes light up. "Did you collect any specimens?"

"No, I thought I'd wait for you."

"I have some running around to do, but maybe this afternoon or evening we'll go explore."

"Make it afternoon," I say, already forgetting my vow to not hike today. "Evenings in the forest aren't my cup of tea."

"Oh Ginnie," Gran says. "By the way, in answer to your question, people die everywhere. When I die, it'll probably be right here. That doesn't mean I'm going to haunt the place."

I walk to the lake and situate my towel over a lounge chair. I start to read but set the book down after a few minutes. Too much is on my mind. I study the scene around me. Birds create a chorus in the trees, a soft warm breeze is already blowing, and the sun already beats down without a cloud to suffocate it. In the daylight and out in the open, it seems as if I'm nothing more than a paranoid city girl.

But the problem remains that I can't discredit what I experienced. And the picture. It shows…something. I glance back up at the deck where Dad and Gran still sit. Maybe I can talk to her later when I have more concrete evidence.

"Are you loony?" I say out loud.

I don't want concrete evidence! I want to stay away from the woods. At least by myself, and especially at night. But the questions are already sizzling in my head, demanding correct responses. I am, after all, a scientist's daughter. And when there are questions, that means there need to be logical answers.

I pick up the book to read again. And try not to think. I check my cell phone for messages. There are none.

Before I talk myself out of it, I call Mum. It goes straight to her voicemail.

"Hi, Mum. Was wondering about you. Call me back."

I stare at the phone and then call Alisa. When she doesn't answer her cell phone either, I try her house phone.

"'ello, there." It's Alisa's Mum.

"Hi there, is Alisa home?"

"Ginnie? Where've you been?"

"In America, but I should be home soon."

"Well, come stay with us, of course. Alisa isn't here though. She's been a busy bee. I'll have her call you."

I manage to say good-bye and hang up. As I lay in the sun, I imagine Alisa at parties, having the time of her life. Grant it, I had only been gone for two days. I imagine Leo and wonder if he's called her back. But I know Alisa would never like him the way I like him. I do still like him, at least I think I do. Then I think of Isaac, and I smile.

So, there's not total despair. Only a bit of despair.

It doesn't take long to start to doze, especially with the restless night I had. I sleep until a shadow covers my face, blocking the sun. I peek open my eyes to see Ian standing over me.

"I have a Welcome to America present," he says, then he walks over to the dock, sits down, and lets his legs dangle in the water.

"A present?" I sit up and stretch. "That was nice of you."

I get up from the lounger and sit next to him on the dock, placing my feet in the water, too. I can feel the seaweed tickle the bottoms of my feet and decide to sit cross-legged. Ian hands me a large brown grocery bag stuffed with items. "It's a peace offering mostly. Mom said to say it is a Welcome to America present, but it really isn't. A peace offering is when two or more sides are conflicting, one side makes a peace offering in hopes that the other side will accept."

"Oh, well, thank you. I didn't know we were conflicting sides."

"I was upset at Isaac, then you were upset at Isaac, then Isaac was upset at everyone. Conflicting sides. So I brought a peace offering."

I smile. His earnestness is refreshing. "You are right about one thing, Ian. I should have stayed and played *Spoons*."

"I am right about a lot of things. This was my idea. Not Isaac's. He wanted to bring it to you, but he had to work. He told me to wait until later, but I snuck out now."

"Should we let them know you're here? I don't want them to worry."

"No. They'll know. Isaac only works the morning shift today, so he'll be home by noon." Ian grins mischievously but doesn't make eye contact.

I had slept until past ten, so I check my phone to see the time. "It's already past noon," I say. "Maybe we should make that call."

"Open the bag. It's a peace offering."

I set it down between us and open it up. It's a hodge-podge assortment of food. "Pringles? Nutty bars? A case of Vernor's Ginger Ale?" Some of the items we have back in England, but not Vernor's.

"And look," Ian said, rifling through the bag. "Bazooka Joe bubble gum, and here." He shoves a big plastic container of chicken at me. "Left-over Kentucky Fried Chicken!"

Ian seems so pleased with himself, that I start to laugh. "This is fantastic! Thank you."

The dock creaks, and I look over to see Isaac heading to us. My heart slams into my chest at the sight of him.

Isaac says, "Ian, you're a dead man."

Ian jumps up. "Not if you can't catch me." Ian runs to the edge of the dock, but Isaac is fast. Ian dives into the water with Isaac at his heels. Both guys splash and fight as they come up.

"It's my peace offering!" Ian yells, before getting dunked again.

I set the food down and run to the edge. "Ian? Are you all right?"

Ian is sputtering but grinning. "My peace offering to end the conflict."

"Yes, I agree. The gift is Ian's peace offering. Not Isaac's." I stick my tongue out at Isaac to show him whose side I am on.

Ian cackles in delight.

Isaac swims over to me. "Will you help us back up?" He extends his hand.

"All right, but no pulling me in. I actually did my hair this morning."

I reach for his hand and grab it. Isaac yanks as I scream. I fall into the water with a dreadful splat. The water is thick with weeds, and it pulls at me. A shock of cold water slams into me, taking my breath away. When I come up, I'm coughing and sputtering for the second time today.

Isaac and Ian find it quite funny. But I'm shivering.

"I can't believe you fell for that," Isaac laughs.

"I trusted you," I say, forcing myself not to spook again. It's only cold water. I splash Isaac. "Now my stomach hurts because I belly-flopped. Not to mention my hair!"

They both find it amusing, so I splash both of them. When that doesn't work, I attack.

I lunge for Isaac and shove him under, but he's deft. He has me in his arms and under the water in seconds. Ian comes to my rescue, and we dunk Isaac together. When we all break the surface, we're panting and laughing, and yes, I'll admit it, even with the seaweed and the spooky vibes, I'm having a riot.

Ian swims away from us out toward the middle of the lake. "Come on, guys. How far can you swim?"

Is that okay?" I ask, still trying to gather my breath.

"He's fine," Isaac says, just as breathlessly. "We've been swimming this lake since we were boys. He's probably a better swimmer than I am." He swims closer to me, and my nerves are all aflutter. "How's your stomach? You had quite a belly-flop."

"No thanks to you."

"Sorry. I only wanted you in the water with us."

I smile because I can't help it. He makes my toes tingle and my stomach flip and my heart tremble. "It's refreshing."

"Can you swim deep? We could swim out a little."

But I'm not really hearing him. I'm too busy looking at the water drops running down his chest.

"Virginia?"

I turn so fast, I lose my balance and half-fall in the water. Isaac catches me until I'm upright again.

"Hi, Dad."

Gran stands beside him, and she doesn't look too pleased either. "This is not a swimming lake." She speaks before Dad does. "You need to get out of the water."

Dad still hasn't spoken. He keeps his eyes on Isaac. "Don't make me not like you."

"Yes, sir."

"Dad, it's not like that. We are swimming."

"You need to come out of the water," Gran repeats. "You promised you wouldn't go in it."

"It sort of happened, Gran, but I'm fine." My teeth began to chatter.

Dad keeps eyeing Isaac. Gran's watching me. Soon Ian splashes over to us.

"I thought you guys were going swimming?" Ian asks.

"We are," Isaac says. "It's good seeing you, Mr. Paxton." He turns and swims out toward the deeper water.

I move toward the shore, officially grossed out by the water. "You're right, Gran. The weeds are thick."

"And leeches." She pointed at my feet.

Sure enough, three leeches are attached to my feet. Two at the toes, and one at the ankle. Scientist's daughter or not, this disgusts me. "Get them off, Dad."

But Dad has actually knelt down to inspect them. "Will you look at that? How fascinating."

"Dad!"

"I'll get some salt, but don't say I didn't warn you." Gran leaves us for the house.

"Look, Virginia. These leeches have the same markings on them that the beetle does."

"They look like nasty leeches to me. We don't have to investigate every creature, Dad."

Dad goes to flick one off my ankle, and it easily falls away. "That's not a leech." Dad flicks the other two off.

"Are those beetles?"

"What are they doing underwater?"

All three are moving back toward the water.

Chills erupt all over my skin, and I nearly have a meltdown. I shake myself and swipe at my arms and legs. "Are there any more?"

Dad looks me over. "I don't see any. By the way, I came down here to let you know I'm going into town. I'm meeting someone for lunch. Would you like to come with me?"

"No, I'm good. Who are you going out to lunch with?"

"Just an old friend."

"An old friend? Ain't that just fine," I mutter and head to

the dock where I can watch Ian and Isaac swim. I still feel the willies after those bugs on me. I shake out my hair and braid it.

"Wait," Dad calls out. "What does 'fine' mean?"

"It means *fine*. As in *whatever you say*."

"You act like you're upset."

"Dad, you sent me packing to another continent telling me my Gran's on death's door, and she seems pretty healthy to me. And now, you're going out to lunch with a friend. I'm glad you're enjoying your vacation."

"I invited you to mass. You went hiking all day instead, remember?"

"Fine."

"And I invited you to lunch."

"Fine."

"Stop saying 'fine'."

"Okay. *Whatever*."

Isaac and Ian swim to the dock and climb onto it.

"Check for leeches. Or beetles. I had three on me."

"They're harmless," Isaac says and scans his legs and Ian's.

Ian has two between his toes, but Isaac has none.

"Here's the salt!" Gran yells from the end of the dock.

I bend over to study the leech, and it doesn't look like a beetle at all. "This is a leech."

"Of course, it is." Ian walks past me, takes the salt from Gran, and pours it on his toes.

"Do you need the salt?" Gran asks me.

"I didn't have leeches. They were beetles."

Gran frowns but doesn't say anything. Instead, she heads back to the house.

"How would beetles survive in the water?" Isaac asks.

"I have no idea. There's a lot about this place that is confusing."

"Let's snack on some of that food we brought." Isaac goes to the bag and sits down beside it.

"The food *I* brought," Ian clarifies.

"What makes you think I'll share?" I take the bag from both of them and start rifling through it.

Isaac smirks. "You'll share or you'll get thrown in the water."

"No, thank you." I shiver just thinking about it. Gran's right. No more lake for me.

"One person cannot eat all that food," Ian states matter-of-factly, not paying attention to us. "Unless that person was used to eating several thousand calories in one sitting, which isn't the case here. A body wouldn't know what to do with it. You definitely would get sick."

"I'm going to share, Ian. I was just teasing."

"It doesn't make sense," Ian says again and sits on my other side.

"Sorry about earlier," Isaac says quietly.

"Don't worry about it. I don't know what my Dad was doing, other than embarrassing me."

"He was being a protective father. Nothing wrong with that."

I lean back and pretend to scrutinize Isaac. "Are you a pothead or coke addict or do you punch little children or steal their candy?"

Isaac does not hide his confusion. "No…why?"

"Because you're too nice. What kind of guy sides with the girl's Dad? No guy I've ever met."

Now Isaac laughs. "I sometimes pull my dog's tail," he mockingly confesses. "And I always eat the last bite of everything…without even asking. And I drink from the juice containers and put them back in the refrigerator."

I roll my eyes. "That's *not* what I'm talking about."

Still, he makes me smile.

Ian hands me a drumstick. "Don't worry. It's still good. It's been in a Tupperware container with a cooling pack to keep the chicken fresh. You have to think about these things. Getting salmonella poisoning is not good. People die from it."

"Don't spoil our lunch," Isaac reaches for a fried chicken breast.

"It's not spoiled. That's what I'm saying. I put the chicken in a Tupperware container with a cooling pack." Ian sighs in exasperation. "You need to listen."

"Okay, okay," Isaac jokes. "Have you ever eaten a Nutty Bar?" He hands over a package with two chocolate bars. "It's chocolate and wafers and peanut butter. Basically, it's heaven."

I set my unfinished chicken leg down, open the plastic wrap, and take a bite. "These are amazing."

"I eat one layer at a time," Ian says. "That way it lasts longer."

So, I follow his suggestion with the second one. Then I have to force myself not to grab another package and devour it, as well. I'm thankful that I'm still wearing my swim cover-up, even if it got wet.

"Now for Vernors." Isaac hands me an opened can. "I know for a fact you don't have this over there. Not even all of the states have it here."

"It tickles my nose." I laugh and take a sip. "It's Ginger Ale."

"It's better than Ginger Ale. It's Vernors." Isaac opens another can and takes a long drink.

We sit on the dock and finish our sodas and chicken, then open the Bazooka Joe gum package and have a piece. The brothers are funny, and I find it sweet that they're so close, even if they tease each other. I glance over at Isaac, who is currently wrestling Ian for the Pringles, and realize how much I like him. He takes the edge off homesickness.

"I've got to go." Isaac stands up. "They need me at the Golf Pro shop this afternoon."

"Me, too," Ian says. "I don't work in the Golf Pro Shop, but sometimes they call me to be a caddy."

"Do you golf?" Isaac asks me.

"No."

"I'll have to take you."

"Okay."

"And me," Ian pipes in. "I'll take you, too."

"Okay."

"Hey," Ian says and jumps in the rowboat. "We should row this to the beach across from our house, so we don't have to walk all around the lake to get back home."

"You walked over to my house?"

"I jogged." Isaac shrugged. "It's not like I'm going to drive a car over here when it's only a mile away."

"You did last night."

"I was thinking of the time last night." He stuffs the food in the bag and sets it on the lounger. "Let's go row, row, row the boat."

A boat is safe, I reasoned and piled in the boat after Isaac. Ian unties it from the dock. Isaac rows, and it's all I can do to not stare at his muscles straining against the shirt he threw on. So, instead, I play thumb war with Ian. Or, I try to.

"You're cheating!" Ian says as I try to pull my thumb out of his grasp. "Isaac, Ginnie's a cheater!"

What I don't expect is Isaac asking Ian to switch with him. The boat wobbles as they move. Ian starts rowing and Isaac sits across from me and holds out his hand. "Trying cheating with me." He has a twinkle in his eye.

"I didn't know I was cheating," I defend myself. "I was trying to get away from his thumb! Isn't that the point of the game?"

"You have to hold hands the entire time. And no standing up to maneuver a better advantage."

I grab his hand, and our fingers interlock together with our thumbs ready for battle. The strength and warmth of his hand are distracting, but I focus enough to chant with him, "One-two-three-four, we're gonna start a thumb war."

He beats me four times in a row.

"Help," Ian says.

We glance up and see Ian straining against the oars.

"Why are you rowing this way?" Isaac asks and switches places with Ian.

"I tried not to." Ian is panting, and his face is red and sweating. "The boat wouldn't turn."

Isaac is paddling with such intensity, his forehead has broken into a sweat, too.

The boat keeps moving in the same direction.

"Stop paddling," I say. "You need to catch your breath."

Isaac stops. "What is going on? It's like something's dragging us along."

My stomach drops to my feet. Now that neither guy is paddling, I can feel the pull of the boat toward the shore.

The three of us look at each other and don't say anything.

Finally, Isaac says, "Well, at least the current is taking us back to shore. Even if it is out of the way."

"Do we have a cell phone?" I ask. "I left mine on the deck."

"Yes, I've got mine. I'll call Mom and have her meet us here." Isaac smiles reassuringly to Ian.

While Isaac talks to his mother, Ian's frown deepens. "You forgot your phone yesterday, too."

"I know. I'm forgettable sometimes. But don't worry. Your Mum will pick you up once we get to shore."

Isaac ends the call. "She's going to meet us at the north boat launch. It seems that's where the current is taking us. Or at least close enough to it."

"There's not this strong of a current in the lake," Ian argues.

"That's what it has to be," Isaac says. "Because nothing else makes sense." He tries one more time to maneuver the boat, but it's pointless. The three of us try to paddle together with Ian on one side of Isaac and me on the other. Then I feel the force pulling us, and I let go of the paddle.

I swallow the lump in my throat, sit back down, and grip the sides of the boat. Whatever is dragging us to the shore is not going to change its mind.

11

"There's nothing here," I say as Isaac hops out and into the shallow water where he drags the boat to shore.

"I know. It's weird. I'll have to tell my Dad about the current. He might know something about it."

He helps me down, and we wait for Ian.

Ian is unusually quiet and looks like he's unsure as to whether or not to get out of the boat. "That was *not* a current." Ian has repeated that same sentence at least a dozen times.

"Until we learn more, let's just say that it is," I say, more for my benefit than for his.

Isaac shakes his head and laughs, calling us both "crazy", but I see the questions behind his eyes, too.

Once Ian steps out of the boat, we stand on the shore and look forward. Other than overgrown vegetation and a steep dirt wall, there is nothing here.

"This is the same spot I saw you hanging from a tree," Ian says and steps forward pointing toward a tree, looming over us.

I take a quick look around the lake and wonder if Ian could be right. Then again, so far Ian has been right with just about everything.

"Let's grab some tree roots and climb up. Then we can head to our house," Isaac says. "I'll call Mom. We're closer to our house here than to the boat launch."

We walk to the incline. I grab some roots and try to pull myself up, but I'm still only wearing my bathing suit and cover, which means dirt and debris are getting everywhere. I drop my hands and step back, brushing the dirt off of me.

"I'll climb up," Isaac says. "Then I can reach down and pull you up, too. How's that sound?"

I nod and wipe at my foot, where a bug landed. I take a second look, and my stomach lurches.

It's one of the beetles, and it keeps trying to climb up my leg.

Not again.

"Hurry!" I cry and rush back to the dirt wall. I grab a root and decide I'm not waiting a second longer. I pull myself up and force myself not to think about the dirt and debris. Halfway up, another beetle crawls on my hand.

I shake it off and force the scream back down my throat. I refuse to act like a nutcase again.

Isaac is up the incline now and holding his hand out to me. "Just climb a little more and grab on. Ian, a little help, please?"

I glance down and Ian is staring at something to my right. I turn my head to the right and see the line of beetles crawling down the dirt wall to something under the debris at the bottom of the incline.

"Come on, Ian!" He snaps his head up and rushes to the wall.

Goosebumps have erupted all over my skin.

Another beetle crawls over my hand. I grit my teeth, trying to hold on with one arm. Then I feel one crawl on my ankle.

Just like my dream!

Isaac's reaching as far as he can, but I can't shake these

beetles off of me. I hear Ian climbing beside me.

Another beetle crawls over my other hand. By now I'm hitting, swiping, kicking, and then snap.

The tree root breaks, and I plummet down.

Isaac yells my name.

I fall on my back with a thud, smashing something underneath me. The beetles are everywhere. It might not be as bad in my dream, but close enough. I stand and start rubbing my body to get everything—visible and invisible—off of me.

That's when I notice the hand.

I stop and stare at it, telling myself it's not there. But it is.

It's a skeletal hand and arm, and it's connected to something under the debris.

That is when I forget everything about acting like a crazy person, and I scream.

Isaac and Ian have come back down. I hear Isaac say, "Oh, sweet Jesus."

Ian gasps and releases a whimper, and then walks backward, away from whatever—or whoever—is under the leaves and beetles. I stay close beside him, wanting to be far away, as well.

Isaac comes over to us. "It's okay. I mean, it'll be okay. We'll call the police."

I cover my mouth, to keep from throwing up, and to contain my sob.

"It's old," Ian says. "Probably surfaced because the lake levels are low."

Isaac takes out his phone, tries to make a call, and then sighs. "No signal here. We had signal on the boat."

"Let's try to take the boat back to our dock. Maybe…the current…isn't as intense." I don't believe my words, but it's better than standing on shore with a dead body a stone's throw away.

"I don't want to waste time on the boat, especially with the current."

"It wasn't a current!" Ian crosses his arms.

"Listen, we need to get out of here. I still think climbing this incline is the fastest way. Ginnie, can you manage?"

I nod and wipe at a couple of leaked tears. He touches my cheek softly.

Steering clear of the body, the three of us start to climb up the cliff. It may have been embarrassing to have Isaac climbing up behind me with a nice view of my backside, that is, if I had been in my right mind.

Luckily, I'm not myself, and embarrassment is the farthest thing from my brain.

I'm almost there and try to push myself to the landing. Isaac says, "I'm going to help push you the rest of the way."

He places his hand on my upper thigh and pushes up. I'm able to pull myself up and onto the landing.

"Help Ian," he says, as he pulls himself up with little difficulty.

Ian's doing well, too, but I still give him my hand and help pull him up.

Once we're all there, we sit for a few seconds gathering our breaths. I look at both guys and have to battle against tears again. They both appear shaken; Ian especially. But I sense whoever is down there was beckoning *me*. Not them.

The cold wind had bothered me. Not them. I saw the girl in the forest. Not them. The beetles had been crawling all over me. Not them.

"I'm sorry," I say. "Somehow I feel it's my fault."

"We're in this together." Isaac stands and helps me up, then checks on Ian, whose face is pale with a sheen of sweat over it. "Let's go home," he says to his younger brother. Isaac had mentioned last night that Ian isn't quite fifteen. Now he looks every bit a child, and my heart breaks at the sight of him.

We can't get there fast enough. The guys would have run the whole way home, but they have on swim shoes, and I am barefoot and feeling it.

Still, I don't complain and try to keep up with them.

When we make it to the road, Ian runs across it to his house, yelling for his parents. Isaac grabs my arm and asks, "How are you holding up?"

"I'll be fine," I lie. I'm far from feeling *fine*.

Ian is talking so fast, his parents look over at Isaac for clarification.

"We found a body. It must have been underwater and the low lake levels uncovered it. Him. Her." Isaac wipes his hand over his face. "We've got to call the police."

Mrs. Fulton drapes her arm around Ian and escorts him to the house. I feel badly at how hard Ian has taken this.

"He'll be fine," Isaac whispers to me.

Mr. Fulton is already dialing on his cell phone. "Beatrice, this is Sergeant Fulton. We've located a body at Pigeon Lake. Send out Pollarski and Hutchings along with a team…." He looks over at Isaac and raises his eyebrows.

Isaac promptly responds, "Northeast side, about a half-mile from here going diagonally."

His father says, "Go change, then take Ginnie back home. I want you back in ten minutes."

It's an order, and Isaac is already running into the house before I realize his Dad wants him changed and me dropped off in under ten minutes.

"How are you holding up?" Mr. Fulton asks the same question as Isaac.

Now that the boys are gone in the house, my resolve crumbles around my feet. I shakily shrug, but tears appear and before I know it, I'm sobbing. Mrs. Fulton is out of the house, and her arms are around me. "There, there. It took strength and courage to come back here to get help."

I slobber all over her shirt and have to wipe at my nose, which isn't helping the mess.

"Here," she hands me the dish towel she's been holding.

These people have already seen me at my worst, so I don't hold back when I blow into the rag. At this point, I don't care. I just fell on top of a dead body, hundreds of beetles tried to crawl all over me, and I am pretty sure that something—or someone—had wanted me to discover it.

"Who found the body?" Mr. Fulton is all business.

I swallow and bite my lip.

"Would you like me to question Isaac instead?"

I shake my head. Too much already rests on Isaac's shoulders. I *can* do this. "I found it. I fell on top of it. We were climbing up this huge cliff, and the tree root broke. It was a hand and partial arm. Everything else was covered under leaves and sticks and mud. And bugs. Lots and lots of bugs."

"Why were you guys over there? That's not public property."

"We took the boat across to save time. The current was really strong, and that's where we ended up. Kind of accidentally. So, was that person buried, or did someone dump her in the water."

"How do you know it's a female?"

I look into Mr. Fulton's eyes for the first time during this conversation and say without a doubt, "I just do."

It's a female, and she wanted me to find her.

Isaac is running back over to us. "Ready, Ginnie?"

I nod.

"Hurry, son. I want to head over there and check it out."

"Yes, sir."

Once we're in Isaac's Jeep, I ask about Ian.

"He's pretty shaken up, but that's part of his Asperger's. If anything is outside of the norm of his expectations, he freaks out. He wasn't expecting the boat to hit the current, and he certainly wasn't expecting what we discovered."

We are at Gran's house way too fast.

"I'll come over as soon as I can and tell you everything, okay?"

"Please, do." I hope that didn't sound like I was begging.

He tucks a strand of my hair behind my ear and lets his hand linger. "I've got to go." He drops his hand. "But I'll stop over as soon as I can."

I slip out of the Jeep and watch him drive off. Then, I can't get into the house fast enough. I bound up the stairs and start the shower, peeling off my bikini and jumping into the hot water.

It can't blast hard enough or hot enough. I scrub my body…again…reliving the beetles of my nightmare and my reality. Eventually, I sit down on the shower floor, pull my knees in, and cry.

I'm not sure how long I sit in the shower, but my skin turns pruny, and the water cools down. I turn off the shower and step out, wrapping a towel around myself and wiping the steam off the mirror. My hair is a mess, but that seems to be its constant state, and my eyes are red and puffy. I comb my hair out and braid it, sticking clips in to keep it out of my face.

A knock on the bathroom door makes me jump.

"Virginia?"

"What?"

"Are you okay?"

"Why?"

"Because the police are here and want to speak with you."

I throw open the door, startling Dad, and head for my room.

"Is it drugs?" He follows me.

"Seriously?"

"Did you steal something?"

"Turn around," I tell him. He turns and I quickly throw on shorts and a t-shirt minus the underclothes. "Okay."

He turns around again to face me. "Well? Some answers, please."

I take a deep breath and say, "I found a body across the lake."

Dad's eyes widen. "A body? As in a human body?"

"Yes. Isaac, Ian, and I took the boat out, and we got stuck near someone's private property—I guess, that's what Mr. Fulton said—and while we were climbing our way up the cliff thingie, a tree root broke and I fell. Onto a body." I hug myself to keep from crying again.

But Dad knows me. He walks over and hugs me. And I melt.

I cry, and he consoles.

It's at this moment, I realize how much I've missed him these last few days. I let him hug me for a long time. When he releases me, I try to hold on some more. "The police are waiting, Virginia. They probably want a statement. I'll be right there with you."

Gran is downstairs entertaining the two police officers. Isaac is not with them. She sees me enter the front sitting room and says, "There's our popular girl. Would you like some iced tea, Ginnie?"

"Ma, sit down. The doctor wants you off your feet as much as possible." Dad sounds exasperated. "I'll get her some tea. I'll be right back."

I nod. I want him to stay, but I also want iced tea.

"Hello," I say to the police officers.

They stand up and shake my hand, introducing themselves, but I don't catch their names, and I'm not about to ask. Instead, I sit next to Gran.

"Isaac Fulton said you were the one to discover the body?"

"Yes. A hand and arm. I'm assuming the body was underneath the debris."

One of the officers is young—early to mid-twenties—and he smiles in my direction.

Dad walks back in the room, hands me an iced tea, and sits on the other side of me. I guzzle the tea, answering basic questions, but purposefully leaving out the freaky stuff.

"What did they discover?" I ask before they leave.

"We don't have too many specifics just yet, but it looks to

be an older child, maybe a teenager if she was petite."

"She?"

"Yes, it looks like the body is a female."

A wave of grief dumps itself on me, and I close my eyes. I feel Dad's arm around me. "That poor girl," I whisper.

The police leave, and Gran asks what we want for dinner.

"It's only two o'clock, Mom," Dad says. "And we'll take care of dinner."

"I'm not dead yet, mister!" Gran snaps. "You'll not treat me like some invalid. Lord, you're getting just as bad as Sue." She walks out of the room purposefully kicking the wheelchair, muttering under her breath.

"What's with her?" Dad asks.

"She's probably worried about what happened."

"How about you and I get some dinner later? Just the two of us?" Dad asks.

"What about Gran?"

"I'm sure she won't mind, plus she has a few friends coming over later in the evening for cards. I guess it's a Saturday night ritual."

A dinner date with my Dad? Normally, I would say yes, but I feel emotionally drained, and want to not leave the house. "Can we take a rain check?"

"Sure. You still want to go exploring for some bugs?"

"No, Dad. I want to stay away from outside at least for the rest of today. And maybe the rest of forever."

He hugs me again. "Okay, go relax, and do whatever you want to do. If you change your mind, let me know."

Dad decides to hike without me. "Oh no, you're not going alone." Gran slips into her hiking boots and begins to tie the laces.

"Mom, you are not going with me."

"Try and stop me." She steps outside and starts marching to the woods.

"Looks like you're going on a hike with Gran."

Still, he smiles and shrugs. "There's no stopping that woman. You'll be all right for a little bit?"

"Yes. I'm going to relax and not think about anything dead."

When he leaves to follow Gran into the forest, I only watch for a few seconds. I shudder and quickly turn away. I've had enough of these woods and lake for a long time.

After checking my phone and texting Alisa and Mum, I scroll through Instagram and see pics of the first party of the summer. But most of the kids I barely know, and I admit to myself that a big part of me is simply not a party girl. Alisa has always pushed us to go to parties. "We need to do this," she'd say. "We need to break free from our nerd status."

The pictures don't entertain me for long, nor do they fill me with longing. Instead, my mind gets distracted by today's events. Now that I don't have beetles all over me, and I'm not landing on a dead body, my interest is piqued. I wander into Gran's office and turn on her computer. My thoughts keep going back to that girl who probably died a horrible death. What had happened? And why are these strange things happening to only me?

As a scientist, I rationalize that there is a logical answer for most everything. What I had experienced, however, was far from rational. And that's what interests me. The unknown.

I log onto the internet and click on a search engine. I do find information on Indian burial grounds in Pigeon Forest, but it doesn't fit what I'm looking for. That girl was not buried. If what Ian says is true, and the lake is low this season, then the girl drowned.

I stay lost in thought for over an hour, staring at the computer screen, reading about the area, and any other old news I could find. Neck deep in a conspiracy theory about ancient burial grounds in the Pigeon Lake area, I hear Dad and Gran come inside from the back deck. They're arguing, which is odd. Dad rarely argues with her.

"I'm paying for the ticket. End of discussion," Gran says.

"You need to respect that I'm her father, and I make the decisions here."

"She wants to go back. Let her go. At least ask her and let her make the decision. She's practically an adult."

"I know."

"Then stop treating her like she's a little girl."

There's a pause before Dad shows up in the office doorway. "How are you doing?"

"Good. How was the hike?"

"I wish you'd have been there. This is a bug lover's heaven."

"It's no wonder you're single," I tease.

"Did you hear the conversation with Gran? I'm assuming you did."

"It's not like you to argue with her. And over me?"

"She's insisting you go back home. That this traumatic experience would have never happened if I'd have let you enjoy your summer with friends." He raised his eyebrows as if waiting for me to agree.

"Gran's a smart woman."

Dad enters the room and sits in the same armchair that Gran sat in the night before. "Is it wrong for a father to want his daughter to hang out with him before everything changes?" He asks the question quietly, and I don't answer because I know what he means. College starts in the fall, and if Gran has her way, I'll be stateside. Dad wouldn't live in Ann Arbor with me. He'd be up here. And if I have my way and stay in London, then there still would be change. "Gran's right. I'm not a little girl anymore."

Dad reaches for my hand. "You'll always be my little girl, which is partly why I wanted you here with me. The thought of being so far apart goes against my fatherly ways. Especially with all those parties you had planned."

"You sent me to Michigan to keep me from partying?"

Dad's expression showed his guilt. "Don't hate me?"

"I don't hate you. At first, I was miffed, but I'm getting used to being here. Besides, I don't think I'd make much of a party girl anyway." We stay lost in our thoughts for a moment. "Want to see the pictures I took yesterday? They're not the best pics, but there are a couple of good shots."

Dad scooches his chair closer. "That's right. Show me what you got."

I close out the search window and open up my photo files. Together, the two of us sit side-by-side, and for the rest of the afternoon and into the evening, it's our own little world once again.

12

Two days pass without incident. One of those days was Sunday, and Gran pressured me into mass. Not a big deal. I sat in the back with Dad and used the opportunity to take pictures of the old sanctuary and cathedral. The three of us ate a delicious lunch from a Chinese buffet, and then spent the rest of the evening downstairs in the home theater with a marathon Harry Potter viewing. And on Monday, Isaac and Ian surprise me with a visit. We avoid the lake, and they teach me how to play *Spoons*.

No ghosts. No beetles. No dead bodies.

That night, Isaac and I stay up until three in the morning texting back and forth, and I fall asleep with my phone beside me and a smile on my face.

The knock on the front door brings me out of sleep. I roll over and hope someone answers it. The steady knocking doesn't let up. "Somebody answer the door!" I yell, then throw the blanket over my head.

But no one answers me or the door. I glance at my phone. Eleven a.m. Not in the mood to be cheerful, I trudge out of my room and downstairs. "Dad? Gran?"

No one's home.

"Fine. I'll see who it is," I mutter.

I open the door and come face-to-face with a tall, older man with long black hair and a brown, weathered face. His eyes seem almost black, and the look on his face isn't happy. When I open the door, his countenance softens a little. "Excuse me, miss, I'm looking for Rose Paxton."

"You have no right," Gran says from behind me. At first, I'm not sure if she's talking to him or me.

"He knocked on the door. And where were you that you didn't hear it?"

She ignores me. "You have no right at all coming on my property again."

His face turns again, and he stares at Gran with absolute contempt. Still, he says, "Maybe we should speak alone."

"Maybe you better get off my property before I get my shotgun."

"That would be an interesting twist, wouldn't it? Would I be the second Indian you killed, or would there be more?" His words slice through the air.

"How dare you. Ginnie, I'm stepping outside. Please call the police and tell them to get over here now."

Without coffee, my gears are turning too slowly to quite understand what is happening. "What? Why? I'm not understanding."

"Ginnie, go. Now." She steps outside and shuts the door.

What I really want is to pour a cup of coffee. Instead, I go into the office. This way I could be close. I slide the window open to get a better listen into their conversation. Unfortunately, they've stepped away from the house, so I can't hear what's being said. But their body language says everything.

He is stepping closer to her, pointing his finger at her. His words seem to be coming out fast. Gran is shaking her head and holding her chest. Panic seizes me. I call 9-1-1.

"Stop!" Gran shouts and steps back. I hear her voice shaking.

Anger takes over. I am already outside and moving toward them when I hear dispatch. "We need police assistance at 7289 Pigeon Lake Drive. The residence of Rose Paxton…The reason? We have a man on our premises that is making horrible threats to my grandmother. He's been asked to leave several times…Yes, I'll stay on the line." I take a stance next to Gran and glare at him with disgust. "What kind of man threatens an old woman?"

He looks from her to me and shakes his head. "All deals are off the table," he says to her before opening his truck's door. It's one of those monster trucks with tires almost as tall as I am. The engine roars to life, and he backs up and speeds out so fast, gravel spits at us.

The dispatcher is talking in my ear. "Yes, that was the man threatening us."

"Hang up the phone," Gran says, still shaken.

When I don't do it immediately, she takes it from my hand, says into it, "False alarm, everything's fine," and cuts off the call.

"You told me to call the police."

"Yes, it was a scare tactic to get him off the property. It worked."

"You should file a report."

"The police already have enough on their hands to worry about me."

"What are you talking about? I'm worried about you! As soon as Dad finds out, he's going to go bloody ballistic! That man threatened you!"

"You can't tell your Dad."

"Oh yes, I can."

"Ginnie, I'm serious. That man's not going to harm me. I told you already that he wants…my property."

"What did he mean when he said all deals are off the table?"

"I'm not sure."

"If you want me not to tell Dad, you better give me a bit more information than that."

"Why were you listening? This doesn't concern you. I will take care of it, and I will tell your father when I'm good and ready." She walks to the door. "And for the record, I'm not *that* old."

She can argue all she wants. But this is serious. I pace outside, waiting for Dad to arrive. Gran wants me to not tell Dad. Yeah, right.

Gran calls from inside, "If you're waiting for your father, you'll be waiting a while."

I stop pacing and look over at the driveway. The Mustang is gone. "Where'd he go?"

"I'm not telling."

I march to the house. "Where'd he go?" I repeated.

"I heard the Mustang start-up and leave about thirty minutes ago."

"Where'd he go?" I ask again.

Gran raises her eyebrows.

"Dad is going to find out one way or another, Gran. Either I wait here until he comes back, or I go to him right now."

"You can't go to him. You don't have a car."

"You do."

"You don't know how to drive. Having the wheel on the left is kind of tricky."

She's right about that. "I don't get it. Why are you keeping secrets? We're your family. We can help. You're shutting us out, and that guy looked like he could snap you like a twig."

Gran scoffs, but it's half-hearted. We are at a stand-off, and she's about to see how stubborn I can be. "All right, if I promise to talk to your father when Aunt Sue gets here, would you allow me to handle it? There are things I need to tell both of them."

"When does Aunt Sue get here?"

"Tomorrow night."

"I don't think that guy is going to give you until tomorrow

night."

"Yes, he will."

"How can you be so sure?"

"Because Ginnie. That man wants something from me. If he does what he's threatened to do, then he will never get what he's wanting. So, you see? If anyone is in control of this situation, it's me. Not him."

I don't believe her. There's something about that man that's desperate enough to do something crazy. Oddly enough, my stomach chooses that moment to growl.

"Your father is spending some time with a friend. He said something about lunch at Manny's Steakhouse," Gran says. "I'm finishing up some trays for this evening's pinochle club if you want to stick around."

Her normalcy surprises me. Here it seems everything is in absolute chaos, and she is fixing food for pinochle club.

"I don't see how you can keep this quiet until tomorrow night."

"Please." She grabs my arm and squeezes gently. "Please, trust me." When I nod, she continues, "How about some of that food I made?"

"First, I need some coffee."

Once I'm seated at the table and drinking my coffee concoction, Gran sets a plate in front of me. "I know you just woke up, but it's technically lunch. Have some homemade spinach dip and pita bread."

"You're trying to soften me up." I take a bite. "Mmm, this is good."

Gran sat at the table with her plate. "Just trust me. I'll talk to both my children tomorrow."

I nod and keep eating.

"Want to explain why you're up so late? Half the day is gone."

"I stayed up late."

"Another movie marathon?"

"No." I blush and focus on my coffee cup. "I was up talking with Isaac."

Gran chuckles. "Oh, those were the days. Your Grandpa and I would stay late on my front porch until my father would kick him off it. We'd sit and talk and do some necking, and then talk some more." Gran gazes off in the distance, as she smiles at the memory.

"It's not often you meet the one person you're supposed to spend the rest of your life with. Most people go through a couple before they get it right. Some people, like my Mum, will probably never get it right."

Gran's gaze lands on me. "When you get it right, it's something special, Ginnie."

"Do you miss Grandpa?" I ask, then add, "Okay, that's a silly question. Of course, you do. I do, too. You both always came to London in the summer."

"I miss him every day. And I was planning on coming out this summer, but your father told me to stay here. He said that you two were taking a special trip here. He wouldn't listen, of course. He's getting just as stubborn as Sue."

"Wait, what?" The pita bread is suspended in mid-air, as Gran's words hit my ears. "Dad was planning on coming here? Before you got sick?"

Gran's eyes widen as if she realizes the information herself. "I don't know. I'm not sure why I would say that." She stands up quickly.

"Gran? What are you keeping from me?"

"You know what? I need to run to the store. I have a list of ingredients I need for my pineapple upside cake."

"Gran!"

She sighs and looks at me. "Ginnie, I honestly don't know. It could be that he was planning on coming up in July. I don't remember the particulars. Didn't he have a conference first?"

"Yes, he had a conference." The thought of Dad lying curbs my appetite. But Gran is right. He hadn't made plans to come here because he had to attend the conference. Still, it will drive me bonkers until I ask him and get a straight answer. "I think I'll try driving to the restaurant. How difficult can it be, right? Do you want me to run to the store for you? Since I'll be out anyway?"

Gran does not look convinced that it's a good idea, but she goes to find her purse. I wonder if I should leave her. Would that angry man come back?

"Do you want to go together?" I call out to her. "Maybe you shouldn't be here alone." I still haven't decided if I'm going to keep her secret. Dad will be livid if I keep this from him. Then again, it seems like there are lots of secrets in the family. What's one more?

When she comes back, she says, "It's a good thing I'm insured," and hands me the keys. "And I live alone twelve months out of the year. I'll be fine. I was out back gardening, and I didn't finish."

"Okay, I guess. Let me go throw on some clothes."

"And you'll give me until tomorrow night to tell your father, correct? You're not heading to see him to tattle on me, are you?"

Something inside me nags not to agree, but I find myself saying, "You have until tomorrow night." I hold out my pinky. "I pinky promise."

Gran holds out her pinky, and we pinky-shake. Once she hears the answer she wants, she hums to herself as she pilfers through the cupboards. I shake my head as I watch her. She acts completely unruffled.

On a whim, I go to her and hug her from behind. "I love you, Gran. I hope I'm like you. A strong, independent woman."

She turns around and hugs me hard. "My Ginnie girl, I love you to pieces. And no matter what happens, always remember that."

I go change and then walk to Gran's car. I pause and study

the vehicle for a moment, talking myself into driving it. "Piece of cake," I say, taking one of Dad's expressions. But her car is this mammoth Lincoln that reminds me of one of those pontoon boats I've seen on the water, so I don't know how much of a "piece of cake" it's going to be. I open the driver's door—which is on the wrong side of the car—and slide in. I sit there and try to get used to the bizarre feeling of the wheel on the left side. The car starts up as soon I turn the key, and I've put it in reverse before I can talk myself out of it.

That's when my cellphone rings. I back up onto the road, then slam the brakes so I can answer the phone. I put it into drive and answer at the same time. "Hello?"

"Hi. It's Isaac."

I swerve and nearly hit a tree.

"I was calling to make sure you fell asleep okay?"

"I slept great. Once someone stopped texting me."

"At least you got some decent sleep. I've been up since seven this morning because some of us have to work."

"Oh no! That's horrible." I nearly side-swipe a mailbox.

"You seem distracted. Want me to come over? I've got some news if you're ready for it."

"Get out of the way!" I yell at a stray dog. "A dog's in the middle of the sodding road."

"Are you driving?" Isaac sounds shocked.

"Not very well, I'm afraid. I wanted to go see my Dad up at some steakhouse, but I'm questioning whether or not I'll make it alive." A delivery truck goes sailing by me. I drop the phone. I hear Isaac talking, but the phone is on the floor in the passenger area. I make it to a stop sign and slam on the brakes. I pick up the phone. "Sorry. It slipped."

"Drive the car back to your grandmother's. I'm coming to pick you up."

"No mudding, right?"

"No mudding…for tonight."

"Okay, but hurry. I'm famished." I turn the big boat around—after reversing and maneuvering about a half dozen times—and drive back to the house. Good. I'm not too sure about the whole driving on a big road.

I park the car and am running up the steps to drop off the keys when Isaac pulls up. I turn and yell, "Give me a second. I've got to give Gran her keys!" Stepping inside, I head to the kitchen. "Hey, Gran? Isaac's going to drive me to town."

I set the keys on the counter and freeze in my tracks. "Gran?"

She is lying on the floor unconscious.

13

Isaac holds my hand and tells me to try and relax. Any other time I would be a pool of warm liquid. Right now I want to tell him to shove off. Instead, I stand up and start pacing again. He's smart enough to not say anything.

The hospital is small, and the waiting room is smaller. I can only pace about four steps before I have to turn around and pace in the other direction. It's a good thing my stomach stayed empty because it would have all came up again. I wring my hands as the one sole thought runs through my mind. *It's my fault.*

I left her alone. I should have waited until Dad showed up. I should have just stayed and helped her prep for her card party. I should have *been there*. Tears keep leaking, and I have to blink several times to keep them to a minimum. No time for tears. Police will be here any minute. Dad will be here. Aunt Sue is driving up. Gran's in the hospital bed. They'll want answers. From me.

And what do I say?

"Ginnie, if you wouldn't have come back and found her when you did, it could have turned out so much worse," Isaac says.

I stop and stare at him. As if I'm looking at a stranger. Then again, I met him only several days ago. Is that all? Yet he's here. At the hospital with me. Gran had told me he was a good guy. "Thank you," I manage to say. "I can quite honestly say that you've seen me at my worst on more than one occasion."

"I'm just sorry that all this is happening."

I nod and have to blink back tears again.

The door bursts open, and Dad rushes to me. I notice a blonde woman walk in with him. She goes toward the nurses' work station. His arms are around me. I smell perfume on his clothes.

"What happened?" he asks.

Where do I start? What do I tell him? "She was on the floor in the kitchen."

"How long had she been there?"

"Not long. Only a few minutes."

"Thank God you were there, Virginia." Dad holds me close. He releases me and sees Isaac. "You were there?"

"I had only arrived to take Ginnie into town. I heard her yelling for help. When I ran in and saw Ms. Paxton, I called 9-1-1."

"Can we see her yet?" Dad asks me.

"No, I don't even know if she's okay…" I stop and cover my mouth with my hand.

Dad hugs me again. "We'll get through this. She'll pull through. We have to believe that."

This time when the door opens Mr. Fulton walks in wearing his police uniform. He's not alone.

Mr. Fulton is all serious when he approaches me. "Ginnie, I'm sorry for all the bad luck you're having."

I give a humorless laugh. "You and me both."

"We do have a few questions if you're up to answering."

"Come on, Ted," Dad says. "Do we have to do this? Ginnie's worried about her grandmother."

"This isn't about Ginnie's discovery of the body. It is concerning Rose." Mr. Fulton asks me, "You had made a 9-1-1 call not twenty minutes earlier. Can you explain those events?"

Dad looks from Mr. Fulton to me.

"A man came over to the house. Gran told me to call the police. Then she stepped outside to talk to him." I pinky-promised Gran to keep the secret, but I can't lie. Not about this. Not with Gran in the hospital. "I couldn't hear what they were saying, but the man appeared angry. He was pointing his finger at her. She kept shaking her head. So, I placed the call and ran outside to tell the guy to hit the road."

"How did he threaten her?"

"I overheard Gran saying 'Stop,' and he said something like 'All the deals are off.' When he left, Gran took the phone from me."

"What are you talking about Virginia? This sounds like something off of Law and Order." Dad is acting more shocked than I anticipated. Somehow that makes me even more nervous.

"It's exactly as I said. I don't understand it either. She told me I couldn't tell you or Aunt Sue until she had a chance to explain things."

"What things?" Dad and Mr. Fulton ask at the same time.

"I'm not sure. She didn't tell me. Last night she said something about people wanting her property. Some Indians said it was their property, and well, maybe that's who showed up today." Well, I just let the cat out of the proverbial bag. But if it gives them a clue to some bad guy, then I'll do what it takes. Somehow that guy is responsible for what happened to Gran.

Mr. Fulton asks me for a description of the man, and we spend some time going over the particulars of what he looks like and the make of his truck. They end up leaving, but Mr. Fulton gives me his card and tells me to call him if I think of anything more.

The blonde lady who came with Dad now enters the waiting room. She goes to him and rests her hand on his arm. "She's stable."

The gesture seems more intimate than it should be. Who is this lady?

Dad sighs in relief and hugs the woman. Not the kind of hug where there's a pat or two on the back, but the kind of hug that shows there's more of that when they're alone.

Maybe because I'm tired or because I saw a dead body and an unconscious grandmother all within a week's time, but the sight of them makes me really pissy. "Hello, I'm Ginnie, Sam's daughter. If you can release my father, I'd be able to shake your hand."

They unglue themselves from each other. Dad doesn't seem sheepish or embarrassed. If anything, his eyes are doing that warning look with me. So, I look away and glare at the woman.

"Virginia, this is Laura. She's Gran's family practitioner and an old friend of mine."

"Hello, Virginia," she says and extends her hand.

"It's Ginnie." I shake her hand.

She smiles, but I don't. It may be her long golden hair in all its perfection or her bright blue eyes perfectly outlined with eyeliner and smoky eyeshadow or her high cheekbones or the fact that she has the body of a lithe model, but I don't like her. At all.

The other doctor enters the waiting room—the real doctor from the emergency room—and I step around the Laura woman and go to him. "How is she?"

"She's stable."

I act like that's not exactly what Laura said.

"What happened?" Dad comes up beside me.

"Hard to say. We'll run some more tests overnight to see if it was a minor heart attack, but she has a large bruise on her temple."

"Someone hit her?"

"I don't think so. She passed out, fell, and hit her head. That's why she was unconscious. Now we have to find out why she passed out. So if it's all right, we'll go ahead and run those tests and rule out some things."

I breathe a sigh of relief and make a mental promise to the

good Lord that I will attend mass at least once a week with Gran as an expression of thanks.

Dad finishes talking with the doctor, and then places a call to Aunt Sue. "Hey there, Sue," he says. "No need to rush up here. She's stable…No, no, it's okay, I promise…You were already coming up tomorrow. That will be fine. I'll stay with her tonight…" When he ends the call, he says to me, "Why don't you go back to the house? I'll stay here with Gran. You've had enough happen."

"Will you be back tonight?" I don't want to sound like a needy child, but I'm not sold on the staying-at-Gran's-by-myself idea.

"If Gran is stable and sleeping peacefully, I'll head home. But I should stay here a while in case doctors have questions or the test results come back."

"Let me know if anything comes up, okay?"

"Of course." He gives me another hug, and I recognize that perfume again.

I want to say something witty and sarcastic, but it can wait. The fact remains that finding a dead girl, possibly seeing her ghost, and finding my grandmother on the floor is enough to shoulder. I will deal with my secretive father and his blonde bombshell doctor girlfriend later. "We've only been here for a little under a week."

"I know. I'm glad we're here though."

"I'm sure you are," I say a little too snottily.

"Virginia, please. We can talk about things later."

I stare at him and shake my head. "Gran's right. You are keeping secrets from me." I spin on my heel, needing to leave immediately.

He calls after me, but I keep walking away before I say anything more.

Isaac's playing a game on his phone when I call to him. He glances up and says, "Ready for a break?"

"Yes. Would you mind taking me home?"

"Of course not."

I don't say good-bye to anyone mostly because no one's paying attention when we leave. I do make eye contact with Doctor Blonde Bombshell, and my frown deepens. I look away quickly and keep walking.

As we walk to the Jeep, Isaac grabs my hand. "How are you *really* doing?"

We stand next to my door. Isaac doesn't release my hand. This time my insides do turn to warm liquid. And for some reason, I decide to be completely honest. "Just a week ago, I was in London, planning the greatest party of my life. Dad was going to be gone for three weeks to a conference, so Alisa had this huge adventure of parties and boys and…oh well, that seems very far away."

"Don't look at it as a bad thing," Isaac says. "Think of everything that's been *accomplished* since you've been here. We met each other, and I think that's a good thing. You found that girl's body…"

The thought makes me shudder.

"I know it was creepy, but now she can be properly buried. Her family can have closure. And if it wasn't for you, how long would your grandmother have been on that floor? And that man might have taken it too far if you hadn't stepped outside to defend her."

His words do uplift me a little. "I guess. It's a lot to process though."

He opens my door. "We could always go mudding. That helps alleviate stress."

I slide into the seat and think about how much fun we had before the Jeep stalled and the ghostly girl showed up. "It *is* daylight."

"Exactly. The woods aren't spooky during the day." He shuts my door, goes to his door, and gets into the driver's seat.

"How's the jeep?"

"She's purring like the well-oiled machine she is." Isaac

reaches out and pats the dashboard. Then he turns to me and starts to taunt in a sing-song voice. "Come on, it'll be fun."

Maybe I shouldn't have fun at this moment, but I realize how much I want it. I want nothing more than to spend the afternoon with Isaac. "Let's do it."

Isaac lets out a whoop and puts the jeep into drive.

***

Two hours later, the jeep has been baptized in mud, as have we. "It just had to rain." I squeeze the water out of my hair and onto my Gran's driveway.

"I could have put the top on, but what was the point." Isaac is also wet and covered in mud. But not like me. I got the worst of it.

"There's mud in my nose!" I lament, needing a tissue. And a shower.

"There's probably mud everywhere. Just saying. Especially with you falling in it."

"Ha, ha. You told me that the jeep purred like a well-oiled machine."

"She does. The mud hole was deeper than I anticipated. The poor girl got stuck."

"And this poor girl fell face first trying to push her out."

Isaac starts laughing. I roll my eyes but start to laugh too. It's hard to be upset when I had a great afternoon. Isaac was right. Mudding helps relieve stress.

"I'm going to clean up. Thank you for a great time. It definitely helped me forget things for a little while."

Isaac steps closer to me and places his arm on my shoulder. At first, I think he's trying to be romantic, and my insides release butterflies. Then he cracks a smile and tries not to laugh, but it escapes anyway. Romantic moment gone.

"Oh, shut up," I say good-naturedly. I head over to the front porch. Isaac had a blanket that he let me use to clean the worst of it, but there is dirt residue all over my body.

"Want me to stop over after I wash up? I never did get to talk to you about what I was going to share."

Alone with Issac?

"Yes," I say quickly. "Come over."

He waves and leaves, and I hurry into the house and up the stairs.

I wash as quickly as I can, not wanting to miss the knock on the door. I throw on the cutest top and shorts I own and opt to leave my hair down. I run downstairs and check outside, but he hasn't arrived. I immediately call Alisa and beg her to pick up.

"Ginnie!" she yells into the phone. There's music in the backdrop and a lot of chatter.

"Are you at another party?"

"Yes, hold up." There's a pause, then I hear her open and shut a door. The background noise is significantly muffled. "Hey there, my long lost best friend. Why aren't you here keeping me from boredom?"

"That hardly sounds boring."

"It is when you're not here."

Her words make me smile. "I wish I was there," I say half-heartedly because, in all honesty, I haven't thought about London all afternoon. "But I have to tell you something, and I have to hurry."

"What is it?" I can tell by her voice that she's intrigued.

"I met a guy."

Alisa squeals. "An American? Oh, I'm positively jelly."

"His name is Isaac, and he's nineteen, and tall, and—"

"He sounds like a magnificent creature."

"He is. And he's coming over. Any minute. And I'm nervous!"

"Is your Dad there?"

"No, he's at the hospital with Gran. So, I'm at Gran's house. Alone."

Alisa squeals again right as Isaac knocks on the door.

"I've got to go," I whisper. "He's here."

"You must call me back and tell me everything."

"I promise!" I end the call, take a deep breath to calm my nerves, and open the door to Isaac…and Ian.

14

"Oh, hello." I try not to sound disappointed.

"Isaac said you fell in the mud." Ian looked at me briefly before looking aside.

"He's right. I was covered in it. And he laughed and laughed." I glance over at Isaac, and his laughter from earlier has long left. He looks as disappointed as I feel. "Well, come in. My Gran has a ton of food she prepared for her friends."

Ian comes in, and I point toward the kitchen. Isaac touches my arm before I follow Ian. "I am so sorry. Dad is still working, and mom had a ladies meeting at church. After what happened, Ian doesn't want to be alone. I didn't know what to do. Mom says she'll pick him up in about an hour."

"Don't worry about it." I mean the words. I may be disappointed, but Isaac's relationship with Ian is one of the many reasons he's a quality guy. "You should never have to apologize for being a brother."

"It's a little annoying."

"We'll survive. Now come on, there is a smorgasbord."

The three of us set out all the trays and bowls from the refrigerator and discuss what to eat first.

"Do old ladies need this much food?" Ian asks. He watches me as I pile a plate with pasta salad, ham rolls, a buttered croissant, and a handful of raw carrots.

"My eyes may be too big for my stomach, but right now, hunger wins." I bite into a carrot and sit at the table.

There's a lack of conversation mostly because our mouths are stuffed with food. We glance at each other and stifle a laugh. "It's as if we haven't eaten," Isaac jokes and shovels another forkful of pasta salad into his mouth.

"Well, I had some mud earlier."

We laugh again and keep eating.

The front door opens and shuts. "Virginia?"

"Dad?" I get up fast as if I've been caught.

He walks into the kitchen. "I've tried to call you all afternoon!" He sees Isaac and Ian and changes to a friendlier tone. "Hi, guys."

The brothers say hello but find their food immensely fascinating.

"Can I see you in the other room?" Dad asks, then leaves without waiting for an answer.

"Are you in trouble?" Ian asks.

"Evidently." I follow my father into the study. "How's Gran?"

"She's doing fine, not that you care." The words are harsh, and they sting.

"Of course I care."

"I'm sorry. I'm tired, and I've been calling you. You need to answer your phone." When I don't respond, he continues, "She wanted her yarn basket and her blanket from the bed. But since you never answered your phone, I had to leave the hospital and come get it myself."

"Who's with Gran?"

"Laura is sitting with her until I get back."

"Well, then see there, you don't need me."

"What I need is for my daughter to answer the phone. That's what I need. Got it?"

I can count on one hand the number of times Dad's raised his voice at me. It's rare, and it stings every time. "Is that all?" I say, with some bite to my words. "I have company."

Someone knocks on the front door, so Dad walks past me to open it. "Hi, Charlotte. Come on in."

"Hey Sam, I'm only here to pick up Ian. I promised Isaac I would get him as soon as I could."

"Oh, Ian isn't going to stay?" Dad turns and looks at me in irritation.

I cover my face with my hands. This is bad.

"No, I needed to run to ladies group tonight, but it didn't last long. It's not fair to Isaac to be the babysitter, especially when he had something special planned with Ginnie."

Dad looks at me again. Now would be a good time for the earth to open up and swallow me whole.

Mrs. Fulton calls out to Ian to get his things and head to the car. She waves good-bye to Dad, sees me, and gives me a wink.

"Bye Ian," I say, as he leaves.

"Bye. I'll see you later."

Isaac now stands in the front hall. Dad slowly turns to both of us. "Is this why you didn't answer the phone?"

"Isaac took me mudding. For stress relief. I didn't even hear the phone."

"I'll get going." Isaac says to me, "I'll call you later."

"Don't go," Dad says the words before I do. "Not on account of me. Now if you'll excuse me, I need to get a few things for my mother." He leaves Isaac and me in the front hall without another word.

Going to Isaac, I whisper, "I need to talk to him and make sure he's all right. But don't go."

"Are you sure? I don't want to upset him anymore. He's acting pretty intense."

"He's worried about Gran. Hold on. Let me talk to him. Stay put."

"Yes, ma'am."

I go to Gran's bedroom and see Dad's already folded up her large quilt. It was one Gramps had specially made for her years ago. "How's Gran?" I ask.

"She's got a partially blocked artery, hon. We're looking at a biopsy. It's pretty serious, but she'll make it. She wanted me to tell you how thankful she is that you came back and found her."

"She's awake?"

"Sleeping at the moment, but yes, she's been awake and demanding to go home for pretty much the entire evening."

"Do you need me to go with you?" I finally ask.

"No, stay here." Dad busies himself with Gran's basket of yarn.

"I don't mind."

"You have company."

"Are you still mad?"

Dad sets the basket down and looks at me. "When you don't answer your phone, I worry. You take hikes and don't take your phone, and then you're going on adventures only to discover a dead body, and then today, not answering for hours."

"I've always been horrible with my phone. I remember my camera but not my phone." It's a pathetic excuse. "Sorry."

"Just please answer your phone."

"I will do better."

"And I don't care how old you are, you'll always be my little girl. And that young man makes me nervous."

"Isaac? He's a nice guy. We're friends."

"I know. And I'm glad to see you've made friends here. But I'm not used to seeing guys around you."

"Thanks." I roll my eyes.

"You know what I mean." Dad comes over to me. "It's always been you and me. Two peas in a pod."

"Two worms on a log," I joke, reminding Dad of the tacky phrase he'd always say to describe us.

Dad laughs. "Virginia's first boyfriend. I guess I better get my baseball bat ready."

"He's not my boyfriend. And if he was, he wouldn't be my first."

"Sure, Virginia. Scotty doesn't count as a boyfriend."

"Why not?"

"What were you? Twelve?"

"Eleven, but that's beside the point."

Dad laughs and so do I.

"All right, I don't have lots of boyfriends, probably because half our house is decaying bugs!"

"They are not decaying, but it's not exactly a charming hobby. Sorry."

"Speaking of decaying bugs, who's the blonde twit?"

"Virginia, be nice."

"All right, who's the blonde bombshell?"

"Her name is Laura Westgate, and she and I went to school together here, and then we went to college together at the University of Michigan."

"Like *together* together?"

"No. In high school, she was a popular cheerleader, and I was a nerd with a bug fascination. We ran into each other at a frat party a couple of years after high school, and I had grown up a bit. At least I wasn't hugely awkward. We hit it off, but then my internship started up in London. And the rest is history."

"You met Mum, had a wild fling, found out she was pregnant, and got stuck."

"I don't look at it in that way, Virginia. I've never felt stuck with you. You're not a burden or a bother. You're my daughter. And nothing's going to change that."

I feel the knot in my throat because I hear the sincerity behind his words. "Well, are you dating Laura, or what?"

"We are restarting our friendship."

"What does that mean?"

"It means stop asking so many questions."

"So, we're good?"

Dad leans over and kisses my cheek. "Go, have a good time with your *friend*. But not too good of a time. I'd hate for his life to be shortened on account of his hands being anywhere near my daughter."

"Dad!"

He chuckles, then goes to retrieve Gran's things.

I wait and follow him out of the room. Isaac, who's been sitting at the table, playing on his phone, jumps up. "Need some help, sir?"

"Yes. Help me with this basket of yarn."

Dad's easily carrying the folded quilt and yarn basket, but Isaac obliges. I watch them as they go outside. They chat briefly, then Isaac runs back to the front door.

I open it for him. "He threatened your life, didn't he?"

"Pretty much. But I reassured him that you're safe."

"Ready for some dessert? I think my Gran has cookies somewhere. She was supposed to bake a cake, but then, well, you know."

"Cookies would be great."

We stare at each other for another minute, before I give an awkward laugh and go inside. I'm a nervous mess, and I fumble with some cookies from the jar. I am keenly aware of being alone with Isaac.

And then there he is, standing beside me, reaching for a cookie. "I have news about the body. If you think you're ready for the information."

"What's the news?" I bite into a cookie to keep my mouth occupied.

"The body belongs to a girl."

"So, the police are sure it's a female?"

"Yes. An older child or a teen, if the teen was petite."

"That's sad," I say, thinking about what might have happened for a girl to lose her life like that.

"I know. There was a girl who went missing about forty years ago. They've only done preliminary tests, but they do think it may be her."

"Forty years ago?" I remember Gran saying something about moving to the area around the same time. I wonder if she would have any recollection of the disappearing. Suddenly, the older man from earlier today pops into my head. *Would I be the second Indian you've killed?* There can't be any connection, I refuse to believe it, but it still destroys the rest of my appetite. I push the plate of cookies away.

"Don't you think it was weird that the current brought us to that spot?"

"I'm having a hard time believing it was a coincidence."

"Yeah, me too. Ian is positive it wasn't a current."

"He made that obvious."

We make eye contact and smile.

"I'm starting to think there's a connection to a lot of these details," I say the words out loud.

"What details?"

I hesitate, wondering if I should share recent events. First, I dream about those beetles, then I see them at several different times and locations. When we went mudding, I saw a girl staring at me, and that's not counting the cold wind I felt right before. Then there's the blurry photo, the *current* leading us to the body, the same bugs being on the dead body—and on me—and now something happened forty years ago, the same time my grandparents bought property in this area. Instead, I ask, "If I show you something, will you tell me what you see?"

"Sure. Is this like a mystery?"

I set our plates in the sink and lead him to Gran's office. "Yeah, I think it might be."

As I sit at the computer and wait for it to open my file, Isaac studies my framed photo on the wall. "Great shot of the lake."

"Thanks."

"You did this?"

"Yes, during holiday. It had just snowed, and the scene outside looked so picturesque, that I decided to snap it. Gran framed it. I didn't know she was going to do that." I push back from the desk. "Here. Take a look at this and tell me what you see."

Isaac kneels at the desk beside me and studies the shot for a moment. "I'm not sure what I'm supposed to be seeing."

"I don't want to help you." Looking at it tonight only solidifies what I saw, but I want to see if Isaac can observe it too. I'm hoping so. I'm hoping that I'm not turning delusional.

"It's like a white light of some kind that's smudgy in the middle, but the outside of the picture is not. Look, is that an arm? Whoa, that looks like a hand."

And the heebie-jeebies are out in full force. So, he does see what I see. "That's what I'm thinking."

"When did you take this?"

"When I first arrived, during my hike. Right before I met Ian. The wind kept blowing from behind me, so I turn to check it out and accidentally took the picture." I'm glad I shared the picture with him. I still don't want to tell him everything, but having someone who can share some of the mystery is a relief.

Isaac gives a low laugh. "That's kind of cool and kind of creepy. It looks like we might have a ghost in these woods after all. Not that it'd surprise me."

"Tell me about it."

"This is the kind of thing that would fascinate Ian."

"Really?"

"He is a genius when it comes to trees and nature, but he also likes history, especially local history and lore."

"Like ghost stories?"

"He knows dozens of ghost stories just in Northern Michigan. I'm telling you, Ian would freak out if he saw this picture, and in a good way."

"He's not afraid of them?"

"There's an Indian legend that says ghosts are souls that were taken before their purpose was fulfilled. So, the 'Great Spirit in the sky', or whatever they call Him, gives them time to finish that purpose. At least that's what I've heard Ian say."

"I'm impressed. Ian's a smart guy."

"What about me? I'm pretty smart, too." Isaac acts all offended. "Didn't I fix the Jeep with only a shaky flashlight as my guide?"

I swat at him. "Hey now. Don't pick on those of us with shaky hands."

Isaac reaches over and tickles my side, making me squeal and jerk my arm. The picture on the screen changes to the one I took of the beetle.

"What—?"

"It's nothing," I say, pressing the arrow key. Unfortunately, it's moving in the wrong direction.

Isaac wrestles me for the keyboard and presses the arrow button, allowing him to flip through dozens of bug pictures.

And there goes any fleeting romance I may have had with this tall hunk of a guy.

"Did you take these?"

I don't answer. Embarrassment has done something to my tongue.

He comes to one of a spider. It's a zoomed-in shot. A ray of sunlight highlights the glistening web, as one leg of the spider is up and ready to move. "This is talented, Ginnie."

"They're only bugs." I finally find words. "Well, not the spider, but..."

Isaac has leaned forward to inspect the pictures, his hand

right next to mine. If he turns his head, our lips would almost be touching. Yes, I'm thinking about kissing Isaac. A girl's hormones don't necessarily shut off just because life throws a ghost and dead body at her. He turns and catches me watching him. He doesn't look away. This may be the moment. But my nerves take over, and I bite my lip and turn back to the computer.

Inexperience will do that.

"I want to be a photographer," I say because he's still looking at me. "Since my Dad's an entomologist, I help him by taking pictures."

"So, you enjoy nature, but not so much at night with a broken-down jeep?"

His voice is low, but I'm not so daft to ignore that he's baiting me, so I clarify, "I enjoy nature, and Jeeps, and certain guys, but not at night in the middle of a haunted forest." I glance over at him, and he's still watching me.

"That's good to know. So if a certain guy with a Jeep wants to ask you out on a proper date, would you be inclined to say yes?"

"I'd be inclined…definitely."

We're so close I can feel his breath on me. He swallows and gives a half-grin. "How about I pick you up tomorrow evening for a proper date?"

My cell phone rings, and the moment is gone.

I want to ignore it, but I remember my promise to Dad. "I have to answer it."

"Well, answer it already." Isaac stands up and heads outside. "I'm going to go sit on the porch."

I nod and follow him, taking out my phone. It's Cassie. "You better be on your way," I say as a greeting.

"Ginnie! The best cousin ever. I'm coming soon. I have stupid laundry and chores and whatever else my mother comes up with, but I'll be there. I wanted to know if you'd like to go in with me and get a gift for Gran. I feel horrible that she's in the hospital."

"That's a great idea." I sit beside Isaac who raises his

eyebrows in curiosity.

Who is it? He mouths.

"It's my cousin. Cassie."

Isaac's eyes widen, and he motions with his hand to be quiet.

"Who are you talking to?" Cassie asks.

"Um…"

Isaac must have heard the question because he's adamantly shaking his head.

"No one. Just myself."

"So, do you trust me to get a gift from both of us, or do you want to shop with me when I get up there?"

"It's up to you. She's coming home tomorrow morning."

"I'll wait until I'm there. Maybe we could take one of your nice pictures and frame it. You always do such a good job."

My heart warms at the compliment. "Just get up here!" We talk for a few more minutes before ending the call. I lean back and scrutinize Isaac. "What was that about?"

"Nothing. I didn't want to interrupt the conversation."

"Do you know her?"

"Not really. I think we met when we were little kids. You know what? I'm exhausted. Someone kept me up last night, and I had to get up early." He smiled at me, but it felt forced. "How about I stop over tomorrow? Or give you a call?"

"Sure." I'm stumped as to what happened. He had acted like he wanted to stay, but that was before the phone call. "Is everything all right?"

"Of course." But he's already down the front porch steps and heading toward his jeep. He says over his shoulder, "I didn't realize how tired I was until after I ate all that food. I'm kind of going into a food coma."

I glance at my phone and look back up. I want to ask more questions, but I don't know which ones to start with.

He at least pauses at the driver's door and says, "I had a

great time today, Ginnie. And I mean that. See you tomorrow evening." He waves good-bye before getting into his vehicle and pulling out of the driveway.

It isn't until he's gone that I realize I am very much alone. I go back inside, shut the door, and lock it.

15

Right before waking up, I dream of a voice. A girl's voice. She calls to me. *Ginnie…*

I open my eyes to the sunlight on my face, my name still echoing in my ears. I sit up and stretch, remembering my decision to sleep on the couch. I attempted to be an adult, going upstairs after Isaac left. But as I lay down, I noticed the box with the bug in it was open, and the beetle had disappeared.

Instead, I sleep on the living room couch with blankets wrapped around my entire body and toilet paper stuffed in my ears, not taking any chances. Obviously wrapping myself up in blankets didn't help. I can't shake the foreboding. What does this girl want with me? I know it's her. I'm not a ghost expert, shoot a couple of days ago I would have scoffed at the idea, but for some reason, this girl is trying to make a connection, and I'm the lucky recipient.

I know what I need to do, but I sigh anyway. I've been contemplating the idea since yesterday when I found the body. I had told myself that I would not step foot in a church for the entire summer, but whether I want to admit it or not, priests know a thing or two about this kind of weirdness. I run my fingers through my hair to see if I need to shower first when my fingers touch something hard and insect-like. No way! I jump up and shake my hair, flinging the beetle onto the floor.

Ugh. Nasty! How long has it been on my head? It starts to scurry away, but I fall on the floor and capture it with my hands. "Ha, ha, sucker, try to escape now."

It's trying to get away, which makes my skin crawl, and I have to resist the urge to act any more *girly*. This thing needs out of this house.

Opening the door is a challenge, but my chin is up for the job.

I place the beetle on the railing of the front porch. Now it doesn't move. It stays still on the railing.

"Go away," I whisper to it. "Leave me alone."

At that moment I glance up and see a man at the edge of our driveway. He doesn't look too much older than me, but he resembles the man from yesterday, which sends a warning message in my brain. He's watching me talk to the bug. Anger boils up in me. "Get away from here!" I march over to him, which probably isn't the brightest thing to do since:

1. I don't any shoes on, and I'm still in my shorts and tank combo
2. He's a pretty solid looking guy who would have no trouble knocking me cold in under a second and
3. I didn't bring my cell phone in case of an emergency.

But thinking of my Gran in the hospital keeps me marching.

"You better leave before I call the police!"

His reaction surprises me. He walks forward with both hands held out, as if in surrender. "I'm sorry. I didn't mean to startle you," he says. "I'm Mitchell Blackstone." He extends one of his hands.

"Mr. Blackstone, you have sixty seconds to get off this property before I call the police again."

"That's why I'm here. You're the one who called the police about the dead girl, right?"

"Yes, I did, and right after I did that, my grandmother was found unconscious on the floor and was sent to the hospital. So, if you think for one second I'm going to let some jerk onto this property again, you're messing with the wrong English girl."

"I realize you've dealt with a lot of inquiries about the body, but I don't know anything about your grandmother's hospital visit."

Everything halts as I zero in on what he said. "What are you here for?"

"To see if you're the girl who found the body. Isaac mentioned something about it yesterday at work. He couldn't tell me much, so I wanted to talk with you. If it's the girl the authorities think it is, she would be my mother's sister."

My jaw drops. Now I notice the Treetops Resort polo that the guy is wearing. That's the same place Isaac works.

"I found the body. I don't have a lot of details. Isaac probably knows more than I do."

"Are you from here?"

"No. I live in London. We're just here, visiting my grandmother."

Mitch's eyebrows furrow as if he's trying to decide what to say next. After a moment, he shakes his head. "Sorry to have bothered you." He opens the door to a small pick-up truck with more rust than paint, pauses to look back at me, then gets in the vehicle and drives off.

Before I can even think about what happened, Dad pulls into Gran's driveway.

"Where's Gran?"

"She's not released yet. I'm only here to hop in the shower and change clothes."

"Oh." I go to walk back into the house.

"What are you doing out on the front lawn?"

I'm not sure how to answer that. I decide not to tell him

about Mitch. The guy seems harmless enough. "I thought I heard something. Being here alone had me hearing things. That's all."

Dad's not listening. He's observing the property, shaking his head. "This place is going crazy. There seems to be something happening every few minutes."

"Tell me about it."

We go inside the house together. Dad sees the blankets and pillows on the couch.

"So, are you going to explain why every light is on in the house, and why your blankets are on the couch?"

"It's a big house, Dad. I found a dead body. It's all strange. For the record, Gran's right. None of this would have happened if I had stayed back in London. Just stating the obvious."

"It would have happened. Maybe not to you, but it would have happened. And, I'm glad that you're here. You are experiencing something very scientific. I'm surprised you didn't sneak over to take pictures before they took it away."

I make a disgusted face. "It's a *dead body*."

"I know. It saddens me, but as a scientist, I want to know the truth. I want to know her story. What happened? What led to her death? Her body holds clues. Just like when I investigate insects and figure out their evolutionary timeline."

"Wow," I say in mock fascination.

"What?"

"My father is such a nerd."

He grabs me, puts me in a headlock, and rubs my hair with his knuckles.

"Stop!" I squeal. "You're not a nerd! You're not a nerd!"

Dad lets me go and wipes his hands against each other as if the mission is accomplished. "Don't mess with an entomologist. Now I need you to clean the house while I take a shower, then I'll head back to the hospital to get Gran. Can you do that?"

By the time Dad has showered and changed, my blankets and pillow have been put away, and the kitchen has been cleaned.

When he leaves, I find myself going through Gran's cabinets in her office. I tell myself I'm dusting, but it's not as if the cabinets open on their own or the file folders open miraculously. There are several photo books. One with pictures of Aunt Sue as a child, and one with pictures of Dad. From birthday parties to Christmas holiday to swimming at the lake, there are pictures to document everything.

I go to shut the bottom file cabinet but see something resting beneath the files. I push the file folders aside and see it is an old Bible with rosary beads on top. Leaving it where it is, I run and grab my camera. I take a few pictures before taking it out of its resting place. The rosary beads seem to be made out of ivory, the cross turning in the light. I make a mental note to ask Gran about it when she gets back. I let the rosary dangle while I focus on a good angle.

When I open the Bible to set the rosary inside, a newspaper clipping is nestled between the first pages. I pick it up gingerly. It's a small clipping, no bigger than a single half-column. It's old and faded, but what I see takes the breath from me.

It's from forty years earlier about a missing fifteen-year-old girl. Barbara Blackstone. The same last name as that guy who visited this morning. But that's not what stole my breath away. It is the school picture they put in the newspaper. The girl has long, black hair with overgrown bangs, a small smile, and sad eyes. And she looks familiar. She looks just like the girl I saw in the woods.

***

Talking to Gran is out of the question. When she arrives from the hospital, she will need to stay as stress-free as possible. If I ask her a bunch of questions, that will not help her. But I've got to talk to someone.

I pause before texting Isaac. He left in such a hurry last night, and I haven't heard from him all morning. Then again, it isn't as if we are together. We are friends. And friends can text each other. Before losing my nerve, I text him, *Mitch Blackstone stopped by this morning. He said he knows you.*

I see Isaac is texting back, and I sigh in relief. *He told me. Said he scared you. I should have told you about him.*

It's good. I text back. *Have him call me. 'K?*

Minutes later my cell phone vibrates. "Hello? Mitch Blackstone? This is Ginnie Paxton."

"Hello," he says. "I'm sorry about what happened today. Isaac filled me in a little about what happened yesterday with your grandmother. I feel like an idiot for just showing up this morning."

"Don't worry about it. That's why I'm calling. Can you find some time to come over here and talk?"

"Are you sure?"

"Yes, I am. I need to talk to someone about it, and since you came to me first, I'll take it as a sign."

"Signs are good," he agrees. "I'll see what I can do. Since I just got here, maybe I can leave for a few minutes before my first round begins."

"Do you work on the golf carts like Isaac?"

"No, I'm a golf instructor. I have a pee-wee session in about an hour, but my schedule's pretty flexible before that."

After I hang up, I run upstairs to get dressed. Once in the shower, I scrub my head with shampoo in case that nasty beetle peed or pooed on my scalp. A girl can never be too careful.

Halfway through brushing my hair, there's a knock at the door. I'm only in my panties and bra, so I throw on a t-shirt and shorts before heading downstairs.

I open the door to find Mitch on the other side of it. Now that I'm not so angry I can truly check out his features. The first thing I notice is his eyes. Something very familiar about them. I think of Barbara Blackstone and assume that's the connection. "Hi," I greet him and step outside. Since I'm home alone, it's probably not a good idea to invite a strange man inside. Not that I'm any more protected outside, but it at least seems like safer ground.

"How about we walk to the docks?"

I don't know him at all, but there's something about him that draws me. Maybe because I feel bad his aunt was discovered. Still, I follow him down the steps and around the house.

We don't speak until we're almost at the docks. "So, how old are you?" I ask, trying to break the silence.

"Twenty. What about you?"

"I turn nineteen in a couple more weeks."

"Cool. Maybe we can get a group together and take you to the casino."

"That sounds fun," I say, truly meaning it. "So, you play golf?"

"Yep. Started by being a caddy as a kid. I liked being outside and watching people play the game. One day, I picked up a club and started swinging. My boss bought me a bucket of balls, placed me at the driving range, and said, 'Let's see what you can do.' I've been golfing ever since."

"I don't golf."

"We'll have to change that."

Just like that, we were talking like two chums who were catching up. We sit on the dock and look out across the lake. I feel reassured now that I can truly ask this guy anything. "My grandmother told me that most of this land is Indian territory."

"Yes. The written pact between the tribes and government goes back at least two hundred years. The verbal one between the two tribes goes back much longer than that."

I think of something I have read and ask, "Is the land cursed?"

"Some say it is." His face becomes somber. "This lake has secrets, and it wants to keep it that way. Or at least that's what some say."

"What do you say?"

"Legend has it that two Indian tribes battled for the land.

One tried to negotiate peacefully, the other violently. The violent tribe won. They had a powerful witch doctor who cursed the tribe and its land. That was before the white man invaded. The tribes are gone now, but a few believe the curse is still real. Anyway, that's what I know, which isn't a whole lot."

"Are you a descendent of one of those tribes?"

"Yes. I am a part of the Apache tribe. Most of our people live in the southwest, like New Mexico and the desert, but a small band explored north. We were outnumbered and lost that vicious battle. The curse supposedly still plagues us."

"What is the curse?"

"That we will always turn to violence, and the greatest battles and loss will be between our own people. Those of us who are still in these parts have very little to do with each other. In part because of what happened over there." He points down at where the body was discovered.

"Do you know what happened to her?"

"Only speculation." He stops and turns toward me. "Can *you* explain what happened? It's probably a difficult topic, but it may bring peace to my household. How did you stumble upon the body?"

"Our boat—I was with Isaac and Ian—got stuck over there, we tried to climb up that dirt cliff, and a root snapped and I fell onto the body."

"Is that the whole story?" he asks quietly.

Before I can respond, a bug crawls across my foot. I don't even need to look. I shake the beetle off and shudder.

Mitch, however, stares in the direction where the beetle landed. When he finds it, he carefully picks it up. "This is different."

"Why?"

"I've never seen a beetle-like this before."

"I know. My Dad and I can't figure them out either, and Dad's an entomologist."

"In my tribe, insects like this signify a warning. Stay away. If you see them often, well, that doesn't matter."

"If you see them often, what?" my eyes nearly bug out of my head.

"It means they have attached themselves to death, and death has chosen you. It's probably more tradition than anything, but I still don't kill them."

I think I let out a squeak, but I'm not sure.

He is too perceptive, and says, "We also believe that a soul manifests itself as an animal it most connects with. But why would a soul want to connect with an insect that represents death? But I may not know what I'm talking about either."

But I do believe him, and I sense it's the latter. "When I fell on the body, these beetles covered it, and they were all over me. I've been shaking them off since I got here. One was even on my head this morning." I shudder again.

Mitch's mouth falls open. "Oh my God."

"Please don't look that freaked out because it's going to freak me out in a huge way. Am I going to die? Is the ghost going to kill me?"

"Ghost? Do you see her?"

Before I know what I'm doing, I'm babbling. "I'm probably losing my mind. Please don't tell Isaac."

"But do you see her?"

"Once I did. And before that, I felt her. I can't describe it. A cold wind blew at me. I even took a picture—I didn't mean to—but she sort of showed up on the picture."

"Whoa," he says and stands up.

His reaction isn't helping. I stand up, too. "Give it to me straight. Am I going to die? Are these beetles going to come and kill me? I'd like a heads up, you know?"

"It sounds like it wasn't an accident that you were the one who found my relative." He says the last sentence more to himself.

My heart bangs against my chest, and I press my palm to it.

"That's ludicrous. I'm from London. Not here. I don't want this. I want the beetles to leave me alone, and the girl to stop haunting me, and I don't want to be sucked into some bloody murder mystery. I mean, I'm sorry about your aunt, but she needs to rest in peace."

"That's not possible. She died because of the curse."

"So, there's no peace for her?" I stop thinking about myself and dying and think about the girl instead. I always thought that there was some peace with death. I can't imagine this much unrest for eternity.

But Mitch doesn't seem to hear me. He's shaking his head and glancing across the lake where we can faintly see the yellow tape.

"Please tell me what's going on?" I try again.

"It doesn't make any sense." Mitch turns and stares out at the sight. I wish he would stop ignoring my questions. "That only means one thing," he finally says. "I don't understand how or why but it has to be the case." He turns back to me and sighs. "Every forty years a life of a tribesman is taken by the curse. It's always some calamity or misfortune, but the curse has never missed its appointment since the witch doctor of the Comanche tribe chanted it. I'm not sure about it though. Our legend also has it that ghosts can only visit those of our blood."

"Then your legend is wrong. I'm not your family."

"I don't get it either. Your father and mother?"

"My Mum was born in South London and was raised in Ireland for a bit. My father was born right here to Rose Paxton. I was just looking at baby pictures this morning. Trust me, I'm not related."

Mitch presses his lips together as if thinking about how to say something. He blows out a breath and says, "Ginnie, I don't know how to tell you this, but these events can't be a coincidence. I don't know all the answers yet, but if all of this is happening to you for a reason, then you and I might be somehow related."

16

The rest of the day I am, once again, a jumble of nerves. Maybe it's because these nasty beetles symbolize death, and they're coming to get me. Or, because this girl has chosen me for whatever reason. Or, because I am somehow related to a cursed Indian tribe, and the curse is about ready to rear its ugly head again. All I know is that London keeps looking better and better.

Mitch is gone by the time Dad gets back. I'm looking at Dad differently now. His skin is whiter than most Indians, but he has thick black hair and dark eyes. Then again, Gran has dark hair, and so does Aunt Sue. Sure, Gran's has a lot more gray in it now, but they still resemble each other in that face. As I hug Gran, I notice her blue eyes. Now that I think about it, Aunt Sue has blue eyes, but Dad's have always been a deep brown. Did Gramps have brown eyes? It's possible.

"You seem lost in thought," Dad says.

"I'm looking at your eyes," I say and smile in what I hope is a disarming smile. "They're almost black."

"My brown-eyed boy." Gran sits next to me at the table since Dad's making us both lunch. "That's what I've called him since I first laid eyes on him."

"I bet labor was difficult."

"Well, I don't recommend it until you're married, so don't get any ideas."

Dad finishes up the chicken salad sandwiches and says, "Let's eat on the deck, ladies. It's beautiful out there. Virginia, grab the plates while I wheel your grandmother out."

"Oh, dear Mary, mother of God," Gran says. "I'm not dead, and I'm not going to be confined to a wheelchair." She gets up, grabs a plate with food on it, then pats Dad's cheek. "Thank you for lunch, my son."

I take the other three plates. "Why do we have an extra plate of food?"

"Laura's coming over for lunch." Dad's holding the door open for Gran and me.

"What? Why?"

"Because I want her to meet my lovely daughter now that we're not in a hospital waiting room. Please be nice." He takes two of the plates and walks outside.

"You could have warned me. I'm dealing with too much to have to put on my nice face. My talents only go so far."

"I'm warning you now."

And speaking of the devil, who rings the doorbell at that moment? "I'll get it," I say. "Since I'm standing and all."

Dad gives me a warning look.

I go to back inside and walk to the front of the house. When I open the door, I smell that perfume that had been on my Dad's clothes in the hospital. I decide I don't like it.

"Ginnie," she says with a warm smile. "Did I get it right this time?"

"Yep. Come on back."

As we walk, she tries her hand at conversation. "Your father was telling me that you get to go to college a year early."

"Yep."

"Have you decided on a major?"

"No, not yet."

We make it to the back deck area. Finally.

"There she is," Dad says. I realize he's not talking about me. He stands up, kisses Laura on the cheek, and leads her to sit between my plate and his.

Gran's watching me. I'm pretty sure she can read my mind. "Anything happen while I was gone?" she asks me as I sit down and begin eating.

"Not really."

"I caught Virginia with Isaac Fulton."

"Dad!" I drop my sandwich. "It wasn't like that and you know it."

"Relax," he says. "I'm teasing."

I pick at my food, letting Dad and Laura do the talking. I hear my name but don't pay any attention.

"Virginia."

I glance up at Dad. "What?"

"Laura's talking to you."

I swallow. "Oh, sorry, I was in my own little world."

"I was asking if you might follow in your father's footsteps and become an entomologist."

"Probably not."

Dad acts genuinely surprised. "Why not? I think we make a great team."

I shrug. This whole situation has put me on edge, so I blurt, "I want to study photography."

"That's a good profession," Laura encourages. "Is there a specific type?"

"I don't know yet. I just want to get through the summer without thinking about it."

"You need to start thinking about it," Dad says. "University of Michigan starts mid-August."

"If I go there."

Gran gasps.

"Sorry, Gran, I don't want to upset you. Let's change the subject, okay?"

"No other school will do," Gran says. "My money goes to the Maize and Blue."

I refuse to get upset at Gran. She needs to limit her stress. "Don't worry, Gran."

Gran deepens her frown. "Ginnie Paxton, please stop treating me like I'm on death's door. We've got a doctor right here if there's a problem. Now talk."

"Talk about what?"

"Talk about your future," Dad says. "It seems you've got ideas that you're keeping from even me. I thought we talked about everything." He doesn't mask the hurt in his voice.

"Fine," I say. "You want me to talk? I'll talk. I don't want to go to college."

Dad stops chewing the food in his mouth and stares at me.

I feel guilty, so I look away. "I want to go into photography, and I don't need a degree for that. What I need is a good apprenticeship. If I can get under some experienced photographer, I can learn from them and then work my way up."

No one says anything.

When Dad does finally speak, he asks, "So, do you want to do this here in Michigan or back in London?"

"I've never wanted to leave London, Dad." I throw my napkin on the table. "That's always been your dream. Not mine." I stand up and grab my plate. Just to be saucy, I add, "Thanks, Laura, for bringing me into the conversation."

I walk back into the house, close the door, drop my plate in the sink, grab my camera bag, and head out the front door. I need to walk and think.

I hear the screen door slam before I've left the front yard.

"Virginia, wait."

"I need to be alone," I say, even though now that I'm nearly surrounded by trees, I'm questioning the statement.

"All right. I'll leave you alone. In a minute."

I stop and turn to face him. "I know what you're going to say. You want me to go in there and apologize for my poor manners, and I will. After I take the walk and cool down."

"Yes, I do want you to do that, but that's not why I'm here."

I wait for him to go on.

"Virginia, all I've ever wanted was for you to be happy. If photography makes you happy, then go for it."

My heart seems to fall out of my chest. "But what about college?"

"I *want* you to go to college. It's paid for. If you go to Michigan, your Gran will cover everything. If you decide to go to school in London, I'll pay for it. Either way, as your father, I'm asking you to please earn at least a preliminary degree. I know you don't think it now, but having those credentials helps when it comes to getting jobs. Not only that but that's the best place to meet professional studios or photographers who are looking for someone to study under them."

I stare at my Dad in shock. "You mean I don't have to go to Michigan?"

"No, of course not."

"And I can stay in London?"

Dad pauses and presses his lips together. "Yes."

"Yes, but what? I can tell you're holding something from me."

"When you go to college, you won't need me. Now that I've raised you, it's time for me to think about moving back here."

"Of course I need you! You're not leaving me, are you?"

"I thought we had it worked out that you would be at the University of Michigan, sweetie. That's why I was surprised at your admission today. It doesn't mean you can't go to school in London, but I may still decide to move back here."

I swallow that big lump as the weight of his words falls on

my shoulders. I should have seen this coming. Dad's always wanted to move back.

"Our family's here," Dad says quietly. "Your mother's parents passed away over ten years ago. Other than for some distant relatives of your mother's that you've never met, everyone is over here."

"Then why stay in England at all? Why didn't you just bring me back to the states? You've had sole custody since I was a tot. Why keep me somewhere where I'll develop friendships and a lifestyle that's not American?"

"Because your mother asked me to stay. She wanted us to be close in proximity. I hoped that you two could develop a relationship, but Virginia, how long am I—I mean, *are we*—supposed to wait?"

This time, I don't say anything.

"Has she called you since we've been here?"

I shake my head.

"Come here." He pulls me to him and hugs me. "We'll work this out, okay?"

I don't say anything, but I do hug him back. I can't imagine living in London without him.

"Let's go finish lunch. I worked hard on that chicken salad sandwich, and you've only eaten half of it."

Deciding I would rather apologize to Barbie than face the woods by myself just yet, I walk back with him. "Can I ask a question without you laughing or thinking I'm nuts?"

"I'll try to resist."

"Do we have any Indian in our blood?"

Dad chuckles.

"Hey! No laughing!"

"I'm not laughing. It's only that I wasn't expecting that question. But no, I don't think so. We can ask your grandma, but I doubt it."

"You look like an Indian. Sort of."

"You mean, Native American? Thanks, I guess." We enter the house, but Dad grabs my elbow before we get to the kitchen. "And will you ease up on Laura?"

I shrug and walk back outside.

"There's my girl," Gran says and reaches for me. I give her my hand, and she squeezes it.

When I sit down, everyone seems to be waiting expectantly for my apology. "I'm sorry that I stormed out of here even though I felt I was being attacked." There. That is as good as that apology is going to get.

"I would have felt attacked, too," Laura says. Then she continues a conversation with Gran.

Thankfully, I'm able to eat the rest of my lunch in peace. As we clean-up, a fancy speed boat drives up to our dock. "Hey, all you crazy people!"

"Uncle Doug!" I am running down to the docks in glee. Finally, Cassie will be here!

I scramble in the boat and throw my arms around my burly Uncle Doug. He's only an inch or two taller than me, with a paunch belly and a toothy, mischievous grin. Cassie gets her bubbliness from him.

"There's my London girl!" he says and returns the hug.

Dad's on the boat now, and the two men exchange a handshake and hug. "Where's Sue and Cassie?"

"They'll be here tonight. Sue had to work, but I got off a day early. Since I have to leave in three days, she told me to head up early and put the boat in the lake. I thought we could do some fishing."

"But what about Cassie?" I ask, trying to hide my disappointment.

"Oh, she got in some trouble with your Aunt Sue because none of her laundry was done. She was planning on coming up with me and doing her laundry here, but her mother would hear none of it. Said that your grandmother didn't need any more stress. We both know Cassie would have dumped the laundry, and your grandmother would wash it."

"Of course I would. She should have come up with you." Gran stands at the dock. Laura stands with her.

"Well, you can reason with Sue about as good as I can," he says. "Want to go for a ride?"

"You bet I do. Why do you think I came down here?"

Dad helps her in, and then Laura climbs in. I may be bummed about Cassie, but I am excited about a boat ride. A boat ride that hopefully won't result in me finding a dead body. Uncle Doug maneuvers the boat away from the dock and punches it almost full throttle. The wind whips through my hair, and I lean back to let the sun kiss my face.

We zip around the lake for about a half-hour as Dad fills Uncle Doug in with the craziness of the last couple days.

He looks at me wide-eyed. "Oh Ginnie-girl, I can't even imagine."

"Dad thinks I should be more scientific about it. I am glad that she'll hopefully be given a proper burial, and that her family will have some closure." I think of Mitch. "But just the same, I'm hoping that never happens to me again."

Laura, who's sitting beside me, shudders. "You have courage, Ginnie. That's for sure."

The compliment seems sincere, but I don't feel very courageous.

Uncle Doug slows a bit as we near the sight. The yellow tape seems out of place at a lake, but it glares in the afternoon sun. Dad says something about stopping, but I quickly say no. I'm not ready to be scientific. Still, my eyes are drawn to the area where days ago I found the body of a young teen. It's now empty and seems void, but I feel the pull inside of me.

Ginnie...

Goosebumps erupt on my skin as I hear my name being called in the wind. No one else seems to notice, which means two things.

I know she's there, and she's waiting for *me*.

17

Isaac waits at the door for me. "Hi."

"Hey there," I say, trying not to awkwardly smile at him. But I'm glad to see him. "You doing better than last night?"

"About that, I shouldn't have left so quickly. I'll make it up to you tonight."

I close the door behind me before Dad embarrasses me. Isaac walks me to the passenger door of his old Jeep and holds the door open for me.

"It's washed," I tease.

"Just trying to impress. Besides, it makes mudding that much more fun."

My stomach is nothing but jitters. I chose to wear the summer dress I packed and even put on some mascara and lip gloss. I hadn't trusted myself with doing anything more. I wish I could call Alisa super quick and have a squealing session. This is squeal-worthy.

As Isaac walks to the driver's side, I check out his fancy dark blue polo shirt and khaki pants. I swallow the big lump in my throat and try to breathe normally as he slides in next to me.

"Work uniform?" I ask.

"Yeah. I didn't have time to change."

"You look nice." Before he can respond, I blurt, "I will never get used to this. The driver's wheel should be right here." I pretend to be driving with a phantom wheel.

"Tell you what, maybe I'll come to visit you over in London, and you can drive."

"You want to visit me? I mean, yes, of course, I'll drive you all over." I stop myself from rambling.

"Are you okay? You seem on edge."

I sigh. "Just nervous." Not about to tell him this is my first date.

"Don't be. It's just me." He finds my hand and intertwines his fingers with mine.

I very well may melt right there.

"How about we get to know each other a little bit? I'll give a piece of information about myself, then you give a piece of information about yourself, then back and forth. For instance, my name is Isaac Fulton, I turned nineteen about a month ago, and I have a thing for cute girls with British accents."

He gives me a devilish grin. I think I say something like, "Uhhhh…"

Isaac laughs. "You should see your face! Okay, I'll start with something that's not going to have you turning twenty shades of red. I love oranges. I eat at least one a day, sometimes two or three. My next favorite food is pizza, then macaroni and cheese, then juicy cheeseburgers with all the fixings. Foods I can't stand would include mushrooms and bananas."

"Bananas? They're delicious."

"Makes me gag every time. I've tried them in pudding, in fruit salads, mixed as a smoothie. Gag, gag, and gag some more."

"I don't fancy pineapple or peanuts. But I love peanut butter. Go figure."

"You don't *fancy*…" Isaac mimics me. "*I'm from London,*

and I like tea and crumpets."

His attempt at my accent is so horrible that I'm in stitches. "I wouldn't try that again."

"Fine, but you have to give me more of an answer than pineapple and peanuts."

"I wasn't finished when you interrupted me. As I was saying, I love peanut butter and pretty much anything my Gran cooks. Shepherd's pies are delicious when done right, but I've tasted a few that didn't win any medals. Oh, I don't like onions. That's it. Your turn."

"I just graduated high school, and I signed up for the National Guard. It sort of upset my Dad because he wanted me in the army, but I want to stay put for a while. Ian might not adjust well with me being gone for a long time."

"The National Guard lets you do that?"

"Yep. I have to do basic training just like the army, but then I can come back home and go to school, live my life, that kind of thing. I have to volunteer one weekend every month and two weeks every year."

"Where's basic training?"

"California."

"Wow. When do you leave?"

"August. Enough about me. You have to give me more info on you."

Still, I look at him and smile. "You're a good big brother."

He stops at a red light and smiles back at me. "I hope so."

We pull into the parking lot of Manny's Steakhouse that has a line of people waiting.

Before we get to the line, a group of kids notice Isaac and call him over. He greets his friends, but I'm uncomfortable, especially because it seems Isaac is quite the popular guy.

"This is Ginnie," Isaac says when one of his friends asks about me.

"Not from around here?" a guy asks.

"She's from London," Isaac answers.

They all wait for me to say something, so I stuff my nerves down inside and say, "Nice to meet you."

Isaac says good-bye and pulls my hand to come with.

"Sorry, the steakhouse is busy on a Friday night, and when you're a local, you know everyone."

Isaac has already reserved a table, so we bypass the line and sit down by a window overlooking some marshlands. We both order cheeseburgers then continue the info-dump game (that's what I dubbed it). I tell him about Catholic school and how Gran is determined to see me at the University of Michigan. He tells me about how much he loves golf, and fishing, and hunting, and that he can't wait to vote in the next presidential election because it'll be his first.

"Have you thought of moving here?" he asks as our drinks arrive.

"Funny you should mention it," and I proceed to tell him about how I finally came clean with what I wanted to do with my life, and how Dad still wants to move here.

"Could you do that? Be over in London while he's here?"

I shake my head. "I don't know. We've been two peas in a pod since I was a baby. I know that girls need to spread their wings and fly, but being that far apart will be hard for us. Hard for me, at any rate."

"Well, there's one other person who would like it if you stayed here."

I smile. "When you say it like that, you almost convince me."

"I have a couple more weeks to do some more convincing."

After we get in the car and head back home, I say, "So, I met Mitch Blackstone."

"Yeah, he told me he scared you this morning."

"I wasn't scared. I was pissy. There's a difference."

"His mother is taking it hard. She has never been a social

person, but Mitch said that she's called into the library today and refused to get out of bed."

"Are they for sure that it's that Blackstone girl?"

"There're not many indicators to go on at this point, but I think dental records confirm it."

I exhale slowly. "I'm not one to believe in supernatural stuff and all, but ever since I arrived, weird things have happened to me…" I shut up because I realize I sound like a whacko.

"I was there." He glances at me then faces the road again. "I'm sorry you had to be the one to experience it."

"Not my greatest moment."

Isaac reaches up and tucks my hair behind my ear. His touch sends fire to my blood. "I don't think it was any of our finest hours."

"Ian looked gray," I say, remembering how terrified he was. "You sure he's doing better? He seemed okay last night."

"Mom knows how to handle him when he has an episode. He did well, considering everything that happened. He didn't lose it until we got home. I wonder if you had something to do with that."

"His episode? Like a tantrum."

"Not really. When he gets nervous, like when something outside of his normal happens, he can't be relaxed. He'll start talking fast and high-pitched. If we can't calm him down at that point, he'll start repeating the same word or phrase over and over again. He'll start to tremble and shake, and sometimes he even convulses. Most of that didn't happen. After we got back from our discovery of the body, he started to get frantic, but Mom calmed him down. He did keep repeating your name though."

"I hope I wasn't what was making him frantic."

"No. Whatever words he repeats calm him down. Normally, it's Mom, Mom, Mom. Last week it was Ginnie, Ginnie, Ginnie. I think it's safe to say he has a crush on you, too."

Isaac pulls into Gran's driveway.

My heart skips a beat as I realize what he has just said.

"Too?"

Isaac shrugs. "Two brothers have a crush on the same girl. Do you think the older brother has a chance?"

I stare at him in shock. I can't believe those words came out of his mouth. And those words refer to me. Me. Unfortunately, my mind comes unglued when faced with the boy of my dreams. "Maybe I should go." I open the door. "Good night."

Isaac reaches over me and shuts the door. He stays close. So close, I can feel his breath. "If you want to leave, then I'll walk you to the door. But you don't have to leave just yet."

"I'm a little nervous," I admit.

"I'm nervous too. But I still want to kiss you."

I bite my tongue to keep from telling him that this would be my first kiss. Unless you want to count Scotty who stuck his tongue down my throat when we were eleven, and I definitely don't want to count him. "I want to kiss you, too."

Isaac leans in and kisses me gently at first. His mouth is lovely, and I want more. I pull him closer and the kiss deepens.

Until the front porch light turns on and off a few times.

"That's my Dad," I whisper against Isaac's mouth.

"I gather that." Isaac leans back into his seat and sighing, opens his door to get out. "Stay there. I'll walk you to the door."

"Hello, Isaac," I hear my Dad call from the porch. Uncle Doug walks out too and gives a beady-eyed stare, but he's also smiling, so I know it's not too serious. Isaac heads toward my passenger side. "Hope I wasn't interrupting anything."

"No, sir," Isaac says. He opens my door and walks me up to the porch.

Dad doesn't look too thrilled. "I can take it from here," he says. "Have a good night, Isaac. Tell your father Doug and I will meet him tomorrow morning for eighteen holes."

"Yes, sir. See you tomorrow?" Isaac asks me.

"Sounds good."

Isaac hesitates, then turns to leave.

Once Isaac is out of earshot, I say, "Geez, Dad. Will you relax?"

"Relax? The second a man's daughter is born, he is incapable of relaxing."

Without the distraction of Isaac's lips on mine, I notice another two cars in the driveway. "Who's here?"

"Laura. She came back after her rounds. I hope you will behave a little better this time."

"I'll be a little angel," I smile devilishly and open the door to go in.

"Virginia," Dad warns.

There's no one in the front sitting room, so I walk to the kitchen. No one's there either.

"We're at the bonfire," Dad says from behind me. "Aunt Sue is up, plus Cassie. We're making s'mores. Cassie's been going nuts."

"Where's Gran?"

"In bed. She said hello to everyone, but she was tuckered out. Here. Take the graham crackers."

I take the graham crackers and head outside the back entrance toward the fire pit. I'm excited to see Cassie, not so excited to see Laura, but none of that matters. What I want to do is say hello, then go to my room and relive the kiss over and over. I also need to text Alisa. I'd call her, but it's way too early in the morning. Then again, if ever there was a time to wake up my best friend, it would be to squeal together over my first kiss.

"Ginnie!" Cassie throws her arms around me, nearly knocking me over.

"Hi, Cassie! It's about time you got here to entertain me."

"Not that you need entertaining." She releases me and raises an eyebrow. "Uncle Sam told me about the little mystery you unraveled today. Tomorrow, you'll have to take me to the sight. That would be sweet."

"S-Sure."

"And who was your date? Uncle Sam said a local boy took you out for dinner. You have to spill, girl!"

"Okay, okay," Aunt Sue says. "Let her say hello to everyone else first." Aunt Sue hugs me. "Hi, again, sweetheart."

"Hi, Aunt Sue."

"Sorry, it took us so long to come back up here. Cassie had to finish her laundry."

Cassie rolls her eyes. "But I'm all done with that and want to spend time with my favorite cousin."

"I'm your only cousin."

The three of us laugh and find seats around the fire. I notice Dad has already sat down next to Laura, who is staring up at my Dad with stars in her eyes. I'm no expert at love, but it looks like Laura has a thing for my Dad.

"What's up with your Dad and the blonde?"

"I'll tell you later." We smile at each other knowingly.

That's another thing. Cassie has the most beautiful smile. Wide, sparkling teeth, cute dimples. Her blonde hair is cut shorter than normal, framing her heart-shaped face nicely. She is always emailing me about a new boyfriend.

Cassie yawns and stretches. "I'm going to bed. Come on, Ginnie."

"Sure you are," Aunt Sue teases. "You want to get the scoop from Ginnie."

"Of course. C'mon, Ginnie. We've got a lot to catch up on, and we can't be around all these adults."

"Technically, you and Ginnie are adults," Uncle Doug pipes up.

"I was trying to be nice and not call all of you *old people*."

I grin and say good-night to Dad. As I stand, a cold wind blows against me with such force, I stumble over the bench and fall backward.

"Virginia!" Dad's up and over me. "Are you okay?"

I grab his hand and nod. I give the lame excuse, "It's too

dark to see anything."

Everyone agrees, and then Uncle Doug starts teasing me about easing up on the drinking.

Dad goes back to his chair. Cassie's already on the deck calling for me.

Stepping away from the fire pit, I leave the adults and head up the path toward the deck. The cold wind hits me again, but I keep my ground. It's darker now that I'm away from the fire. I tell myself to keep looking forward, but my curiosity has a mind of its own. It's as if I have to challenge myself.

The girl is standing in front of the tree line, holding up her hand in my direction. Her mouth is moving, but I can't make out what she's saying.

"Come on!" Cassie grabs my arm, only to release it. "Why is your arm like ice?"

All I can do is stare in the direction of where the girl stands. "Do you see anyone by the trees?" I hope she sees what I do, and that I'm not completely losing my mind.

But Cassie has already run inside.

I shake so hard, I have to grit my teeth to keep them from rattling. I look one more time toward the trees, but the girl is gone.

18

"What do you think?" Cassie twirls and poses, modeling her new bikini.

I'm flipping through my missed calls, trying to pay attention to Cassie while listening to voice mail. Alisa's voice pulls me into her message. "I've tried to call you a hundred times today. You never called me back after your date! I want details!"

"Hello? Ginnie?" Cassie pulls me back to the task at hand.

"You look fabulous. When did your melons get so big?"

Cassie stuck them out even further. "You like them? I'm in a size D now. Can you believe it?"

"They're about to fall out of the little pieces of material. Of course, I believe it."

"Oh, don't be jealous. You have nice perky ones. Besides, I don't have your gorgeous hair. Mine is thin and straight."

I press a number key and hold up my finger to Cassie. She rolls her eyes. I hope Mum's called, but no, it's Alisa again. This time I hang up.

"So, are you going to tell me about what you saw in the woods? You looked freaked out."

Cassie takes off her bikini right in front of me and throws on her shorts and tank combo. She plops herself on my bed with some nail polish and starts painting her toes.

I don't know how to answer her. My family will think I'm nuts if I talk about ghosts and beetles, but I know what I saw. I know who it was. Barbara Blackstone.

"I've been told the land around Pigeon Lake is cursed. It's done a number on me."

"Ooh." Cassie's eyes widen at the news. "Cursed? No one's ever told me that."

"Anyway, I found a dead body the other day, and it's wigging me out."

"I know. Tell me everything."

"Not much to tell. I went on the aluminum boat with Isaac and Ian and we got stuck—"

"Isaac Fulton?"

"Yes. Anyways, I tripped and fell and saw a hand."

"I can't wait for Isaac to see me in that bikini. He won't be able to take his hands off!"

I pause and wonder how to approach this. Surely, Cassie will leave him alone if she knows I like him. "How do you know Isaac?"

"We've had a thing the last couple of summers. He is an amazing kisser."

My stomach drops to the floor. I have no words.

But I don't need to say anything. Cassie keeps talking, "He's a ladies' man, if you know what I mean, but two summers ago, we sort of hit it off."

"You were fifteen."

"And he was sixteen. Trust me. He taught me a lot of stuff."

I get up from the bed. I need to do something fast. I grab a brush and start brushing my hair.

Isaac has to know that Cassie is my cousin. Is he messing with me? My heart, that had been elated just an hour ago, now feels ripped in half. I stop brushing my hair when I remember how quickly he left yesterday evening. He didn't want me to tell Cassie I was with him. I drop the brush, feeling hurt and disgust at the same time.

"Did he say anything about me?" she asks. "When you were in the boat with him? And when did you meet?"

I start braiding my hair.

Cassie catches on. "Oh, he made a move on you, didn't he?"

"What?" I ask, fumbling with the braid. I turn around and face her. "No. No, he didn't. Not at all."

"Oh, good, because that would suck. I've been crushing on him forever."

I smile tightly and nod. I need to tell her. But I can't. Does he even qualify as a boyfriend? We went on one date and shared one kiss. He's nineteen now—a man—and probably has more girls he's interested in. That leads me to wonder what he's doing with them.

"Sit down and let me paint your toenails."

Sighing, I go back to the bed and give her my foot.

"If I tell you something, you have to swear to never tell."

I don't want to know what she's about to say.

She tells me anyways. "He's the one. You know, the one I want to…"

I put my foot down on the floor. "I forgot to call Mum. I've got to do it before I forget."

"Won't she still be sleeping? London's eight hours ahead of us, right? There's no way she'd already be up."

"She's waiting for my call," I say and leave before she can say anything more.

I fly down the stairs and open the door to go outside. I stop when I see Dad and Laura over by her car. Her arms are around him, and they are in quite a passionate embrace.

Not that I'm one to be hypocritical, but didn't we just arrive? And now he's sucking face with little miss blonde doctor?

Sure, Isaac already kissed me, but that was before I knew that I may not be the top girl on the totem pole.

I go back inside and walk to the kitchen. I open the icebox and stare. Grab the ice cream, take a bite, put it back. That's not what I want. I walk to the back door and think about going out onto the deck. The deck should be safe from ghosts. Still, I stand there and look out the wide windows that face the lake.

Before I think twice, I dial Alisa. She, at least, won't kill me for calling so early.

"Hello?" she mumbles sleepily. "What do you want at this God-forsaken hour?"

"It's me, Ginnie."

"Ginnie? I've been calling you. But can you ring back at a reasonable hour?"

I'm on the verge of tears just thinking about what that entails. "I need to talk to you. Don't hate me for waking you up."

There's a pause. "What do you need to talk to me about?"

Alisa's up. I hear her moving around. I also hear the guilt in her voice. Alisa could never hide anything from me.

"Why don't *you* tell me what's going on?" I try. Knowing her, she's been partying up, having the time of her life without me.

There's another pause.

"It was only coffee. Well, first the party, then coffee. But I won't talk to him anymore. I promise. Pinky promise. Besides, you have your American boyfriend, right?"

I feel my world crumbling down around me. "Leo?"

"The American is named Leo? How bizarre is that?"

"No, his name is Isaac, and I was wrong about him."

"Oh, Ginnie. Okay, I'm awake now. Tell me everything."

I should have known. I shouldn't be upset. It's not like I own Leo. The guy's never talked to me, and I was just kissing Isaac, but my chest still hurts.

When I don't say anything, Alisa says, "Ginnie, I'm sorry. Mum wasn't supposed to tell you until I did. I can't believe her.

You should be here. I wouldn't be doing this if you were here, yelling at me."

"I wish I could come back."

"You can stay here. I'll talk to Mum."

Before I can respond, I cover my mouth as I see the girl at the top of the deck's steps, her hand still up as if in greeting. I close the cell phone and watch Barbara. She seems to come in peace, but I can't shake the chills and foreboding I get around her. "What do you want?"

The front door opens, and Dad enters the house. I keep my eyes on the ghost. Dad walks into the kitchen. "Hey, what are you doing?"

She turns and stares at Dad.

"What?" he asks.

Of course, the girl is gone, but I am shaken to my core as if the coldness of her spirit has found a permanent home inside of me.

"Did you see something?"

Instead, I cry. I didn't ask for *any* of this. My entire world was going fine until now. It's been smooth with very little bumps. But not now. It's a mess. I mentally shake myself. I won't be a wimp. If that ghost wants me dead, I'd be dead already. Shoot, those beetles could have sucked the soul right out of me if they desired. I even out my breathing and wipe at my eyes. "Sorry. Just feeling a little like a basket case."

"Virginia, I need you to talk to me. You look like you've seen a ghost."

What can I say? I can't tell him the truth. He wouldn't believe me. Dad's too sensible to believe in ghosts. I had been, too, until this summer. "I miss Alisa. And Mum. Not that she ever calls."

"How about we go to bed. Tomorrow will be a busy day with all the family here. That should help with the loneliness. Cassie and you always have a good time together."

I smile tightly, but I know it doesn't reach my eyes.

Dad touches my arm. "Virginia? If you need anything, let me know."

"Sleep. I need to sleep. Good night." I go up the stairs to my room, contemplating what I'm going to do. Obviously, the ghost knows where I'm staying, and is it only a matter of time before that crazy guy comes back? In all honesty to myself, I don't want any more ghosts or jerk boys who pretend to be nice and lovely or Dads who forget about their daughters to be with blonde bombshells or cousins who ruin whatever romance this girl might have had. So, maybe I should focus on the mystery of this missing girl. Like Dad said, begin to look at it from a scientist's perspective.

"What's up?" Cassie asks as I enter the room.

"I don't want to talk about it."

"You've been acting strange since I've got here. What gives?"

"It's been a long day, and I think I need some sleep."

Cassie sits cross-legged on her bed and gives me a look that says, I-don't-think-so. "You can tell me anything. You know that, right?"

I think of Isaac and know that's not true, but I need to tell someone something. "Do you believe in ghosts?"

"My friend Beth lives in a haunted house. It's one of those big, turn-of-the-century ones. She says that doors slam all the time on their own, and that she wakes up to someone literally shaking her bed." Cassie's eyes are huge.

"I'm seeing things," I admit.

"What kinds of things."

"A girl, mostly." I leave out the bugs part.

"Like a ghost?"

"Yeah."

Cassie watches me in either curiosity or shock or a mixture of both. "Why?" she finally asks.

"I don't know. Some guy came over today and said that girl whose body I found that her soul still needed to fulfill her purpose."

Remembering the picture, I say, "I even caught her on film. Want to see?"

"Yes!" Carrie can barely contain her excitement.

Okay, I guess she's not afraid of ghosts. We wait until Dad has shut his bedroom door. The hallway is filled with sounds of snoring from the bedrooms, so we sneak downstairs. Once in Gran's office, I start up the computer and wait to show her the pics. "Want to see something twisted?" I ask and pull out the old Bible. I take out the newspaper clipping and show Cassie.

"Is this the dead girl?" she whispers.

"Yep. That's the girl I'm seeing."

I find the blurred picture and show Cassie. "What do you see?"

She studies it before taking a step back. "Oh my word, I can't believe this is what you've been dealing with the last couple of days."

"Do you see it?"

She nods. "In all my years of coming here, this has never happened to me."

"My first summer, and it's like everything is unleashed all at the same time."

"Then it's a good thing I'm here." Cassie puts her arm through mine. "You and I have a mystery to solve."

"You mean, you don't think I'm crazy?"

"Ginnie, this picture is proof enough. I saw on that Ghost Raiders show that when a ghost is in the room or close by and you take a picture, there will be a blurry type of light, just like this. Not to mention, you are the most down-to-earth realist I know. You wouldn't lie to me about this. That's not you."

"So, you'll help me?"

"Yes, where do we start?"

We go back up to the bedroom, shut the door tight, and talk about how we were going to free the ghost and solve the dead girl's mystery.

Cassie eventually crashes and sleeps like a log. I, on the other hand, am a different story. My brain won't shut off. Plus, my body trembles most of the night. Any noise makes me cling to the blanket. When I do fall asleep, it's fitful and full of nightmares about beetles.

My head doesn't come out of the blanket until I hear noises downstairs that morning has come. Cupboard doors close, someone is talking. I peek my head out and check around. The morning sky is shaking off its gray, which means it's early. I'm about to throw the blanket over my head again when I realize it is Dad's voice coming from downstairs.

I get up and tiptoe out of the bedroom and down the stairs.

"I don't know what's going on," he's saying. When there's a pause, I realize he must be on the phone.

"Ever since she discovered the dead girl, she's acting strange. Not herself. Have you tried calling her? She needs to hear from you."

Another pause.

"There has to be time in your schedule, Melinda. Make time. It's your daughter."

I press my lips together to keep from balling up right here on the floor. Dad's trying to push me off on Mum. It should make me happy. It's what I want, to get away from this ghost-and-beetle-infested place.

"Maybe if she hangs out with Alisa, spends some time with you, she'll calm down…No, I've got to stay here for another two and a half weeks, at least…No, I haven't told her, not yet, but she knows I want to move back when she's finished with school…I'll take care of it. I've been taking care of her for eighteen years, I just need her to hang out with you for a few weeks while I set up some kind of home health care…"

I step into the kitchen, mostly because I feel guilty for eavesdropping on my parents, but also because the more I think about it, the more I'm itching for Mum to let me come home.

Dad sees me, smiles, and waves. He looks like he hasn't gotten any sleep either. Gran leans against the counter, sipping coffee. I go and make myself a cup.

"All right," he says. "That's fine. I'll book a flight back at that point." He gives me a thumbs-up sign.

When he hangs up, I ask, "What's going on?"

"I know you've been wanting to go home, so I thought I'd try your mother again. She said yes, we could work something out."

"But Cassie just got here. I can stay for a few more weeks. I don't mind."

Dad eyes Gran. "I thought this is what you wanted."

"It sort of feels like you're pushing me off on her. Especially now that you've got the hot babe."

Dad runs his fingers through his hair. "Gran thinks it's a good idea for you to spend some time with your mother, so you can make a sound decision about college. Melinda said that she's finishing up a project, but in a couple of days, she'll be free."

I glance over at Gran who is finding her cup immensely fascinating.

"Do I get a say?"

"Of course."

"Then, I want to stay here. I'll let you know if I change my mind." I leave them, and as I walk by the office I see the computer screen is up and running that scanned ghost picture. Gran's Bible also lays out on the desk. Did I forget to put that back?

When I go to keep moving up the stairs, I stop when I see Gran watching me. "Ginnie, I love you, and I want you protected. You need to fly back to London."

"Is something wrong?"

"I can't tell you, but I will say that it would be so much easier on my heart if you were to be in London where it was safe."

"So, you did call me? Before we left?"

She doesn't say anything, but she doesn't need to. "You know I love you, Ginnie-girl," she says again. "Please, do this for me. Once it's all settled and over, you can visit as long as you'd like."

"What about Dad? Is he safe?"

"He's not the one I'm worried about," she says.

London. Alisa. Mum. Home.

"How do you know the girl?" I ask. If I'm going to leave, I might as well ask.

"I was a substitute teacher in her class. She was a dear, sweet child. I took her death hard because that was around the time your father was born."

Dad walks to us, stifling a yawn.

"When do I leave?"

"I have to call the airline and see if I can book a Wednesday flight. Can you handle being here another couple days?"

"I guess." Gran hugs me, then says she's off to get more sleep. I decide to pour some coffee that Dad must have made.

"I'm going to go crash for a little bit," Dad says and kisses my forehead. "You probably should, too. It's only six in the morning."

When he's up the stairs, I set the creamer down and sip my coffee. An enormous weight should have been lifted; I get to go home. Instead, I feel frustrated at myself, like I'm quitting.

I toast an English muffin, layer on the peanut butter, and decide to brave the deck. The sun is coming up, streaking deep pink across the sky. I tell myself ghosts don't visit during the daylight.

The coffee doesn't keep me awake. Spread out on a lounger, the fresh morning air and chirping birds are therapy for my soul, and I find myself drifting into sleep.

It seems as if I've just shut my eyes when someone shakes me. "Ginnie, there's some hot Indian guy here."

I peek my eyes open and see Cassie leaning over me. "What?"

"There's some guy here to see you. And he's not bad. Was that your date? I need to know because I can't flirt if you've got dibs."

I sit up and rub my eyes. "How long have I been sleeping?"

"Don't know. It's past ten o'clock though."

"He's in the front?"

"Yep. Is he your boyfriend?"

I'm still in my pajamas, but I trudge through the house to the front. I stop at the screen door and recognition hits me. "Hi, Mitchell."

"You can call me Mitch."

I step outside.

His hair is pulled into a small ponytail, but other than that and intense dark eyes that remind me of my Dad's, he's dressed like any other guy on the weekend in a t-shirt, shorts, and sandals.

We stand for a second. I hear Cassie cough behind me. "Are you going to introduce us?"

I hardly know him myself, but I quickly say, "Cassie, this is Mitch. Mitch, this is my cousin, Cassie."

He nods at her and says, "Hey." To me, he says, "Can we talk?"

"Sure. I'll meet you at the dock in a few minutes."

Mitch glances at Cassie before heading around back.

"Oh. My. Word. Am I drooling?"

We run upstairs and both throw on clothes. I don't do anything with my hair. Cassie stops me. "Oh no, you don't. Don't go down without me, and don't go down there looking like that."

I brush through my hair and braid it, placing sunglasses on my head. "Done."

"It will have to suffice," Cassie says, as we make our way outside.

"Oh, by the way, if we're going to be mystery-solvers, we better make it quick. Gran is sending me back to London."

Cassie stops me just past the deck. "What? Why would she do that?"

"She says that I would be safer back home. She found that

blurry picture, and I must have left her Bible out last night."

"That doesn't sound like Gran. She loves it when you guys come during Christmas. Something is not adding up."

"Maybe it's because I was witness to that Indian guy coming over and threatening her. Maybe she thinks I know too much. And if I stay longer, I may find stuff out and get in trouble."

Cassie squares her shoulders. "Then I guess we have our work cut out for us, but you don't have to go if you don't want to."

"She practically begged me. What was I supposed to say?"

We keep walking.

Mitch has been watching us stop and start and now smiles at us. With a laugh, he says, "I wondered if you two would ever make it down."

"Family business," I say. "So, what's up?"

Mitch's face turns serious. "Last night, I hiked to the sight. To pay my respects, check it out, that kind of thing. Well, this huge monster truck was parked near the forest, and I got this weird vibe about it."

"A monster truck? With humongous wheels? And black paint with a red streak?"

"Yes, that's the one."

"That's the same guy that came to the house and threatened Gran!"

Cassie stops batting her eyelashes at Mitch. "Are you sure?"

"Positive," I say.

"I found that same guy at the top of the cliff, right before it drops down to the beach."

"What was he doing?"

"He acted upset. Said that he knew the girl, and was paying respects, too. But he said something that made me pause. He said something about a baby."

"A baby?" Cassie and I both ask the question.

"Yes, he said that the girl had a baby or was expecting a baby. I'm not sure. Like I said, he was upset."

My brain starts crunching numbers. Forty years ago. A baby may have been born. "We need to find this baby," I say.

Mitch says, "I have a suggestion, but please don't hate me."

"What?"

"We need to get the DNA of your Dad and your grandmother."

My eyes widen. "Why would we need to do that? They have nothing to do with this."

"Do you know for absolute certain that your grandmother carried and delivered your father?"

"That's absurd," Cassie says. "Of course she did."

"All I know is that what's happening to you, shouldn't be happening. Unless—"

"Unless what?" I ask, not sure I wanted to hear it.

"Just get their DNA. The local police post will run it for a small fee. It will rule out our theory of possibly being related."

"Why are you doing this?" Cassie asks, all niceties gone. "Are you trying to destroy my family?"

"My family's already destroyed," Mitch addresses her with an urgent glint in his eye. "And if we don't hurry, your cousin may share the same fate."

19

I feel sick. Mostly because his words ring with some truth. The easiest thing to do is to take something they've touched and drunk from and place it in separate baggies. Simple to do, but do I want to find out the answer?

"Are you okay?" Cassie whispers as the three of us walk to the house. "The test results will show that Gran and Uncle Sam are related. I know it. There's nothing to worry about."

"I hope so. I won't worry as much about being this guy's blood relative."

"It just seems weird to not trust Gran."

"I know," I say. "I do trust her though. Whatever her reasons, I trust she loves us and wants what's best for the family."

Cassie nods and places her arm around me. "I'm so glad I came. What would you have done without me?"

I think of Isaac, and my heart nearly breaks all over again. But she's waiting for an answer, so I squeeze her shoulders and say, "I'm glad you're here, too."

We slow as we hear the raised voices. It's Gran and Aunt Sue.

"Brace yourself," I warn Mitch. "Maybe they'll stop when they see I have a guest." But I know that won't happen before the words are done leaving my mouth. Cassie goes in first, sits at the table flipping through a magazine. When I come in with Mitch, she looks over at Gran and Aunt Sue and rolls her eyes.

"Traitor!" Gran yells. "I can't believe my own daughter—my flesh and blood—is a traitor!"

"Mom, Cassie gets part of her tuition covered because I work there. Plus, she won't have to stay in the dorms. It's a no-brainer."

"No family of mine is going to that…that… *place*. It was bad enough when you accepted a job there."

"I have to feed my family. And that *place* is Michigan State. It's a good school."

"Lies!" Gran yells. "I'm paying for my granddaughters to go to the University of Michigan. That's always been the plan. Why is everyone changing everything?"

"Save your money. I can take care of my daughter."

"Save my money? For what? I'm almost dead!"

Dad walks in, looks at me with a what-in-bloody-blazes-is-going-on, and steps in front of Aunt Sue. "Let it rest, sis."

"She started it!"

Gran sticks her tongue out at her daughter. When she sees me with Mitch, she raises her eyebrows.

"Everyone, this is Mitch. He's a friend of Isaac's and mine."

"And mine!" Cassie pipes up.

"Mitch Blackstone," Gran says and pours herself a cup of coffee. She pushes her hair away from her eyes and says, "My condolences to your family." She drinks from the cup, and the three of us watch her with hungry eyes.

"Thank you."

"Oh, is that a relative?" Dad asks, pointing across the lake. "I'm so sorry."

Aunt Sue nods at Mitch, but she quickly leaves the kitchen,

still in a huff.

"Why do you have to start stuff?" Dad turns to Gran. "It's not good for your heart to get that worked up."

"Me? I'm trying to defend my family's traditions."

She sets the cup down, and Cassie is already up and at the sink. "I'm going to help with dishes. Gran, why don't you relax? Uncle Sam, where's your coffee mug?"

"Oh, it's over there at the table. Ginnie, help your cousin clean up."

Dad leaves the kitchen with Gran.

I hurry and grab the sandwich baggies. I hand one to Cassie and one to Mitch. Mitch looks at three mugs on the table. "My Dad is the only one who uses cream."

Mitch inspects the cups. "There's two with cream." He holds up a green one. "There's this one, and there's a red mug with cream in it too."

"The one you're holding is Uncle Sam's," Cassie says. "I saw him drinking from a green mug this morning."

"The red one's mine," I say. "I had it outside this morning and brought it in when I went to get the door."

"And this cup has black coffee hardly touched," Mitch says, looking at a striped cup.

"That's my mom's," Cassie says. "She never drinks all her coffee."

We place Dad's green cup in one baggie, and Gran's large mug in a separate one.

"Easy-peasy," Cassie says. "What's next?"

"I'll keep you posted on the results." Mitch goes to leave.

"I don't think so," Cassie acts offended. "We are going with you. Right, Ginnie?"

"Sounds like a plan. I want to be there for the results."

Someone knocks on the front door.

"I'll get it!" Cassie runs past us to the front door.

"Busy place," Mitch says.

"Yeah, it's even busier when my Uncle Doug's here, but he's fishing pretty much all day today."

"I don't know what it's like to have a regular family. It's been my mother and me for twenty years, and she suffers from depression. It's been lonely."

His words pull at my heart. "When I'm in London, it's mostly just me and my Dad. But I've never felt lonely with him."

"I turned to golf. That was my escape. Now it helps me earn my keep. So, it all works out."

"Oh, I almost forgot. I've got a bunch of news articles I unearthed yesterday. I haven't had a chance to read through them all."

"I could stay and help."

"Yes," I say. "I mean, I wanted you to, but I didn't know how it would sound."

"I get it." He grinned. "But look at it this way, if we're right, you and I are related somehow."

"Don't take this the wrong way, but I think you're going to be disappointed."

"Why is it so hard to believe? It's a small world. I've heard that we're only six people removed from every person on the planet."

I motion for him to follow me and lead him down the hallway toward the front of the house and Gran's office. I stop when I notice Isaac standing in the entryway. His mouth is curved down like he's displeased Cassie is here.

I bet.

When he sees me, he smiles, then notices Mitch. "Hey, Mitch. What are you doing here?"

"Just wanted to talk to Ginnie."

"It's a long story," I add, then stop myself. Why am I defending being with Mitch?

"Want to go see a movie tonight?" Isaac asks me, completing ignoring the other two people in the room. "I have to be at work in a few minutes, but it's only a five-hour shift. I could pick you up around seven?"

Cassie is staring at me with a look that says I'm supposed to be helping her. Even if she is exaggerating about their relationship, the fact they had one and Isaac hadn't told me sets me on edge. But I should at least talk to him about it before I assume the worst. His body language shows that he's not enthused about Cassie being here. "Sure. That sounds fun."

Cassie jumps in. "I know. Why don't we all go on a double date? Ginnie and Mitch, and Isaac and me. The movies sound fun. There's that new Channing Tatum movie."

Isaac seems so tense, I almost feel sorry for him. He keeps glancing at me like he wants to say something, but I'm still hurt. So, I turn to Mitch and say, "Let's go check out those articles."

I walk into Gran's office while Mitch says something quietly to Isaac. Once we're in the office, I shut the two French doors. Cassie is already talking nonstop to Isaac. I make eye contact with him, and my heart breaks all over again. I turn and go to the computer desk.

"You know he doesn't like her, right?"

"Hmm? Who?"

"You know who. Why are you letting your cousin torture Isaac?"

"She's not torturing him. Plus, she has a crush on him and made it clear to me last night that there was some history between them. I don't want to get involved in all that. I've got a ghost spooking me, remember?"

"Whatever you say," Mitch shrugs. "Is she eighteen?"

"Yes."

"If she ever gets tired of him, let me know."

"Why wait until then. If you're interested, go for it."

Mitch watches her from the computer desk and smiles. "Maybe. Show me the articles."

I hear the door shut and sneak a look out the window. It

takes every ounce of will power to keep my butt firmly on the seat and not chase after him.

"The articles…"

"Sorry." I hand him half the stack of papers. "Most of the stuff is internet articles and blogs on ghosts and paranormal activity. My grandmother has an article on the actual missing girl. I open the file cabinet, but the Bible and rosary are gone. "She took them," I say. "They were right here."

"That's okay. I know the article. My mother has it. Eventually, everyone forgot about her," he says in resignation. "But my mother has never forgotten."

"Oh Mitch, that's awful."

My cell phone beeps with a message. It's from Isaac. *Please, lets' talk.*

"It's Isaac, isn't it?"

"Yes."

"My suggestion is to just tell your cousin the truth. No harm, no foul. It's going to come out eventually." He sets the article, along with the others, down and looks at me. "The library will have better archives. Besides I need to talk to my mom and get her DNA sample. Want to come with?"

"Why do you need her DNA sample?"

"Because she and Barbara were identical twins. My mother will have the same DNA."

"Your mother works at the library?"

"Yes." He stands and stretches. "She needs to know what's going on. And she'll want to meet you."

"Sure, let me change."

I run up the stairs as Cassie comes down. She walks into the office and starts chatting with Mitch. Poor bloke. She'll talk his ear off. Then again, maybe he'll make a move.

Aunt Sue is sitting on her bed with her laptop on her lap, typing feverishly. Her door is open though, so I decide to see if she remembers anything.

"Hi, Aunt Sue. Are you busy?"

"Hmm? No, dear. Not really. Just typing my assistant a message. If I don't leave him clear details, nothing will get done." She finishes, then shuts the hand-held computer. "So, what's up? Sorry, you and your friend had to walk in on that little disagreement."

"Oh, no worries."

"Your father says you're leaving soon. Is everything okay?"

So, they omitted that Gran wanted me leaving? "I just miss Mum, and my friends, and London."

Aunt Sue smiles in understanding. "It probably was very difficult for a girl your age to pack and leave, especially so quickly, but we love to have you here. We don't see you enough."

I nod because I don't know what to say to that. After a few seconds, I blurt, "Do you remember anything from when Dad was a baby?"

Aunt Sue leans her head back in surprise. "No. Not really. I was only two when I became a big sister. Why do you ask?"

"No reason."

I say thanks and turn to leave. Aunt Sue stops me and says, "I remember your Dad was fussy. Very fussy. If I'm not mistaken, Gran hired one of her students to help watch us because we were so hard to manage. I like to blame that on Sam."

"One of her students?"

"I don't remember much about her, other than she liked holding Sam a lot. I don't think she gave me that much attention." Aunt Sue smiles at the memory.

Cassie's laughter carries up the stairs. I wonder how Mitch is doing down there with her as company.

After I'm dressed, I brush my hair and put some gloss on my lips. If I do go to the movies tonight, I'll have to try a bit harder than this, but for now, it'll do. I run down the stairs and pause. Mitch is telling Cassie this elaborate story, and Cassie is hanging onto his every word. He must get to the punch line because Cassie starts laughing again. Mitch's grin spreads across his face, no doubt in delight. Cassie is quite a catch.

But that makes me think of Isaac, which makes me frown. I take out my phone to text him, but I pause, not knowing what to say. I'm horribly awkward already, and I don't know how to broach the topic with Isaac or Cassie. So, I shove the phone back in my pocket. "All right, I'm ready."

"There you are!" Cassie exclaims. "We wondered what happened to you." They start snickering again. "Mitch says I can come, too. This is going to be so much fun!" Cassie runs out of the room and yells up the stairs to Aunt Sue.

I raise my eyebrows at Mitch. It's weird because technically he's a stranger, but I feel like I know him.

He grins and shrugs, "What? She's cute. Besides, if I keep her occupied, you can have time with Isaac. It's a win-win."

"What's a win-win?" Cassie asks as she slips into her shoes.

"Going to the library and meeting Mitch's mother," I say quickly.

Mitch walks past us to the door and holds it open for us. Cassie looks at me quickly and whispers, "Do I look all right?"

"Of course. What a silly question."

She smiles and heads outside, her blonde hair bouncing with each step as she bounds for Mitch's truck. Mitch watches her, too. "Boy, she's something."

I sigh and follow her. "She sure is."

Luckily on the ride to the library, Alisa calls me. Cassie chose to sit in the middle between me and Mitch, so they don't seem to mind when I take the call.

"Hey there," I say into the phone.

"You are such a ninny!" she yells in excitement. "How can you call yourself a close mate of mine and not tell me you get to come home!" She's squealing, and I would squeal, too, but Cassie and Mitch can already hear Alisa through the phone, so I'm not going to add to that.

"I haven't had a chance to call you, but yeah, Dad's buying the ticket for a couple of days from now. I guess he got Mum to agree."

"We ran into her at one of the record shops. She says that we can chum it up the whole summer! I'm already planning a party."

"Why was Mum at a record shop? Why were you?" I laugh because Mum's idea of music is listening to herself sing off-key in the shower, and if it isn't a Korean boy band, Alisa isn't interested.

"She was flirting with the owner. They might be an item, I'm not sure."

Mitch pulls into the library's parking lot.

"I've got to go," I say as we scramble out of the truck. "I'll let you know the exact times as soon as I find out."

When I end the call, Cassie's watching me. "I still can't believe you're leaving. Not if I have anything to do with it. I don't ever see you, other than at Christmas."

"You come out and visit."

"Not since I was twelve!"

I press my lips together, not knowing what to say. I guess I never realized how much Cassie wanted me there. She turns and walks into the library without saying another word.

Mitch has watched the whole scene with a serious expression on his face.

"What?" I ask. "You don't want me to leave either?"

I'm being sarcastic, so it surprises me when he says, "No, I don't. If you are related to me, it's going to suck not getting to know you."

The guilt is annoying me, so I snap, "We don't know that we're related," and I walk into the library. Then I feel bad for my behavior. It's not their fault that I have to leave. And it's sweet they want me to stay. What's wrong with me? I feel completely torn in two. One part of me longs for London and home, but there is another part of me. That part feels I belong here. That I owe it to this ghost to figure out what's going on.

"Ginnie?"

I glance over at Mitch who's standing next to a beautiful Indian woman. Her black hair shines down her back, her skin looks years younger than her probable age, and there's a wisdom and shyness to her persona that pulls at me. But none of that makes my knees tremble or my stomach flip. It's the resemblance to the ghost that has me nearly passing out.

"This is my mother, Bonnie Blackstone."

"N-N-ice to meet you," I finally say after I regain some composure.

"It's nice to meet both of you." Bonnie turns to Mitch. "I have to get back to work."

"But we need to ask you some questions."

"Now? What could it possibly be about that you need to speak to me right this second?"

"About Barbara," he whispers. "Ginnie is the one who found her."

Mrs. Blackstone turns back to me as if seeing me for the first time. "Go to the back meeting room. I'll be there in a minute."

There's a sadness in her features as she walks away that pulls at me.

"This way," Mitch says.

We make our way to the back room. I sit in one of the leather chairs that surround a conference table.

"This is nice," Cassie says. She goes on to talk about how she might decide to major in media technology so that she can be a librarian, but I am still squeamish by the resemblance of Mitch's mother to the ghost. It makes the ghost all the more real to me.

Mrs. Blackstone walks into the room and shuts the door behind her. "I only have a few minutes." She sits directly across from me. "You found my sister?" She seems as much in disbelief as Mitch was.

I nod. "It felt as if something was pulling the boat. We tried to paddle away, but nothing worked. We just let the current—or whatever it was—lead us to the shore."

Her eyebrows raise in apparent shock.

"She's seen her ghost," Mitch says quietly. "She has to be a descendant of our tribe."

"She's not just a descendant," Mrs. Blackstone says. "She's a full-blood."

"No, I'm not." They don't seem to hear me, so I say again, "My Mum is full-blood Irish. So, even if my Dad is full-blood, I can't be. And, I don't know if my Dad is related."

She nods slowly, then lets out a long breath. "It can't be," she says to herself.

"What?" the three of us kids ask together.

"How old is your father?"

"He's turning forty this week."

Mrs. Blackstone gets up from the table, shaking her head. "I have to get back." She studies me for a few seconds. "Let me think about this. Thank you for finding my sister," she says before she walks out.

"You upset her," Cassie says.

"How?"

"No, my mother always does that when she has to think about something. Come on, let's check the archives."

"Don't you have any pictures or anything at your house?" Cassie asks Mitch as we head out of the room.

"Some, but Mom hid everything that reminded her of her sister."

"I feel like we're detectives or something," Cassie says. We've sat at a set of computers labeled *Archives*. "What do we search for?"

"One of us type in Barbara Blackstone. Someone else should research any other deaths at or near the lake. No matter how far back you have to go," Mitch says. "I'm going to research my tribe's customs and see if I can discover anything new about the curse."

"Sounds good," Cassie says. "Which one do you want to research?" she asks me.

But I'm already typing in Barbara's name. "You find out about any other deaths," I say while scanning the computer screen for relevant information.

The three of us stare at our screens, silently reading articles as the minutes tick by.

"I found something that might help you." He clicks the print button and walks over to the printer.

"I didn't find anything here. Maybe I'm doing it wrong."

"I didn't find anything either," I say with some disappointment.

Cassie heads over to the printer where Mitch is looking over some papers.

As I leave, I say to Mrs. Blackstone, "I'm sorry about the loss of your sister."

She nods and says, "Thank you."

I start to walk away when she grabs my arm.

"You won't find anything."

At first, I'm not sure what she means, but then she continues, "I searched for…years. One day we're walking to school together. I didn't see her for the rest of the day. She never came home that night. She went missing. Rumor was that she was pregnant, but she never kept secrets from me, and I never knew about that. She didn't have it in her to run away. She was always the chicken, and I was the brave one." Mrs. Blackstone chuckles softly at the memory. "So I kept looking. I didn't want to believe in a curse. I wondered if she was alive somewhere, but I think my heart knew all along."

"I'm sorry," I say again for lack of anything better.

"Anyways, there's nothing there. It's like she vanished."

Mitch and Cassie walk back over. "You ready?" Mitch asks.

Before I leave, I ask her, "If you think of any reason why

she is trying to communicate with me, will you let me know?"

"I want to find out myself. So, you keep me posted, too, okay? Be safe out there."

A heaviness tugs on my heart as I walk out with Mitch and Cassie. Maybe it's because we leave the building with more questions than answers, but, more importantly, I know that it's because if I want to find the truth, I'm going to have to go to the source.

20

No one is having a good time. Other than Cassie.

With Isaac around, she is in full swoon mode, which makes everyone uncomfortable. Isaac looks at me occasionally, and my heart leaps into my throat. Even Mitch acts like he'd rather be anywhere but here. He keeps watching Cassie openly flirt with Isaac, and I swear he seems jealous. Maybe he's developed a bit of a crush.

Needless to say, the night is awkward. And miserable. And, *well*, awkward.

I barely remember anything about the movie. Isaac decides he's tired and doesn't want to eat anywhere afterward. Cassie pouts. We all pile in Isaac's Jeep. Yeah, not fun.

On the way back, Mitch and I keep the conversation going between us to pretend things aren't as weird as they are.

"What did you think of the article?" he asks while Cassie is talking faster than a squirrel on crack.

"I found the info about the beetles, but there wasn't anything there about a specific curse."

"I know. I asked my mom about it, and she said that it only

affected the tribe of this area, so that's why we can't find it in the literature."

"What are you two talking about back there?" Isaac asks, looking directly at me through the rearview mirror.

I look away, but Mitch answers, "We researched some stuff about my tribe. We're trying to find out if we're related."

"That would be so cool," Cassie gushes. "Would that mean I'd be related to you?"

"No," Mitch says too quickly.

I glance up and Isaac is still sneaking peeks at me through the mirror. He coughs loudly. Mitch reaches into his pocket for something.

"So, you two might be related? How's that?" Isaac asks as if nothing happened.

Mitch leans forward to talk to him and maneuvers himself toward the middle. "Well, we don't know yet."

As Mitch talks, he drops something in my lap. I realize it's a note, and that it's probably from Isaac. Why wouldn't he just text me? Then again, he's texted me three times today, and I have yet to text him back. I can't stop my heart from beating wildly. I want to read it right there, but it's dark, and I don't want Cassie to see. I stuff the small paper into my pocket and look out the window.

We can't get to the house fast enough. Once Isaac pulls in, he makes no effort to get out. "Well, see you all later."

Mitch says good night and heads to his truck. "We'll talk tomorrow," he says to me before getting inside.

I shut the back door to the Jeep, and Isaac makes eye contact. "Bye, Ginnie."

"Bye."

"You can come in," Cassie offers.

"Nah, I need to get going." Isaac puts the Jeep into reverse.

It's becoming clear that Isaac wants nothing to do with Cassie, but is that because she puts him in an awkward position? But he knew she's my cousin. Wouldn't he assume Cassie would tell me everything?

"What was up with him?" Cassie says as we enter the house.

"You heard him. He's probably tired from a long day at the golf course."

"Yeah, I guess. Maybe I'll call him tomorrow. Or even better, maybe I'll surprise him with a visit. What do you think?"

We shut the front door and lock it, then head up the stairs. The note is burning a hole in my jeans. I'm certain of it.

"What about Mitch?" I ask. "He seems to like you."

"Really? I mean, I couldn't do that to Isaac."

"If Isaac doesn't pay you attention, but Mitch does, then sometimes a girl's got to move on."

I can't believe I'm manipulating my cousin. But that's exactly what I'm doing. Before I can stand it, I excuse myself to the loo. Once the door is locked—and I've checked it three times—I venture a look at the paper. I unfold it, and sure enough, it says, *I can explain. Meet me at the docks. 12:30 a.m.*

My knees give out and I fall onto the toilet seat. I am so giddy. I know I should be hurt or angry or frustrated, but the thought of Isaac sneaking this note to Mitch to give to me is enough to have me at least go out to the docks and see him.

Then it hits me. The docks. At 12:30 at night.

I will have to walk in the dark. By myself.

Despair hits me like a sledgehammer to the stomach. I can't go. There's no way. I know I might have thought about seeking out the ghost, but who was I kidding?

I shove the note in my pocket, deciding to send him a text. But being at the docks with Isaac sounds deliciously romantic. I'm undecided as I go to the bedroom.

Cassie has her phone out. "I'm snapchatting," she says without looking up. "I mean, Instagram is great, but I don't know, Snapchat has better filters." She poses and takes a pic. "Here. Pose." I place my hands on my hips and stick my tongue out. She laughs. "I'm posting that."

I crawl into bed with my clothes still on, trying to talk myself into going.

Isaac will be there…The ghost hasn't hurt you…If she wanted to hurt, it would have already happened…*Isaac will be there*.

"So, you believe you saw a ghost?" Cassie turns off her phone.

"Yeah, I think so."

"You should videotape it and send it to that one show that investigates places where ghosts are located. Oh, what's it called?" she snaps her fingers. "Ghost Hunters! That's it! Maybe we could get some money for it."

Cassie keeps talking, so I turn off the light, to let her know that I want to go to sleep. She doesn't, however, get nonverbal communication. I glance at the alarm clock. It's already midnight.

"So who do you think I should go for? Isaac or Mitch?"

"All I know is Mitch seemed jealous tonight. It seems like a waste of time to try and flirt with a guy who's going to be a wanker about it."

"Mitch was jealous?"

Cassie takes the bait, but I fake tired and yawn. "I need to crash."

"It's still early," she says in a huff. Still, she lies down in bed. For a few minutes, everything's quiet. Then Cassie says, "I think I'm going to flirt with them both. There's nothing wrong with having a little fun with two guys."

I don't respond, hoping she thinks I'm sleeping. Then I battle it out in my mind. Brave the ghost for Isaac or stay safe in bed? But as 12:30 hits, I already know what I'm going to do.

Cassie's been quiet for about twenty minutes. I don't take any chances and slip out of bed as carefully as I can. My bed squeaks though as I stand up. I stop, then tip-toe to the door.

"Where're you going?" she asks sleepily.

"To the loo. My guts are killing me."

I shut the bedroom door behind me and let out a breath. I go and turn on the light in the bathroom and shut the door, just in case she comes looking for me. As I tip-toe down the stairs, I listen for any movement coming from our room. Nothing.

Before I walk to the kitchen, I go to the linen closet and grab a flashlight. I can*not believe* I am going out there in the dark. If Isaac stands me up, I swear to everything holy, he will suffer.

I've already wasted five minutes. I cross myself and recite a quick prayer. *Saints, don't fail me now!*

Opening and closing the door as quietly as I can, I refuse to look anywhere near the woods. I move quickly down the steps, across the fire pit area, and as I get closer, I see a figure on the docks. My breath catches.

It's not a ghost. It's Isaac.

He stands at the edge of the dock, looking up at the sky, and my heart thumps thickly. When I step on the dock, he turns. There's no smile, only worry, and agitation.

"Ginnie…I don't even know where to begin…"

I walk to him, closing the distance.

"I didn't think you'd come out here," he says. "I hoped you would, but I wasn't for sure."

I can't say anything yet. I press my lips together to keep my emotions in check.

"Nothing happened between me and Cassie. I don't know what she's told you, but I promise I'm not lying. She's just very exuberant in her flirting."

My eyes have been looking down only because I know I will get lost in his gaze, but he lifts my chin anyways. Our eyes make contact, and I feel I'll melt right there.

"She's had this silly crush on me since forever, and a couple of years ago, I was immature and stupid and kissed her. Nothing major. Just a peck. Big mistake. Every summer I think she'll grow out of it. I just assumed…I don't know what I assumed. I hoped she would get the hint if she saw us together." He trails his fingers across my cheek faintly, sending goose pimples down my spine. "Please, say something."

"I want to be angry," I finally answer. "But all I can think about is kissing you again."

Isaac rests his forehead on mine, brings his hands to my hands, and intertwines our fingers. We pause before our lips find their way to each other. Nothing else matters. He wraps his arms around me, and I cling to him. We come up for air, only to go under again.

"This is going to be difficult," he says, pulling away.

"Just the same, if you keep me kissing me like that it won't be difficult for much longer."

"Ginnie, Ginnie, Ginnie, please don't say stuff like that to me. It makes me crazy." He leans in and kisses me again. It's an urgent kiss filled with need. I am loving this! Isaac stops, then says, "I'll take you back inside."

I nod. "I should remain a good Catholic girl for a while longer."

Isaac laughs softly. "Yeah, all right, as long as everything's okay between us."

"Yes."

"Do you want to tell Cassie? Or should I?"

"I hadn't thought about that."

"I don't want these next couple weeks you're here to be like tonight, so someone's got to say something."

My stomach drops when I realize I'm leaving in a few days. I squeeze my eyes shut and inwardly swear at my stupid self. I can't fathom leaving Isaac. I'll have to talk with Gran.

"I'll tell her," I say.

Isaac takes my hand and walks with me back to the house. I decide to not look anywhere else but straight ahead.

"So, I've decided we should try mudding again." We approach the deck and take the steps quietly.

"Sure, why not. I'm in good hands."

"As long as you don't face-plant in mud again."

"Ha, ha." My insides haven't yet calmed down. From the kiss or the threat of the ghost showing up. Still, I wrap my arms around him. Ghost or no ghost, I'm not ready for Isaac to leave. "Today was miserable without you," I confess. "Thanks for the explanation."

Isaac rests his hands on my hips and pulls me closer. Our lips are not even an inch apart. "How am I supposed to leave?" he asks, his breath mingling with mine. When we kiss this time, everything leaves my brain and I simply enjoy the taste of his lips on mine, the amazing sensation I feel when he touches me. Too soon, Isaac pulls back. "I need to go."

We kiss again.

Isaac sighs reluctantly and takes a step back. He rubs his hand over his face and chuckles to himself. "Your father's never going to trust me if I sneak you out of the house and then make out with you all night."

"I'm willing to risk it," I dare say.

He looks at me with such longing, it takes my breath away. "I need to go," he says again. "I have the day off tomorrow. Want to hang out with me and Ian?"

"Of course."

"I thought we could take you golfing. Ian may like ghost stories, but he's determined he only likes to read about them and is not quite ready to be near the lake."

"I don't blame him."

"Okay. I'll stop by around eleven." He pauses, then says, "You should probably get in the house while my self-control is working."

I bite my lip but can't stop my grin. "Bye."

I open the house door and shut it, waving at Isaac that I'm safe and indoors. He gives me one last smile before jumping off the deck and running around the side of the house. Without Isaac there, I no longer want to be near the door or outside. I quickly turn

around and walk as quickly as I can away from the door.
And run right into Cassie.

21

The hurt and confusion on her face are the first things I register.

"I can explain."

"I've been up waiting to make sure you're okay, and here the whole time, you've been out stealing my guy."

"Cassie, he's not your guy. What happened between you was years ago."

"Why didn't you tell me? Why have me make an idiot out of myself tonight?"

"I…"

"Oh, I get it now." Cassie's becoming more upset. "Throw me on Mitch, huh? Was that the plan?"

"No, yes, it's not like that. Mitch seems to be into you. I wouldn't lie."

"You wouldn't? Because it looks like you just did." She snatches the flashlight out of my hand and storms to the back door.

"Where are you going?" I say in a panic.

"None of your business."

"Cassie! Don't go outside. Not now. Please."

But she's already slammed the door.

I groan in exasperation. "I'm not going after you!" I say to no one. I can't go after her. One step outside, and I'm sure the ghost will reappear.

Still, I go to the window and barely make out Cassie stumbling into the woods.

"What is she doing?" I am so exasperated, I pound the countertop. "She knows I see a ghost out there. Stupid girl. I'm *not* going after her."

But the hurt I've caused her is more than I can take, and I run outside before I lose my nerve. "Cassie!" I call. "Cassie!"

"Leave me alone!" I hear her not too far away. Good, maybe she's chickened out.

I take a deep breath before I walk through the tree line. "Where are you at?" I ask, completely spooked. "Can we go back to the house and talk about this like normal, rational people?"

I hear her crying.

"Come on, Cassie," I plea, tentatively stepping toward the sound of her sobs. "Isaac and I liked each other before you got here. After you told me you liked him, I was going to leave him alone."

"Then why didn't you?"

I'm almost to her. At least she's staying in one place.

"I don't know. He wrote me a note to meet him, and…and I like him, okay?" I see the small light coming from the flashlight. I push past some ferns, and see Cassie sitting up against a dead log.

"You think you're so special," she spits out. "*I'm from London, I've got a cute accent and a cute body and cute hair.*"

She reminds me of Alisa. Neither one of them can mimic me very well.

"What are you talking about? Have you taken a look at yourself, you big loony? You're the one with blonde hair and big jugs. You're every guy's Barbie fantasy." I don't want to sit down next to her, but she's not budging. "Can we please go back to the house? You know this place creeps me out."

"Oh yeah, the mysterious ghost you keep seeing," she says, and it's like I feel her eyes rolling in annoyance. "Comes in handy to get the guys. Sure wish I would have thought of that."

I run my fingers through my hair and count to ten, trying to keep my cool. "What do you want from me, Cassie? I'm sorry you found out that way. I was going to tell you. But, I'm not going to apologize for liking him. You know I haven't had a boyfriend…ever. Can't I enjoy this one guy who likes me?"

"He's just using you!" Something in the woods skitters away in surprise. I hear her sigh, "I wish you would have told me. Now I'm embarrassed."

She seems to be calming down. I decide to risk it and sit beside her. "You're right. I should have. But you shocked me when you mentioned him. I didn't know what to think."

We're quiet for a moment, and I'm about to lose my bloody mind out in these woods. Cassie doesn't seem spooked at all.

"I've always had a crush on him," she admits. "I guess I wanted something to be there."

"What about Mitch?" I ask. "He was so jealous tonight. I can't believe you didn't notice."

"That makes me even more embarrassed!" She giggles, and I know we're over the worst of it. "I could have been spending my time with him. I wondered why Isaac kept looking at you. Boy, I'm such an idiot."

"No, you're not. I should have told you earlier. That was stupid. Forgive me? I can't have my only cousin pissy at me."

Cassie rests her head on my shoulders. "I love you, and you know it. So, is he a good kisser? You two looked like you were about to get it on right there."

I shove her playfully, and she's giggling like a schoolgirl. "What? He may have kissed me, but definitely not like that!"

She has me blushing just thinking about it. "Well, I don't have tons of experience to go on, but let's just say he turns my insides to mush. Like a million gazillion butterflies all at once."

Cassie is laughing so hard, she gets me giggling. "What?" I ask.

"Who says that? *He turns my insides to mush.*"

"Please stop trying to imitate me. You're horrible at it."

But she's laughing so hard, she's doubled over.

I stop laughing as soon as I feel it. "Cassie, we need to go." I jump up, forcing myself to push past the cold. But the ghost is pulling at me. Grabbing Cassie's arm, I yank her up.

"What? What is it?" She may act like a complete airhead, but Cassie is as perceptive as they come. She shines the flashlight all around us.

"Stop that," I whisper. "Let's move." I pull her toward the house, which isn't too far away. I see the porch light through the trees.

"Oh my God." Cassie stops.

I take in a shaky breath and turn back to grab her arm again.

The ghost stands right beside us. Her eyes on mine. She extends her hand, her palm up.

"Do you see this?" I whisper.

Cassie grabs my hand and squeezes it.

I can't take my eyes away from the ghost. "You're Barbara Blackstone," I say. I don't know why I'm not completely freaking out at this moment, but any fear I felt is gone. Something about this girl tugs at me.

She doesn't move, but the cold pushes at me.

"Touch her hand." Cassie turns to me as calmly as if talking about the weather. "She wants you to touch her hand."

"I'm not touching her."

"You need to hurry. I read today that ghosts can only expend so much energy at a time."

Something about what Cassie says makes sense. Plus, I reason that this ghost is never going to leave me alone unless I do this. I slowly reach my available hand out. It's shaking, and I have to steady it.

"It's okay," Cassie says. "She doesn't want to hurt you. At least I don't think she does."

Before I can change my mind, my fingers meet the ghost's hand. The cold seeps into my blood, and I feel frozen. Suddenly I feel her pain. Her anguish. A young life gone.

"Ginnie…" her words course through my body, reverberating every cell. Suddenly she pulls away and disappears.

Cassie takes the lead and helps me get to the house. I go to open the back door when a beetle crawls onto my hand. I swallow back the scream and shake it off.

Cassie opens the door for me and shuts it closed once we're inside. I lean against the wall and collapse onto the floor. I hold myself to quiet the tremors. Taking deep breaths I cover my face and focus on not hyperventilating.

Pain. I felt it. Her pain.

I glance up and see Cassie pacing the kitchen floor. She's talking to herself. "It's not like I didn't believe her, but well, I didn't believe her. This is crazy." When she sees I'm watching her, she breaks into a grin. "That was…*awesome*!" She doesn't even try to be quiet.

Awesome? I am still unable to stand, my knees are still rattling.

"She said your name!" Cassie keeps going. "How does she know that? Oh my God, did you see how young she was? It's like a riddle and we have to find out what it means."

I put my hand up to stop her. My head might spin-off if she doesn't stop. "I know what the ghost said." I stop, then wonder, "How do you know what she said? I heard it…inside of me."

Her words still echoed in my head.

"We were holding hands." Cassie sits down on the floor across from me. "I felt her through you."

I close my eyes as overwhelming exhaustion blankets me.

"What are you going to do?"

I had just started to doze. "Right now, I'm going to sleep."

"Here?"

But I had already laid down on the floor, using my arms as a pillow.

You'd think I would have nightmares, but I don't have any. I sleep so soundly that when my eyes open, I'm surprised to find a pillow underneath my head, a blanket over me, and Cassie sleeping beside me. I lean up on my elbows, squinting at the bright sunlight, and see Aunt Sue standing over us. "Why are you sleeping on the floor? In the kitchen?"

I sit up all the way and rub my eyes, forcing my sluggish brain to work. But there's a crick in my back, and I need coffee, so I hold up one finger, signaling her to wait. I stretch a few times, then stand up and groggily trudge over to the coffee pot. Once a hot cup of coffee is in my hands, and I have sipped a few times to get everything sort of moving, I remember.

I stare at my hand and immediately feel the sensation of the cold touch, of the unbearable, heart-wrenching pain she endured, of her message to me.

"Well?" Aunt Sue prompts.

"We thought it'd be fun... you know, to try something new."

Aunt Sue snorts. "I will never understand how sleeping on a hard floor constitutes as fun, but that's beside the point. It's nearly ten. I have to get going, and your Dad's not back yet, and neither is your grandmother."

"Where'd they go?"

"Your grandmother left a note this morning that she went for a hike, which doesn't make me happy. The coffee pot had turned off automatically by the time I got downstairs, meaning she had to have left around five this morning. I've tried to call your Dad, but he spent the night at Laura's, and well, he's not picking up or returning my calls."

"He stayed where?"

"Laura's. I thought he would have told you. Obviously from

the look on your face, he didn't."

"No, no he didn't. He neglected to mention he would be rendezvousing with Miss Blonde Bombshell."

Aunt Sue started chuckling. "Yeah, she's something, isn't she?"

"Do you think her knockers are real?"

Aunt Sue keeps chortling, but I'm quite serious. "It's pathetic," I add. "He's nearly forty years old, out all night, yet trying to protect my virtue. The nerve."

"For the record," Aunt Sue pauses as Cassie mumbles at us to be quiet. "Get up," she orders her daughter. "I'm leaving, and I want to say good-bye. Anyways," she looks back at me. "What was I saying? Oh yes, for the record, Laura's genuinely nice. She and your Dad were close back when we were all in school. She might look like a shallow model, but she's not." Aunt Sue realizes what she said, and adds, "I don't think that your mother is shallow—"

"It's okay," I say with a shrug. "Mum is a shallow model."

The back door opens, and Gran comes clomping in with her filthy hiking boots.

"Where have you been?"

And Aunt Sue is off. I'm still thinking about my Dad sharing Laura's bed. Sure, it's been a while for him, but what about his little 'stay pure until you're married' speech he gives me. Well, he wasn't married to Mum. Or to Laura. The hypocrite. What a way to set an example.

Aunt Sue interrupts my thoughts. "What part of 'heart condition' do you not understand, mother?"

"Exercise is good for the heart, daughter. Ginnie, pour me a cup of coffee, will you? And toast me an English muffin with some peanut butter." She takes off her boots, opens the back door again, and sets the boots outside.

"You've been gone for hours! You could have been out there, passed out, with no one to know where you were."

"I'm fine. Now, will you stop yelling? You're the one liable to have a heart attack with all your caterwauling."

"Did you see anything out there?" Cassie is sitting up and very lucid all of a sudden.

I shake my head at her. She sees me. Hopefully, she understands I want her to keep what happened under wraps.

"Just God's creation. Why?"

"No reason."

I let out a breath and keep spreading the peanut butter on the English muffin.

We hear the front door open and close.

"I'm telling him," Aunt Sue says to Gran as a threat.

Gran pretends to be frightened and says, "Ewwww. I'm scared."

"Mature," Aunt Sue is saying as Dad walks in. "Real mature."

"Hey, everybody," Dad says, exceptionally chirpy.

"Deal with your mother," Aunt Sue says, as she walks out of the room. "I have to finish packing and get out of here."

Dad looks at Gran, who is now at the table, sipping her coffee and munching on her English muffin. I'm at the counter making myself one and avoiding any eye contact with my traitor father.

"I went for a walk," Gran says with a sigh. "She is so uptight."

I sit beside Gran and begin to eat breakfast. Cassie's up and making toast for herself.

"So, where've you been?" Cassie asks Dad.

"Oh, um, Laura and I stayed up talking late last night, and she let me sleep there. On the couch."

Gran and I snort at the same time.

"So, how are you?" he asks and walks over, planting a kiss on my forehead.

"Lovely. Never better."

Cassie snorts. Soon, Gran's chuckling. Cassie starts, and

even I can't hold my grin.

"What?" Dad asks. "You know what? Never mind. Virginia, I purchased your plane ticket. You're set to leave in two days. I have to take the Mustang back anyways, so Laura will be following us, and I'll ride back with her. Sound good?"

"You're not leaving now, are you?" Cassie cries from the counter. "We have a murder mystery to solve!"

I shake my head. Big mouth!

"You two stay out of trouble," Dad says. "Let the police do their job."

I know I can't leave. That girl wants my help. If I went back to London, I wouldn't be able to shake her. Plus, there's Isaac. "Maybe I'll just stay here. I'm sorry, Gran, but I feel like I need to be here."

"Virginia Paxton! You can't keep changing your mind like this!" Dad shakes his head. "Make a decision and stick to it."

Gran watches me. Her eyes look frightened. I don't want to hurt her, but this is important.

"Gran, I don't want to upset you, but I want to stay. I know I acted all homesick, but now Cassie is here. I never get to see my cousin."

"Is the ticket non-refundable?" Gran asks.

"That's not the point!" Dad presses his lips together, just like I do. He blurts. "It's…It's just annoying!"

"Right, Dad. I'm sure my being here will complicate your *couch-sleeping* sessions at Laura's."

Dad blinks at me in surprise. Cassie now sits on the other side of me, and none of us at the table can keep a straight face. Then she starts belting out Marvin Gaye's "Let's Get It On…" and Gran starts laughing. I try to hold it in, but Dad looks like the cat that snatched the canary, and soon I'm laughing, too.

"Real mature," he says, which sends us into fits. He leaves the kitchen in a huff, much like Aunt Sue.

22

I finally head upstairs to get dressed. I know I have to contact Mitch. He'll know what to do. Then I think of Isaac. Crazy how just a couple days ago I didn't know either of them.

Someone knocks at the bedroom door as I finish putting on my underarm deodorant. It's not Cassie, she'd just let herself in. I throw on a pretty green tank top to match the jean mini-skirt I put on and call out, "Come in."

Dad walks in and closes the door. "You look nice."

"Isaac's taking me golfing."

"And you're wearing that?"

"Don't worry. Ian's coming with us and probably Cassie, too."

"That's not what I mean. It's kind of hard to golf with a skirt on."

"Well, considering I'm going to be dreadful at the sport any way I look at it, I might as well look good."

Dad shakes his head. "The logic of women."

"Did you need something?" I brush my hair and spray detangler through it.

"I canceled your plane ticket."

"Oh."

"That's what you wanted, right?" He eyes me suspiciously.

"Yes." But I stand there with my brush in hand and think of Alisa and Mum. No, I'm needed here. I mentally shake any pang of remorse out of my system.

"I still have to take the mustang back. I only rented it for two weeks."

"Okay."

"Laura said she'd follow me downstate, then I could drive back with her. We're thinking of making a day trip out of it."

"Okay."

Dad watches me. "Are *you okay* with this? I mean with me and Laura?"

"I don't know," I answer. "You've kind of kept me out of things, and I don't know what to think. I have no idea who she is, for starters."

"I want to change that. Let's go out to dinner. The three of us."

"That's not exactly what I was referring to."

"But it's a start. Virginia," Dad pauses and takes a deep breath. "I like her. A lot. She's a good woman. I don't know what's going to happen or what the future looks like, but I do know she makes me happy."

I swallow and nod, unable to look my Dad in the eye. Why does this bother me? I want him happy. But it hits me that he's been lonely, and I've been too naïve or self-centered to notice. "We can go out for dinner. I'll keep my tantrums in check." It's hard to say the words though. I keep brushing my hair without looking at him. I'm near tears, and I don't understand why.

Then he's right beside me, taking the brush out of my hand and turning my face toward him. "You are my first and utmost love, Miss Virginia Paxton. That's not going to change. Not now. Not ever."

A tear travels down my cheek as Dad says what even I don't want to see in myself. "I don't want to lose you."

"Not going to happen."

"You didn't even tell me you were going to stay over there."

"I'm sorry. It was sort of spur of the moment. One minute I'm here, the next minute she's texting me asking me to come over. And I *did* sleep on the couch. I'm trying to be a good example for you." He gives me a gentle squeeze. "I will try to keep you in the loop. If you promise me the same thing."

"Okay."

He gathers me in his arms and hugs me, and I breathe a sigh of relief. I feel safe in my Dad's arms. "I'm glad you decided to stay here in Michigan for however long it's for. Do you want to call your mother or would like me to call her?"

"I can call her."

Someone knocks on the door downstairs.

"It's probably Isaac and Ian."

Dad releases me and grins. "It's a good thing you have a chaperone, or else I'd have to go with you."

"Hey, Ginnie!" Cassie calls up. "Mitch is here!"

I go to leave. Dad asks, "Who is this Mitch anyways? He shows up out of the blue. It's weird."

"He's Isaac's friends. They work together at the golf club. And now we all hang out." I leave out all the parts of us being possibly related.

Cassie is full-out flirting with Mitch, and he seems to be soaking it up. I'm glad she's letting the Isaac thing go. It makes me respect her and love her even more. Plus we have this bond now that we experienced the ghost together. It's nice that she's in this with me.

"What's going on?" I ask once I'm down the stairs. "Were we supposed to meet today?"

"Cassie texted me last night and told me to stop by today. Said you needed to tell me something."

"Oh, good thinking, Cass."

She beams at me. "Let's go by the lake and talk. I want to layout and soak up some rays anyways."

It's now I notice she's in her skimpy bikini with a towel slung over her shoulders and tanning lotion in her hand. "When did you change?"

"When you were in the shower. Then I came down here to wait for Mitch." She gave him her thousand-watt smile.

"All right, let's go to the lake." I yell up the stairs, "Dad?"

"Yeah?" He walks to the top of the stairs and looks down.

"Could you send Isaac and Ian to the lake when they get here?"

"Sure."

Cassie and Mitch have already walked through the house and are waiting for me at the back door. Gran's on the phone and watching Mitch with a hint of…annoyance? She sees me and turns quickly, pretending to be deeply involved in the conversation.

Mitch, Cassie, and I head outside. As we walk to the lake, Cassie is chattering away at Mitch. They seem complete opposites. Cassie is talkative and bubbly; Mitch is quiet and calm. Yet, they do complement each other. I wonder if anything will happen between the two of them.

We set lounge chairs next to each other on the sand. Cassie spreads out her towel, sits down, then begins to rub lotion on her arms. Mitch sits down beside her as do I.

"So, what happened last night?"

"A ghost!" Cassie exclaims, only to stop herself. "Sorry, Ginnie. You tell it."

"What she said," I joke.

"You both saw her?"

"Yes," we said in unison.

Cassie looks at me, then says sheepishly, "Sorry."

"Cassie came out here last night to get some fresh air."

"You don't have to hide the truth," she interrupts. "I caught

Isaac and Ginnie kissing, heavy-duty."

"Okay, he gets the picture."

Mitch chuckles. "Ouch."

"Tell me about it," Cassie says to him. "So, I overreact and run outside. Ginnie, being the brave, devoted cousin she is, follows me, although I'm sure she was nervous. Go ahead and finish the story."

"We're sitting on the ground, and I feel her."

Cassie sits up and Mitch leans forward. "What?" Mitch asks as if the suspense is killing him.

"I turned around and she stood with her hand like this." I hold my hand out and up.

Mitch sits back in fascination. "She's telling you she comes in peace."

"You skipped the best parts. All of sudden, Ginnie jumps up off the ground and says, 'Come on, we have to go now.' At first, I'm oblivious, but then I get goosebumps all over my skin and the hair on the back of my neck stands up." Cassie is so animated, I decide to let her tell it. "We're running for our lives out of the forest when I see her. I stop, and Ginnie and I grab hands. There she is standing as close to us as you are. She reaches out her hand to Ginnie. It's like I could feel her pleading with Ginnie, so I told her to touch the ghost's hand."

"Whoa." Mitch gets up and starts pacing.

"She said *Ginnie's name*. Right?" Cassie looks over at me.

"Yeah, that's what she said, but it was more than that." I stop to remember the sensation. "At first I felt cold, but there was more. I felt pain. Not just physical pain, but something terrible."

Mitch is staring at me, his eyes wide, his mouth slightly open.

"Say something. What do you think it could mean?"

"I'm not sure," Mitch says, still in shock. "Mom told me about the rumor of her sister being pregnant, but she dismissed it."

"What are you saying?" I ask. "Barbara Blackstone had a

baby? She doesn't look old enough to…well, you know…"

"She was fifteen," Mitch replies. "In our tribe, girls become betrothed before their sixteenth birthdays, so it's possible. I have to ask Mom. But maybe that's where the pain came from, or how she knows your name."

"How does that explain how she knows my name? This is bloody confusing!" Now I stand up to pace.

"I told you. She wouldn't be pursuing you if you didn't have matching bloodlines." Mitch says it so quietly that I stop to look over at him.

"How's is that possible?" I ask though I think I know where he's going.

"You're blood relation to Barbara Blackstone. As in her blood runs through your veins. That's why she's able to communicate with you."

"But I…have a…Dad and a…Mum…" I'm trying hard not to hyperventilate.

"How old is Uncle Sam?" Cassie asks.

"He'll be forty on Friday."

"Almost forty years ago, Barbara Blackstone disappeared."

I turn to Mitch as his words sink in.

"No way," Cassie whispers.

"That doesn't mean anything." I remember Aunt Sue's recollection of a girl in the house. "Barbara went into hiding," I say as the truth unraveled before me. "Oh, hell…My grandmother took her in. My Dad…"

"…is Barbara Blackstone's son," Mitch finishes.

"Hi, guys!" Ian's greeting makes me jump, along with the other two. We stay quiet for too long because Ian says, "When someone greets you, you are supposed to greet them back. It's called manners."

"Hi, Ian," I say, as do Mitch and Cassie.

"Are you ready to go golfing? Do you have a set of clubs? We have some to rent if you don't." He turns in my direction but doesn't look me in the eyes.

"I brought Mom's," Isaac says as he walks toward us. We make eye contact. My stomach alerts the swarms of butterflies to begin their chaotic flight. "What's going on?"

"Oh, nothing much," Cassie says a little too sweetly. "Just discussing the ghost encounter from last night and how Uncle Sam is Barbara Blackstone's son."

"What?" Ian tenses up. His eyes dart from one spot to another, and he wrings his hands while moving from one foot to the other. "How do you know that? Nobody knows that for sure. You shouldn't say things like that if you're not sure. That doesn't make any sense."

I tap Cassie's leg with my toe and shake my head. She mouths "sorry", but I'm more than annoyed. Poor Ian can't handle the stress of the body we discovered, let alone ghostly visits.

"It's all right, Ian. Cassie's playing a joke, that's all." Isaac rests his hand on Ian's shoulder. Ian calms down a little, but his face is still drawn in and crestfallen.

"I was just teasing," she adds. "Because Ginnie was so scared last night. I'm sorry."

The awkward pause dangles over us.

Finally, I blurt to Ian, "Let's get out of here. I don't know about you, but I'm ready to go whack at some golf balls."

A laugh escapes from Cassie. "Whack at some golf balls? You don't have the slightest idea of how to play golf, do you?"

"How complicated can it be? Take a golf club, and then take a swing at it."

My reply has garnered an eye roll or a look of disbelief out of the four of them. Even Ian makes eye contact with his brother before they both commence an exaggerated eye roll. "Fine, all you fancy pants, let's golf. I'll show you how easy it is."

"Easy?" Isaac repeats. I'm not sure if he knows I'm only being annoying to get Ian's mind off what blabber-mouth Cassie had just said, but...*I don't think so.* "Want to wager how easy it will be for you to quit?"

"Quit? Me? Never."

"She won't make five holes," Mitch says.

Now I look at him in disbelief. "You're betting against me?"

"I believe in her," Cassie says.

"Thank you."

"She'll go at least six or seven holes before she's busted every one of her clubs in a fit of rage," Cassie adds with a twisted smile.

"Hey!"

"And I say she'll give up after three holes. Shall we say twenty bucks?" Isaac asks Cassie and Mitch.

They agree, but so do I. "What about me? Don't I get a say?" I ask. "I bet I'll finish the whole course or holes or whatever it's called."

"Without any help," Isaac adds.

"Without. Any. Help." I cross my arms to prove my point.

"I'm going to get dressed." Cassie jumps up and runs to the house. "Don't leave without me!"

"I guess I'm going golfing, too," Mitch says. "I'll need to collect my money."

"And to watch Ginnie try to *whack at some golf balls*," Isaac says, mimicking me, to which Mitch starts laughing.

"People need to stop mocking me. They don't do a good job."

Isaac and Mitch laugh louder. Ian comes over to me. "I know what you did," he whispers.

"What? What did I do?"

"You changed the subject and got everybody mad at you."

At least one person knows what I was trying to do. "Well, Ian, I wouldn't worry. I enjoy a challenge." I take his arm, and we walk up to the house. I hear Mitch and Isaac follow behind us. "So," I say quietly to Ian. "Do you think I have a chance at winning?"

"No," he answers curtly. "Not at all."

23

It's official. I hate golf.

"What is the purpose of hitting a ball to the other side of the course and whack at it until it falls into a little hole?" I munch on a French fry angrily. It didn't make it any better that the other four had played golf many times and were fairly good at it. Even Cassie knew what she was doing.

They made it look easy. But it wasn't easy. Since they didn't help, I royally sucked at the game. The only thing they did accomplish was to make me look like a complete buffoon.

"Don't be a spoilsport," Cassie teases.

I glare at her and stuff another fry in my mouth. Mitch grins at me, and I make a face. He laughs. "Let me give you lessons."

"Never."

Isaac is still talking to the managers about getting his money back because after the sixth hole I refused to play. In my defense, not one golf club was hurt during any of my fits of irritation. I'm sure looking back on it I will find it comical.

"I guess I'm out the money," Isaac says with a smirk and sits beside me again.

"Good. That's what you get for not giving me any instruction."

"It was worth it. You're cute when you're angry." He winks at me, and I have to look away in embarrassment.

It's a wonder he is still talking to me at all, after the way I behaved, but they all found it funny to see a British girl yelling at the golf clubs…and the trees…and even the golf balls.

Not my finest moment.

The only thing I accomplished is getting the attention off of Barbara Blackstone, and even I am grateful for that.

My cell phone vibrates, which is a nice pause from all the attention. I excuse myself to answer it.

"Hello?" I answer as soon as I'm outside.

"Hey there, sweetie. Just wanted to let you know that Laura and I are headed back to the airport to turn the car in."

That could have been me going home. The twinge of doubt quickly fades as I glance through the window and see my friends at the table. I need to stay here. So I say, "Okay, Dad. Have a good time. Don't do anything where you'd be embarrassed if I caught you."

"Ha, ha, Virginia. I am a gentleman. And the rest is none of your business."

"Don't be so defensive."

"Be good," he says, ignoring my comment. "I'll be back tomorrow. Oh, how was golf?"

"It's a pointless sport."

"Not so good?"

"Understatement."

Dad laughs. "All right. Call me if you need anything. I trust you and Cassie to keep an eye on your Grandmother. Make sure to take her to mass."

"Dad!"

"It won't kill you."

"You sure about that?"

The restaurant door opens and Isaac steps out. I say good-bye to Dad, then hang up.

"Everything okay?" Isaac asks.

"Other than making a complete ninny of myself on the golf course, everything's daisies."

Isaac gives a crooked grin that nearly does me in.

"Sorry I lost my cool out there. It's a very frustrating game."

"Ginnie, you don't have to apologize. I knew what you were doing all along."

"What's that?"

"You changed the subject back at the house," Isaac says quietly. "And it worked. Ian avoided a meltdown. I…we…wanted to say thank you all day, but we haven't been alone."

"So, you don't think I'm a big ogre?"

"No, it was funny. You are cute when you're angry or annoyed. Your forehead pinches together, and your mouth slightly frowns. Kind of like what you're doing now." He steps closer to me as I alter my facial expression. "Thanks," he says again. "I mean it."

"You're welcome."

He kisses me gently.

Before we go inside, he asks, "Is what Cassie said true about last night?"

Those words bring back a flood of memories. A shiver shoots up my spine. "Yes."

Isaac looks grim. "Let me drop Ian off at home, then you can tell me what happened."

We walk back inside, and I notice Cassie watching us. We make eye contact. She gives a wink and a half-smile, but I can tell it bothers her a bit. I make a mental note to talk to her in private when we are alone.

Isaac stays true to his word and drops off Ian. Ian is entirely too perceptive for his own good. "You're getting rid of me, aren't you?"

"No. Well, yes, but only because I want to spend time alone with Ginnie."

"You're lying. You always glance down and to the right when you're not telling the truth."

Isaac doesn't contest it. Then again, Ian doesn't let him. "I know what you're all doing. You're going to talk about the ghost, and you don't want me to hear. But I can handle it. And help. I've read enough Sir Conan Doyle to know how to be a sleuth."

"If we decide to talk about the ghost, we'll have Isaac tell you." I hope my lie goes undetected.

"Will you tell me if you need help?" Ian asks. "I'm good at discovering."

"I promise." I hold out my pinky. "I'll even pinky promise."

Ian links his pinky with mine, and we shake on it.

When Isaac pulls into his driveway, Mitch comments, "What's my mother doing here?"

It's then I notice Bonnie Blackstone with her arms crossed, appearing rather agitated, and talking rapidly to Mr. Fulton. She acts like she can't stand still and keeps moving from one spot to another only to walk back to Mr. Fulton.

Mitch opens the door before the Jeep has been put into park.

"Wait," I say to him.

The worry is all over his face, but he waits for me.

"Let's not say anything until we're 100 percent sure," I whisper.

"Why?" his face falls. "My mother would be ecstatic to know she has a nephew and a great-niece. Family's everything to us."

"Please. We're making educated guesses. Just wait until we have actual proof."

"You have proof enough."

"Not to my father and grandmother."

"She's right," Isaac says to Mitch. "They will take us seriously when we have scientific data."

Mitch seems to mull it over. "Fine." He shuts the door and jogs over to his mother.

Ian gets out of the car, too. He's watching Bonnie Blackstone with intense fascination.

"Well, let's go see what's going on," Cassie says.

I'm the slowest of all of them to walk over simply because even though forty years have passed, Bonnie strongly resembles the fifteen-year-old Barbara. Her words replay over in my mind, but I continue to walk over to the group, shoving the heebie-jeebies to the side.

"There has to be something," Bonnie is saying.

"You have a right to be frustrated," Mr. Fulton says. "But none of that information is available to the public yet. When it is, you will be the first person I contact."

"So, there is information, then? Police have discovered some kind of clue?"

Mr. Fulton sighs. "Bonnie, I cannot disclose anything to you at this time."

She rubs her arms as if cold, and her face briefly crumples. Then she composes herself.

I am almost tempted to tell her what happened, but something stops me. What if we are wrong? Even though I don't think that's the case, I still hold back. We need more proof. Mitch's gaze meets mine. He acts torn, too.

Before either of us can say anything, Bonnie Blackstone turns to leave. "Mitch, I'm glad you're here. I need your help at the library."

Mitch nods and follows his mother to her car. "Where's your truck?" she asks him, as they walk away from us.

"Ginnie's grandmother's house."

"I'll drop you off there, then follow me into town."

Mitch turns to us. "I'll stop by later if I can."

They get into the vehicle and back out of the driveway. A few minutes pass before Ian breaks the silence. "She's hiding something."

Isaac, Cassie, me, and Mr. Fulton turn to Ian, who shuffles from one foot to another. "I don't think so, Ian," Mr. Fulton says. "She's most-likely grief-stricken."

"No, you're wrong." Ian glances at his father, only to look away. "Her eyes are shifty. She couldn't make eye contact for long. That is classic body language for hiding something."

"All right, maybe I'll look into it." Mr. Fulton waves good-bye at me and Cassie and walks with Ian up the porch steps and into the house. "I'm assuming you're going to be at Mrs. Paxton's?" he asks over his shoulder.

"For a little bit," Isaac answers.

Mr. Fulton sticks his head out the door. "I know you all are curious, too, but make sure to leave the crime scene alone. Understood?"

We agree and head back to Isaac's Jeep. Once inside and on the road, Cassie's cell phone beeps. "It's Mitch," she says. "He texted to say that he's waiting at the house."

"So much for following his mother," Isaac jokes.

"He must really want to talk," I say.

Mitch sits on Gran's porch when we pull in her driveway. Cassie jumps out before Isaac has the key out of the ignition. "I don't think she's quite ready to embrace us as a couple," I say quietly. "I mean if we are a couple. That was a bit brazen. I didn't mean to suppose—"

"Suppose all you want to." He leans over and gives me a quick kiss. "At some point, I would like to be alone with you."

"We'll figure something out." I'm relieved that I didn't put my foot in my mouth like I thought I did.

As we approach Gran's house, Isaac calls out, "So much for helping your mother, huh?"

"Ha, ha," Mitch laughs with no humor. "I told her I needed to talk to Ginnie, and I've waited all day to do it. She says to come when I'm finished here."

"Sorry," I apologize. Now that I think about it, Mitch probably has been waiting all day for us to finish the conversation from this morning. "I didn't want to upset Ian, but yeah, that did take a little while longer than anticipated."

Mitch shrugs. "I'm not complaining. Mom probably has boxes full of books that need moving. I have no problem delaying that for as long as possible."

Cassie already sat next to Mitch on the porch swing, so Isaac and I sit in the two available wicker chairs. "Tell me what happened," Isaac starts.

Cassie nods at me, so I explain the story again. Just repeating the words brings the memory of the girl and her pain fresh into my mind. "We think my Dad might be her son."

"Wow. It makes sense. A DNA test will tell us for certain."

"What about the father? If he's alive, that could eliminate a lot of questions," I say the words, thinking about some man out there who is my biological grandfather and doesn't even know it. "I'm not sure why I didn't think of it before." I try not to get excited, but I do anyway. "My grandfather could still be alive."

"He's not."

I stop and look over at Mitch. "Sorry, Ginnie. He's not alive. My mother told me one time that he took it hard when Barbara disappeared. He left town soon after. His parents left town not long after."

"How do you know he's dead?" Isaac asks.

"Mom said one of their mutual friends told her a few years back. He was drunk one night and got hit by a car."

Any excitement I had felt fizzed out. "There goes that idea."

"You guys are missing the point!" Cassie jumps off the swing and throws her hands up in the air. She startles all three of us, mostly because she has sat there so quietly. I should have known that there's nothing quiet about Cassie. Now she paces back and forth, sighing in exasperation. "You act like Barbara Blackstone's main objective was to reunite her family. That's an awful lot of unrest the last forty years just for Ginnie to meet her biological grandmother!"

I think of Barbara and the intense pain I felt inside of me when I touched her hand. "Cassie's right. Something happened and Barbara wants me to figure it out."

"It probably has to do with the curse," Mitch adds. "If you and your Dad are truly related to her, then your lives may be in danger, especially his."

"The curse. She has to be warning me about the curse."

"Are you in danger?" Isaac asks me.

"Yes," Mitch answers. "Well, maybe not her."

"My Dad."

"Wait a second," Cassie interrupts. "Why is only Uncle Sam in danger? What about Bonnie Blackstone? She's in danger, too."

"Whoa," Isaac throws his hands up. "The curse exists? I mean, literally exists?"

Mitch nods.

"Can someone please answer my previous question?" Cassie asks. "Who all is in danger?"

Isaac shakes his head, ignoring Cassie. "No, Mitch. It doesn't make sense. If there is a curse, when does it take place, how does it happen, who does it involve? I've heard about the curse my whole life, but it's just a legend."

"Tell that to Barbara Blackstone."

"There are other things that could have happened," I add. "What Isaac said makes sense. When I was researching here at the house and at the library, there wasn't any kind of questionable disappearances or deaths."

"It happens every forty years," Mitch says impatiently. "I told you that."

"The county has had a newspaper for over a hundred years. My Gran writes a column for it. I scrolled back as far as I could. There's been a few fishing accidents, and a hunter accidentally shot himself, but nothing about any Indian deaths or an ancient curse. That's got to mean something."

"What are you saying?" Mitch asks with a flash of temper. "That my mother's a liar?"

"No," I say quickly. "I'm just thinking out loud. A curse doesn't have to mean only death. You said the curse was about the tribe warring within each other. Somewhere I read that it's never having peace. Does your mother have peace? See, maybe the curse is plaguing your people every day. It doesn't have to mean death."

"But in this case it does."

"Maybe your mother got misinformation," Isaac says. "She was only fifteen when her twin sister died. Maybe she clung to the legend as the only explanation for what happened."

The screen door bangs open, as Gran steps out onto the porch. "Which one of you girls is taking me to mass?"

Cassie and I glance at each other, neither wanting the honor.

"Well, don't argue over it. You can both go. Boys, you need to leave. The girls are taking me to church."

Isaac tells me he'll text me in a few hours, and Mitch asks if he can come by later on.

"I'll call you," Cassie tells him.

Once they have left, Gran sighs, "Okay, go get changed. I'll wait for you."

"What's wrong with what we're wearing?" Cassie asks.

"Ginnie's skirt is far too short and your shirt is far too revealing. We're going to the house of God, and since He is the one who created you, He doesn't need to see all your body parts. He already knows what you've got. Besides, we have plenty of time." She sits down in one of the chairs. "I'll wait for you."

Cassie and I make eye contact, both knowing it's a battle that we won't win.

"Come on," I say in defeat and open the screen door. "It looks like we're going to mass."

24

"How much of it do you think she heard?" I whisper to Cassie as we're heading up the stairs. Once in the house, I notice we still have an hour until evening mass. Saint Mary's Catholic Church can't be more than five minutes away. "Do you think she broke it up on purpose?"

We walk into our bedroom, and Cassie shuts the door. "Why would she break it up? She's just being Gran, that's all."

I decide to tell Cassie about my suspicions. "I think she's hiding information from us."

Now Cassie raises her eyebrows. "I don't know," she finally admits. "But Gran wouldn't lie to us, Ginnie. You know that. She's just as much your grandmother as she is mine."

My heart feels the pang of guilt. Cassie's right. "I'm probably overanalyzing everything," I say. "I didn't mean to implicate Gran as untruthful."

Cassie hugs me, rubbing my back. "We've got a lot of stuff swirling around us right now, but Gran? The woman is incapable of keeping secrets."

I smile in response to Cassie's smile and push the thought

aside. But not for long. Something nags at the back of my mind, and I can't fully rule out Gran. She is hiding something. I don't just know it. I *feel* it.

"Do me a favor?" I ask as I'm changing outfits. "Don't say anything to her. I don't want to upset her."

"Of course not," she says. "You know, it's too bad that Barbara's boyfriend isn't alive anymore. It would have made things a lot simpler."

"Tell me about it."

"I wonder if he was murdered, too."

"So, you think Barbara was murdered?"

"Yes. Didn't you feel that?"

"Yeah, I did." It should be a relief that Cassie sensed the pain of the girl, as well, but instead, it creates a tension in me. I had wanted to be wrong. "I need to figure out what this curse is all about."

"Seems convenient, doesn't it?" Cassie says what I'm thinking. "Someone kills that girl, then blames it on an ancient Indian curse. I'm not buying it."

I grin over at my cousin. "Are we like Sherlock Holmes?"

"Yes, there is a mystery here that needs to be solved, and it would be cool to be Sherlock, especially the Robert Downey Jr. version of Sherlock."

"Hey! What if I wanted to be Sherlock? I am British, after all. You be the Watson character."

"Okay, okay, we can both be Sherlock."

We start giggling. I brush out my hair, set down the brush, and sigh. "Well, there's no getting out of it. Come on, Gran and mass are waiting."

Cassie groans, and we leave the room. "Why can't she be a Christmas and Easter Catholic?" Cassie asks as we go down the stairs.

Gran is standing at the door and smirks at us. "You two act like I'm about to pull out your teeth. Lord have mercy."

"You know there is a beauty to worshipping God at home," Cassie tries.

"Nice try. Let's get a move on."

Cassie drives because I'm uncomfortable driving on the wrong side of the car. Once on the road, I watch as Gran reapplies her lipstick and checks out her hair. I ask, "Why are you getting all gussied up? There might be ten people there."

"Well, now there will be twelve since you two are going. Besides, there aren't many events I get dressed up for anymore. Let me at least look nice for mass."

We arrive forty-five minutes early. "What are we supposed to do now?"

"Pray." Gran gets out of the car and heads inside.

"You know, prayer might not be a bad idea," Cassie says and follows Gran.

"For forty-five minutes?" I ask, not that either of them is listening.

Inside, the church is dark and quiet, and I find myself relaxing. Being here with Gran and Cassie is much different than being forced to attend with a couple hundred school kids. Gran is already lighting a candle and kneeling. Cassie watches her and follows suit.

I light a candle for Barbara Blackstone and pray for her soul. But, just like in school, it doesn't take long for my mind to wander. From bugs to ghosts, I try to connect the dots. What does science say?

Science says that a decomposing body would elicit feeders. Beetles liked eating dead things. Dad said he'd seen those beetles around this area when he was little. Maybe the beetles were just that. Beetles. But what about my dreams? I had my first nightmare before I ever set foot in Gran's house. And then there was the one on my head, and the ones around my ankle when I fell in the water.

And the ghost? What does science say about ghosts? What would science say about my picture with the ghost captured in it, or about the ghost sightings? Cassie saw the ghost, too, which legitimizes all of these freakish things that defy science.

A shiver shoots up my spine.

"No more thinking about bugs or ghosts," I whisper to myself.

"Shh," Gran says from beside me. "Some of us are trying to pray."

I glance over to Cassie who's already finished praying and is now flipping through her phone.

Gran sees her and clucks her tongue. "We're in the house of God," she whispers at Cassie. "Put that away."

"Sorry, Gran," she says.

Gran looks at both of us and shakes her head. "Let's go and wait for mass to begin."

As we enter the large sanctuary, the priest stands by the doors, smiling at Gran. "There you are," he says, before blessing her. "We prayed for a speedy recovery, and I'm glad to see the Lord has heard our prayers."

Gran introduces me and Cassie to Father Wayne Briggs. "These are my granddaughters I've told you about."

"You are all Ms. Paxton talks about. One of you graduated early, did you not?"

"That would be my Ginnie." Gran pats my arm. "She's to go to the University of Michigan where she wants to study photography." Gran acts pleased with herself. "And Cassie will attend my alma mater, as well."

Father Briggs addresses me. "I think it's wonderful that you completed your studies early. God does not honor the slothful."

"Thank you, Father." I slightly bow my head, all my religious education at the forefront of mass etiquette.

He blesses me, but Cassie has already left us to sit in a pew. I go to her while Gran chats some more with the Father. "Why does Gran have to act like that?" Cassie whispers in my ear. "It's like she's not giving us a choice."

"Don't worry about it," I tell her. "Just smile and nod, and let our parents handle the details with her."

Finally, mass finishes, and Cassie and I wait while Gran goes to greet the priest. I watch her and notice she's not going over to the priest, but to an older gentleman at the organ. I nudge Cassie and point toward Gran. Now we're both watching. Gran is full-out flirting with the man, tossing her hair back, smiling, and even batting her eyes.

"Are you seeing what I'm seeing?" I ask.

"Oh, yes, I am."

The man seems to soak up the attention. He's at least a head taller than her with gray hair and matching mustache.

"He's not bad," I whisper. "She could do worse."

"That suit looks like he's been wearing it since the 1970s."

I look over at Cassie, as she watches disapprovingly.

"What's wrong?" I'm surprised at Cassie's reaction.

"Nothing. Other than she drags us out here, pretending it's for her salvation, only to find out it's because she wants to flirt with the musician." Cassie rolls her eyes. "Wait till I tell Mom."

Gran waves us over.

"Behave," I whisper to Cassie, who snorts in response.

"These are my lovely granddaughters I was telling you about," Gran says as we approach. "This one is my Ginnie, and this one is my Cassie. Girls, this is George Hodgens. He's been a friend of your grandfather's and mine for many years."

"Nice to meet you," I say. "You play the organ beautifully."

"Thank you, and it's nice to finally meet Sam and Sue's daughters. Your grandmother cannot say enough good things about you." He smiles over at Cassie. "How is your mother doing?" he asks her.

"Fine, thank you." Cassie is all decorum and politeness, and I have to hand it to her, she plays the part well.

"How about some dinner?" he asks the three of us. "My treat."

Cassie's mask of politeness falters for a split second, but she quickly agrees.

"That sounds delightful," I add, poking Cassie in the ribs.

"I will ride over with George," Gran tells us. "We like to go to Big Boy."

"Big Boy," Cassie repeats, then looks over at me with eyes that say she's clearly not thrilled.

"What's wrong with Big Boy?" I whisper as we walk away.

"Nothing, if you enjoy eating out at a place populated by senior citizens!"

"At least we'll have each other."

Still, on the way there we try to come up with excuses to get out of dinner. We can't think of anything plausible, so we vow to make the dinner go as fast as it can. As we pull in to the restaurant, Cassie comments, "See? Check out all the Lincolns, Cadillacs, and Taurus's! Told you!"

I am just about to ask her what any of those cars have to do with Big Boy and senior citizens when I see Bonnie Blackstone leaving the restaurant. "What is she doing here?"

Cassie notices her. "Maybe because she's old, and this is where old people go to eat."

"She's fifty-five. That's not *that* old."

"Old enough."

Cassie goes to get out of the car, but I hold her back. "Stay here for a sec."

It's too much to see Bonnie Blackstone, and I especially don't want to talk to her. I can barely contain the grief I feel over Barbara. God knows what Bonnie is enduring right now. Cassie seems to understand because she doesn't fight me over it. Unfortunately, Gran and George are already out of the car and notice us still in ours.

"Girls?" Gran calls. "What are you doing sitting in the car? Let's get some dinner."

Bonnie Blackstone stopped right outside the restaurant door

to rummage through her purse. As I step out of the car and shut the door, I feel her gaze before I even make eye contact.

The emotion on her face is conflicted. "Ginnie," she says though she doesn't appear too happy when the words leave her mouth.

I wave and hope I can go into the restaurant without any more of a conversation.

"Mitch told me."

Now I stop.

"Told you what?" Gran asks.

"It's not true," Bonnie directs the comment to me. "The more I thought about it, the more it didn't make sense."

"What are you talking about?" Gran asks again.

But I know. "It's the only way any of it makes sense," I say.

Bonnie shakes her head. "I'm her twin, remember? After I met with you and Mitch at the library, I couldn't stop thinking about it. I've even started researching again. But there's nothing. No evidence she was pregnant. And she wasn't pregnant when she vanished. I'm sure of it."

"All right," Gran says, clearly annoyed now that she knows what the conversation's about. "That's enough. We're going to get dinner."

"It's probably best you leave this alone. My heart can't take much more." She presses her hand to her chest, and her face barely contains her emotions.

"Of course they'll leave you alone." Gran barely acknowledges Bonnie. She's motioning for us to follow her. "You heard the lady. Let's respect her privacy."

"If I may," I hesitate because I'm trying to best word it. "May I stop over after dinner? I have questions, but I won't stay long. I promise."

"That's not a good idea," Bonnie says quickly. "You can ask Mitch, and he can relay them to me." She gives Gran a pointed look, then turns and leaves in a huff.

"Can't you girls leave well enough alone? She asked for privacy."

George has been holding the door open the entire duration of the conversation, and now Gran has walked into the restaurant, talking quietly with him.

"We'll talk to Mitch after dinner." Cassie shakes her head.

"Do you think she's hiding something?"

"The ghost—Barbara Blackstone—all but told you that you were connected to her," Cassie says before we walk into the restaurant.

What Cassie says is true, which means one thing. For whatever reason, Bonnie Blackstone is flat-out lying to me.

25

"You seem to be thinking hard," George says.

I stop ripping the napkin to shreds and glance up. "Sorry. I'm not the best company at the moment."

Dinner at Big Boy hadn't been too shabby. And for all of Cassie's griping, she ate her burger and fries like a champ. She and Gran left for the restroom, leaving me with George.

"There is just too much information. My head feels like it's about to explode." I bite my lip, shocked I said it out loud.

"Your grandmother told me about you finding the body. It's a lot to deal with. I should know, I used to be the sheriff."

That is enough to get my full attention. "Really?"

"Yes. I retired about five years ago."

"So, you knew…Barbara?"

He nods. "I was one of the cops who searched for her when she was reported missing. That was a sad day for our entire Pigeon Forest area. The Blackstones took it very hard, especially Bonnie, but the worst one was Mitchell."

"Mitch? You're not talking about Bonnie's son, are you?"

George gave a half-chuckle. "No, no, of course not. I'm

talking about Mitchell Hunt. He was Barbara's boyfriend when it happened. I believe he had already asked her father for her hand in marriage."

"That's what I heard, too. Do you know anything about his death?"

George sits back surprised. "No, I didn't know he passed on."

"I guess he got drunk and got hit by a car. It was a while back."

"That can't be right. Mitch was a recovering alcoholic, but he had been sober for at least ten years. How long ago did you say it happened?"

"Oh, I'm not sure. Mitch told me. The other Mitch. Bonnie's son."

George nods. "That's odd. I just saw him about a month or so ago. I have friends who live about ten miles out of town, and he was putting on a new roof for them. I teased him about moving back to the area, and he said, 'No way. I'm only traveling this far because I owe Joe Longhorne a favor.' He didn't show any signs of the bottle then."

Gran and Cassie return. "Are you ready?" Cassie asks me.

I'm momentarily speechless. Could this man who might very well be my grandfather, be alive? I don't think Mitch would purposefully lie to me, so who's right?

"Too much information," I say again.

"What I was going to say is to not worry about all this information," George says. His eyes are kind, and his smile is genuine. "This is summertime. Go, have fun. Let the police deal with all of it."

"Those are wise words indeed," Gran agrees.

Cassie's pulling on my arm.

"So, I'm planning a surprise birthday party for your father tomorrow night," Gran says to me. "I'll make a few phone calls, but I will need you two to be the errand girls and pick up the groceries and help with the cleaning.”

“Yes, Grandma,” Cassie says. Her polite façade had taken all of about two minutes to crumble once we were inside the restaurant. Now she rolls her eyes. “We will be back in a little bit.”

“Here’s the grocery list?”

I place the folded up paper into my purse.

“And Ginnie, don’t forget to get him a birthday present.”

I want to make a snide comment that Laura is birthday present enough, but I keep my snarky comment to myself.

As soon as we are out of earshot, Cassie asks, “So? Are you going to tell me what you and George were talking about?”

“He knows Mitchell Hunt. That’s Barbara’s fiancé. He doesn’t know anything about his death.”

We get into the car and Cassie starts it up. She shakes her head as she backs out. “Mitch wouldn’t lie.”

“I’m not saying that, but he could be misinformed.”

“Or you could be misinformed.”

“George used to be the sheriff. He doesn’t have any ulterior motives for telling me he just saw Mitch—that’s the old Mitch—about a month ago.”

“Unless Grandma asked him to.”

“Wait a second, you told me back at the house that I should stop supposing about Gran. That she wouldn’t or couldn’t lie to us.”

“And yet how surprised we were to meet George.”

“It’s not that big a deal she has a beau. If he makes her happy.”

“A *beau*…Who says that anymore?”

“Me. Everyone. I don’t know. Why are you hostile all of a sudden?”

“Because it’s not Mitch. He’s not a bad guy. You already took Isaac. You’re not taking Mitch…off to jail!”

“I’m not taking Mitch anywhere! For bloody sake, the guy might be my cousin or uncle or something.”

Cassie takes a deep breath. “Sorry, I kind of like him, that’s all. And I don't know what to believe anymore. To top it all off seeing Grandma with another man other than Grandpa felt weird."

I think of Dad with Laura and completely understand. "No worries. Let's see if what George says is true. Let me have your phone."

Cassie hands it to me. "What are you going to do with it?"

"You have GPS on it, right? Now that I know the guy's full name, I'm going to see if he's still around."

"Good idea," Cassie says excitedly.

"What are some towns outside of Pigeon Forest? George said he lived away from here."

She lists off a couple of towns, and I get to work. "Wow," I say after a few minutes. "There are a lot of Mitchell Hunts."

"Forget GPS. Try the internet first. It'll give you ages of the names. We need a Mitchell Hunt who is between 55 and 60."

"And I need a pen and paper." I scrounge around until I find the back of an envelope and a broken pencil at the bottom of my purse.

"Well?"

"Shh!" I scroll down on the screen and begin to write.

"You better tell me something," Cassie warns.

"There are seven Mitchell Hunts in the surrounding areas that fit the age group."

"Wow," she mutters. "Popular name."

I start dialing.

"You're calling them now?"

"How else are we supposed…Hello? Yes, this is Ginnie Paxton from the… Pigeon Forest newspaper…"

I glance over at Cassie and shrug. She's giggling with her hand covering her mouth.

"I'm calling to investigate the disappearance of Barbara Blackstone. Your name was given. Were you a former acquaintance? Okay, thank you."

"No luck?"

"Nope. On to number two."

"I like your disguise as a newspaper reporter," she whispers because I'm already on the phone.

On the fifth call, I hit jackpot.

"What do you want to know?" The voice is deep and gruff, and interestingly enough seems filled with grief.

I have to think. I didn't know I would get this far. How do I come out and ask if Barbara was pregnant?

"Were you engaged to be married?"

He pauses. I hear his breathing. "Yes. I had asked for her hand. I heard her body was discovered. Do you know if any type of memorial service is planned?"

Cassie's waving her hand at me. "Ask him if he got drunk and got hit by a car."

"Hello?" he asks. "Did we get disconnected?"

"No, no, I'm here." I scramble to think about what we were talking about, but Cassie keeps distracting me. She's currently miming drinking from a bottle then acting all loopy. "Um, we were under the understanding that you had a bit too much to drink and were hit by a car. I take it you're okay now?"

Cassie gives me another thumbs-up sign seemingly pleased I asked the question.

"Who are you?" he demands. That snaps me back to the phone conversation.

"I'm from the…newspaper…?"

"Are you the one who charged after me? I swear to God, if you think you can scare me, think again. I'm alive and kicking, and if you come near me, I'll put a bullet through your heart!" I hear the click and the dial tone.

I stare at the phone in shock.

"What happened?" Cassie asks.

"I must have said something wrong. He wigged out on me."

"You asked him about getting drunk and being hit by a car."

"He threatened to shoot me if I come near him. Something

about charging after him and scaring him and next time I'm dead."

"He's obviously not referring to you. Someone charged after him though?"

"That's what he seems to think. Like maybe someone charged after him in that car. On purpose."

Cassie nods. "Exactly. You're on to something. He feels that someone hit him on purpose."

"He assumed it was me."

"Maybe because no one else knows."

Cassie slows the car down, and we stare at each other as each of us appraises the situation now in a different light.

"Ginnie?"

"Yes?"

"I don't know what to believe anymore."

"That's why we need to go and see this Mitchell Hunt. Right away."

"What about the grocery list and birthday present?"

"We'll get to it."

"After we visit Mr. Hunt?"

"Exactly."

"Type in his address in the GPS."

I do so, then hold up the phone for her to see the coordinates. We make eye contact again, and I give a slight nod, completely in sync.

"Looks like we're going on a little trip," Cassie says, as she turns the car around.

"Let's hope he's out of bullets."

26

Over an hour later, Cassie turns onto what seems like the umpteenth two-track; this one full of potholes and mud puddles nearly the size of small ponds.

"Are you sure the GPS is talking about this road?"

"This is the only road to turn left on," I answer, looking in all directions to verify my response.

"And I thought Grandma lived in the boonies."

"It's almost like he's hiding," I say more to myself.

"I think you're right."

"Let's hope we find it soon because my cell phone lost signal about an hour ago, and yours has only one bar."

We bounce and jiggle with the two-track and more than once I pray that we don't get stuck in any of the mammoth mud holes.

"It's saying we've arrived at our destination." I look at the GPS again because it has to be wrong.

"There's nothing here," Cassie says what I'm thinking.

The two-track keeps going along with thick forest on both sides. Up ahead the two-track narrows. "Go to where it narrows."

Cassie inches the car along until we reach the narrow path. My gaze follows the path. It's then I notice the path diverges. "There's a walking path that veers off to the right," I say and get out of the car. Once Cassie's out, we venture on foot.

"This is creepy, Ginnie," she whispers.

And she's right. I've been trying not to think about that. We've been driving in the middle of this dense forest for several miles with nothing to assist us should something happen. But something pushes me to keep going. I know we're close. It's weird because it's like I sense a nearness to whatever or whomever it is I'm looking for. Still, Cassie seems to wait for a reply, so I say, "If we can handle ghostly encounters, we can handle creepy woods."

"Creepy woods that very possibly hide an angry man with a gun. A ghost can't shoot us."

The woods have no sounds of any kind of human life. There's a soft breeze blowing, rustling the trees, and I hear the insects whirring in different locations. Birds chirp happily. All in all, it's lovely. Other than the hair that stands on end at my neck and the chill that shoots up my spine with every snap of a twig, of course.

"Holy crap!" Cassie shoves herself next to me, nearly making me jump out of my skin. "A snake!"

Now she has my attention. I follow the direction of where her finger points. Then sigh. "It's just a gardener snake. Don't alarm yourself."

"You sure?"

"Positive."

We walk further, but Cassie still stays close by me.

"What happened to the girl who storms into the woods in the middle of the night with no flashlight?"

"That was different. I was acting on emotion and not thinking clearly."

"But you weren't freaked out at all by the ghost. You were the one who told me to touch her hand."

"Shh! Can we please not talk about ghosts here? Besides, it's not ghosts I'm worried about. It's psycho killers lurking behind trees."

"There are no psycho kill—"

"Don't move." The gun barrel snaps in place, and I feel the tip of it against my head.

"What were you saying?" Cassie whimpers.

"I warned you," the man is saying. "Give me a good reason why I shouldn't shoot you right here."

Cassie's whimpering all-out and clinging to me. So, I say the first thing that pops into my head. "You might be my grandfather."

The gun barrel is no longer pushing against my head. I swallow down some nerve and turn in his direction.

Mitchell Hunt is tall and lean with dark hair, dark skin, and piercing eyes. The eyes of my father. The connection stirs something inside of me. He still watches me warily, but I know he senses it, too.

"Forty years ago, you loved a girl. I'm just trying to find out what happened."

"Why?"

"Because she wants me to."

"I don't have time for childish games," he says, but this time there is no meanness in his words.

"It's true." This time Cassie speaks up. "I was with Ginnie when she saw the ghost."

Mitchell Hunt does not take his eyes off mine. "There's no such thing as ghosts."

He reminds me so much of Dad that it's making me a wreck.

He sighs and lowers his gun. "Where'd you say you were from again? The Pigeon Forest newspaper?"

I nod.

"Well, we know that's not the case."

I nod again.

"Where are you *really* from? Your accent gives you away."

"London, but my dad's from here. Pigeon Forest. His mother is Rose Paxton."

"Yeah, I know the Paxton's. They bought up a bunch of my family's land. For a while there, they were the only white folks in Pigeon Forest. Now, it's nothing but white folks, and all the Indians have disappeared. My brother's mad about it."

"Because of the curse?" Cassie asks.

"Curse?" Mitchell Hunt gives a slight, humorless laugh. "So, let me guess. You think that Barbie disappeared because of the curse." He said it like a statement and not a question.

"I don't know what to believe, other than whatever happened to Barbara was painful and horrific." I shudder just thinking about last night. Had it only been last night when I touched her hand?

"That's because what happened to Barbie wasn't a curse. It was murder." His face appears haunted.

"Do you know who did it?" I ask.

"I have my suspicions, but…" he glances down at his gun.

"George Hodgens said he saw you about a month or so ago."

"My day job is roofing. That's how I own this place free and clear. I worked on Hodgens' roof years ago. Then he had me put on a new roof at the police station, and well, we've been friendly acquaintances ever since."

"About that accident," I start again.

Mitchell Hunt's face clouds over. "Where did you hear about that?"

"From a friend. He's helping us figure all this out, too."

"How would he know that? No one knows what happened."

"He said his mother told him," Cassie answers. "His mother is Bonnie Blackstone, Barbara's sister. Do you remember her?"

His facial expression sets in a grim line. "Yeah, I know her. She's the one I've got suspicions about."

"Bonnie Blackstone?" I nearly laugh until I realize he's not joking.

"It's hard to believe they were twins. Aren't twins supposed to be close? Not those two."

Cassie leans forward as if the story's about to get good. "Family drama," she says with understanding. "Been there, done that."

"Especially Bonnie," he tells her. "She was always jealous. About everything. Didn't matter what. If Barbie found a quarter on the street, Bonnie would trick Barbie into giving it to her. If Barbie ever earned praise, Bonnie would twist it so that the praise went to her. Barbie let her because she loved her. I never understood that. That's what drew me to Barbie. She had the heart of a saint. But Bonnie, there was nothing saint-like about her."

"Bonnie wouldn't hurt her sister, would she?" Cassie asks.

"Well," he rubs his face. "That makes this story even more interesting. See, Bonnie was my girlfriend."

Cassie and I both exchange glances.

I go to speak, but Mitchell Hunt stops me. "Let me explain," he says. "Bonnie is the oldest twin, so her parents and mine worked out an arrangement of sorts, and it was a silent agreement that we would get married."

"Your family's from the Apache tribe?"

"Yes. As a teenager, I rebelled against the idea of marrying Bonnie. I couldn't flat out treat her poorly, so I picked on Barbie. All the time. Since they were two years younger than me, I would pull on Barbie's pigtails, or knock her books out of her hands. Bonnie would taunt her, too, which irritated me. If anyone should look after Barbie, it should have been her twin sister. But not Bonnie." He pauses.

"They were that different?" I ask, having a hard time seeing Bonnie Blackstone in that light.

"Like night and day. It irritated me so much because Barbie would never…react. Now I can see how much I wanted her to notice me." He stares off with a slight smile on his face. "One day, Bonnie dared me to trip Barbie. I thought it was cruel, but I wanted to see if Barbie would react, so I accepted. It was horrible. She landed face-first in the dirt. Bonnie laughed, and Barbie started to cry. I'll never forget that. I looked from Bonnie to Barbie, and I knew. At that moment, I knew that I didn't want Bonnie. Nothing could make me want her. Who I wanted was Barbie. I picked her up and carried her home. She cried on my shoulder the whole way."

The three of us sit quietly for some time.

"Could Barbara have been pregnant?"

"Not to change the subject," Cassie's voice pulls me away from Mitchell Hunt's moving story. "I'm still wondering why you threatened to harm us? What happened with the car accident? Mitch says that you died from it."

"Mitch?"

"He's Bonnie's son. He's the one helping us with this mystery."

"Bonnie's son?"

"Yes," Cassie says slowly.

"How old is he?"

"Maybe twenty," I say. "I think I heard him say that."

"I think that's enough for today. Recounting all these painful memories has taken its toll."

He holds out his hand and gives me a guarded handshake. I don't want our meeting to end this abruptly, but I don't know what else to say.

"I have a feeling we'll see each other real soon," he says and gives my hand an extra squeeze.

"I hope so."

Dusk has settled onto the landscape. Mitchell Hunt decides to walk us back to the car.

"How do you get back here?" Cassie asks, pointing at his truck.

"Behind the house is Tomahawk Trail. My driveway, if you

want to call it that, takes me in that direction."

"Oh, I wonder why our GPS didn't give us those directions," Cassie says to me.

The older gentleman laughs. "Don't put too much stock in technology, ladies."

When we reach the car, he opens my car door. "If you could not tell anyone about me, I'd be appreciative," he says it so quietly I almost don't hear him.

"You mean, for now?"

He pinches his nose as if what he's about to do is painful. "I know you think that I may be related to you, and I'm not saying I doubt you, but…Let's just say that I have buried the past, so to speak. Sometimes it's best to leave it buried."

"Wouldn't you want to meet him? My Dad? If he's your son, you'd want to, right?"

"But he's not my son." His words sink deep into my soul, as he continues, "Whoever killed Barbie all those years, closed that path for my life. It's closed for a reason. I'm not about to open it back up."

"And meeting my dad will complicate things?"

He nods and smiles sadly.

I want to ask, *What about me?* Both of my grandfathers are dead, and yet here this one turns up out of the woodwork. "I feel slighted," I admit. "If we're related, you are just as much my history as any of the other people in my life."

I slide into the car and shut the door before he can respond, but our eyes meet as Cassie backs up. And for a second, I see regret in his eyes. I wonder if he can see the disappointment in mine.

27

We stay quiet in the car at first. There so much going through my mind, but sadness is the recurring emotion. I'm surprised at how much I like Mitchell Hunt, and how disappointed I am that he wants nothing to do with me.

Once we drive onto the main road, both of our cell phones come to life. Cassie checks hers. "Five missed calls and six missed texts. Yep, we're screwed."

Mine has even more. Dad alone tried to ring through at least ten times. Cassie tries to drive and text one-handed. I give my father a call.

"Where are you? Are you all right? Please tell me you're not halfway dead or in the hospital!"

"I'll tell you I'm fine if you let me get a few words in."

"You're fine?"

"Yes."

"Then you're grounded."

"Where's the concern from two seconds ago?"

"It went out the window the second you told me you were fine and have only been rude these last several hours while we've been worried sick and even contacted the police!"

"I'm sorry. We didn't mean to be rude. We didn't have a good cell phone signal."

"No excuse, Virginia. You have no idea how worried we've been."

I sigh and rub my forehead. I am so tired, but I do hear the worry in his voice, so I say, "All right, fine. But I'm eighteen. Isn't that a little old to be grounded? And from what?"

Dad pauses. "I don't know. I haven't thought that far in advance!"

"Why are you there? Weren't you supposed to take a trip with Laura?"

"Yes. We were going to take our time and tour a winery. Until my mother called me up worried sick about where her two granddaughters were, and how neither one of you were answering the phone. She was short of breath and everything. You do remember you were supposed to be looking out for her?"

I'm feeling guiltier by the second. I glance over at Cassie, but she has already shut her cell phone off. When she sees me watching her, she shrugs. "We both don't need to get reamed out. I can hear Uncle Sam from over here."

"Is she okay?" I ask Dad.

"She'll be fine. We're just glad you two girls are okay. Where are you at?"

"I'm not sure exactly."

"Outside of Pellston," Cassie tells me.

"Pellston," I tell my Dad.

"Why are you up there?"

"We were visiting one of Cassie's friends."

Cassie nods like that's a good answer.

"Unbelievable," Dad says. "Just get back here as soon as possible. It's going to be about midnight by the time you get here."

"Sorry," I say again, but he's already hung up.

"That's amazing," Cassie says.

"What?"

"I've never heard Uncle Sam that angry. He's always so mellow."

I scoff. "You haven't been around him as long as I have."

"Obviously."

My cell phone rings again. This time it's Isaac. The butterflies in my stomach immediately take off.

"Hello?"

"Hey, your Dad hung up before I could ask to speak with you."

"You're at Gran's house, too?"

"Yeah, she called my dad and said she wanted to report missing granddaughters who don't answer their phones."

I could hear the humor in his voice and could envision him smiling that crooked smile of his. "We were in Pellston, where there's no cell phone signal."

"Your Dad told us. Who's Cassie's friend?"

"Is anybody around you?"

"Yeah."

"Am I on speaker?"

"No."

"Cassie and I decided to see if what Mitch said about Barbara's boyfriend was true. Ends up, he's still alive."

"No *way*," Isaac stops himself. "I mean, wow, are you sure?"

"Positive. We've been talking to him this whole time."

"Why would Mitch say the guy was killed?"

"Because his mother told him. Turns out Bonnie Blackstone wasn't Miss Nice."

"Okay, well, we'll talk when you get back." Isaac is talking loud.

"Are people listening?"

"You bet," he says in a false-friendly way.

I start laughing. "We'll see you later."

"Nice talking to you." Still loud.

"You're weird."

"Bye." Isaac chuckles as he hangs up.

I don't realize I'm smiling at my phone until Cassie says, "You've got it bad."

"Yeah, I do," I confess. "The other night I was scrolling through Instagram, and I saw pics of Alisa at a party, and Leo's arm is around her. Not too intimate, but friendly-like. A week ago, I'd have been in tears. I'd have called her and wigged out. But not now."

"What are you going to do when you have to go home?"

"I don't know. I haven't thought that far ahead."

"Long-distance relationships can work," Cassie tries to encourage me. "Besides, you're coming state-side to go to college, right?"

"I guess. I don't know. A part of me wants to, but then again, my life is back in London. Mum's there."

"Looks like you've got a pretty good life over here," she says. "You've been over here for over two weeks, and you're already Miss Popular."

"Thanks to a ghost."

"It's not that."

"Fine. It's my accent."

"Yeah, maybe it's that." Cassie looks over at me and grins.

I know what's coming. "Please, Cassie, no. Don't try to—"

"What?" she says in a horrible English accent. *"I was going to say how bloody fabulous it is back in London with Queen Elizabeth and Big Ben and Hugh Grant and crumpets!"*

"Hugh Grant? Really?" I'm giggling as Cassie fluffs her hair and bats her eyes. She looks ridiculous.

"Hugh Grant and crumpets!" She wiggles her eyebrows. *"London is sooooo fabulous. How could I possibly leave there and live in the drudgery of Northern Michigan? It's far beneath me."*

"Stop it!" I can barely get the words out amid my laughing

hysterics.

After another hour of Cassie's wackiness, we are nearly at the outskirts of Pigeon Forest.

"Man, it's dark out there," I say, staring out the window.

"Not a lot of lights in the country."

"That's one thing about London. It's always so bright. Can't see very many stars, that's for sure."

"For the record," Cassie says, "I would love to have you here. Maybe we could be roommates at U of M."

"I thought I heard Aunt Sue say you were going to Michigan State."

"I'd rather go to Ann Arbor. No offense to my mom and dad, but they want me at State, so I can still live at home. Where's the adventure in that? If you go to Michigan though, I know they'll let me go there with you. Just think of how awesome it would be! We could major in crime scene investigations. You could be the photographer, and I could be the cute blonde that asks all the questions."

I smile at her. "Is that what they'd put on your degree? But yeah, it would be awesome. Gran would cry tears of joy."

We both glance at each other, then start laughing all over again.

Neither one of us notice the headlights coming up from behind. But we do feel the impact of the vehicle as it smashes into our bumper. Cassie swerves, and I'm afraid she'll lose control.

I turn around and see a huge monster truck accelerating from behind us to our side.

"Oh my God, Cassie!" I yell. "Watch out!"

But the truck's tires, which are as tall as our car, smash into Cassie's side of the car. The car swerves again. Cassie tries to slow down, but the truck seems to read our minds at the same time. It smacks us again, and this time doesn't let up, pushing us to the side of the road.

"Ginnie, I have no control!" Cassie's screaming.

We are completely at the truck's mercy.

The truck comes at us again, and like a schoolyard bully, shoves us off the road. We barrel down a steep hill, increasing in speed, and screaming what may be our final breaths.

***

My name is being called from far away. It seems like I'm in a dark tunnel, and the person calling me is trying to find me. I try to yell, "I'm here!" but nothing comes out. I gag because something is choking me. I clutch my throat, my airway clogged. I hear my name again. It's no use. Despair settles in. With one final effort, I try to purge whatever's in my throat. With a violent push, my mouth opens and my throat releases a stream of beetles. They pour out of my mouth and onto me.

It is then that I scream.

When I come to, I gasp and start flailing to get the beetles off.

"She's with us!" someone yells. "It's all right," the person tells me. "You're going to be okay."

"Virginia!" My Dad leans over me, patting my forehead and arms, tears freely running down his face. "I'm right here."

He calms me down, but I still tremble. It's then I notice the throbbing in my head. "I'm so glad you're all right," he's saying. He kisses my forehead.

"We're going to strap her in," the voice says to my Dad.

"I don't think that's necessary," he says.

"We can't have her injuring her head anymore, sir. It's just a precaution."

Dad looks down at me. "They're going to strap you to the gurney just until you get to the hospital. I'm going to be right here next to you the whole time."

I wrack my brain trying to put the pieces together. I'm lying on my back on what must be the gurney. Now that I've got more of my wits about me, I see a bright light shining over me, yet when I turn my head, which I can't do for long because it hurts too much, it's dark.

"The accident," I remember. I try to get up. "Where's Cassie? I've got to find her."

Several pairs of hands push me down.

"It's okay," Dad reassures me. "You got the worst of it. She's cut up a bit from the shattered window, but her airbag worked."

"No airbag for me?" I ask, wincing at the continual throb of my skull.

Dad's face clouds over. "No. It didn't release. Thank God you had your seat belt on." He does not hide the emotional upheaval he's going through, and my heart lurches.

"Does this mean I'm not grounded?" I joke. I can't bear to see him this upset.

Now he smiles. "It's negotiable."

"We've got her strapped in, sir. Let's get her in the ambulance and to the hospital."

Dad nods to them.

They begin to move the gurney, and I can tell it's an effort to move me through the terrain. "How far from the road are we?"

"Not too far. The trees stopped you." Dad squeezes my hand, and I can see how emotional he still is. "It could have turned out a lot worse."

I think of the monster truck that came out of nowhere and charged at us before shoving us off the road. "Whoever it was wanted to hurt us," I say out loud. "It was that man in the monster truck."

Dad's face freezes. "I'll take care of it. The police will get a statement later. Right now I want you to focus on getting better."

The paramedics, along with Dad, have to carry me up the hill that leads to the road. I'm jiggled back and forth, which makes my body scream in pain, but I don't say anything. What would be the point?

Once we make it to the side of the road, I notice how many people are here. Three police vehicles close off this portion of the road, not to mention there are a fire truck and two ambulances. If that wasn't enough, a crowd of people hang along the background, curiously looking around.

"In small towns, any news is big news," one of the paramedics says to me as they lift me into the ambulance.

Mr. Fulton appears in the ambulance doorway. He's in full police uniform. "How is she?" he asks Dad.

"Looks like she'll be okay. Possibly cracked or broken ribs. Maybe a concussion. They've got to run tests and make sure there's nothing internal to worry about."

They both look at each other a moment longer, communicating something in silence. Mr. Fulton nods briefly at Dad. Then he says to me, "I had to make Isaac leave. It was too much to see you knocked out. Still, he wouldn't go home. Just to let you know he's waiting at the hospital."

I smile. It hurts, so I stop.

"Glad you're okay," Mr. Fulton says. "We'll talk later, Ginnie, but I promise we'll find out what happened and take care of it."

He glances again at Dad and then leaves.

The paramedics shut the ambulance doors.

"Why did his eyes look like they were threatening you?"

Dad is sitting beside me as the ambulance takes off. He takes my hand again, chuckling to himself. "Let's just say when I heard from Cassie about someone running you off the road, I vowed that I would find that person and take care of the situation myself. Ted overheard it."

"Don't do anything crazy. I don't want to have to visit my father in prison."

"Did someone really run you off the road?"

"It was the same truck from Gran's house. The truck came out of nowhere and plowed right into us. Kept at it until we were barreling down that bloody hill. Stupid truck. He did it on purpose."

"There, there, leave the vendettas to me. That way, only one of us goes to prison."

"Dad?"

"Hmm?"

"When we get to the hospital, can I not have any visitors? At least until morning? I need to collect my thoughts."

"Of course. I'll keep everyone at bay. Even Isaac."

"Well, he's already there. He can see me." Then again, I think of what I must look like, and say, "You know what? Just tell him I'm doing fine, and I'll see him tomorrow."

With a sigh, I close my eyes and tune everything out. I need to think. Without any interruptions or questions or curious glances. This is something I have to sort out myself. Why would that man want to hurt us? Meant to maybe even do more. I shudder at the thought. Who would shove Cassie and me off the road? What kind of person would want us dead?

But someone did. Someone who must be getting annoyed at my picking around some swept aside secrets. The more I think about it, the more I agree with Mitchell Hunt. There is no curse on that land or on the tribesmen. No, what I'm dealing with is much worse. I'm dealing with a murderer. One who has no hesitation to murder again.

28

I feel something flick my nose.

"Psst, Ginnie. Wake up."

My eyes peek open to see Cassie's face inches from mine. "I'm sleepy," I say before I drift off to sleep again.

Another flick at my nose.

"Stop," I murmur and try to turn over. But I'm strapped to a few machines, which makes turning over complicated. Plus, Cassie's sitting on my covers. I let out an exaggerated sigh. "I was sleeping without any weird dreams." I open my eyes and glance around. "Where's Dad? He was supposed to protect me from people like you."

"I told him he could go get a cup of coffee. I had to promise not to disturb you."

"Go figure."

"We have to talk." Cassie's voice lowers. "Someone tried to kill us."

I sit up, knowing my night of sleep is over. The sun shines brightly in the room, so I must have slept for several hours, but I'm still annoyed at being woken up. "Looks that way."

"When I looked over and saw you knocked out, I thought you were dead. I was yelling your name, shaking you, but nothing." Cassie looks down, her voice shaking.

Okay, so I'm not so annoyed now. I reach out and hug her. "I'm fine. I'm right here. You're stuck with me." After I release her I notice the cuts and bruises on her face. "Oh my word, Cass…" I touch her face.

"It looks worse than it feels. Laura and the other doctors said that it won't leave any permanent scarring, so that's good. And no offense, but you are the one everyone's worried about."

"Why? I feel okay. My head is kind of sore."

"Yeah, but you were out for a long time."

"How long?"

"At least an hour. After the accident, you were unconscious and our legs were pinned under the smooshed dashboard. You should see the car. The front half smacked a tree, and even though I slammed on the brakes just before we hit it, the car is totaled."

"So, what happened after that?" I prod her along.

"Luckily, your phone was within reach. I grabbed it and called the first number I found, which was Uncle Sam. I was hysterical, of course, because I thought my only cousin was dead, and he took care of everything else. He told me to sit tight and say a prayer for you. Next thing I know, not five minutes later, I hear sirens. Which was good because being in the car with what I thought was a dead body was weirding me out."

"How bad do I look?" I ask. I touch my head and feel the bandaging around it.

"Not horrible. You have a cut right here by your left eye, must have been glass from my window."

"My window didn't bust?"

"Nope, just mine. Anyways, you'll probably have bruising on your forehead, maybe even a goose egg."

"Thank God." I breathe in and out, trying to calm my nerves. Just talking about it makes me nervous. "That guy tried to kill us. The same one who threatened Gran."

"That's what I've been trying to say. Mr. Fulton's going to want to talk to you, but I told him and the other police officers everything I remember. It's a big mystery. Why would that man purposefully want to hurt us?"

"I wonder if it's the same person who hit Mitchell Hunt and left him for dead? Whatever the reasons, Gran might know about why he's targeting us."

Cassie's eyes widen. "I never thought about that, but it makes sense. Do you think he's trying to get at her?"

Before I can answer, Dad walks in with a cup of coffee in one hand, a cell phone in the other, and Laura beside him. "You woke her up?" he asks Cassie.

"She was already up."

His look reveals his disbelief. "Yeah, right." He comes over to me and kisses my cheek. "How're you doing?"

"I'm alive." I hear someone on the other end of his phone. "Is that Mum?"

"Your mother's on the phone, having a panic attack. Are you up to talking to her?"

I reach my hand out.

"You sure?" he asks again.

I nod and take the phone. "Hello, Mum. I'm all right."

"Oh dear sweet *Jee-ssuuss*, Mary, mother of God, I've been worrying like a cat without a tail! How's my love? What happened, dear?"

She's still loud, but the emotion in her voice touches me. "It was a car accident…"

"You weren't driving, were you? Those American cars can be a bit tricky."

"No, Cassie was, but it wasn't her fault. Some truck smacked into us."

Mum throws out a slew of profanity. I have to hold the phone away from my ear. Dad takes the phone. "Let me have her call you back. She just woke up. Yes, Melinda, I will have her call you. Thank you." He sighs in annoyance. "Yes, I realize that if she would have got on the plane, none of this would have happened. It was her choice." He pulls the phone away and blinks. "She hung up on me."

"She's prone to tantrums," I say.

"No one knows that more than me." Dad looks over at me. "Want some coffee?"

I take the cup and sip. That's when I notice Laura at the end of the bed with a clipboard. She's shuffling through some papers, making notes.

"How does it look, Doctor?" Dad jokes. "Will the patient live?"

Laura smiles and looks up, giving him a wink. "More than likely."

"Oh, spare me," Cassie says and pushes herself off my bed. "That's enough middle-aged flirting this girl can handle."

"I'm not middle-aged," Dad argues.

"You're forty now, aren't you? That makes you—"

"Oh my WORD!" I shout, interrupting Cassie. "Happy Birthday! I can't believe I forgot!" I look at Cassie. "We didn't go to the store last night! I forgot to get him a present!"

"Relax." Laura comes up next to me. She checks my bandages, then my eyes. "Follow my finger," she says. Once she's done, she adds, "You'll be released soon. Thankfully, the concussion is healing nicely. I'll check up on you at the house, but I know you'd like to be with your Dad today. Plus, there's the party, which I can tell Rose not to cancel. How's that sound?"

"Thanks for letting the cat out of the bag," Cassie says annoyed.

"I found out last night when your grandmother slipped and said you were supposed to go to the store to get supplies for the party. It doesn't take a rocket scientist, Cassie." Dad turns to me. "What do you say? Want to get out of this joint in a little bit?"

"Yes, but I have to stop by the store."

"No, you don't. You being alive and well is enough of a gift for me." Dad kisses me again on the cheek. "I don't need anything more."

For some reason, this gets me emotional. I swallow back the tears.

"I'll go let the nurses know," Laura says, looking from Dad to me. "It might take some time, but you should be out of here in the next hour or so. Come on, Cassie. Didn't you say you were leaving?"

Both Cassie and Laura leave the room.

"Happy Birthday," I say quietly.

Dad sits beside me on the bed and leans his head next to mine. "Thank you. And thank you for not dying. That would have made today a horrible birthday."

We stay quiet for a few minutes. "Thanks for keeping everyone away."

"It's been difficult, but they wanted to respect your wishes. Other than Cassie."

I stifle a laugh. "She's a slithery one."

"That she is."

"She's wanting to be my roommate at Michigan."

"Really?" Dad tries to mask his interest, but I can tell he's hopeful. "Does this mean…?"

"I don't know just yet, but I'm leaning toward it. If you're over here, I can't see being in London without you. And Cassie, well, let's just say she's more than a good cousin."

"She's a good friend?" Dad adds.

"Yeah. We're thinking of doing some kind of criminal justice program. I'm thinking I might be able to find something that has a focus on detective work with photography. I don't know. Do you think that's kind of cheesy?"

"I think it's a great idea, and what a great birthday present to know my daughter might move to the states for me."

"And Cassie."

"Of course."

"And for myself."

"Even better."

Someone knocks at the door. Mr. Fulton sticks his head in. "Is now an okay time?" he asks Dad.

"They're needing a statement," Dad says to me. "Should he come later?"

"Now's fine."

Mr. Fulton enters the room. He's intimidating even when he's not wearing his uniform, but with it on, he's quite the looming presence.

"You're staying here, right?" I ask Dad.

"I'm not leaving, hon."

Another officer enters the room, and I see that it's Pete from before. He nods in my direction and says hello to Dad. It's clear though that Mr. Fulton runs the show.

"Cassie provided a lot of information last night, so we shouldn't take too long," he starts. "Before I go through what she said, I will ask questions of you to verify the information we received from her. Does that make sense?"

"Yes."

"Where were you yesterday at 11:50 at night?"

"I was driving back to Gran's house with Cassie. She was driving actually. I was the passenger."

"Where were you coming from?"

"Pellston, or just outside of it. I'm not sure of the exact directions."

"Were you going north or south on 27?"

"We were going south. I remember commenting on how dark it is up here and how bright London is at night. We were in the middle of nowhere, but a sign said that Pigeon Forest was only five miles away."

Mr. Fulton nods. "Why were you in Pellston?"

I swallow and glance at Dad. "We were visiting a man by the name of Mitchell Hunt."

Now Mr. Fulton looks up from his notes. "You were?"

He acts surprised, and I start to panic. Isn't that what Cassie said? Did she say we were visiting her friend? Why would she say that without telling me?

"Virginia, Mr. Fulton asked you a question."

"Cassie made it sound that you were visiting a friend more your age."

I bit my lip. Wow, this complicates things.

"We need the truth." Mr. Fulton taps his pencil on his small notepad.

"We only said that to my father because we didn't want him to worry. Yesterday I had talked with a man named George Hodgens, and he said that the guy who was Barbara Blackstone's fiancé at the time of her death was still alive. This was different from what we heard earlier."

"What had you heard earlier?"

"That he had been hit by a car and died."

"That's what I had heard, too," Mr. Fulton says.

"Who told you that? Wouldn't you investigate it?"

"It was out of my jurisdiction. Still, he has quite the troubled past, I can understand why he wanted to fade into the woodwork. So, are you sure you met with him?"

"Yes, I think so. He lives in the deep woods, but he knew a lot about Barbara Blackstone, which is why we went out there. We had questions."

"Okay," Mr. Fulton puts his hand up like he wants me to pause. "One thing at a time. Let's discuss the accident first, then we will discuss…Barbara."

I can see why Cassie decided to lie about where we were at. It certainly would have been easier to explain!

"Do you remember what happened on the road last night?"

"Cassie and I were talking about schools. Headlights appear

behind us out of nowhere. Really bright. They smash into us from behind. Hard enough that Cassie swerves. It comes up to the side of us. That's when I realize it's this enormous truck. The ones where the tires come up to here." I indicate with my hand how tall the tires are. "It's the same one that was on our property the day I found Gran. It rams into us and doesn't let up. We were virtually at its mercy."

"Did you get a glimpse of the driver?"

"The tires were huge," I say again. "But I couldn't see that high up. The next thing I know we're flying down a hill."

"Did Cassie upset anyone on the road? Was she driving crazy? Could it have been road rage?"

"No. Like I said, this truck appeared out of nowhere. It's that guy. I'm sure of it. He told Gran 'All bets are off.'"

"Did you get a clear look at the make and model of the truck?"

"It was a dark color because it matched the night."

Mr. Fulton glances at Dad. "All right, Ginnie. That's enough for now. If I can talk to your father outside—"

"Wait!"

He stops.

"What aren't you telling me?"

"Nothing I can disclose right now." He looks at Dad and motions to the door.

As they leave, Mr. Fulton says, "Oh, Isaac insisted on coming. He doesn't have to come in, but he wanted me to ask if he could see you."

"Of course. How's Ian?"

"Good. We haven't told him about you and the accident. He's taken a liking to you, and we didn't want to alarm him."

"Won't he know eventually? I mean, look at me."

"Yes, but it will be easier for him to handle when he sees that you are okay and that the bruises will heal."

They leave, and I'm alone again. I sigh and lean back. The

thought crosses my mind—again—that maybe I should have gone back to London, but I don't let it stay. The more I discover and find out about the mystery behind Barbara's disappearance and death, the more determined I am to figure it out. Going back to London is a safe thing to do. It's my comfort zone. But if I'm honest with myself, the more I'm here, the more a part of it I become. There's a history here, a history that is a part of me. Still, with someone out there who is determined to take me out of the picture, it definitely takes this up a notch.

There's a knock at the door.

"It's open," I call out.

Isaac walks in and watches me before moving closer. He doesn't speak, only takes my hand in his. He can barely look at my face.

"It probably looks worse than it is. I'm doing much better this morning."

"I stayed up all night. I couldn't sleep, not until I saw you." He reaches down and hugs me. His arms are strong, and he smells of soap, which does a number to me, which makes me conscientious on how pathetic I must look at the moment. "Is it true? Your father said that some truck knocked you off the road?"

"Yes. It's true. The question is why?"

"No, the question is how am I going to find this person and beat them senseless?"

"You'll have to get in line."

He smiles, but not for long. "Ginnie, it could have been worse. Do you have any idea who it could be?"

"That man who threatened Gran has a monster truck. It has to be him. Who else do I know? I've only been here a week, and Cassie arrived after I did. It's not like we know people."

"Did the man you visited offer any clues?"

"He thinks Bonnie Blackstone might be involved somehow, but I don't see how."

Isaac shakes his head. "No. I've known Ms. Blackstone

since forever, and Mitch is my friend. I've spent the night over at their house a couple of times. That just doesn't make sense."

"I know, but that's it. I've got no other leads. Mitch did tell me that he saw that same man with the monster truck at the sight where I found her. So, he is connected."

"I wonder…" Isaac stops and rubs his chin. His forehead crinkles, and he stares off past me. "Well, you might not like the idea."

"What?"

"Do you think you could talk to Barbara?"

My eyes widen. "You mean the dead girl? Are you serious?"

"That dead girl's been pursuing you. Maybe she would have some concrete answers." Isaac shrugs.

"A ghost?" I repeat. "A ghost would have concrete answers?"

"It was just a suggestion."

Before I respond, the door bangs open, and Cassie enters in a hurry. "I've got it!" she says. "You need to visit Barbara Blackstone. She'll have answers. I just know it!"

I look away from her excited expression to Isaac's expression of I-told-you-so, and accuse, "Did you two talk before coming in to see me?"

"No," they say simultaneously.

"Well, I'm not doing it. One time was creepy enough. I'm not going to go and actually pursue a ghost. That would be absurd."

Cassie and Isaac simply look at me.

"I'm not doing it…No…Stop looking at me…" Then I simply sigh and say, "Fine, but I'm not going alone."

29

The party vibrates the walls as I lay in the dark bedroom. The noise of conversation mixed with the music of Dad's favorite 80's bands rise pleasantly through the floorboards. I should be down there. But I'm not.

For starters, I *was* downstairs, but I had to sneak out once it got going. The music and noise make my head throb. Everyone acts overly concerned, which means I have to lie and say I'm quite all right, thank you. But I'm not.

It doesn't help that I have yet to get Dad a birthday present. It's embarrassing to see the stacks of gifts and know that not one of them comes from his only daughter. I could have gone to the store last night, or even this afternoon. But I didn't.

None of these reasons are the entire picture though. I am mostly up in my dark bedroom because, in a few hours, I am going to go look for a ghost. I'm going to try to communicate with her. I have already made contact with her, and I'm still here, so that should mean something. This shouldn't freak me out, right? But it does.

There's a gentle knock at the door. It can't be Cassie; she'd just plow in. "Come in," I say, but stay lying on the bed.

The door shuts, but the light doesn't turn on. Someone walks closer to me. Now I sit up to see who it is. "Dad?"

The person sits on my bed beside me, and I see through the faint moonlight that it's Gran. I quickly exhale the breath I'd been holding. "I was just headed downstairs," I say, knowing she came in to scold me for not helping in the kitchen.

She shakes her head and looks down at her hands. "No, no, you stay here and rest."

Still, I sit up and hug my knees. "I'm sorry I never got those items you needed. I didn't even get a present for Dad."

Gran laughs softly. "Silly girl. You being alive and well is gift enough for us."

It's not often that Gran is so sentimental, so I stay quiet.

"Ginnie, I came in here to tell you something." Gran pauses, glances out at the window, and turns back to me. She squeezes her eyes shut, then adds, "I haven't been honest with you. Or your father."

The admission hits me like a rock to the stomach. Even though I suspected, I never expected this.

"I swore on my life that I would take the secret with me to the grave."

I can barely breathe for want of hearing the truth. Gran's eyes bore into mine. I whisper the word that hangs over us. "Barbara."

Gran presses her lips together, closes her eyes again, and slowly nods. "She begged me to tell no one. She was in danger and so was her baby. Your grandfather and I couldn't leave the poor girl destitute. Sam was born right here. In this very room."

A chill shoots up my spine. "Why haven't you told us?"

Gran seems hesitant to answer. "I don't know. From what she told me years ago, if word got out that her baby was born, she would be hated and ridiculed. She wanted to go into hiding for a while, have the baby, give the baby over to us, then show up at her home like she had run away and decided to come back. We worked with Father Roy and Catholic Human Services to make the adoption legal, but even that was very secretive."

"Why did you believe her?"

"The fear in her eyes. She was afraid of something. Or someone."

"How'd you know?"

Gran takes a deep breath. "Well, I first met Barbara—I knew her parents, of course—when I was hiking around the lake. Taking pictures, talking to God. That's when I stumbled upon her. She was sitting on that tree ledge near where you found her. Later on, she told me she always went there to think and get away from everything. But that day, she had her arms wrapped around herself and was sobbing. I heard her before I saw her. That encounter started our friendship. I'd worked with her at the school, but nothing serious. Still, I invited her to the house where I served her some tea and homemade soup. Eventually, she opened up and started talking. It became routine. Every Friday after school. Sometimes she skipped school and showed up early. Sometimes she showed up on days other than Friday. Didn't matter."

"So, she acted afraid?"

"She seemed jittery a lot, that's for sure. But she didn't talk much about any of that. She did mention her betrothed, and how happy she was, but that happiness didn't seem to last long. Eventually, I picked up on the fact she was pregnant. The way she ate! Holy cow, that girl could put it back! Her clothes became baggy, and she wore this long jacket that just hung on her. When I came out and asked her, that's when I saw the fear."

"Why?"

"She said no one could know. Begged me to keep it a secret. Said her parents would kill the baby if they found out. I said I wouldn't tell anyone, but that she would have to one day. About a month later, she shows up on the doorstep late in the night, all banged up. Her nose was bleeding and everything. Asked if she could hide for a while."

"You let her?"

"What was I supposed to do? I took one look at her and knew that she would be safer with me than with whoever was doing that to her."

"But her parents…"

"I know, I know. She vowed to go back once she healed. They didn't have a phone in the home back then. I had her at least write a letter to her parents and inform them that she was okay. I delivered it myself. I knocked on their door for some time. When no one answered, I left the letter stuck between the screen door and frame. I planned to send her home within a day or two. A week later, she went into labor."

I feel the chill go up my spine again. "Dad?"

"We made a promise that night to each other. She promised to let me raise Sam with no interference, and I promised that I would take her secret to the grave. But desperate times call for desperate measures."

"But you lied…to Dad, to me."

"I'm sorry, Ginnie. I never expected anyone to find out. Truth is there are secrets in these woods that are best left untouched. Look at what happens when you go messing with secrets. But I blame myself. If I would have told you when you asked, or had taken care of Henry when he first showed up, the accident might not have happened."

"Henry?"

"Yes, he's the only one who knows about Barbara staying here. He followed her to report back to her sister. It was horrible. He still feels tremendous guilt to this day. Yet, he blames me for the death. He thinks I had something to do with it. Your grandfather and I have tried for years to be patient with him, giving him money here and there to make sure he didn't do something rash. But he went after my grandchildren. There's no excuse." Gran seems angry and shaken.

"You don't have to lie to us anymore. Barbara Blackstone is dead, and she wants me to find the truth."

"And what if the truth is dangerous, Ginnie?" Gran asks in a low voice. "What if the truth will cost you your life? Or your father's life? That Mitchell Hunt…" she stops herself and presses her lips together as if to keep the words in.

"You know him?"

"I used to. He used to be horrible to Barbara. He and Bonnie. Just torturous. He was livid that he had to marry her."

"Right. He told me that. Said he fell in love with Barbara. Bonnie was jealous because he ended it with her."

Gran acts confused. "No. He didn't love either one of them. Barbara saw through him and ignored him, which is why he was so horrible to her. Bonnie was madly in love with him. He used her. They both deserved each other though. Mean, mean people."

"How can you stand being in the same town as Bonnie? Are you suspicious of her?"

Gran quickly stands up and distractedly kisses my forehead. "That's enough conversation for now. I only wanted to apologize for not being open with you. I will find a way to tell your father, too." She walks to the door and opens it. "But Ginnie?"

"Yes?"

"Do your old grandmother a favor and leave the woods alone, okay? Let the secrets stay uncovered. Sometimes that's for the best."

I nod and watch her leave the light from the hallway leaving with her as the door closes.

So, Barbara Blackstone is my grandmother.

Gran had known all along, yet I completely understand why she had to keep it a secret. Gran made a promise to the young girl. It would have been fine if I had left everything alone. I shake my head and get up from the bed. "No, she found me. I wasn't looking for her."

My mind wanders to Mitchell Hunt. Is there a side of him

that I refuse to see? Could he have been lying to me, too? He had commented that his brother was the one with the monster truck. Who else knew where we were at?

I sit back onto my bed and hold my head.

The bedroom door opens.

"There you are!" Cassie says. "We're getting ready to sing, 'Happy Birthday.' I thought you might want to come downstairs."

"I didn't get him a present."

Cassie gives me a look that says you've-got-to-be-kidding. "I'm sure your Dad isn't worried about a present."

"You're right. Let's go." I leave the room and wait for her. I want to tell her about my conversation with Gran, but hold my tongue. I'm not sure how Cassie will take it when she finds out Gran has been lying to us. "I'm not sure about tonight."

"It'll be fine," she says with a wave of her hand. "We're all going to be there. Even Mitch, who's here, by the way."

"Is Bonnie?"

"No, I don't think so, but that George Hodgens guy is."

"There she is!" Dad calls out as I approach. He wraps his arms around me and lifts me up. When he sets me down, he says to the guests, who have piled into the large living room area, "For those of you who haven't met her, this is Virginia, my daughter. I'm so lucky to have her."

Everyone claps or cheers, which embarrasses me, especially since I still have a large gash on my forehead. Cassie brushed my hair and tried to cover the gash as best she could, but it still probably sticks out like a beacon in the night.

Aunt Sue and Uncle Doug bring out the cake—they arrived late last night while I was still in the hospital—and we begin singing "Happy Birthday."

Laura stands in the crowd, but I see her watching Dad. Her smile seems genuine, her glances almost shy. I can't deny the feelings that are evident on her face. I look at Dad, and although he's smiling at everyone, I notice him make eye contact with her.

He blows her a kiss.

I swallow back the raw emotion I feel inside of me because I know what I need to do. Something that will make a great birthday present. I wait for Dad to blow out the candles, then slip out and run back upstairs. Once there, I search for an envelope or box and a piece of paper. I find the small box the beetle was in. "This'll work," I mutter, snatching it up. Finding some pretty paper in Cassie's things, I write out,

> *I may not have been able to buy you something tangible,*
> *but I still have something to give. My blessing.*
> *I want you to be happy. If Laura makes you happy, then*
> *you have my blessing.*
> *It's not much, but it's all I have. Happy Birthday to the*
> *best father a girl could ask for.*
> *Love,*
> *Virginia*
> *XOXO*

Once the paper is folded, I place it in the box. I write *To Dad* on the outside. Once in Dad's room, I place it on the end table next to his pillow. Since his bedroom is on the other end of the house, the window overlooks the road. I pause. I step back from the window to take a closer look without being seen. A truck sits at the cross street, its headlights on, with a person still sitting in the driver's seat. Their face is not visible.

My anger grows as I think of the accident. Could the culprit be in that truck watching the party? Ready to make his move?

Without a second thought, I decide to see for myself. It doesn't occur to me to bring someone with, my only forethought is to bring a flashlight. I have to head out the front door, which is risky but I don't want to talk to twenty people at the party on my way to the kitchen's back door. Still, after I creep out of the front door, I walk around to the side of the house, and in the darkness, turn course and head toward the road.

Now that I'm closer I crouch down. I see that the person is

definitely observing Gran's house. The face still stays hidden in the darkness. I have to risk it. It's the only way to know. I get up from my crouched position and walk out of the trees. With flashlight in hand, I'm ready to turn it on to see who it is that has to hide in the shadows.

I take a deep breath to strengthen my resolve. The person hasn't noticed me yet. I walk closer. Before I can lose my nerve, I flip the switch on the flashlight and shine it at the person.

The person turns in surprise and looks right at me. I drop the flashlight. The face staring back at me is Bonnie Blackstone.

30

I back away slowly. If she's staking out the house, she may want to hurt me. I need to get to safety and then call law enforcement.

She rolls down her window. "Hello, you startled me."

Do I respond?

"S-Sorry," I stammer. Why am I apologizing? "I saw the headlights and wondered who it was?"

"I'm waiting for Mitch. He's supposed to bring me out a house key. I left all my keys locked up in the house."

I hear footsteps behind me.

"Hey, Ginnie, what are you doing out here? Your Dad's looking for you."

I turn to Mitch. "Hi, I just came out to see who was in the truck."

Stupid, stupid Ginnie! She was waiting for keys! The accident must have shaken me up to the point of idiocy.

"Here," he says to Bonnie and hands her a key set. "I'm staying here for a while, and then I'll probably crash at Isaac's." He leans in and gives her a quick kiss on the cheek.

"Okay," she says. "Be careful. Don't go in the woods. Bye, Ginnie," she says to me. "My apologies if I frightened you."

"No," I say too quickly. "Not at all. Would you like to come in for cake?"

She smiles sadly. "That's a thoughtful gesture, but I think I will go home. I'm not a big crowd person. Tell your father I said 'Happy Birthday.'" She starts the engine and drives off.

Mitch watches the truck leave before turning toward me. For a moment, he just stares into me. "Cassie told me everything. It's not my mother."

I nod.

"I'm serious, Ginnie." Mitch seems to have to keep his emotions in check. "Her life hasn't been an easy one. I'm not saying she's perfect, but she isn't a murderer. And last night she was with me at home. We were watching the Late Show when I got the call about the accident."

I nod again, blinking back tears.

"It's not her," he repeats. We stand silent for a few seconds. He eventually asks, "Do you want me to step back from all of this? I don't want to make you uncomfortable."

"No! Why are you asking that?"

"Because I don't want you to feel obligated to hang out with me, especially if you feel my mother might be guilty. That's going to drive a wedge between us. Maybe I should just back off, and leave you to your own devices."

I shake my head. "No, don't go away. I don't know what to think. Someone tried to kill us last night. It's been tough. I'm just trying to figure out why and who."

Mitch steps closer to me and rests his hands on my shoulders. "I'm sorry," he sighs. "You've been through a lot. I shouldn't have attacked you like that. Its just…Mom won't even kill spiders. She places a cup over them, then slides a paper under the cup to trap the spider, then releases it outside. She's harmless."

"I think Mitchell Hunt might have messed with my mind.

He said stuff about how mean Bonnie was as a child, and I don't know. It got me confused."

"That doesn't sound like my Mom at all." He shakes his head. "So, that guy's still alive?"

"Yeah."

"I'll have to ask my Mom what she had said about him. I thought she said he had died, but I'm not too sure now."

Could Mitch be completely blinded by his love for his mother? Or, is she as innocent as he believes her to be?

"Go with us tonight," I say. "Hopefully we'll find out more answers."

"Still friends?"

"What are you talking about? We're potentially cousins."

He smiles. "That's right. We're family."

A Jeep pulls up beside us. "What's going on here?" Isaac jokes.

I am relieved that Isaac has finally arrived. He had to work at the golf course, but told me he'd come to the party as soon as he showered and changed. I rush over to him and see Ian stepping out of the Jeep, too.

"Hi, Ian."

"Hello, Ginnie. I had to work at the golf club today with Isaac. I got to caddie two different golf groups. They tipped me a total of forty dollars."

"Nice. Do I get a cut?"

"You did not work for it."

Isaac, Mitch, and I laugh.

"What?" Ian asks. "I made a factual statement."

"Come on," Isaac grabs his brother and messes with his hair.

Ian pushes him away. "Ginnie, your forehead is worse than Isaac told me."

"I'm fine. My seat belt worked."

"Seat belts protect lives. Do you know that only one percent of them malfunction in an accident? That means that they are an effective device for protection."

"Yes, I agree."

As Ian climbs the steps, Isaac says to me, "That went well."

As we head in the house, I place my hand on the railing to climb the porch stairs. A bug crawls across my hand.

"Another beetle," Mitch whispers to me.

A part of me is grateful he saw it. Sometimes I feel like I'm completely losing my mind. "They won't leave me alone. They're even in my dreams."

Mitch grabs my hand to stay back. Then he says, "Ginnie, you may not be out of danger."

"I know."

"What are you two whispering about now?" Isaac asks.

"Bugs."

"Yeah, that's right," Isaac teases. "You're a bug collector. When are you going to show me your collection?"

"It's at home. So, you'll have to come to England."

"Sounds like a plan," he says and moves out of the way as some guests leave.

When we're back inside, we see others getting ready to leave.

Dad pokes his head from the kitchen entryway. "There you are! Why do you keep disappearing?"

"I went outside to greet Isaac and Ian."

"A few people are staying. We'll be out back having a bonfire."

"We're going for a boat ride," Cassie says. She's coming down the stairs with a thin jacket zipped up.

Dad raises his eyebrows. "Is today a good night for that? The last thing I need is for any of you to get injured."

"Isaac and Mitch are going, too. We'll stay in plain sight. I promise."

Dad's looking at me, and I'm looking back and forth from

him to Cassie.

"I'm a skilled boater," Isaac adds. "She'll be safe."

Dad lets out a sigh. "I'll put my overprotective father mode to the side and trust you." He's not looking at me now; his eyes are boring into Isaac's.

"She'll be safe," Isaac repeats.

I know Dad. He wants to say no. And I don't blame him. I don't want to go at all. My head still has a slight throb to it, and after my encounter with Bonnie and then Mitch, I want to crash onto my bed and not think about any of this murder stuff. At least until tomorrow.

"We won't be gone long," I say. "They want to show me the stars from the lake. With the full moon, it should be beautiful."

"I won't relax until you're back," he finally says. Before walking away, he adds, "And where a life jacket."

Once he's gone, I turn to Cassie. "Does it have to be tonight?"

"Yes. This problem isn't going away. We need to figure it out. The longer some murderer is out there running around, the more danger we're in."

I'm surprised at how strong and emphatic she is. "Okay, I guess. Why the boat ride?"

"Because you and I both know there's no way they would let us walk in the woods right now. Plus, who wants to walk a couple of miles to where we're going? It's a lot faster to take the boat across."

"Is that necessary?" Mitch asks. "Hasn't the ghost shown up here on the property?"

"So, what are you saying? Just throw Ginnie out there and see if Barbara pops up?" Cassie teases him.

"I don't think you guys should do this," Ian says this quietly, without looking at any of us. He's wringing his hands though. He seems to realize he's doing that because he crosses his arms and stuffs his hands in his armpits.

None of us say anything, probably out of guilt. I had completely forgotten Ian stood beside us.

"Ian, go hang out with Mom," Isaac says. "We won't be gone long."

"You're not listening to me." Ian is trying not to get agitated. "Don't pursue that ghost." He makes eye contact with me. "She's manipulating you."

Isaac rubs his face.

But something in Ian's words makes my skin crawl. "What do you mean?"

"I felt it when our boat was being pulled toward her. It was even stronger when we found the body. It's not good. It doesn't feel good."

Isaac gently touches Ian's shoulder. "You're right, Ian. It gave me the heebie-jeebies, too. Come on. Let's go find, Mom." Isaac leads Ian through the kitchen to the back door.

Ian glances back at me.

"Finding a dead body would freak anybody out," Cassie says. "You and I both felt her pain and sorrow. It'll be okay."

Mitch chuckles to himself. "You know what my mother told me about pain and sorrow? They're cousins to anger and hate."

I rub my arms to get rid of the goosebumps.

"Not helping," Cassie says to him. "Ginnie, we are all going to be there. We need to find out who hurt her. That's it."

The way Cassie says it, it sounds like it's nothing. Jump on the boat, go say hello to a ghost, find out who killed her, jump back on the boat, head home. "If we're going to do it, let's do it before I change my mind." I walk past both of them and find my jacket on one of the coat racks. After throwing it on and zipping it up, I go out the back door and walk toward the dock. Isaac whispers something to his Mom and runs up next to me. Ian won't look in my direction.

"Is he okay?" I ask.

"I'm stupid for forgetting he was there with us."

"Don't beat yourself up. We all forgot."

At the docks, I notice the big speed boat floating. "Cassie said Uncle Doug brought his boat back. I'd forgotten about that."

"This is nice."

"That's not the one we're taking," Cassie says from behind us. She carries a tub of supplies. "We have to take Gran's boat."

"Great," I say and glance at the boat I'd been on just a few days earlier.

"Let's get this over with," Mitch says and climbs in.

Isaac follows and gives me a hand, while Mitch helps Cassie. The boat wobbles as we situate ourselves.

"Here," Cassie says. "I brought a floodlight. The moon is bright, but I didn't want to take a risk. I also brought two blankets, some food, and my cell phone in a plastic baggy. With Gran's LED lanterns at the dock, we'll be fine."

I take a deep breath.

"Don't look so freaked out, guys," Mitch says. "We're being watched."

I turn around and see Dad, Uncle Doug, and a few other people walking toward the docks.

"Go, before they ask questions," Cassie whispers.

Isaac and Mitch untie the rope and push us from the dock. They have just begun paddling when we hear Uncle Doug call out, "Don't run into my new boat or get a scratch on it from one of the paddles!"

"We won't, Dad!" Cassie calls back.

I wave at my Dad, and he waves back. Even from here, I can see the worry in his eyes. Who knows? Maybe he can see the worry in mine.

Once we're in the middle of the lake, Cassie says, "You know, if we weren't trying to talk to the dead, this would be really romantic. Of course, Mitch would have to be sitting next to me, and Ginnie next to Isaac."

"Have you figured out what you're going to say?" Isaac

asks as he pushes the oar against the water.

If I wasn't so frightened, I would revel in how sexy he looks right now. But I'm terrified. My stomach is clenched tight, and I bite my lip to keep from ordering them to turn around. It kind of annoys me that they are making me do this right now, one day after the accident, but I know it's because we need to figure this out. Before…well, before something worse than last night happens.

"I'm just going to ask her if she could reveal who did this to her."

We reach the taped off beach shore in what I think is record time. The goosebumps won't go away. I hope I don't get sick again. There's an eeriness that settles on a lake at night, and it's not making me feel reassured.

Mitch and Isaac jump out of the boat first and pull it to shore. Isaac helps me out. "I'm right here," he whispers in my ear. "Nothing's going to happen to you."

I step under the tape and into the closed-off area. I close my eyes, steady my breathing, then begin to walk toward where I found her.

"Oh my God," Mitch says before grabbing my arm and pulling me back.

That's when I see the beetles. There must be hundreds, if not thousands, moving toward me.

But I'm already stepping backward. The beetles follow me. They begin to swarm around my feet.

"Ginnie, get out of here," Mitch is yanking me back. "Stay back!" Mitch yells to Cassie.

Isaac grabs my hand. "What do we do?"

Mitch and Isaac are pulling me back, but the beetles are swarming around my feet despite my stepping on them. They crunch where I walk.

My back hits the yellow tape. Isaac and Mitch lift it and push me through it. The swarms stay back, but I still don't stop until my feet are touching the water.

"What was that?" Isaac demands. "Why did they only swarm around Ginnie?"

"This is serious, Ginnie. We need to go see my mother. She'll know what to do."

The three of them discuss and argue, but all I can do is stare at the beetles. The cold wind blows at me suddenly, and I know. My gaze lands on Barbara standing in the same spot where I found her lying dead. Her hand is extended as it was before. "Mitch," I whisper.

That's all I have to say. The three of them follow my gaze.

"I don't see anything," Isaac complains, then I feel him grab my hand.

Not a second later I feel Cassie grab my other hand.

No one says anything. I should be reassured that the three of them are with me, but I'm not. Every part of me trembles in trepidation. Ian's words course through my veins. *She's manipulating you.*

Should I push the uneasiness aside and go to her? She hasn't hurt me before.

My attention shifts to the beetles. As I study them, something clicks. These are the same beetles from my nightmares. The beetles try to submerge me. I wake up in terror every time.

Why would I want to communicate with a ghost who is surrounded by them?

She's manipulating you.

I don't know how Ian knows this information, but he has yet to be wrong.

I turn around and go to the boat. "Let's go. We're getting out of here."

The three of them sense the urgency in my voice and move quickly. Once we're in the boat, Isaac has to jump out to push us into the water. I go to help him get back in and see Barbara standing right next to the shore, her hand extended. "We're trying to help you," I say to her. I'm standing in the boat as Isaac and Mitch paddle away from the beach. "Please rest in peace." I watch her arm fall to her side. She fades into nothing.

"What's happening?" Cassie asks. "Ginnie? Mitch? Somebody tell us something."

I notice I'm still standing in the boat. When I turn to sit down, Isaac is the one paddling while Mitch watched the encounter. Mitch's eyes find mine.

"*What*!?" Cassie yells to the both of us.

Despite the intense heebie-jeebies I'm feeling, I can't help but smile at Cassie. "Chill out. It was Barbara."

"Where?"

"She showed up right next to the boat. I told her to rest in peace, and that we were trying to help her."

"That's it? Why'd you make us leave? We could have found out some important information."

"Because…" I start. "Because Ian is a pretty smart guy. He told me that this ghost was manipulating me. I don't know how or why he would know this, but I trust Ian more than I trust that ghost."

"I agree," Mitch says. "Those beetles mean something. I have to talk to my mother. Please, Ginnie. We can't keep this from her. Our bloodline is the reason. My mother would know more. She could explain what the heck is going on."

I can't tell Mitch I don't trust Bonnie. There is so much that is unknown, that the only instincts I trust are my own. "Let's sleep on it, and talk about it in the morning."

"He's right, Ginnie," Isaac pipes in. "Ms. Blackstone needs to know this. What just happened is freaky. You're in over your head."

"What's that supposed to mean?" I ask, trying not to get bent out of shape. "I didn't ask for any of this!"

"That's what I'm saying. Let other people help you. Ms. Blackstone might have the answer."

"Or she could have been the one to kill her sister!" The words are out before I can catch them and shove them back in.

Mitch's face immediately clouds over. "I'm sorry. I can't rule anything out. And my head is throbbing." I rest my head in my hands and avoid making eye contact with Mitch. "I'm sorry, Mitch. I don't want to upset you. Let me get some sleep, and I'll be good tomorrow."

"Here's a thought," Isaac says. "Why don't you let the police do their job, and we can all go and enjoy the summer. I don't know about the rest of you, but that's enough ghostly encounters for the rest of my life."

We're silent for the rest of the way back. Even Cassie doesn't talk. I'm about two seconds from crumbling into a thousand pieces. I am no closer to an answer than I was when Barbara first sought me. And now, I'm alienating myself from people—friends—who are only trying to help.

"I'm sorry," I repeat. "Mitch, I shouldn't have said what I said. She's your mother. That was wrong of me."

He doesn't look me in the eye, but he nods. Isaac says, "You've been through a lot, Ginnie. Just remember who your friends are."

Our gaze lingers, and I give a half-smile. At least Isaac doesn't hate me.

As we drift to the dock, the four of us hear the commotion at the same time. A few police vehicle lights blink in the darkness.

"Why are the cops here?" Mitch asks, trying to get a better look.

"I have no idea," Isaac answers.

We dock quickly and scurry off the boat. Most of the party has been deserted, save for Gran and Aunt Sue and Laura. "What's going on?" I ask as I run to the back porch.

Tears stream from their faces. Gran is sitting down, rocking back and forth.

"It's Ian," Laura finally says. "He's disappeared."

31

"Tell me everything," Isaac demands.

"One minute he's by the fire, the next minute he's gone. Ted thought he might have tried to walk home, but he's not there. Search parties are all over the place."

Isaac is checking his phone. "This can't be happening," he whispers. "It was on vibrate." He covers his mouth, then says, "Okay, I'm going to look for him. He'll answer my call. Mitch, are you coming with?"

"Right behind you." Mitch takes the floodlight from Cassie.

"I'll go with you," I say and follow them.

"No." Isaac turns quickly and adds, "Leave this alone, Ginnie."

I stop cold, telling myself that he's worried and agitated. He has to know that all of this is completely out of my control.

He runs as if he can't get away fast enough. I see him dialing a number on the phone as he runs. "Dad? Where are you?" he asks into it.

Then he's gone into the trees with Mitch right behind him.

"He's worried," Laura says from behind me. "We say crazy

things when we're worried. Maybe you should go inside and rest. Your Dad wanted us to watch you once you returned."

"They'll find Ian. Everyone knows these woods. He can't be far." Aunt Sue places her arm around Cassie. "Mom," she says to Gran. "You should be inside. This can't be good for your heart."

"Being inside isn't going to make me worry any less," Gran snaps. "This entire summer has been nothing but chaos. Ever since…" she stops herself. "I think you're right, Sue. I'll go inside and make some tea."

Once she's inside, I say, "Ever since I got here, right? That's what she was going to say."

"No, of course not," Laura tries to mollify me. Aunt Sue looks like I hit the bulls-eye.

"I didn't ask for any of this." I keep saying the words, hoping someone will believe me. I move past them and head to the dock. What I need to do is lie down, but that's not going to happen. Not with Ian missing. My heart hurts more than my head. *Ian.*

Once at the dock, I gaze up at the sky and say a silent prayer. A tear leaks down my cheek. I hear Cassie coming up behind me. I don't even have to turn around. I just know it's her.

Cassie grabs my hand. "No one's mad at you. And no one thinks any of this is your fault."

"You know that's not true," I say, still staring at the night sky. "If they're not mad, they're at least annoyed. Even Gran. She wanted me to go home, begged me to, and I went against her wishes. I was told to leave this alone, and I didn't. And now, Ian is missing."

"It's no one's fault."

"Tell that to Isaac. To Gran. To everyone." The tears flow freely at this point.

"Then let's do something about it. You and I both know where he probably went."

"Where?"

"Let's put two and two together. He likes you. He's worried

about you. He told you not to go to where you found the body. You go anyway."

"Cassie, you're a genius. Let me call Isaac and tell him."

"We don't need him. We'll take my Dad's boat across. I know where he keeps the spare key."

I shove any hurt I feel aside. The chaos may have started since I arrived, but I wouldn't give up now. "Let's do it."

We hop in Uncle Doug's boat. Cassie scrambles to find the key.

"Aunt Sue just came back outside," I whisper.

"Found it!" Cassie starts up the motor, turns to me, and says with a grin, "I hate paddle boats."

"CASSIE!" Aunt Sue is racing toward us. "Get back here right now!"

I undo the ropes as Cassie guns the motor.

"Cassie!" Aunt Sue yells.

"We'll be right back!" she calls out to Aunt Sue.

We move across the water in record speed. Even with Uncle Doug's boat lamps, the lake is ominous. But Cassie doesn't seem to care as she rips across the water. "You know," I say, "last time you drove, you nearly killed me."

"Thought I'd get it right this time," she teases.

"Why is all this craziness happening?" I ask. "Gran's right. It started when I got here. How messed up is that? It's like I'm responsible."

"Stop it." Cassie touches my arm while one hand stays on the wheel. "Everyone is freaked out, stressed; there are a lot of emotions right now. But that doesn't change the fact that we're on a mission. We're not doing anything wrong. This ghost sought you out to help her. People aren't going to understand that."

I look at Cassie and feel the tears well in my eyes. "Thanks."

"For what?"

"For believing in me, you twit."

We laugh, and I wipe at my eyes.

"We're in this together," she says quietly and slows the engine. We're near the shore. "Ginnie, you're going to have to get out and secure the anchor."

I nod and push down the fear. I jump into the shallow, murky water.

"Here." She hands me the anchor. "Make sure it sticks."

Once it's in place, Cassie turns off the motor.

We walk to the beach and stand, looking at the yellow tape.

"Let's look outside of the yellow tape first," I suggest.

Cassie hands me a flashlight. "Okay, but that's not going to stop her. She's been on Grandma's property, for Pete's sake."

"It's not her I'm worried about."

"Yeah, you're right. Sorry. Let's stay away from those creepy bugs."

We start calling Ian's name. I'm not too scared because I can hear the groups of people in the woods. His name is being called from all directions.

I move the flashlight all over, even where the bugs were from earlier. Nothing is there now.

"He would have come from up there," Cassie says. "Right? He didn't take a boat."

"You're right. Should we climb up?" I shine the flashlight above us to the tree ledge.

"Ian?" someone yells. Whoever calls his name is very close.

My flashlight shines across the ledge. I notice a tree limb that's broken and dangling. It looks like the same tree limb that I had caught on to on my first hiking trip. My heart freezes as the flashlight travels down to the beach we're at. A lump lies on the ground. "Ian?" I rush to it, moving the yellow tape and heading into it. "Oh," I gasp as soon as I see it's him. "Ian?"

No response.

"He's here!" Cassie yells with all her might. "*Ian is here! Hello, everyone! Ian is here!*"

"Where are you at?" someone calls out.

"Where the yellow tape is!" she calls. "At the bottom of the tree ledge!"

"On our way!"

There's more yelling, but I have tuned it out.

"Is he all right?" Cassie asks.

"He has a pulse." My voice quakes. "But he's not responding. He fell, Cassie. Do you think he was up there when we were here? Could he have been watching us? In his own way trying to protect us?"

Flashlights shine from above.

"We're here!" Cassie yells. "Ian must have fallen! He's knocked unconscious!"

I look up to see Mr. Fulton scaling down the tree wall.

"You got him?" someone yells.

"Get an ambulance!" Mr. Fulton yells. "Stat!" He jumps halfway down and lands on his feet. He's over to us and cradling Ian's head.

"He has a pulse, Mr. Fulton."

Mr. Fulton feels the back of Ian's neck, check's his head, lowers his head to gauge his breathing. "Ian?" Mr. Fulton isn't rough, but quiet and calm. "Ian? Can you hear me? It's Dad. Time to come out of it." He gently slaps Ian's face. To us, he says, "It doesn't appear too serious. Ian will panic occasionally and seizure. It takes him a while to come out. Let's hope that it's nothing more."

I hear more people coming down the tree ledge. "How is he?" It's my Dad. We make eye contact. "He was with you?"

"No. Cassie and I took Uncle Doug's boat out here after we got back and found out what happened. We thought Ian might have tried to follow us."

"You came here?"

"Yes."

Dad doesn't look happy. His jaw sets in a firm line. He turns to Mr. Fulton, "How's he doing?"

"It's too soon to tell. I think he might have panicked and

slipped into an epileptic coma. We'll see."

Ian's head moves suddenly.

"Ian?" Mr. Fulton tries again. "Ian, come on now. I'm waiting to talk to you."

A boat's motor slows as it comes to shore.

"Cassie, go tell them where we're at," Dad orders.

She moves without a word. Dad glances at me then looks down at Ian. "Ginnie, you need to go back to the house. We'll take care of it from here. Cassie needs to go with you. Stay there."

I nod. I should be relieved that Ian is found and will probably be okay. But once again, I feel as if I'm going to get blamed for this.

"Ginnie?" Mr. Fulton calls to me. "I'm glad you found him." To Dad, he says, "It's probably fastest if we use the boat and take Ian across. We're too far in the woods here. Could you have first responders meet at Rose's house?"

"I'm on it," Dad says. "Do you need help getting him on the boat?"

Mr. Fulton doesn't answer because he's already lifted his son and carries him to the water.

I follow, and soon someone else approaches who helps lift Ian safely into the boat. I pull up the anchor and climb on board.

"Are you good to drive it?" Mr. Fulton asks Cassie.

"I think so." Cassie starts the boat and drives it to the other side of the lake. I make a point to keep my attention on Ian. I've had enough of that ghost for the time being.

Cassie slows the boat as we approach the dock and cuts off the engine. The gentleman who came with us to help with Ian helps to tie the boat to the dock, while Cassie puts the key back into its storage space.

Together the gentleman and Mr. Fulton carry Ian across the dock and around the house to the front.

Aunt Sue is waiting for us. "Both of you, in the house. Now."

"We found Ian," Cassie snaps. "We had a feeling he followed us earlier, so we wanted to check. And I'm already eighteen. The time has ended where you get to treat me like a child."

Aunt Sue points up to the house.

"Come on, Ginnie," Cassie says with dripping sarcasm. "Looks like our efforts were *so* appreciated."

When we get to the house, I don't wait for anyone. I don't want to think about anyone or anything. I walk straight to our bedroom, take off my shoes and jeans, pop one of my pain killers into my mouth, and fall face-first into my bed. The clock beside the bed says it's past one in the morning, and that's the last thing I see before I drift off.

32

The next time I open my eyes, the clock beside my bed says it's past noon. I think about last night, and it all comes flooding back. Sitting up, I check Cassie's bed. She's still sleeping soundly, so I leave her alone.

I throw on a pair of sweats and leave the room. Before heading downstairs, I see if Dad is in his bedroom. His door is open, but he's not there. I notice my box has been opened, and the note is resting beside it. Somehow, I doubt that will spare me from a sound verbal lashing.

Voices come from the living room. I walk in and see Dad, Gran, Aunt Sue, and Uncle Doug all sitting down. Gran looks guilty, and Dad tries to wipe any emotion from his face. It's then that I realize Gran must have told him the secret.

"I'll come back later," I say and step outside the room.

"No, you'll get in here now." Dad's voice is stern and unmoving.

Here goes.

Once in the room, Uncle Doug and Aunt Sue excuse themselves. Aunt Sue doesn't look at me, so I know that I'm still in the doghouse.

"How's Ian?" I ask.

"He's home. He came out of the coma and was in his right mind. He has a broken ankle from the fall, but once they had the cast on him, he got to go home. Ted said he would cope better in his own environment."

"Good." I sigh in relief.

Dad barely pauses. "We've decided that you should go back to London," Dad says without looking up. "Too much is going on here, and I need to know that you're safe."

"And London will make me safe?"

"Being here seems to be dangerous for you," Dad says sharply. "Especially when you won't listen, and then lie to cover your tracks."

I can't recall the last time Dad has truly raised his voice at me. He's been annoyed before and short-tempered but never this unflinchingly angry. "You don't understand."

"Understand? What's there to understand? You've got some bug up your craw about some dead girl and how she's related to us? You sound like you've lost your mind!" Dad is standing and bellowing at me. I grip the arms of my chair to hold my composure. "Not only have you put yourself in danger, but you've put other people in danger. Other people are getting hurt, Virginia. Because of your thoughtlessness and impulsiveness! And if that's not enough, you're tearing this family apart!"

"Sam, go easy on your daughter. You're taking your anger at me and directing it at her." Gran speaks calmly, but there is emotion in the words.

"I have purchased your plane ticket. We leave for Detroit in the morning." He storms out of the living room and slams the front door shut behind him.

My fists are clenched and I can't control my shaking. I start to sob. My body trembles as I cry. I feel Gran's arms around me. I want to tell her to leave me alone. She lied to Dad, and I got blamed.

Instead, I lean into her until I have no more tears to shed.

"You're right, Ginnie," Gran says in my ear. "It's not your fault. Your father is rightfully upset at me, and he's taking it out on you. Give him time to cool off. Until then, there's somewhere I need you to take me."

"I have to pack."

"It won't take long. It's somewhere I should have taken you when you first started asking questions."

"Can I go, too?" Cassie stands at the entryway. "Sorry, I didn't want to interrupt, but I'd like to go, if that's okay?"

I stretch out my arm and Cassie sits down on my other side and hugs me and Gran. "I've never heard Uncle Sam yell like that."

"He's had a lot thrown at him. Give him time to process," Gran says. "It's why I kept his birth a secret for so many years. It was simpler. But you know what they say about secrets, the truth has a way of revealing itself."

"I thought the truth set you free." I know the Bible verse from all my years at Catholic school. Unfortunately, the truth doesn't feel so free at the moment.

"It does, but it takes time for us to realize the freedom that comes with it. Now, go get dressed girls. Pandora's Box has been opened. I might as well show you something that could be useful. I'll go tell Sue and Doug, you're coming with me."

As Cassie and I go up the stairs, I ask, "I thought you were still sleeping?"

"After you went downstairs, Mom and Dad came up to the bedroom, woke me up, and told me if I ever pull a stunt like that again, they won't be paying for my car insurance. They'll take away my keys."

"I'm going to London tomorrow."

Cassie stops surprised. "You can't leave. We haven't figured this thing out."

"What am I supposed to do? Maybe Dad's right. Everyone's getting hurt. Maybe it's better this way."

"If you leave, I leave. This summer will suck if you're not here."

"I don't have a choice in the matter. You know it's bad when Dad thinks I'm safer with Mum."

After we're dressed, we leave with Gran. First, she takes us to Monday morning mass—she refuses to let either of us get behind the wheel. But I don't mind too much. I go and confess my sins and feel much better. Gran gives me a wink and says, "That's a good Catholic girl."

Right when Cassie's about to snap from boredom, Gran piles us in the car and drives us to the newspaper's office.

"This is where you wanted to take us?" Cassie asks.

"Shh."

Once inside, Gran brings us past the main office and through a set of security doors. She stops and chats with a few people, but tells them we're on a mission. We follow her down a flight of stairs. "Here's where we keep the archives." She unlocks another door and lets us in a room packed with filing cabinets.

"Haven't you ever heard of a computer database," Cassie mutters.

"We're a small newspaper, so our digital records only go back a couple of decades. The rest is stored in multiple places. This is where we keep our really old archives." Gran goes to a set of filing cabinets and opens a few of them, skimming through the folder tags. "Jackpot!" She pulls out a musty file. "Look at this."

Gran hands me the image of Barbara Blackstone that I had first seen in the newspaper. It's an eight by ten and is truly a better quality image. I glance up to see Gran walking down the narrow path to cabinets on the other side of the long room.

"Come over here," she calls.

"Why didn't she show us this earlier?" Cassie whispers.

"Maybe she didn't think we'd figure out as much as we did. She told me she was planning on taking the secret to the grave."

Gran's digging through more folders. "These are where

more recent photos are kept."

"Isn't it just downloaded onto the computer from the camera?"

"Yes. When our photographers take the picture, it is. But sometimes community members bring photos in. We store them here." She pulls out a photo and hands it to us.

It's a picture of Bonnie Blackstone, holding an award of some sort. She looks into the camera with the same shy smile that the girl does in my other hand. "This was taken a few years ago."

"They look a lot alike." Cassie sighs, "I don't get it."

"Take a look at the mole."

At first, I don't see it, but then I notice a small, dark mole just above her right eyebrow. When I compare it to Bonnie Blackstone's, she has the same mark.

"After Barbara went missing, everyone noticed a change in Bonnie. It was strange. Bonnie had always been a mean girl. The way she treated Barbara, especially. After the disappearance though, Bonnie did a complete turn-around. Almost like it was a different person."

I keep looking from one picture to the next. I think of Isaac and Mitch and their fierce denial that Bonnie Blackstone could possibly be a murderer. So then, who is staring at me in the pictures?

"I've always wondered," Gran's speaking in a hushed whisper. "The way Bonnie completely avoids me. Wants nothing to do with me. Won't even look me in the eye. The real Bonnie wouldn't act that way."

"Unless she was guilty," Cassie says. "Or unless her sister's death caused her to change her ways."

Gran looks at me and raises her eyebrows. "Barbara promised me that she would not interfere in my raising of Sam. It would be just like her to honor her word forty years later."

"So, what you're saying is that the girl and woman in these pictures is the same person?"

"It's just an educated guess. I've always wondered."

"So, if this is Barbara Blackstone, who's the ghost?" Cassie asks.

A chill shoots up my spine as I think of the beetles, of Ian's warning, of my uneasy premonitions. "I think it's time to talk to Bonnie Blackstone."

"Which one?" Cassie asks warily.

"We'll start with the living one first."

33

We pull into the driveway of Bonnie Blackstone's house. She's another one who lives away from town. Gran turns off the engine, but none of us move.

"She and Mitch must like seclusion," Cassie says. "A lot of these other houses look deserted."

"This is tribal land. Many have left. If I'm not mistaken, Bonnie inherited this stretch of land from her father. He didn't live long after Barbara's death. Neither did their mother."

"Probably died from a broken heart," I whisper. I think of my Dad and how much I've put him through. "Dad has every right to be upset. I can't imagine the pain he'd have endured if what happened to me had been more…permanent." I touch my forehead, the wound still tender.

"Don't blame yourself," Gran says. "Please, Ginnie. Things are beyond our control sometimes. I realize that now. It's almost as if the universe aligned to have all this happen at this moment in time. There's a verse in the Bible that says your sins will find you out, and I believe it. It was only a matter of time before you and your father learned the truth. Secrets like this can't be kept forever."

She grabs my hand and squeezes it. "I thought if I didn't say anything, even with all your questions, that it would just go away. I shouldn't have done that. This is as much my mess as anyone else's."

"I only hope he can forgive me." I rub my eyes.

"Uncle Sam isn't like that," Cassie consoles me. "He's upset, but he'll cool off. We all know that. Let's go and see what's up with this Barbara/Bonnie mystery before you get shipped back across the ocean."

"I'll stay in the car and wait for you," Gran says.

"Are you sure?"

"Yes, it's better this way."

Cassie and I step out of the car. Mitch must have seen us pull up because he stands on their small porch. I hope he has forgiven me, too.

I swallow back the guilt I'm feeling. "Hey," I say with some hesitation.

"Hey," he answers. "Are you here to interrogate my mother? Because I won't let you."

"No, I want to talk with her about the ghost."

"I thought you said we weren't going to tell her." Mitch's words are layered with sarcasm.

"Didn't you already tell her?" I ask. "I saw her outside of the restaurant two days ago, and she said you had told her."

"I only told her that we thought you were related. That's it. I didn't say anything else."

"Please. I'm tired of the ghost wreaking havoc in my life…in all our lives. I think you were right, your mother can help."

"Mitch," Cassie steps up beside me. "You need to get over yourself. Why don't you just tell your mother that we're here, and see if she wants to talk with us?"

He shakes his head and scoffs. "Women." Still, he turns and goes into the house.

"Nicely handled," I tell her.

"Thank you." She flips her hair and gives me a dazzling smile. "I'm not about to let Mitch or Isaac mistreat us. They're a bunch of jerks as far as I'm concerned."

Isaac.

I have to block out the hurt for a while longer. Sometime today, I will need to go to their house and say good-bye. If he'll even let me in their home.

The screen door opens. Bonnie Blackstone steps out, holding a dishcloth. "Hello, girls. What a nice surprise. Please, come in."

"Thank you," Cassie says and glares at Mitch.

We enter and Bonnie offers us a seat. The four of us sit in her living room. I notice the small mole above her eyebrow.

"Would you like anything to drink?"

"No, thank you." I realize that I'm the one who'll have to start the conversation. "There's been a lot going on, Ms. Blackstone. We wouldn't bother you other than we think you can help."

"I'm afraid I don't know much more than you."

"The ghost of…the girl has visited me on several occasions."

Bonnie Blackstone drops the dishcloth on the floor. She gives a half-laugh as if she's unsure whether to believe us or not.

"It's true, Mom. I saw Barbara with my own eyes." Mitch looks over at me and nods. I see the relief on his countenance. It must have been difficult for him to keep this a secret.

"Wh-Wh-What? Why? This is impossible."

"No, it's not. You told me about the curse. How we're in danger. And Ginnie is blood. She's one of us, which means she's in danger, too."

Bonnie Blackstone doesn't say anything at first. Her features display a variety of emotions, mostly disbelief and possibly fear. She eventually covers her face with her hands. "Barbara wasn't pregnant."

"Yes, she was," I say. "Forty years ago, she was pregnant with Mitchell Hunt's baby. She feared for her life. My grandmother, Rose Paxton, took that girl into her home. They reached an agreement that Rose would adopt the baby, and Barbara would act like the baby never happened. She feared that the baby would be in danger if members of her family knew."

Bonnie Blackstone stares at me in shock and trepidation. "How in the world do you know that?"

"My grandmother told me."

"Mom, don't you see? Ginnie and her Dad are related to us. Doesn't that mean they might fall to the curse?"

Bonnie stands up quickly, startling us all. "I'm sorry. You need to leave. This is too much."

"Please, I need help. I don't know what to do about the ghost. She wants me to find out what happened, but every time I try to figure it out, bad things happen. First, the car accident and last night, Ian was seriously injured. I don't know how to find the answers."

"And going to her isn't an answer," Mitch adds. "Not after all those beetles."

"Beetles?" Bonnie asks.

"Yes," I answer. "Since I've been here, these beetles have found me. As soon as I landed from the airport and was on my way up here, I dreamt about them for the first time. Last night, there were hundreds of the beetles at the gravesite."

"Thousands," Mitch corrects me.

"Millions," Cassie adds.

"Oh my God." Bonnie presses a hand to her heart and acts like she's short of breath. "This is not happening."

My cell phone rings. I see it's Cassie's number. "Why are you calling me?"

"Oh, I left the phone in the car."

Gran.

"Hello?"

"Police just pulled into the driveway. I thought I should let you know."

"Police? In what driveway?"

Bonnie and Mitch go the window. With one glance, Bonnie turns and pushes herself against the wall. "What am I going to do?"

There's a knock at the front door.

The four of us stand like we've been caught red-handed. I don't know what to think anymore.

The knocking continues. Bonnie Blackstone takes a deep breath and opens the door. "Ted? Hello, what brings you here?"

"Hello, Bonnie. I'm sorry to bother you at your home, but could you please come to the station with us. We have some questions."

"About what?" she asks, but I can see her hands shake.

"We can discuss this at the station."

"You can at least give me the courtesy to explain why you're hauling me off to the police station."

I hear Ted sigh. "We arrested Henry Hunt for reckless driving and attempted murder. He has released a statement about the true identity of your deceased sister. We need to confirm some new details."

Bonnie Blackstone looks at her son and embraces him. There are tears in her eyes. "Whatever happens, know that I love you."

"Mom?" Mitch is shaken, too. "What's going on?" he asks Mr. Fulton, as his mother leaves.

"I'm sorry, Mitch," Mr. Fulton answers.

I stand at the door. When Mr. Fulton sees me, he says, "I just sent Pete out to your grandmother's house. We have the suspect in custody who caused the accident. You need to get home."

Cassie and I step outside. "Do you want to come with us?" Cassie asks Mitch.

"No, I'm going to drive to the police station and wait for my mother."

"Everything will be all right," I say and hug him.

"Why did she act…guilty?" The emotion is visible on his face.

I take out the two pictures. "Don't be upset with me, okay?"

He nods.

I show him the two pictures. "See the small mole right above the eyebrow?"

"Yeah. My Mom's always had it."

"Barbara had the same mole?"

Mitch keeps studying the pictures.

"Do you have any pictures of Bonnie…your mother from when she was little?"

"Or any pictures of the two of them together?"

"I'll be right back." After a few minutes, Mitch walks out the front door, holding a picture frame. "Mom keeps this in her top drawer."

Two smiling teenagers pose for the camera. They're twins, no doubt about that, but their demeanor is completely different. The twin on the left smiles shyly at the camera, much like the girl's school photo I have in my hand. The other twin acts much more confident with chin thrust out, her nose pointed up, and a confident glint in her eyes.

"Look," Cassie points at the confident girl on the right. "No mole."

From the angle, I can't see the mole either. I study the twin on the right, and the mole is definitely above the right eyebrow. "Mitch?" I ask. "Which one is your mother?"

He slowly points to the twin on the right, then stops. He takes the frame from my hands and opens the back. "The one to the right is Barbara. The one on the left is Bonnie."

I hold the two photos up while Mitch holds up the picture frame. "What does this mean?"

"Your mother is the girl who went missing," Cassie answers in a way that says she can hardly believe it herself.

"This doesn't make sense."

"It explains why you can't believe your mother would do any harm," I say. "Because your mother wouldn't. The question is if your mom is Barbara Blackstone, what happened to Bonnie?"

Mitch hands me the frame. "Wait right here." He goes back into the house.

Gran calls from the car. "We need to leave, girls! The police are at our house!"

"One more minute!" I yell back.

My cell phone rings. It's Dad. "Hi, Dad. I know I'm supposed to be home."

"The police are here."

"Yes, I ran into Mr. Fulton. We're on our way."

"Where are you right now?"

"Gran asked me to take her to mass."

There's a pause. "Virginia?"

"Yes?"

Dad sighs into the phone. "I just wanted to say…"

"It's all right, Dad. You have every right to be upset with me. I haven't been entirely honest, and that's not good. But I hope you know that I didn't mean for any of this to happen."

"No, stop that. It's…It's not your fault. Let's just talk when you get back. Drive safely."

"Gran won't let either of us drive."

"Smart woman. And Virginia?"

"Yes?"

"I love you."

"I love you, too, Dad."

Cassie's grinning at me. "See? Told you he'd calm down. Face it, Ginnie, you have one awesome Dad."

"Yeah, I do."

"Too bad that calmness didn't rub off on my Mom."

Mitch walks back outside, carrying a yellowed, aged book. "This is one of our tribal legends books. It's a history, so to speak.

I remembered something about when a person dies, an animal will represent a person's soul in the land of the living. The animal that represents a person resembles the true nature of their soul." He flips through pages. "I might be wrong. Mom taught me the pages of this book a long time ago. And I didn't think much about it until last night with those swarms of beetles. Here it is."

He shows us the page.

"We are all one in spirit, soul, and body…" Cassie reads aloud. "Look. The pictures are a butterfly, a deer, a bear…there's no beetles."

"The pictures are just examples," I say. "But Barbara Blackstone wouldn't have those ugly beetles as her spirit, would she?"

"Girls!" Gran yells. "We have to go."

The three of us stand there, looking at one another.

"We can meet up later," Cassie offers.

"It'll need to be tonight because I leave tomorrow."

"What? Why?"

"Dad's sending me back to London. Things have gotten a little crazy around here, and I think he wants me out of this situation."

Mitch sighs, "I hate to say it, but maybe he's right."

"Yeah, I guess I'm a nuisance, huh?"

"No, Ginnie. It's not that. I want you here, but this ghost. If it's not Barbara, then it's Bonnie. And I'm afraid that what she wants with you isn't good."

"He's right," Cassie says. "If Bonnie Blackstone is haunting you, it's not because she's happy you're her niece."

"But what about all of you?"

"We'll figure it out," Mitch says. "But first, I'm going to the police station. It's time I learn who my mother really is."

34

Officer Pete is waiting for us at Gran's house.

Once again, Dad, Uncle Doug, and Aunt Sue are sitting in the living room, only this time Pete sits with them. When we enter, Dad goes first to Gran and hugs her neck. Then he hugs me. "How was mass?"

"Very Catholic," Cassie retorts and sits next to her parents.

Gran goes to say something but instead goes to leave the room.

"Mom?" Aunt Sue calls. "Where are you going?"

"I'm going to lie down. I'm pooped."

Dad leads me to a chair. "Go ahead, Pete."

"We found the man driving the truck from Saturday night. His name is Henry Hunt, and he is Mitchell Hunt's brother. According to his statement, he was trying to scare Ms. Paxton, but he did not want to harm the girls."

"Yeah right," Dad scoffs.

"That's the other thing," Pete says almost like he's apologizing. "It seems Mr. Hunt is accusing Ms. Paxton of the death of Barbara Blackstone."

There's a collective gasp in the room.

"We're looking into his accusations and claims. I wouldn't worry just yet. Right now we're interviewing Bonnie Blackstone, who he also charged with the death."

I leave the room and go out the back door, heading for the dock. Sitting down at the end of it, I stick my feet in the water and look out across the lake to where the yellow tape still marks the spot. It's hard to believe that I have only been in Michigan a little over two weeks. And tomorrow I'll be leaving. A part of me is scared to stay. Bonnie Blackstone wasn't a good person, and she has to have ulterior motives for pursuing me. Even in my dreams, I feel terrified. If I go back to London, normalcy can ensue. There's Alisa and Mum and…who am I kidding? I don't want to leave. Not with everything up in the air like it is. Not with me just now discovering that my biological grandmother is still alive. Not after my friendship with my cousin is flourishing. Not without making things right with Isaac.

"I don't want to leave," I say out loud.

The dock creaks, and I turn around to see Dad walking toward me. He sits down, takes off his sandals, and puts his feet in the water next to mine. I see he's holding the note I wrote him last night. We don't say anything for a long time. There's something about Pigeon Lake that quiets the soul. At least in the daytime.

"Virginia," Dad says. "I can't tell you how sorry I am about my outburst this morning. I took my anger and hurt over what your grandmother had revealed to me, and I took it out on you. I thought if my daughter hadn't been snooping around, I wouldn't be this hurt. I had to cool down before I saw that all you were doing was trying to find the truth. Like a scientist."

"I shouldn't have lied."

"No, you shouldn't have, but I understand why you did. Who knew that such a mystery lay within the forest here? I grew up in this very house and was completely oblivious."

"You were born here," I say.

He nods. "That's what Mom tells me. So, clarify a few things."

"I'll try."

"What happened to bring about all this?" He motioned to across the lake.

"The first hike I went on I felt a cold wind and a presence. I don't know how to describe it. I told myself that I was merely a city girl in the middle of a massive forest, but one of my pictures showed an outline of a person. I didn't think anything of it—or tried not to—but Mr. Fulton and you had discussed at dinner about a ghost in these woods. And it was like I couldn't shut my brain off."

"We've experienced some weird things, but I always chalked it up to being goofy kids. One time when we were teenagers, we were hiking across the lake, and I felt chilled all of a sudden. I was walking near one of the sharp edges of the forest, looking to see where'd be the best spot to hang a rope. You know, for swinging and jumping in the water. Next thing I know, I'm falling off the edge and toward the bottom of the cliff. Luckily, my arm still held one of the thick branches, and I didn't let go."

"You never told me this! Did someone push you?"

"I can't say. Ted swears it wasn't him or Tommie, the other friend we were with. But it happened right after I felt chilled. Anyway, I didn't even think about it."

"At the dinner with the Fulton's, you two talked about what happened after graduation."

"Well, everyone in these parts knew that the forest was supposedly haunted. I don't think Sue ever really ventured into the woods, but I loved them. Your Gran and Grampa always kept a close eye on me, but they never outright told me no, as long as I was with someone. That night after graduation, we decided to camp in the woods, which we had never done before. We decided to see if the ghost stories were real."

"And interestingly, you've never shared any of this with your daughter."

"I wasn't exactly hiding it from you. I didn't think too much about it."

"What was your conclusion? Did you and Mr. Fulton see the ghost?"

"Something was out there that night, but I always wondered if it was one of our friends pulling a prank. I don't know. I'm a scientist. I'm not too superstitious. That said, I'm not so arrogant that I can't admit that there are mysteries of the world that cannot always be explained or solved. That's why I still consider myself a man of faith."

"Right. Which explains making your only daughter endure Catholic school."

"Haha, you survived." Dad pauses. "It was a big blow to learn about...you know, events of the past."

"It doesn't have to change anything. Gran and Grandpa will always be your parents."

"It does change things. Somewhere out there is my bloodline. People who are related to me—people related to you—and for forty years, I had no idea. I could have had relationships and contact with them. It's a big deal."

"I guess it is. I wasn't trying to uncover it. I had no idea. I've only been trying to avoid bugs, dead bodies, and ghosts. How was I supposed to know it led to some humongous family secret?"

Dad and I sit side by side for a few minutes, both lost in our thoughts.

"This is probably really hard for Gran. She loves us a lot." I rest my head on Dad's shoulder.

"I know she does," he says. "I honestly don't know what to do or say."

"You don't have to say anything right now. Just be there for her. No matter what she raised you and took care of you. So just be there."

"My biological mother, she's the girl who passed away?"

"It looks like she's still alive."

"She's not the ghost you keep seeing?"

I stare at him in surprise.

He laughs, "What? When enough people tell me that my daughter sees this ghost, and then I watch how you've uncovered all this dormant evidence, yeah, I don't think you're crazy."

"It's nice to not have to hide that from you anymore."

"So, the ghost? I thought that was my mother?"

"I thought so, too. But Gran showed us these two pictures. One from forty years ago, and one was from a few years back of Bonnie. Only one of the twins has a mole over her right eyebrow. Barbara. The woman alive—who says she is Bonnie Blackstone—has a mole over her right eyebrow, identical to the mole in Barbara's younger pictures."

"Which means Bonnie Blackstone maybe Barbara?"

"Yes."

"My biological mother?"

"It appears that way."

Dad stays quiet for several minutes. "Thank you for finding her. Your grandmother will always be my mother, but I can't explain how I feel knowing that my biological mother isn't only alive, but I know who she is, and I have the opportunity to thank her for giving me life."

A beetle crawls across his hand. He studies it. "Fascinating," he says. "This type of Coleoptera. Maybe Lucanindae? Martin finally got back with me. These are not classified at all. Want to help me dissect it?"

"They've been bothering me since we arrived. That's the animal connected with Bonnie Blackstone's spirit, or at least that's what Mitch's book said. What did Martin say when you sent him a picture of it?"

"Nothing like it. We associated it with the American Carrion beetle, just for classification purposes. It has the most similarities with that one, but it's obviously different."

We're studying the underside of the beetle when the dock

creaks from the weight of another person. I glance up to see Isaac approaching us. I cough in embarrassment and scoot away from my Dad and the beetle.

"I've seen enough of those things," Isaac says to Dad.

"Hey there, Isaac, I was just showing Virginia the sex features—"

"Dad, thanks, don't you need to go to the house or something?"

"Okay, okay, okay, how's Ian recuperating?"

"He's recovering nicely. A little too bossy now that he has a broken ankle, but I don't mind. I'm just glad he was found. Mom wants me to invite you all over for a barbeque tonight. Ian wants to see Ginnie, and Mom and Dad are really grateful for your family's help."

"We'd love to," Dad says and stands up. "Do we need to bring anything?"

"Mom said to bring over some steaks. We have chicken and brats."

"Oooh," Dad rubs his stomach. "I'm getting hungry already." He walks off the dock. "Be good, you two."

I pat the dock beside me. "Come and take a seat. It's a pretty popular spot."

Once he sits down and has his feet in the water, he takes my hand and intertwines his fingers with mine. "Ginnie…" he starts. "What happened last night—"

"You were worried and scared. I understand. I'm sorry it happened."

"We pushed you though. I could tell you didn't want to go and talk with the ghost. Shoot, you're still recovering from a car accident." He gently touches my forehead. "Ian warned us, too. No, it was easy to blame you, but everything is completely out of your control. Sorry, I messed up."

"You're forgiven." I take a deep breath, knowing I have to tell him. "I leave tomorrow."

"I know. Your father was talking with mine. They both think that you've had too much happen and that you need space."

I don't say anything, only continue staring at our intertwined fingers. I finally admit, "This ghost has seriously annoyed me."

"Tell me about it. Last night bothered me. Not about the supernatural weirdness going on, but with Ian. I can't have him involved in this. I have to put aside my feelings until everything gets resolved."

"What do you mean?" My gut already knows where this is headed.

"Maybe going back to London and getting away from here is a good thing right now."

The words hurt. *Isaac wants you to leave.*

"Please, don't be angry. My feelings for you haven't changed. I like you. I really, really like you. But someone tried to kill you the other night. And this ghost, with all her nasty bugs, none of this was around before—"

"Before me." I have to force the tears away. It shouldn't feel like complete rejection. He admitted to liking me, wanting to get to know me, but the rejection is there. And it stings.

"Ginnie…"

"It's fine. I understand." I go to get up, but he grabs my arm. "Isaac, please don't make this worse for me, okay? I do understand. Since I've been here, life's been complicated. It doesn't mean I like your decision. It just means I understand why you made it. So, please leave me be."

"I want to visit. I want us to keep in contact. I want us to be us."

"Please. I need to go." I can't look at him.

He releases me. I hear him say something more, but I've already run off the dock and up to the house. I run through the kitchen and up the stairs to the bedroom. Cassie sits on her bed, her laptop open. "I've been researching," she says. She takes one look at me, then sets down the computer. "What happened?"

"Isaac," I press my hands against my eyes, but I can't help it. This is twice in one day! "He broke up with me. I'm not sure we were boyfriend and girlfriend, but whatever we were is over."

She hugs me. "I will exact vengeance upon him in your honor."

"Ugh! It's because of the stupid ghost. He said he likes me, but he thinks I should go back to London."

"Oh," Cassie releases me. "That's not as bad as I thought. He likes you, Ginnie. Sheesh, why are you crying?"

"Because he's still dumping me!"

"Take it from a girl who knows how to dump a guy. He's probably genuinely worried about you and Ian and this whole situation."

"If it wasn't for that stupid ghost, he wouldn't have to step back!"

"Well then, it looks like we need put an end to Bonnie Blackstone."

"And how do we do that? She's already dead."

"Mitch wants us up at the police station. His mother wants to talk to us. I told him we would leave after you've rested. Are you rested?"

"As rested as I'm going to be."

As we're going downstairs, Cassie asks, "Are you still going home tomorrow?"

"It looks like it." Dad is at Gran's computer. "I'm going to the police station."

"To talk with Barbara?"

"Yes."

"I'll come with." He scoots the chair back and stands up. "I'd like to officially meet her."

Cassie and I glance at each other. "Okay."

We go to leave but are stopped by Gran. "Where are you all headed?"

"We're going to the police station," Dad tells her.

"To see Barbara Blackstone?" she asks. I hold my breath, hoping Gran doesn't get offended or angry or hurt. She simply says, "I'm going, too. Let me grab my purse."

"Shoot, maybe I should ask my mom if she wants to go," Cassie jokes.

"You want me to go where?" Aunt Sue comes out of the kitchen where she must have been with Gran.

"We're going to the police station," Cassie says with extra exuberance. "Want to go?"

"I'm getting ready to go fishing with your Dad. Unless, Sam, do you want me to go?"

"Go fishing," Dad tells her. "I'll be all right."

Aunt Sue nods. "Oh, and don't let either of the girls drive."

"Not a chance."

"For the record, the truck attacked me. I was driving just fine."

"Oh hush," Gran says, as she walks out of her bedroom. "You two girls together are like two sticks of dynamite ready to detonate wherever you land."

Cassie shrugs, "That's because we're hot."

"Oh Lord," Aunt Sue says with a grin. "Look at this youthful arrogance."

"She has to get it from somewhere," Dad teases.

"Ha, ha, get out of here, guys, before I start insulting my brother."

The ride to the police station is anything but ordinary. Gran couldn't be any feistier, and Dad won't stop picking at us, jerking the wheel this way and that, and saying, "Whoa! Hold On!"

It may be because the heaviness of the situation demands we enjoy any moment that doesn't have to be serious, but the car ride makes us feel as if it's all going to work out somehow. At least it does to me.

I wonder how awkward it will be with all of us there to see

Barbara. Will she feel outnumbered? I don't sense that Gran wants to make the woman uncomfortable. On the contrary, Gran seems to want to put everyone at ease. In her own snappish way, of course.

Dad puts his arm around my shoulder as we get out of the car and walk to the front doors of the police station. "I bet this American adventure beats anything you would have done with Alisa."

"Um, yeah, probably. I'm not sure how Alisa would handle ghosts and beetles and car accidents."

Ted Fulton sees us come in and motions for us to come around the desk. "Do you think it's true?" he asks Dad as we approach.

"It all fits together."

"Crazy." Mr. Fulton shakes his head. "I'm not sure what I can disclose right now, but she wants to see the girls." We walk down a long hallway to a closed-up room. "She's in here." He knocks then peeks his head in. "Ms. Blackstone, Sam Paxton, and Rose Paxton came with the girls." He nods at us, "Okay, go in."

Mitch sits next to his mother at the long table in the room. A police officer brings in some folding chairs and places them around the table. Mr. Fulton stands off to the side. Once the police officer leaves, Mr. Fulton shuts the door and leans against it.

Dad seems to look at Barbara Blackstone for the first time. She glances up at him now and then but keeps her gaze mostly fixed on her hands, clasped on the table. I sit down first and the others follow.

"How are you holding up?" I ask.

"There's a weight that gets lifted once the truth is revealed," she says in hushed tones. "But it doesn't make it any easier. Mitch?"

He nods at his mother. "She asked me to explain the situation, this being so difficult. About forty-one years ago, my mother fell in love with a young man named Mitchell Hunt. He was betrothed to her sister, Bonnie, but he asked for the hand of Barbara instead. This made Bonnie insanely jealous and angry. She refused to live under the same roof as Barbara."

Ms. Blackstone wipes at her eyes but nods at her son to keep going.

"Bonnie's taunting only became worse and worse. Barbara would come home with cuts and bruises. One time Bonnie sprained Barbara's wrist by dragging her across the street. Her behavior to Mitchell was only worse. She would spit at him, she keyed his car, even drained his brakes. When Barbara found out she was pregnant with Mitchell's baby, she became desperate. She had already made friends with a beautiful white woman by the name of Rose Paxton."

I look over at Gran and see her staring at Barbara with tears running down her face.

"Bonnie became suspicious of Barbara's weight gain and baggy clothing. She tricked Barbara to come out to the ledge at Pigeon Forest where they used to go as little girls."

"Back then," she interrupts Mitch. Her voice is quiet, but she continues. "Back then, we use to have a rope that dangled from the tallest, thickest tree. We would fly out over the water with that rope and drop into the water. The lake levels were much higher then, but it was still scary and fun." She seems to realize she's talking. "I'm sorry. Continue, Mitch."

"Are you sure?" he asks. When she nods, he goes on, "Bonnie tricked Barbara to come to that ledge, telling her she wanted to make up and put the betrayal behind them. Instead, she beat Barbara senseless out there, demanding she abort the baby. Barbara, of course, lied and said she wasn't pregnant. For added measure, Bonnie kicked Barbara's belly just to make sure. It's a miracle that kick didn't kill the baby." He glances up at Dad.

It's now I notice Dad is crying, too. I grab his hand and hold it. Cassie grabs my other hand, and grabs Gran's available hand, too.

"Barbara went straight to Rose's house. Rose took care of her, promised her a safe haven. Barbara wasn't sure if the baby was okay, but she couldn't risk going to a hospital. If Bonnie knew the truth, Barbara was scared for her life, and that of the child's. The baby was born at Rose Paxton's house."

"On June 21st," Barbara says between sobs.

"At 2:37 in the morning," Gran adds.

The two women look at each other with a smile.

"I vowed I would not interfere with your raising of him."

"And I vowed to keep your secret safe. I was going to take that secret with me to the grave."

Now Barbara turns to Dad. "It was the most difficult decision I have ever made. But I knew the Paxton's would be the best parents for you. I walked away and never interfered, just like I promised. But I watched. I watched you grow up. I watched you play in the woods. I watched you collect bugs. And I was happy because I saw that you were. I may have given you life, but you had quite a fine woman giving you a warm home and lots of love."

Dad looks over at Gran and winks at her. "Yes, she did. She's a pretty magnificent lady. You both are."

"Is anybody going to mention what happened to Bonnie?"

We all turn our attention to Cassie.

"I'm just curious. We do have a ghost that won't leave Ginnie alone…It'd be nice to know…" Cassie stops talking.

"What happened?" Gran asks Barbara. "Why did you go all these years pretending to be Bonnie?"

"After I left your house, it was my goal to leave town and never look back. But I wanted to see Mitchell one last time. To tell him that I was okay. I hoped he would come with me, but I wouldn't make him. When he saw me, he was thrilled. I told him that I would have to leave town, and then I told him why. I stopped at the part where Bonnie kicked me. I thought it would be better if he thought the baby died." Barbara takes a deep breath. "He became so angry. He decided to lure Bonnie to the ledge, make her think he wanted to marry her, then I would be there with him, and she would see that it had been a trick. Stupid, I know, but what happened after that was a complete accident. She charged at me. I truly believe she wanted to kill me. Mitchell threw her off of me, but he threw her so hard that she gashed her head against a rock. That was it. She was gone." Barbara covers her face.

Mitch puts his arm around her shoulders. "They thought since Barbara was already considered missing, it would be easier for her to be the one that died. Mitchell had to dump Bonnie in the lake, hoping that that's where their secret would stay buried. They tied the rock around Bonnie's foot, since it had bloodstains on it, and let the lake swallow her up."

"From that day forth, I was Bonnie."

"What happened between you and Mitchell?" I ask, thinking of the man I met in the woods.

"The guilt became too much for both of us. Plus with everyone thinking I was Bonnie, it kept bringing up the fact that the real Bonnie was gone. He lost himself in the bottle, and then eventually left town."

"Other than twenty years ago," Mitch says to her.

Barbara looks at her son and smiles. "That's right. He knocked at my door that day. Our love was right there. It had never left. Unfortunately, by that point, Mitchell had a lot of demons he was dealing with. He'd have night terrors. Screaming Bonnie's name. I told him he could come back when he sobered up, even though I knew it wasn't the alcohol. I didn't want to lose another son, so I kept my pregnancy a secret from him. I'm sorry, Mitch."

"So, wait," Cassie's grinning from ear to ear. "You're telling me that my Uncle Sam and Mitch are not just half-brothers, but they're whole brothers?"

No one says anything. Mitch and Dad act awkwardly, looking over at each other periodically.

"So," I say to Mitch. "We're not cousins?"

"Technically, I'd be your uncle."

"I hope you don't expect her to call you 'Uncle Mitch.' That'd be too weird," Cassie says.

The tension is broken, but we become quiet again, each of us contemplating the truth.

"What do we do about the ghost?" Cassie asks.

I appreciate her efforts in trying to keep the conversation going.

"Leave the ghost alone," Gran says. "Now that the body is found and gone, she probably has gone to the great beyond."

"I don't think so, Gran. I've seen her. Recently."

"Her spirit and soul are no longer in her body," Barbara says.

"Then her spirit is stuck in the woods?" Cassie asks. "As in forever. Poor Gran has to live in haunted woods."

"I've lived in these woods for over forty years. The ghost has never bothered me."

"Because you're not blood," Mitch explains to Gran, and then turns to me. "But the ghost is bothering Ginnie because she is blood."

"Blood for blood," Barbara adds. "She won't go away because her spirit lives on."

"It's those beetles." As I say the words, it starts to make sense. "She lives on through those bugs."

"For forty years, I have lived in these woods, and everything has been fine." Gran shakes her head. "Until this summer."

No one says anything. I think of Isaac's words. He agrees with Gran. I should go back to London. "Well, I'm leaving tomorrow, so hopefully the ghost and her bugs will go back to being dormant. Since it's obvious I'm the reason she's bothering everyone, I'll take myself out of the equation."

Once again, no one says anything.

A police officer enters and says that we need to leave. As everyone rises to leave, Barbara asks, "May I speak with Ginnie for one moment longer?"

The officer nods and says, "Three minutes. That's it."

Cassie tries to stay behind, but Barbara asks her to leave. "Just Ginnie, please."

Once everyone leaves, I say, "I know this has to be hard, Ms. Blackstone, and I never meant for all of this to happen. Tomorrow, I'll be gone, and it'll all go back to normal."

"Everything happens for a reason, Ginnie. I'm not sorry for any of this. Watching Mitch realize he has family has opened my eyes to how much I've kept from him. Then there's Sam. I've watched him from a distance for years. All at once, I'm given a chance to get to know him…and my granddaughter."

I stare at the floor, keeping my emotions in check. "Well, I'm sorry I have to leave and won't be able to get to know you, but it's for the best."

"I don't think it is."

"What?"

"I don't think it's for the best. I didn't know she was bothering you this much, but it's a sign she's desperate. She identifies with you the most, probably because you are a teenage Blackstone."

"What does she want?"

"I can't be entirely sure, but it sounds like she wants to reincarnate herself in you."

My blood goes cold. I remember the pain and anguish I felt when I touched her hand. Then Ian's words, *She's manipulating you.*

"I've had nightmares of those beetles consuming me, and then, after the accident, they were inside of me, pouring out."

"From what I gather, those bugs are her reincarnated. You have to destroy them, or they'll never go away. And what happens when you come back? Are you going to never visit your grandmother's house again?"

I think of Dad's decision to move back to the states. It's already determined that he's to inherit the house and Aunt Sue is to inherit the acre attached to the east side of the property. That meant my family is here and will be for the foreseeable future. "What do I do?"

"Enough of those bugs have to be destroyed. Her essence must be burned, and those bugs are the manifestation of her essence."

"Go to the source?" I ask.

"Yes. Do you know where that is?"

"Unfortunately, I do."

35

"Are you sure you want to stay back?" Dad sounds surprised.

I stand over my bed, folding laundry. I've already texted Alisa and Mum to let them know the time of my arrival. Dad's giving me the keys to our townhouse, saying that he trusts me to not burn it to the ground. Cassie has been quiet all afternoon, even though we emailed the University of Michigan and filled out the necessary paperwork to be roommates. Gran has stayed in her room for the last three hours. There's a heavy blanket of unspoken words. I wonder if Dad is going to Mr. Fulton's for none other reason than to get out of the house for a little while. But being near Isaac is the last thing I want. He wants space, so I need to give him space. "I've got another load of laundry in the dryer, and I need to finish packing."

"Want some help? I can call Ted and cancel."

"I thought you said Laura would be here any minute?" Before he could answer, I continue, "Go and have a good time. I'll be here when you're done with the barbeque."

He pauses at the door, "I'm going out for breakfast

tomorrow with Barbara. She was released and called, asking if I'd like to meet."

"Good."

"I thought we could go and meet up with her before I drive you to the airport."

"Fine."

"You sure?"

I stop folding a pair of shorts to smile at him. "Yes. Fine. Now go."

He steps into the room, kisses my bandaged forehead, then leaves. "I won't be gone long."

I wait for him to leave the house before I release the breath I've been holding. Gran and Cassie are around somewhere, so I'll have to be sneaky. But it is time to get rid of this ghost, and I refuse for anyone else to be hurt. I make a mental list with what I'll need to take with me. A lighter, some paper for kindling, a water bottle, my cell phone, and of course, my Nikon.

Slipping into my tennis shoes, I pull my hair back into a messy ponytail and slide my cell phone into my front pocket. *Now to get the rest of the stuff and sneak out of the house.* Cassie would want to come, but just thinking of Ian's injuries is enough to have me scratch that idea. Barbara told me I am the one who can stop the ghost. That means everyone else is safer away from me.

"There you are," Cassie says, entering the room and jumping onto her bed.

Wonderful. How am I to escape her?

"Remember how we were supposed to go in on a gift for Gran, and we never did?"

"Yes. We got a little busy." I notice a wrapped package in her hands. "Did you get her something? That's so thoughtful."

"From both of us."

"It's from you. I've been consumed lately with other things, but this gift is all you."

"Not a big deal. I put both our names on the card. Mom

brought the card with her that I had bought while home."

"So, what is it?" I indicated the package.

"Oh, this one's for you. Gran has a duplicate."

"You bought me a present?"

Cassie reaches over and hands me the package. "It's not a big deal. Just a keepsake to take with you.

I open the gift wrap and inspect the framed picture. It's the two of us on the second night of Cassie's arrival. We sit on the floor of the bedroom, surrounded by pillows and a variety of magazines and nail polish. Her arm is around me, and we're both showing off dazzling smiles at her phone's camera. As an added touch, Cassie stuck little bug stickers all over the frame. "I adore it."

"We look awesome, right? Mom printed off the photos, and we framed three. One for Gran, one for me, and one for you. I thought we could give Gran hers before you leave tomorrow."

I hug Cassie, completely touched by her thoughtfulness. "Thank you. And I like the bug stickers. Nice touch."

"You can take them off the frame. I was being silly. I didn't want you to forget."

"Ha, I doubt I could forget even if I wanted to, but I like the stickers. They stay." Now I feel really bad about my decision to sneak across the lake without her. But if Bonnie Blackstone is as maleficent as they say, then I don't want anyone I care about going near her. I release Cassie and set the framed picture down. "Want to watch a movie downstairs? We can make lots of popcorn."

"You're not going to the barbeque?"

"No, it's better I stay here."

Cassie nods in understanding. "Say no more. We will gorge ourselves on junk food and watch some action movies with no romance."

"Deal. I'll make the popcorn. You choose the movie."

Together, we head downstairs, Cassie chatting about all the movies we could watch. "There's John Wick. We could watch all of them. Plus, Keanu Reeves is kind of hot…for an old guy. Or, we could watch any of the Fast and Furious movies. Then again, all the guys are hot in that, too. But nothing wrong with eye candy."

"I'll meet you in the home theater. Do you want extra butter popcorn or kettle popcorn?"

"Yes, to both. And hurry."

I wait until I heard Cassie down in the basement before I search for the candle lighter. With that and some wadded up newspaper, I figure I have what I need. I set a bag of popcorn in the microwave and turn it on.

Once I open the door and tiptoe outside, I run to the docks. I get in Gran's boat and untie the ropes. After I've pushed away from the dock, I check one more time to see if anyone has noticed. But I don't see Cassie or Gran, so I exhale in relief and start rowing the boat to the other side of the lake. Several rows in, I see the ripples around the boat and pause. Sure enough, a strong force pulls me in the direction I'm already headed. "She's waiting for me." I shouldn't be surprised, but a cold dread fills my stomach, and I question if I know what I'm doing.

Not quite to shore, a beetle crawls over the boat's edge and moves toward me. "Go away."

I fumble for the candle lighter, but I lose my grip and it falls to the bottom of the boat. After I retrieve it and sit back up, my heart freezes in my chest. A mass of beetles crawls from the water and into the boat. I scream and try to set the lighter, but it's not working, and my hands are too shaky to hold it steady.

The beetles swarm toward me with purpose as more and more pour into the boat. I scream and use the oar to swing at them, but I'm no match. They move from my shoes to my legs as I swipe at them like a crazed madwoman.

The boat rocks back and forth as I continue to maneuver away from them. "You can't have me!"

Suddenly the boat upends, projecting me into the water. I break the water's surface, coughing and sputtering. I'm close to the shoreline where she wants me to go. I feel it. This is what Bonnie

Blackstone wanted all along.

Me. Alone.

I have no paper or lighter. My cell phone is submerged and ruined. It's just me and her.

A part of me considers staying in the disgusting water. The seaweed is thick, but the beetles get lost in it. If I could swim out to the middle and call for help, maybe I could get away. At least until I can bring back some other fire starter.

But the water pulls me to shore. Her essence is evidently stronger the closer to where her body was. I look in both directions, remembering Mrs. Fulton saying something about a boat launch being close by. If I could stick to the shoreline, I may be able to find it and get help.

Ginnie…

"You can't have me!" I shout and turn to swim as far from shore as possible, but it's no use. She's strong, and the water pushes me the rest of the way.

For a second, I feel myself panic. I shouldn't have come here alone. I'm no match for a ghost who uses nasty beetles to do her bidding. Seeing no other option, as soon as I can stand, I do so. Instead of going to the shore, I sprint across the shoreline, not quite coming to shore. But the lake's floor is uneven and murky, and my feet get sucked up into mud holes, throwing me forward into a patch of seaweed and surrounding beetles.

I push myself to shore, my only option being the root wall that led up the tree edge. I run out of the water, past the bugs, past the yellow tape, and practically throw myself against the cliff's bottom. I grab for roots and pull myself up, ignoring the rustling sound of a swarm of beetles approaching.

With each step closer to the tree edge, I say a prayer, begging God to send someone to my rescue. "I'm not picky," I cry. "Anyone will do."

Ginnie…

"No! Leave me alone!" I grab another tree root and pull

myself up. "I know who you are, and you can't have me."

But the beetles are there, and they're moving faster. Around the tree root, up my arm.

I grit my teeth, but they're now all over my torso, under my shirt, through my shorts. My hand slips…and I fall with a thud, smacking my already injured head.

Just like in my nightmare, the beetles have buried me, and I lose consciousness.

***

When I come to, I sit up and find myself right where I fell. I jump up quickly, shaking my hair and hitting my body until I've expended all my energy.

"They're gone. For now."

She has a quiet and familiar voice, but it now has an edge to it.

I search for a place to climb.

"There's nowhere to go. You're with me now."

I pause and slowly turn toward her voice.

"I've waited for you to be alone. I kept calling to you. Over and over. And here you are."

She stands, no longer faint or ghostly, but not necessarily alive. A heavy fog moves between us. I open my mouth to speak, but nothing comes out. I quickly cross myself.

"Don't do that." She's at the other side of the brush where I found her body. I sense her displeasure. "I need you to let me in. I keep trying to get in on my own, but I'm not powerful enough. You keep resisting."

I still haven't found my voice again, so I fervently shake my head.

"Let me in."

I've yet to stop shaking my head. I close my eyes and begin the Lord's Prayer.

"They killed me. And I've been stuck here…*waiting.*"

When I open my eyes, she's in front of me. Her eyes show anger, her mouth curves in a jeer.

"Together, we can live again."

My stomach rolls as understanding takes hold. Finding my voice, a strength from within me shouts, "No!"

The sound of my voice blasts like a trumpet and throws her across the clearing.

I hear my name being called from a distance. "I'm here!"

"They can't hear you," she says.

"I'm over here! Follow my voice!"

But they keep calling for me as if they can't hear.

"I told you. They can't hear you."

"Why?" I demand.

"Because I'm suffocating you. Now let me in or die."

But the voices are closer. My family and friends. They're coming for me. I feel the strength from within, the same strength that threw her from me, bubble inside and course through me. "You have no power over me," I say, finally understanding. "All this time, you've been trying to force yourself on me, but it hasn't worked."

"*Let me in!*" she screams.

"No." Bonnie Blackstone is thrown back once more, so I say the word again. "No. No. No. Not now. Not ever."

Her body slumps, and her face contorts into an expression of grief and sadness. "I only wanted another chance to live."

Ian's words resounded inside me. *She's manipulating you.*

Dad leans over the cliff, "Virginia!"

"I'm here, Dad!" I wave frantically at him, but it's as if I don't exist.

"No one came for me," she says quietly. "I died here alone. And I've been alone ever since then."

"You don't have to stay here," I tell her. "Go, to where you're supposed to go. Isn't there the other side?"

This time, Bonnie is the one to shake her head. "I don't want to go there. It's worse than staying here."

"Let them find me."

"No. You either let me in, or you die here with me."

"I'm not letting you into my body. That will never happen, but this could be your chance to make the right decision. This could change your fate. Show mercy."

She watches me. By now, this small area by the shore has several people roaming around. All of them calling my name.

"Ginnie!" Cassie frantically searches the ground. Isaac and Mitch help her. "She has to be here."

"Show mercy," I plead with Bonnie. "After all, I am your niece."

But she no longer looks at me. Instead, she turns and faces the water.

Dad is now on his hands and knees, shoving the rocks and branches and other debris away. "Virginia? If you can hear me, say something!"

I feel something stir inside me. It draws me closer to him. I see his tears. I hear the horror in his voice as he calls to me.

The warmth I feel starts to spread, and I become aware of the steady beating of my heart. It turns to electricity as my pulse vibrates throughout my body. The intensity of it brings me to my knees before it explodes all around me in what seems like thousands of stars.

The first thing I notice is I'm on the ground. The second thing I notice is the pain. And the more aware I become, the more intense the pain.

"She's here," someone says from far away.

I try to open my eyes, but I can't. My head hurts too much.

"Virginia, stay with us." It's Dad. He's close.

"I've already made the call." Isaac is talking. "But we need to decide how first responders will get here. It's a pretty remote location."

"Gran's boat is in the water," Cassie says. She sounds like

she's crying. "It's flipped upside down."

No one is saying anything. I want to open my eyes and tell them I'm okay, but my head hurts so much that I can feel the pain down to my toes.

"We've got to do something!" Cassie cries. "She can't die!"

"Help is on the way," Isaac tells her.

"Can't we pick her up and carry her?"

"She's too injured," Dad says. I feel his strong hand pick up mine and press into my wrist. "She has a pulse, and she's breathing on her own, so I don't need to resuscitate. It might do more harm, considering her injuries. Isaac, call your father and request an airlift. We need her at the hospital immediately. Cassie, use my phone and call Laura. Tell her what's going on. Have her meet us at the hospital." Dad must lean down to my ear because I can feel his whiskers against it. "Stay with us, Virginia. You hear me?"

I hear you, Dad.

36

When I'm finally able to open my eyes, I'm in a hospital bed in a darkened room. I hear the beeping of a monitor and see Dad sleeping in a chair beside me. His facial hair is thicker and longer than I remember, and I start to panic. How long have I been out?

I try to speak, but my voice is all crackly, like an old person who never gave up smoking. "Dad?"

He stirs, then takes a second to recognize that I'm awake. Right when he sits up, the door to the room opens, and a nurse rushes in. "The monitor alerted us to a change in activity."

"She's awake." Dad sounds relieved.

The nurse approaches me. "Do you know who you are?"

I once again try to speak, but my throat is parched and hurts. Still, I push out the words, "Ginnie Paxton." She nods, checks the monitor, promises to return with the doctor, then leaves. I turn to Dad, who now sits on the bed, holding my hand. "Water. I'm thirsty."

He gets up quickly. "You had your stomach pumped, so I bet your throat is still quite raw. Let me see what I can do." He goes to leave, then turns and kisses my forehead. "I'll be right back."

While I wait, I assess the situation. I have an IV in my right arm, and I reach up to feel tubes in my nose. My head is heavily bandaged, but the rest of my body—from what I can see—looks like it survived.

I survived. An overwhelming sense of gratitude floods my soul. Had I experienced death? Is that what Bonnie has endured for forty years? Stuck between reality and eternity? Even though I should be angry at her, I'm not. For that brief moment in time, I saw her loneliness. She was angry, yes, but she was also afraid. I think of her words, *I don't want to go there. It's worse than staying here.*

Yet, she let me live. I'm sure of it. I remember seeing the look of resignation when she turned to face the lake, as if admitting defeat. The next thing I know I'm back on the ground in pain and my father finds me.

The hospital room door opens, and Dad enters followed by Laura and another doctor. "They said you can have ice chips right now." Dad hands me the cup filled with ice. I place one in my mouth and feel worlds better.

I'm on my third piece of ice before Laura says, "This is Doctor Shravi. He's our top neurologist and has been monitoring you for the last three days."

"Three days?"

"You've been unconscious for three days," Dad says.

The first thought that pops out of my mouth is, "I missed my flight?"

The three of them smile. Doctor Shravi steps to me and checks my eyes and examines my head. "When's your birthday?"

"May the tenth."

"How old are you?"

"Eighteen."

"Your full name?"

"Virginia May Paxton."

"That's a lovely name," the doctor says, before asking me several more questions.

I suck on the ice and answer whatever question he throws at me.

Before leaving, Doctor Shravi tells me and Dad that I'm over the worst of it. "Her memory is strong, and the MRI shows minimal internal brain injury. I'm hoping for a full recovery."

Dad exhales slowly and covers his face as if that will keep the emotion in check.

"I feel fine," I reassure him. "I didn't mean to be out of it for so long."

"I…thought…I lost…you…" Dad tries to hold back the sobs, but he's unable to do so.

I try to sit up, but there are too many wires and tubes attached to my head. Still, he leans down and hugs me, whispering a prayer of thanks. I notice Doctor Shravi has already stepped out. Laura, however, acts unsure, but she eventually decides to leave. "I'm going to be fine. That's what the fancy doctor just said."

Dad releases me and sits back again, reaching for a tissue and blowing his nose. "They said the longer you were in the coma, the higher the percentage you wouldn't wake up."

"My head still hurts. I must have hit it pretty hard."

"It was an open skull fracture, hon. Some internal bleeding. Very serious."

"If my head is what was injured, why did I get my stomach pumped?"

"You were vomiting beetles."

My stomach flips. "Got it. I don't want to remember that part."

A voice from the hallway catches my attention. "She's awake? Well, why didn't you bloody say so?"

I look to Dad and raise my eyebrows. "Is that—?"

The door opens, and Mum rushes to me in an overdramatic display of affection. "Careful of the medical equipment," I say as she squeezes me too hard.

"Oh, thank you, thank you, thank you, Mary, Jesus, and Joseph." She kisses my cheeks, and her strong perfume makes my eyes water.

"You're here." I glance in Dad's direction to see if he could clarify what my English mother was doing in Northern Michigan. "Mum's here. I assume you know this?"

"Of course he does, you ninny. He bought the plane ticket. Told me to hop over here in a hurry." She blows him a kiss. Dad's cheeks redden.

Mum sits at one end of the bed, and Dad sits at the other. The three of us chat, and I can't remember the last time we were all together. But it doesn't take long for Mum to be checking her phone.

"Are you expecting a call?" I ask.

"Yes, love, Sally's is finishing up next spring's line-up, and I'm going to make the cut. It's not Vogue or Cosmo, but it's keeping me busy." She glances at her phone again. "Oh bother, they called."

"Call them back."

"You sure?"

"I'm not going anywhere."

She kisses my cheek and leaves the room. I turn to Dad who's shaking his head. "Some things never change."

"No, they don't. But I'm glad she flew out here. It means a lot. Thanks for buying her ticket."

"Don't be upset, but I don't think she plans to stay long."

"Of course not. Does she know about Laura?"

"Why would it matter?" Dad doesn't maintain eye contact.

"Actually, it's probably good you don't tell her. Mum has always been competitive. And then she'd start embarrassing us by talking loud, swearing too much, and being obnoxious."

Both of us laugh.

"It's for the best," he says, still not looking at me.

"Especially since we'll be leaving as soon as you get the medical release."

"We? What about Gran?"

"Cassie is going to stay with her through the summer, and then Sue and I will determine our next steps at that point."

"Next steps?" I study Dad who finds the floor immensely fascinating. "What's going on? Dad?"

"Nothing. I've been thinking since all this has been happening, and I think we both need to go home."

"I thought this was your home."

"London has been my home for eighteen years. I have a life there. With my daughter." He stops me from saying anything. "I almost lost you, Virginia. And I almost lost you because my mother kept secrets from us. I almost lost you to a land that clearly has some vendetta. I'm not sure I want to be here. At least not right now. In London, we have a routine. And there are no ghosts or demonic beetles or whatever else is going on here. I'm sorry it took me this long to truly see it."

"What about Laura?"

"We'll see what happens. She understands. Nothing will change our friendship."

"Friendship? Dad, you love her."

"I love you more."

"No." I try to get up, but I can't. How many wires are attached to me anyway?

"Virginia, it's better this way, and you know it."

"But I'm not dead, Dad. Don't you see? I won. The ghost tried to possess me or whatever it was she wanted to do, but I was stronger. I told her no. I'm not afraid anymore. That ghost is a scared fifteen-year-old dead girl whose life ended far too soon. But my life hasn't ended."

"I watched you vomit bugs." Dad grimaces. "They had to pump your stomach to get them all out. They've never seen anything like it. And that would have never happened to my baby girl if I would have let you stay where you belong."

"But I belong here just as much as I belong in London." Dad stays quiet. He walks over to the window and stares outside. I continue, "It's taken me a while to see it, but we can love two places. In London, I have Mum and Alisa and school. I have our townhouse filled with dead bug specimens and our trips to the corner park to take pictures and document more bugs. Not to mention our motorcycle drives. But here, I have Gran and Cassie and Aunt Sue and Uncle Doug. I have Isaac and Ian and Mitch…and yes, Barbara Blackstone. And you have all those things too, as well as a blonde bombshell doctor who is over-her-head in love with you."

Dad turns and sits on the window sill. We stare at each other, both stubborn, until I lay my head back down. Dad's expression softens. "Get some rest. We'll discuss our options later."

He doesn't have to tell me again. I close my eyes and start to drift off. "Don't let Mum wake me up."

"I won't."

I feel Dad's hand in mine, and I fall back to sleep.

***

People move in and out of the room, but I barely register who they are or what they're doing. Whatever medicine I'm on makes me tired, so I sleep often and only wake up for short bursts periodically. Dad tells me at one point that only he and Mum are allowed in the room, and it only takes a couple of conversations with Mum to realize interactions with her only increase my headaches.

After two days, I'm out of ICU and onto a more accessible floor, but Dad insists no one visits me until I'm released. "I want no talk about ghosts or bugs or anything like that," Dad tells me. "And the only way I can make that happen if I keep your friends and cousin away. But don't worry. They ask about you daily and can't wait to see you."

I'm not entirely surprised when I wake up from one of my many naps to see Cassie, Mitch, and Isaac all standing around my bed. Cassie hovers over my face, using a feather to tickle my nose.

"Stop that."

"I'm trying to wake you up. See? Success." When I push myself up to a sitting position—most of the wires and tubes have been taken out at this point—Cassie wastes no time throwing her arms around me. We don't speak for several minutes. She and I stay with our arms around each other, both communicating without speaking a word.

"I'm sorry," I eventually tell her. "I should have never gone alone."

She releases me, and I see the tears in her eyes. "Ya' think?" She smiles while I cringe. "Very clever with the whole let's-watch-a-movie-and-eat-popcorn routine."

"I didn't want you to get hurt. Barbara talked to me in private about torching the place and killing the beetles. That it would basically destroy the ghost of her sister. I thought I'd just go light a fire and leave." I notice Mitch and Isaac shake their heads. "Okay, not my brightest moment, but my intentions were noble. Speaking of intentions, my dad said that he intended on keeping everyone away."

"I got your mother to keep him distracted. I overheard her tell him that they needed to talk, and they went to the cafeteria for coffee. We probably have about an hour."

"Maybe a half-hour."

"So, let me get this straight." Mitch interrupts us. "You were going to light the bugs on fire? And if the fire wasn't contained?" Mitch asks, stepping over to my other side. "What then?"

"I get it. I shouldn't have gone alone. I became well aware of that fact when beetles crawled into the boat and marched toward me in a big angry mob. Not fun."

"The boat was flipped over," Cassie says. "What happened?"

"I don't remember if I was jumping around too much that I flipped it and fell out or if something—or someone—flipped it on me."

"When we couldn't find you, I wondered if you had drowned." Cassie acts like she'll burst into tears.

"I'm right here, and I made it."

"If you would have waited, we would have helped," Mitch says. "My mother told me what she said to you. She wasn't expecting you to run off on your own. She thought we'd work together. As a team."

Before I can respond, Cassie comes to my rescue. "We get it, Mitch. She shouldn't have gone alone. Let's stop harping on her and figure out what we're going to do."

"Nothing," I say. "We don't have to do anything. I won. She wanted me, and I told her no. It was pretty incredible actually."

"You told her 'no.'" Cassie says the words in disbelief. "And she what? 'Oh okay, Ginnie, sorry I've been bothering you. Have a good life.'"

"Not at first, but it became pretty clear that she couldn't have me without my consent. She'd been trying to control me for some time. That's why I've been dreaming about the beetles, and when we got in the car wreck, I had beetles coming out of my mouth."

"Whoa," Mitch says.

I notice Isaac has stayed at the foot of my bed this entire time, not uttering a word. But I ignore him or at least try to. "Exactly. When she couldn't just possess me, that's when she tried to kill me. She needed me at a point where I'd be willing to give her control."

"Those nasty bugs," Cassie stops talking and tries not to gag.

"None of it matters anymore," I say. "Because she lost. You

all found me before, well, you know…"

"Before you died," Isaac says. The three of us turn our attention to him. He isn't acting upset, as much as he's acting angry. Livid, in fact. "When your father found you, you were buried under those bugs. You…were not…breathing." He stops himself and takes a breath. "We saw you airlifted, and you were lifeless."

"I didn't know that it would happen like that."

"Yes, you did! It happened to Ian."

"Ian fell from the tree ledge. What happened to him was an accident. She sought me out. I didn't know that the ghost planned on killing me or taking over my body. I wasn't privy to that, Isaac."

"She doesn't know," Mitch says to Isaac.

"What don't I know?"

"Ian went to confront the ghost," Mitch says. "It wasn't his first encounter."

"The forest around the lake always fascinated him, especially when he heard the ghost stories," Isaac explains. "I told you a little about his reading of all those books. But when you started having serious issues with the ghost, Ian decided to investigate. Then when he knew we were going to ignore him and go out to the ghost, he thought he'd be your knight-in-shining-armor, so to speak, and protect you."

"I didn't know that."

"Neither did any of us until after he calmed down enough from the accident to explain. But now I know that what happened to Ian might not have been an accident. He could have fallen in a similar way to how you did."

I rub my head. I no longer suffer from headaches, but this is still a lot of information to process. "For what it's worth, I don't think she'll bother anyone anymore."

"Do you think you're the only one she's tried to get to?" Mitch asks. "There's a reason my people avoid this forest. It can only be a blood relative, but believe me when I say that I doubt you're the first she attacked, and I doubt you'll be the last."

"So, we kill those nasty bugs?" Cassie asks.

"We torch them," Isaac says grimly.

"With a controlled fire, of course," Mitch adds. "And we do it together. As a team."

I'm not enthused about the idea of going back. "My dad and I are leaving for London, as soon as I'm released. I'd like for this to be behind me."

"Isaac and I are already set up. We've got the fire extinguishers and the torch ready to go. We're going to line the area with a row of rocks. It'll help keep it contained."

"I'm going to have the buckets of water," Cassie says. "We're going today. And we're going to get rid of this ghost once and for all."

"And me? I'm stuck here."

"You sit this one out," Isaac says, gently touching my leg. "Trust us. We're going in together, as a team, and we'll get rid of this ghost once and for all. And then she won't be able to mess with people we care about."

Dad enters the room and places his hands on his hips. "Sneaky. Very, very sneaky."

"You can't keep me from my cousin." Cassie threw her arms around me again.

"We only wanted to say hi," Mitch says.

"Well, you said hello, so let's leave her alone."

"Dad, I'm fine. I don't mind the company."

Cassie releases me and opens up her purse. "See? I brought cards."

Mum walks in, takes one look at Mitch and Isaac, and says, "Which one of you mates has the hots for my daughter?"

While I turn a hundred shades of red, Mitch points to Isaac. "I'm technically her uncle, so that would be weird."

Isaac stretches out his hand. "I'm Isaac Fulton. It's nice to meet you. I can see where Ginnie gets her pretty eyes."

That's all it took to get Mum swooning. "Oh, aren't you

lovely.”

Mitch laughs at Isaac who can't hide his embarrassment. "Have you given her the present yet?"

"Not with everyone in the room." Isaac continues to look everywhere but at me.

"Come now, loves, let the young man have his moment." Mum grabs Dad's arm. "You can stand right outside the door. Or better yet, come with me while I smoke a ciggie."

"Are you sure you want me to leave?" Cassie asks, eyeing Isaac warily. "The last time you two talked, you were super upset."

"Just give us a few minutes," Isaac says.

Cassie raises her eyebrows at me, waiting for permission. I eventually nod my head. My heart isn't ready for another *let's be friends* speech, but I can't help but have hope. I like him a lot more than I've yet to admit to anyone.

Once the door is closed, Isaac steps closer to me. His eyes show a mix of sadness and anger, and I realize he may just yell at me. "I've been so worried. I don't know what I would have done if your father hadn't revived you."

"Well, he did revive me, so there's no need to worry."

"Ginnie, I…" He stops talking and takes my hand. Butterflies immediately release inside me. "I let you down when you needed me the most. I'm sorry. I was upset about Ian, but it wasn't your fault. Please forgive me for pushing you away."

My breath caught in my throat. "I forgive you."

"I texted at least a dozen times that night, telling you how I feel about you. Then we got the call from Cassie that you had left and weren't answering your phone."

"When the boat flipped, my phone got destroyed. I'd like to read the messages, but they're at the bottom of the lake in my cell phone."

He handed me a thick letter stuffed in an envelope. "I wrote it down for you. Don't read it now. Wait until I leave."

"A love note?"

"If you'd let me, I'd like another chance. How about a date where you pick what we do?"

The truth felt heavy on my shoulders. "I'm leaving for London. As soon as I'm released, I'm going to go say good-bye to Gran, get my stuff, and head out the door."

"I figured as much. That's why I thought you could choose the date. Seeing how you know London and all that."

"Are you flying to London?" I try not to get excited, but my insides are not listening.

Isaac smiles and nods. "Before I fly out to California for basic training, my family and I were going to take a big road trip. Mom and Dad agreed to pay half my airfare if I wanted to fly to England. I've never been there, and it sounds fun."

"Yes!" I can't stop grinning. "There are so many places to take you. Oh, I've got to make a list. And you get to meet Alisa. I can't wait to tell her."

"Good." Isaac releases an exaggerated sigh. "I didn't know if you'd want me to, but now that I know you do—"

"A thousand times yes."

Dad pops his head in the room. "Everything okay? What's with the raised voices?"

"Isaac is going to visit me in London!"

"Is he?" Dad doesn't seem as enthused. "Great."

After he shut the door again, I scooted over on the bed and patted the spot beside me. "Want to sit?"

Isaac sat beside me and wrapped one arm around my shoulders. He rested his head against mine. "Is this hurting you?"

"Not at all."

"I still have to work on your father. He's not exactly sold on me dating you."

I lean into Isaac. "Good luck with that."

37

I look out across the water and am no longer afraid. Now I can focus on the beauty of nature and the warm breeze that caresses my face.

"You're in my sun," Cassie complains.

"Fine. I only wanted to see the view one more time before I go."

"It's not like you're never coming to the states again. I'm going to see you in two months."

"Yes, I know. But that's in Ann Arbor, not up north."

"I understand that, but at some point, you're going to visit Gran, right? And what about lover boy? He'll be back up here once basic training is over."

"Okay, okay." I step off the dock. "Well, give me a hug, at least."

Cassie sets her phone down and pushes herself up off the lounger. "Goodbye, my dear cousin." She gives me a hug and a loud kiss on the cheek. "When's Isaac's flight?"

"Early next week. Which is perfect. Gives me time to hide all the bug specimens."

"So gross. And I can't believe you still want to get a degree in forensic science. Haven't you had enough nastiness to last a lifetime?"

"Not at all. Dealing with the mystery and the paranormal elements quite intrigued me. Maybe one day I'll be a detective. As long as I can take the pictures."

"Me too! Sherlock and Holmes!"

I laugh. "You mean Holmes and Watson. Sherlock is Holmes' first name, you ninny."

"Whatever. You knew who I was talking about."

Both of us pause as Gran approaches. She's been quiet since I was released from the hospital yesterday. Dad said that she couldn't get worked up over the situation because of her heart condition, so they only told her I fell and got a concussion. Still, I sense that she knows more than she lets on.

"Hello, girls."

We both greet her.

"Cassie, would let me say goodbye to Ginnie?"

Once Cassie's out of earshot, Gran asks me to sit down. I take one lounger while she takes the other.

"I'd have never forgiven myself if something happened to you."

"Gran, I'm fine. I fell and hit my head. I shouldn't have been over there by myself anyway."

Gran turns to me and shoots me a withering look. "I'm not a dummy. You wouldn't have been in the hospital for almost a week if you had bumped your head."

I don't say anything because what would be the point?

"Barbara Blackstone visited me before you and Sam came up to visit. She was worried, telling me that she'd been having nightmares where her sister was calling out to her. She wanted to know if I'd seen anything or heard anything. But I hadn't. Just the usual forest sounds. She asked if any of my family was coming to visit, and I knew who she meant. I told her no. You and your dad have never visited in the summer. She said to make sure that you stay far away, just as a precaution. Well, it had been years since I had talked to her, so I didn't think anything about it. That same afternoon, I saw her."

"Barbara? Or Bonnie?"

"The ghost girl. She stood in the same spot Barbara had been standing not even an hour earlier. That's when I had my first episode. She startled me!"

"Is that around the time you called me?"

"When I was in the hospital, and I found out from Sue that you and Sam were flying in, I remembered Barb's warning. I'm not one to believe in all this ghost nonsense, but I know what I saw."

"You couldn't have kept Dad or me from coming to see you."

"I should have tried harder. But a part of me wanted to believe that everything was fine. I missed you both so much, which made me keep second-guessing my intuition. And I'm sorry that I didn't take the threat as seriously as I should have."

"It all turned out okay. We're fine. And I'm glad we came. Even with everything that happened, I'm still glad we visited."

Gran stares out across the water. "I hope Sam will forgive me one day. I know that's part of the reason he's going back to London."

"Of course he forgives you." But I remember Dad's words in the hospital, and I know he still has a lot to process. He's running from the truth, but I can't tell Gran that.

Cassie calls my name. I turn to see Mitch standing beside her on the deck. "He wants to say good-bye!"

I wave them over to us.

"Oh, I forgot to tell you that Barbara stopped by this morning. She wanted to see you. She was really demanding, but you were sleeping still. It was strange. I've never seen her so pushy."

Before I could question her further, Mitch and Cassie are

close. I get up to greet Mitch. We exchange a hug. "Good news," he says. "Isaac and I didn't have to go destroy those psycho bugs. I woke up yesterday morning early. I kept hearing drawers bang shut. It was Mom. She told me that she felt awful about what happened to you, and it should be her that confronts her sister, and no one else. She said she knew what she had to do. She came back a couple of hours later and said it was done."

Gran now stands beside us. "She destroyed the bugs? I'm not understanding."

"Those nasty beetles that kept bothering me," I explain to her. "They were the ghost—"

"Think of them as Bonnie's messengers," Cassie adds.

"They were her, more or less." Mitch corrects Cassie.

"And they're destroyed?" Gran still stares across the lake.

"If a person burns them up—destroys them—then that person destroys the ghost's essence."

"There was no fire over there." Gran walks closer to water, her eyes fixed on the other side.

"I'll have to ask Mom, but she said it was taken care of. It took a lot for her to do that. She hasn't been in these woods for as long as I can remember. She's been frightened by them." I can hear the pride in Mitch's voice.

"I haven't seen one of those beetles since I've been back, so your mother must have been successful."

"Technically, your grandmother. She did it for you."

"I'm her grandmother." Gran spins around and glares at Mitch. "Let's get one thing straight. The cat might be out of the bag, but we made a promise to each other. I'm going to keep my promise, and I expect your mother to do the same."

"I was only saying that we're family. My mother set aside her fear and confronted her sister. Because of Ginnie."

Gran swears, which shocks the three of us. "She should have confronted that ghost years ago. That wasn't bravery that sent her over there. It was guilt. She didn't want someone else to get hurt. And then she shows up on my porch this morning, her head held high as if she has a right to claim what isn't hers."

Mitch looks from Gran to me. "I don't want to argue. I only wanted you to know that it's finished."

"Has your mother been acting differently since she's come back?" Gran completely changes her tone. "When she was over here this morning, she had a lot more confidence. She was staring me down, demanding to see Ginnie. Strange, isn't it? That woman has barely looked me in the eyes for these forty years."

"She faced down her ghostly sister. I think she feels a lot more confident." Mitch says. "I have to admit that I was surprised when she didn't go to work today. She said that she didn't want to be at the library anymore. But if she's happy, I'm happy."

"She quit the library?" I ask. Gran makes eye contact with me, and the clues hit me like a runaway train.

"Not yet. She took a day off." Mitch watches us, before saying, "Listen, I'm going to leave. I thought you'd be happy that Mom finished the job for us."

I mentally shake myself and give Mitch another quick hug. "Be safe. I'll see you soon."

"Cassie and I are already planning a meet up in Ann Arbor."

After Mitch waves and walks away, Cassie glares at both me and Gran. "What was that about?"

"There was no fire over there yesterday," Gran says. "So whatever Barbara went over there to do, didn't happen."

"How can you be sure? It might have been while you were sleeping."

"I haven't slept well for over a week. Since my granddaughter was nearly killed. And yes, that's right, none of you fooled me with that 'hurt her head' nonsense."

"There'd at least have been smoke, right?" I ask, feeling the trepidation down my spine to my toes. "Maybe she did something else."

"The woman who came over to see you acted nothing like

Barbara. Why do you think I questioned whether or not she was Bonnie? Because that woman has avoided me for forty years. Always kept her head. Very shy. Just like Barbara. But this morning," Gran pauses and shakes her head. "This morning, the woman at my door was in my face and demanding. I had to put my foot down and remind her of our promise to each other. And do you know what she said? That promises mean nothing to her, and that I destroyed her family. Barbara would have never said that."

"So, if that's not Barbara then who is it?" Cassie asks, then gasps and covers her mouth. "You don't think—?"

"The ghost needed me to let her in. Like she wanted to possess me," I say the words, feeling sick to my stomach. "But I wouldn't let her. Instead, I prayed, which she didn't like, and then, it was weird, I felt really powerful inside. When I said 'no,' it literally threw her from me."

Gran gives a slight smile. "That doesn't surprise me at all. You're strong, Ginnie, and all that good faith teaching helped."

"But what if Barbara wasn't as strong?" I ask. "What if she went over there like I did to destroy the bugs, but instead…" I stop because I can't even say the words.

"That explains it," Gran says. "The woman who came to see you, Ginnie, wasn't Barbara Blackstone."

"It was Bonnie."

THE END OF BOOK ONE